Forward Passes

Jami Davenport

A DANGEROUS SPIRAL

Her new neighbor's door opened. Lavender stared at the most incredibly sculpted though sweaty chest she'd ever seen. Tyler towered over her, naked from the waist up with his faded jeans slung low on his hips. She lifted her gaze to well-defined pecs with a smattering of black chest hair. Muscles bunched, and a Rose Bowl tattoo adorned his right upper arm. Despite the muscles, he looked lean and ready for action. Lavender licked dry lips, imagining the kind of action a man like that might be ready for.

Damn, but he had a fine body. Gorgeous. Absolutely gorgeous. Too gorgeous for his own good.

Or for hers.

Forward Passes

Jami Davenport

www.BOROUGHSPUBLISHINGGROUP.com

FORWARD PASSES
Copyright © 2012 Pamela D. Bowerman

Digital edition created by Maureen Cutajar
www.gopublished.com

ISBN 978-1941260098

To all those children from broken homes who were made to feel disloyal because they wanted a relationship with both parents. Guilt is a powerful thing, but love and forgiveness conquer all.

ACKNOWLEDGMENTS

First of all and always, thanks to my wonderful hubbie for his football expertise, and a special thanks to Boroughs Publishing Group for believing in me and my books. Thanks so much to Chris, Michelle, and Jill.

CONTENTS

Chapter 1

What Goes Up

A man about to make pro-football history should be a lot more excited about it.

Like a well-programmed robot, Tyler Harris zeroed in on his receiver, instinctively calculated the distance, and lofted the ball into the air. The second the football left his hands he knew it'd be a touchdown catch.

His cousin and the Seattle Lumberjacks top wide receiver, Derek Ramsey, blazed into the end zone, spun around at the exact right moment, and caught the ball.

Ty waited for the smugness, the confidence, the satisfaction to surge through him. He waited for the greatest natural high on earth to engulf him, a high better than the best sex, and that was pretty damn, fucking good.

Usually.

But nothing happened.

Two more minutes to glory. The defense took the field and held the Bruins. The clock ticked off the last seconds until the scoreboard displayed: *00:00.*

The stands erupted. Confetti blinded Tyler in a snowstorm of red, white, and blue. The stuff swirled through the air and stuck to his sweat-soaked uniform. Teammates slapped his back. Coaches hugged him. The roar of the fans deafened him. Sportscasters crammed microphones in his face and barked questions at him. Rabid reporters yanked on his Number Eleven jersey and fought for his attention.

He stood frozen in place, staring at the scoreboard. He felt more like a shell-shocked soldier than a conquering field general who'd led his troops to victory in the final battle and won the war.

Except he wasn't a general. He was no fucking hero. He'd never risked his life to save others. He'd never tramped through the desert or the jungle not knowing if his next step would be his last. He'd never sacrificed so others could have a better life or even have a life. He was just a guy gifted with an athletic body and a no-quit attitude. He didn't deserve this: the adulation, the money, the fame, none of it.

But since when did he give a shit if it was deserved or not?

What the fuck was wrong with him?

Every football player lived for this moment from the first second he gripped a football in his hands. It should've been the happiest time of his life, a defining moment in a career of defining moments; two Super Bowls under his belt and a sure MVP of the game. He was a future Hall-of-Famer with a lot of gas left in his tank, still in his prime, not yet thirty years old. The press touted him as the hottest QB in the league.

Nowhere to go from here but—

—*down.*

Nothing had been the same since Ryan died. Try as he might, he couldn't find his passion for the game, for life, for anything. Hell, not even for sex.

Like a disembodied spirit, he observed the scene, detached and way too fucking melancholy in the midst of the celebratory mayhem engulfing him. Jostled around by the sea of humanity, he barely felt them. He stood in the middle of the crowd, numb, apathetic, and alone. The emptiness smothered him, gnawed at his gut, consumed him.

Regardless of his apathy, he wouldn't rain on his teammates' parade.

Forcing a grin he didn't feel and adopting his cocky façade, he faced the television cameras and gave them what they'd come to expect from him, an arrogant, yet entertaining, recap of his performance. Then he stood on the podium, and made one of his typical fist-pumping speeches laced with humor. After which he did every post-game interview with his usual brash panache. No one noticed his mechanical movements or the dead smile.

Was this all there was?

What had happened to his legendary enthusiasm for the game, his penchant for living life on the edge? What happened to *him*? He'd lost himself somewhere between college jock and superstar athlete, yet it hadn't mattered before. He'd lived in blissful ignorance until that fateful night when Ryan died of cancer.

If you stripped away all the hype and his public image, he didn't have a fucking clue who lived underneath.

All this deep shit rattling around in his brain was way too much introspection for a dumb jock. He shook off this momentary lapse into deep thought, took a deep breath, and squared his shoulders. In a week, he'd start the relentless pursuit of winning all over again because losing, for Tyler, had never been an option.

Glancing at his watch, he followed his teammates out of the locker room via a back door, down the long hallway leading to buses waiting to take them to the airport. A couple hours and a few glasses of champagne later the team plane touched down in Seattle. Security hustled them past the large crowds to waiting limos.

Waving and grinning, he acknowledged the hordes of fans crammed into every spare inch of terminal space. He paused and breathed in the crisp Seattle air. His teammates shouted to each other, planning parties which would last well into the morning.

Cass, his long-time fiancée and even longer-time girlfriend, would expect to attend every one of them. She'd already texted him with her location at a teammate's home on Lake Washington.

The Vegas line against them ever getting married had once topped out at fifty-to-one and dipped to fifteen-to-one after he'd set a date for two weeks from today.

Claustrophobia set in, smothering him. He felt trapped, trapped in a career he no longer had a hunger for. His self-created, bad-boy image pigeonholed him in a role he wasn't sure he wanted to play. His upcoming wedding in two weeks weighted him down with doubt.

He needed to escape, clear his head, gain some clarity.

Tyler slid behind the wheel of his sports car and accelerated out of the underground parking garage. His wheels spun on the rain-slickened streets as he turned a corner too quickly. Instead of heading toward I-5 and Mercer Island for a night of celebration, he turned in the opposite direction, dodging in and out of cars on the four-lane street. The light ahead turned yellow, Tyler punched the gas.

And slammed right into the back of a police car.

Chapter 2

Must Come Down

Lavender Mead sniffled and rubbed her puffy eyes. They burned like hell from crying most of the night and into the morning. Hugging herself tight, she blinked back more tears.

All around her, fellow San Juan islanders hunched their shoulders against the incessant February rain, as they gathered in clusters near the shore of Outlaw Bay. The protected bay had been named for all the smugglers, rum-runners, and various other criminals who'd sought refuge there, not to mention the Harris family of the 1920s, renowned for their bootlegging.

Behind her, Art Harris's decrepit mansion clung to the slope above the rotting marina, like a stubborn old lady refusing to surrender to the ravages of time.

Dang, but Lavender was going to miss the old bachelor.

She'd met Art eight years ago, shortly after moving next door to Twin Cedars, his run-down estate. At nineteen she'd just dropped out of college with no future plans, an island-sized chip on her shoulder, and a fondness toward self-destruction.

The crotchety old man had chewed her ass for feeding his fat cat, who was on a diet. How the heck was she to know? The cat had bitched at her door, and she'd assumed he was a stray, a very fat stray. Art's cantankerous attitude hadn't fazed Lavender in the least. Impressed he couldn't intimidate her, he'd invited her to sit on the marina bulkhead with him and fish. They never caught anything, but they talked a lot.

The next day Lavender cooked her five-alarm chili and carried it over to him. One bite and two glasses of water later, he declared it the best damn chili ever. From that point on, they forged a lasting friendship, a lonely old man and a lonely young woman. Art filled a hole left by a dad who chose football over his daughter. In exchange, she became his family. At least, the only family who gave a shit about him.

Now her one rock in the storm was gone.

Another sob welled up in her throat. Funerals were supposed to give closure, help people move on.

Not working so far.

She yanked a tissue from her pocket and blew her nose. Mrs. Malacotty handed her another tissue and patted her arm. Lavender managed a weak smile but nothing eased the ache inside her.

Art died in a nursing home. Alone. She should've been there. Instead she'd stayed on the island, kidding herself he'd recover enough to come back home. No amount of praying and singing gave a person closure on that kind of guilt.

A gusty wind blew in off the water, pelting Lavender's face with rain. The big, fat drops mixed with her tears and left salty trails down her cheeks. Good thing she hadn't bothered with makeup. She pulled up the hood on her raincoat and hunkered down, teeth chattering. In front of her, the minister droned on like a stubborn mosquito buzzing in her ear. His bright yellow raincoat squeaked every time he shifted his fat body. Lavender hiccupped and covered her mouth with her hand.

Meanwhile, Art's only nephew stood at the head of the marina dock, not appearing the least bit grief-stricken, and most likely counting the hours until the reading of the will.

In all the years she'd been Art's neighbor, never once had his nieces or nephew visited him, which branded them as despicable people in her book. Senior citizens deserved to be surrounded by family and friends in their golden years, not discarded and forgotten.

Even worse the nephew happened to be Tyler Harris, a jock to rival all jocks and an entitled asshole.

Tyler stood to one side of the preacher and surveyed the crowd with stony indifference. Dark circles settled in the hollow of his cheekbones giving him a haggard look. Most likely, he'd been dragged out of some party at 3 a.m. and hauled to the island.

Tyler's detached gaze settled on Lavender. Turquoise blue eyes drilled into her until she squirmed. She'd never seen eyes that color before, like a South Pacific lagoon, but not nearly as inviting. Regardless, she couldn't look away, couldn't shake the spell he'd cast on her with one hot, unnerving gaze.

Several locks of dark, wet hair fell across his high forehead. His brows drew together as he squinted through the rain. A day's growth of stubble darkened his cheeks and strong jaw. One corner of his mouth lifted in a half-hearted bad-boy smile. Her heart, already woozy from grief, flopped over and begged for mercy.

Mentally she slapped herself for admiring a piece of eye candy during Art's funeral. What kind of a sorry soul did that? Even if it had been a while. Everything had a proper place and time, and this wasn't it. Wrenching her gaze away, she faked complete attention to the service, all the while fidgeting under Tyler's shameless scrutiny.

The preacher stumbled through his eulogy as raindrops smudged the ink on his handwritten notes. Finally finished, he nodded to a group of Art's cronies who'd christened themselves as the Island Yankee Brotherhood. They shuffled forward in their military uniforms, buttons bursting and fabric straining around their shoulders. Except for big Ed. He'd draped his too small uniform jacket over his shoulders.

Homer, the leader of the Brotherhood, lifted a trumpet to his lips and blew out the first notes of what had to be Taps. The Brothers stood at attention, while the other guests held their hands over their hearts. Even Tyler Harris placed one big hand over his chest, most likely to call attention to the Super Bowl ring on his finger. The diamonds on the gaudy thing cut through the gloom like a light in a lighthouse.

Halfway through Taps, Homer hesitated. His eyes glazed over. He repeated da-ta-da once, twice, three times, over and over like a broken record stuck in one spot. The Brothers didn't budge one muscle, while the rest of the guests glanced at one another. Finally, Jim Miller elbowed Homer in the ribs. He woke from his stupor after one last ear-splitting, off-key note and lowered the trumpet.

All eyes turned to the dock and Tyler Harris. Lavender averted her eyes to avoid another round of disturbing eye contact. Her gaze fastened onto his impressive body. Even hidden beneath a raincoat, his broad shoulders and wide chest were visible, along with his long legs. The rain plastered his wet pants to his muscular thighs. His strong calves and ankles ended at big feet. Really big feet. Which from her experience meant—

Big mistake. Mega big one. This would never—ever—do. Jocks were not on her recommended diet, no matter how delectable they might appear on the outside. She'd sworn off any man with the channel numbers for ESPN worn out on his remote.

Lavender scrubbed her face with her hands and banished her current line of thinking.

The preacher handed Tyler a football-shaped urn, courtesy of a local ceramics shop. He stared at it and wrapped his long fingers around it. After giving it a few practice tosses, Tyler spun on his heel and lurched down the rickety dock. The rotted structure rocked from side to side with each step causing Tyler to stagger like a drunk on a three-day binge.

He stopped near the end and braced his legs apart for balance. The dock groaned and creaked as waves beat at the pilings. The jock's athletic body countered every jolt with ease. He stood in profile, his head thrown back, staring out to the water, like a defiant conqueror. His strong chin jutted out, accentuating a slight cleft. His unruly hair, in need of a haircut, plastered against his forehead, but he didn't bother to pull up his hood.

Cat, Art's orange tabby cat, rubbed around Lavender's legs and meowed, demanding attention. She ignored the prima donna so the tabby head-butted her legs. She pushed him away with her foot. His green eyes bored into hers. He twitched his tail from side to side. "Shhh." She held a finger to her lips.

The cat yowled again. She bent down to grab him, but he eluded her. When she took a step toward him, he streaked toward the dock, weaving in and out of the crowd like a running back heading for the end zone.

"No!" Lavender scrambled after the cat but stopped short of the unstable dock.

Tyler hefted the football urn over his head and cocked his arm. An orange flash darted between his legs. He stumbled in an attempt to avoid stepping on the tabby cat. His front foot couldn't find purchase on the slippery planks and shot out from under him and off the edge of the dock. The urn smashed onto the dock, shattered, and sent gritty gray ash flying everywhere, coating the preacher and anyone within several feet. Tyler's ass followed his foot, skidding across the dock and off the edge. His big body crashed into the icy cold water.

Cat ran back to her and sank his claws in her leg. With a yelp, she leaned down and detached the little brat, cradling him in her arms. "You're in deep shit, buddy."

Cat purred. In the self-absorbed way of most cats, he'd didn't give a damn about all the trouble he'd caused.

Sputtering and cursing, Tyler bobbed to the surface and grasped the edge of the dock. He hoisted himself out of the water and stomped to shore, shaking water from his hair.

Lavender's eyes widened as he headed straight toward her and Cat, his eyes blazing and his shoes making squishing noises. Every muscle in his six-foot-four frame appeared tensed for battle as he towered over her by more than fourteen inches. She tightened her grip on the troublemaking feline.

"That cat just used up all nine of his lives."

Standing toe-to-toe with the arrogant quarterback, Lavender shrugged and tossed him a too-innocent smile. "You're dripping all over my feet."

His body vibrated with restrained fury. Salt water ran off him in streams and puddled on the already saturated ground. He gave her a once-over as the storm in his eyes built to a category five. "I'm not done with him. Or you." Whirling around, he grabbed a towel someone handed him and stalked off.

Lavender didn't know whether to laugh or run like hell. If he thought he was pissed now, just wait until the reading of the will this afternoon.

She'd be replacing Cat as number one on his hit list.

Chapter 3

Animal Attraction

Over the years, Tyler worked hard to cultivate his reputation as an asshole. One hundred percent asshole, from his gorgeous mug to his well-exercised cock, from his fast moves to his irreverent attitude, he practiced the art of being an asshole. In fact, he considered himself a master.

Screw nice. Tyler didn't do nice. Nice guys were pussies, boring pussies. Well, except for his cousin and best friend, Derek. Yeah, Derek could be a pussy at times, especially with his fiancée, but he also had steel in him. He was the guy Tyler would want to have his back.

On the rare occasions when Tyler was caught doing a good, selfless deed, he drowned it in a smoke-screen of self-serving bullshit. The press ate it up. Everyone loved to hate an asshole. So he gave them what they wanted and made money doing it. More importantly, the asshole role kept people at a distance and discouraged them from looking any deeper because Tyler *never* exposed his soft underbelly to anyone. Never let them see the guy who didn't watch sad movies, had a soft spot for animals and old people, and anonymously donated shitloads of money to childhood cancer.

Which was exactly why no one knew about his relationship with Uncle Art. Not even his mother or sisters.

Jim Miller, his uncle's attorney, rifled through the stacks of papers teetering precariously on his desk, leaving Tyler to wonder if the old coot had lost the will. Tyler shifted his butt in a chair made for a guy half his size. He stretched his cramped legs out in front of him and crossed his arms over his chest.

His gaze flicked over the hot little chick with the weird name radiating some serious attitude in the chair next to him. He made a mental note to take a rain check on a more thorough body assessment of the sassy redhead.

Just not now.

Uncle Art's unexpected death had sucker-punched him in the gut. No more secret weekly visits to the VA nursing home to play poker with his uncle and his cronies. No more arguing over who was the greatest baseball player of all time. No more stories about ancestors Tyler never knew. Even worse, he didn't get the chance to say goodbye to an uncle he'd only gotten to know in the past six months.

Just one week ago Tyler had stood on the podium after winning his second Super Bowl and hadn't felt a damn thing but emptiness. He sure as hell didn't have that problem now. He swore a grizzly bear had torn open his chest and ripped out his heart, leaving a gaping cavity and a load of intense, agonizing pain.

But he'd played through pain before, and he'd do it again. He put on his game face and slipped into his favorite role when things got tough, that of a selfish asshole.

The old attorney with bad taste in clothes finally held the will in his pudgy hands. Tyler bit back a few choice words. He just wanted to get on with it and get the hell out of here and back to civilization. He couldn't even get cell-service on this godforsaken island.

Jim glared at him through his coke-bottle glasses, as if Tyler had pissed him off somehow. Hell, Tyler was the one who'd been summoned from his city condo, dunked in the freezing-ass cold waters of Outlaw Bay, and forced to stay on this isolated rock two hours longer than necessary. And for what? To be an unwelcome guest at his uncle's funeral and make a total ass out of himself? To listen to the reading of a will which didn't apply to him? Tyler preferred to do his grieving in private, not in front of several hundred hostile islanders in the middle of a fucking hurricane.

Tyler leaned forward, elbows on Jim's desk, and rubbed his eyes. He hadn't slept in over twenty-four hours, which contributed to his crappier than usual attitude.

The old goat pushed his glasses up his nose and started reading. Tyler tuned him out until he heard his name. "*To my great-nephew, Tyler, as the last of the Harris males, I will to you my estate at Twin Cedars and all of my personal effects therein, including my beloved cat. I'm truly sorry my estrangement from your family kept us from knowing each other sooner. After your father died, I should have been there for you, but I wasn't. At least we had time together at the end.*"

What the fuck? Tyler leaned back in his chair, letting the words sink in. He hadn't seen this coming. Not at all. Especially the cat part.

Hot Chick aka Lavender shrieked one of those high-pitched female sounds that usually sent him diving for cover. She clamped her hand over her mouth, but not before he heard a muffled sob. Oh, crap. Not tears. He'd never been able to deal with a woman's tears, not even his sisters'.

He played dumb, not hard to do with a 1.09 GPA.

Lavender stared at the attorney seated across the table from her as if his words had sucked the life out of her future. "Jim, there must be some mistake. Are you sure?"

"I wish there was a mistake. Artie requested the change six months ago."

"Six months ago?" She made that little heartbreaking sound from deep in her throat, the one women usually followed up with hysterical crying and a big dent in his credit card to make things better.

"Right after Art took a fall and went to the veterans' nursing home in Seattle to recover."

Right after he'd called Tyler out of the blue and asked to see him. Tyler bit back a dose of guilt, even though he'd no reason to feel guilty. He hadn't asked for this. Hell, no one in their right mind would ask for this. The place was beyond repair and a money pit if he ever saw one.

"But-but..." Lavender wrung her hands in her lap. Tyler figured she'd rather be wringing his neck. "Art shared the will with me. We had dreams for the estate—shared dreams once we got the money together. He knew I'd carry on if something happened to him. How could he leave it to this—this person who has no appreciation of the mansion's history or interest in the legacy of one of the island's pioneer families?"

"Which happens to be my family," Tyler reminded her.

She shot him a look that had first-degree murder fantasies written all over it.

"It's quite clear, Mr. Harris inherits it all if he conforms to the requirements set forth in Artie's will."

Tyler snapped to attention. "What requirements?" Jim had better not be messing with him. Tyler wasn't in the mood for bullshit.

"The terms are clear, Mr. Harris. Before you can inherit the property, you'll need to be in residence for ninety consecutive days starting today."

"What?" All those years in loud football stadiums must have screwed up his hearing.

"Ninety consecutive days." Lavender repeated, as if she considered him a fucking idiot or something.

"Not gonna happen." No way in hell did Tyler want to be stuck on this frigging island, not even for five more minutes. At this very moment, a float plane idled at the dock, waiting just for him.

"Then the property passes to the Island Yankee Brotherhood and Lavender Mead."

"Island Yankee Brotherhood? Not the old guys in military uniforms at the funeral?" Hell, they couldn't even get taps right, let alone deal with a big-assed estate badly in need of millions of dollars in TLC or, even better, bulldozing.

"One and the same." The defiant look in Lavender's eyes almost had him smiling. He liked women with balls.

"I'm supposed to get married in a month." Like that was going to happen. Cass wouldn't answer his calls after he'd postponed the wedding once again, and truthfully, Tyler was relieved.

"You'll just have to get married on the island." Jim's helpful suggestion didn't help one damn bit.

"Cass would never come here. She'd hate it."

"Then I guess she'll wait if she really loves you." Lavender was starting to annoy the hell out of him.

Besides, Ty wasn't marrying for love, just convenience and hot, inventive sex. At the thought of sex, his gaze slipped to the woman next to him who wore her displeasure like a suit of feminine armor.

He considered his options. If he left, he'd forfeit the place to a group of geriatrics who'd most likely lose it or sell it. Or, he could spend the next ninety days on an island with no cell service, one stoplight, and no nightlife, unless you counted playing pull tabs and swapping fish stories with the locals as nightlife. He'd be completely isolated from rabid reporters and hoards of nosy fans, which did have its merits. Or he could high-tail it out of Dodge with nothing lost, nothing gained.

Ever since he'd rear-ended the cop car over a week ago, his life had been hell. The press hounded him day and night. Rumors flew about DUI and drug charges, even a possible stint in rehab. Forget that he'd just won the Super Bowl. Nobody cared about that. They wanted dirt. Even worse, some dipshit videoed the entire fucked-up accident, including the aftermath and sold it to a major sports network. The clip started with him ramming into the cop, then taking a breathalyzer test which he passed with flying colors—thank you very much—and ending with him being handcuffed and hauled into jail because he'd given the jock-hating prick of a cop some lip. The cocky son-of-a-bitch had arrested Tyler just because he could. His attorney got him out a few hours later, no charges filed. At least, not yet.

But that didn't stop the speculation. Everyone wanted to believe the worst of him. No one bought that he'd passed the breathalyzer. He'd been the subject of just about every sports show for the past week—ad nauseum, while his agent worked feverishly to do damage control with the league and the team.

Tyler rubbed his thumb across his stubble, considering his options: peace and boredom or mayhem and stress. He pinned Jim with a laser gaze. "So, how much do you think that property is worth?" He kept his attention on Jim, not chancing a look at Lavender, even though he heard her sniff and blow her nose.

"Millions. With that much waterfront, even in this economy, it's priceless." Something flickered in Jim's eyes, immediately rousing Tyler's suspicions. The attorney wasn't being one hundred percent straight with him.

Whatever.

Tyler didn't need a run-down mansion in the middle of flipping nowhere. Yet, Twin Cedars was *his* family's legacy, built over a hundred years ago by his timber baron ancestor, Jackson Harris. Not that he'd keep it in the family.

The land was a different story. *Worth Millions?*

Tyler blew through money like a NASCAR driver blew through the finish line. Being a big spender was all part of his persona. He always figured he'd just earn more.

Yet even before the playoffs, the winds of change had started blowing across his once secure future. That big contract loaded with incentives and the lucrative endorsements could all end tomorrow. Take another mediocre season and add a hot-shot rookie quarterback, and he'd be relegated to backup status. Even worse, an injury could end his career in the time it takes the center to snap the ball. Then where would he be? No source of new income, no marketable skills other than football, expensive tastes, more expensive fiancée, and a family who dipped into his cash a little too often.

He'd seen it happen several times. A washed-up football star goes bankrupt.

Not gonna happen to him. He'd never suffer that humiliation; never do that to his family. They depended on him.

He'd be damned if he'd give up a valuable chunk of land just to get out of ninety days of pure hell. If there was one thing Tyler had never had enough of, it was money. And Tyler always wanted more. His life revolved around an endless pursuit of more: more fame, more fortune, more victories, more women, more parties. More of everything. Because somewhere buried in all the excess had to be the one elusive piece that finally allowed him to say *now I have enough.*

"Did Art say anything about me?" Lavender sniffed and honked her nose so loudly she'd do a Canadian goose proud.

"Yes." Jim felt around for his glasses, stuck them on his fat face. He cleared his throat and sent Tyler the same kind of look Tyler used to get from his dad warning his son to be seen and not heard. *"Lavender, you're probably really disappointed with me and confused. I'm sorry I let you and the Brothers down. You are the granddaughter I never had. I know we had plans for turning the mansion into an affordable vacation resort for veterans. Especially disabled, aging veterans. You have a gift, a great affinity for senior citizens. I wanted to help you get your degree in gerontology—"*

"The study of old people," Lavender added, as if she considered Tyler a moron.

Tyler gritted his teeth but said nothing. He'd never pretended to be a Rhodes Scholar, but he hated being talked down to like a dumb jock, even if the cleats fit.

Jim waited for the two of them to stop their mental stare down then continued. "*—but there's no money, and I can't mislead you anymore. Tyler can afford to do what needs to be done. The Brothers and you can't. I only hope after ninety days in residence, he will come to love the place as much as we did, and do the right thing."*

"The right thing? What the fuck does that mean?" No chance in hell would he keep the rotting hulk. In ninety days, the place had to go on the market, sold to the first buyer with a wad of money. Stuff like family heritage and historical significance couldn't influence his decision. He wouldn't let it. He needed that money, as much as he needed to lay low for a while.

Jim glared at him like this whole mess was Tyler's fucking fault. "You figure it out."

Tyler shifted his gaze to Lavender, who'd gone back to wringing her hands and sniffling. "Look, I didn't ask for this."

She raised her chin and glared at him. Tear tracks were visible on her cheeks. Her lower lip quivered. "But you're going to do it." She spoke so quietly he had to lean toward her to hear. He caught a whiff of her perfume, taking him back to the smell of the spring wildflowers that had grown in the front pasture of his father's ranch. The feisty little redhead met his gaze, wiped at a tear on her cheek and held her head high.

"Yes, I'm going to do it."

"It's settled then. Here are the keys." The old goat attorney slid the ring of keys across the table. "You'll love the island, Mr. Harris."

Tyler grabbed the keys and sealed his fate.

Chapter 4

The Cat's out of the Bag

Lavender hoisted the fat feline into her arms and rapped on her neighbor's door. The orange tabby cat, evil prima donna that he was, purred his approval.

As long as she had anything to do with it, Tyler Harris was going to take care of Art's cat and not shirk his responsibilities. He'd had two weeks to take care of business, now she'd take care of it for him.

After Art went to the nursing home, she'd fed the pissed-off tabby, even smuggled him into her little house, but her landlady grandmother went wacko after she showed up one morning and found the animal drinking out of the toilet. Add to that the claw marks on the back door, cat hairballs on the carpet, and her grandmother's cat allergies. Not a pretty sight by a long-shot. The cat found himself kicked out for good. She'd tried to find him a home, but no one wanted the demanding animal. Besides, Art willed Cat to Tyler, and Art had adored Cat. That must mean something. She just hoped like hell she was doing the right thing.

Bracing herself, she knocked on the door again.

The door opened. Lavender stared face-to-abs with the most incredibly sculpted, though sweaty, chest she'd ever seen. Tyler towered over her, naked from the waist up with his faded jeans slung low on his hips. She lifted her gaze to his well-defined pecs with a smattering of black chest hair. Muscles bunched in his arms and a Rose Bowl tattoo adorned his right upper arm. Despite the muscles, he looked lean and ready for action. She licked her dry lips, imagining the kind of action a man like that might be ready for.

The word *Ryan* was tattooed on his chest, right above his heart. The name rang a bell in connection with Tyler, but she couldn't quite recall why and chose not to ask.

Instead, she focused on the superficial. Damn, but he had a fine body. Standing next to him at point-blank range, he was taller than expected, and gorgeous, absolutely, gorgeous. Too gorgeous for his own good and hers.

A slow, sexy smile softened the hard lines of his face and transformed him from a jerk to a charmer, all the more lethal. "So, Lavender, what brings you to my doorstep? Been missing me?" His deep voice rolled over her like the gentle swell of a tide on the beach.

She found her tongue tied to the roof of her mouth and forced it back into service. "I'm your neighbor, and this is your cat."

His amused gaze washed over her, warming her inside and outside. His blue eyes infiltrated her defenses.

"My cat?" Tyler leaned against the doorframe and hooked his thumbs in the belt loops of his jeans. He crossed one ankle over the other, as he studied the cat. The smile faded from his face. "I know that cat."

"You've met before." Lavender bit back a laugh at the image of the vindictive feline tripping Tyler and sending him and the urn tumbling into the frigid waters of Outlaw Bay.

"Yeah, I remember, and no way in hell is that my cat."

Cat looked up at him and meowed, digging his claws into Lavender's arm.

"That's not what he says."

He stared at the fat lump of orange fur in her arms, his expression skeptical. "The cat lies."

"Cats never lie."

"That one does. I don't have a fucking cat."

"He's not a fucking cat, he's fixed."

Tyler chuckled. "Don't quit your day job. You'll never make it on the comedy channel." His mouth turned up in a genuine grin, making him seem human, almost nice. The man was get-naked-now gorgeous when he smiled like that and way too irresistible. Good thing he spent the majority of his time in jerk mode.

She steeled herself against his many weapons even as her body rebelled. Well, it could protest all it wanted; she'd limit her fantasies to her imagination and her vibrator. She'd learned her lesson when it came to men who played games for a living.

Case in point, her absentee father, who abandoned his family for the fame and fortune of coaching ball at a major college. And the quarterback who dated her in high school just to add another notch in his belt. Then there was the linebacker her freshman year of college who told his frat buddies about their sex life in every vivid detail. The ass even offered to share. That was the end of him. There were more, but those were the lowlights.

She'd been on a jock-free diet for four years now. So what if Tyler happened to be an exceptional physical specimen? Willpower stood on her side. Only willpower didn't have a killer smile, straight white teeth, and a teasing glint in his eye.

Oh, Lord, she'd been staring at him like a lovesick high-school cheerleader. Rattled, she lowered her gaze back to his chest, not a good idea either, so she looked back at his face, specifically his nose, about the safest part on his body.

"This cat comes with the house. He was Artie's cat." At his blank expression, she prodded his memory a little more. "Remember? The one named in the will?"

"Oh, that one." The man even had a gorgeous frown.

"Yes, that one."

"Tell you what? Since I'm such a generous guy, I'll let you have him." She watched as his charm flooded back at full wattage, especially now that he wanted something from her.

"My landlady doesn't allow animals."

"What am I going to do with a cat?"

Lavender could think of a lot of things. Love them. Cuddle them. Take care of them. And when things got tough, no matter what, they'd always be there, purring or licking your face, taking away the hurt. Nothing like a man. "You're not an animal person are you?"

"I love animals. Just not cats." He straightened and glared down at her, like she'd insulted him or something.

That surprised her. Shocked her actually. She never would've pegged him for an animal lover. "Good. Then I won't need to report you for animal neglect."

"Sweetheart, threats don't work with me, but I am open to other types of bribes." The jerk made a show of looking her up and down.

"Not even a threat of castration? It might improve your attitude. It helps with most animals."

"Honey, I'd like to see you try." He threw back his head and laughed, a deep from-his-belly laugh. She liked his laugh, all strong and masculine with an undercurrent of good-natured humor, totally at odds with his usual asshole scowl.

"They grow on you. In no time you'll be drowning in cat hair and loving every minute of it. Give me a call if you need any cat tips." She shoved Cat into his arms and tucked a business card deep in the pocket of his Jeans. Her fingers brushed something hard and—

Oh crap.

Without another word, Lavender hurried down his front steps and out through the main gate.

* * * * *

Tyler stared after Lavender, mouth hanging open, cock locked and loaded, and the furry hunk of lard clutched in his arms.

Her butt in those baggy chinos swayed back and forth. Her tangle of red hair bounced with each step. He liked what he saw from the back, as much as he'd liked the front. Usually, he preferred his women tall and willowy with large, enhanced breasts, Barbie dolls in the flesh, yet his neighbor had it going on for some unexplained reason.

The island must be getting to him. He'd spent two weeks stuck on this rock in the furthest corner of Washington State. Needless to say, he craved some entertainment.

As a result, he didn't disguise his interest when Lavender showed up on his doorstep holding the cat in her arms. Especially after she slid that business card in his jeans and shocked the hell out of him. She'd copped a feel, most likely accidentally, since his pocket and his cock were in the same vicinity. His cock didn't care if it was an accident or not. Desire surged to his dick and turned it harder than that big boulder on the shore near the marina.

Since Cass ignored his occasional calls and text messages, he figured the engagement was off. That being the case, Lavender might prove a welcome distraction if she was interested. And she *was* interested, all right. Her irreverent foreplay said as much.

His mouth tipped up in a satisfied smirk. Most women drooled all over him. Not her. The contempt on her face came through as loud as referee's whistle. No problem, he never mixed physical with emotional. You didn't have to like a person to have great sex with them. Every one of his last several girlfriends proved that theory. Besides, her body didn't hate his body—not one damn bit.

The cat meowed at him, breaking him out of his trance. Oh, shit, he hated cats. What the hell was he going to do with a fur-spreading, litter-box using, flea-infested cat? He didn't want cat fur on his furniture, or headless mice on his front porch, and no way in hell would he clean a litter box.

The fat cat lolling in his arms drooled, rolled its eyes up at him, and smirked, as if to say, "Fuck you, buddy."

"Hey, fuck you, too." He put the cat on the porch.

The cat stared up at him, blinking his green eyes.

"I mean it. Find a new home. I'm not a cat person."

The cat didn't move. Tyler frowned, narrowed his eyes, set his jaw, and glowered at the furry creature with his best you're-in-deep-shit glower. It worked on the biggest, baddest lineman in the NFL.

It didn't work on the cat.

The damn thing yawned and sauntered past him to scratch at the door.

"No way in hell are you getting in my house." Tyler liked things neat and tidy. Claw marks on his antique leather furniture and orange cat hair on his black leather jacket didn't do it for him.

The cat stared at him. Tyler got the impression the cat knew something he didn't. It rankled him. He hated being out of the loop, even with a damn cat.

"Okay, I'll cut you a deal. I'll buy cat food if you agree to live in the barn. And that's my final offer."

The cat blinked again.

"Canned cat food?"

The cat meowed.

With an annoyed sigh, Tyler opened the door. The cat slipped past him and led the way into the old mansion as if he owned the flipping place. His orange and white striped tail waved like the flag of a conquering army.

Damn. Damn. Damn. He didn't need a fucking cat. What the hell was he doing letting the damn thing in his house? Someone might see it and accuse him of being a softie under his asshole exterior. That would fucking never, ever do. The guys in the locker room would eat him alive.

He followed the cat into the kitchen. The little shit sat down and waited while he poured milk in a bowl and placed it on the floor. The cat sniffed it, lapped at it a few times, and sat down again, staring up at him.

"Aw, hell. What now?" Tyler pulled a ham out of the refrigerator, cut it up in small pieces, and put it next to the milk bowl. Finally satisfied, the cat finished the whole thing and rubbed against his legs. Tyler leaned down and scratched the tabby behind the ears. The cat arched its back and danced around him. Tyler shook his head and smiled. "Don't get any ideas, buddy. I don't like cats."

The cat rested on its haunches and yawned as if he knew Tyler was full of shit.

Shaking his head, Tyler remembered the business card and pulled it from his pocket. Printed on one side was the name and address of a local veterans club. On the other she'd scratched a phone number. He rubbed his chin, wondering which mixed message this female meant to send him. With a shrug, he left the card on the counter and went to bed.

A few hours later, Tyler woke from a sound sleep and spat out a mouth full of cat hair. The cat purred loudly on the pillow next to his. Rolling over, he closed his eyes and tried to go back to sleep.

Tomorrow he'd get rid of the cat.

Chapter 5

Tripped Up

Tyler looked down at the random pieces of paper scattered on the roll-top desk. Startling numbers swam across the old-fashioned ledger pages, painting a more dismal picture than he'd ever imagined.

Jim Miller failed to mention his uncle's extreme financial straits. What Art owed could bankrupt a small country. He'd be lucky to realize one penny out of this money-sucking monstrosity based on the fucking liens and mortgages on the property. In fact, in this economy, the value could very well be upside down. No wonder Uncle Art dumped it on him, rather than his cronies and Purple Lady. Only Artie had no way of knowing that Tyler wasn't exactly flush with cash either.

What a fucking mess.

He could walk out right now and leave it to the vultures to pick the bones clean. Let Lavender and the Brothers deal with the frigging disaster.

Tyler sighed and massaged the back of his stiff neck with one hand. His problems weighted him down. He still hadn't heard anything on possible charges related to his traffic incident. The cop claimed he'd assaulted an officer, even though Tyler never used his fists, only his big mouth. That worst case scenario would catapult the press into a feeding frenzy, the NFL into punishment mode, and the Lumberjacks front office into a panic. He'd be up a fucking creek, possibly fined to the hilt, and wasting his Super

Bowl bonus money on attorney fees and spin doctors. Add to that the rumors about drug and alcohol rehab and the alleged DUI.

Crap. He stood and stretched, grabbed a coat and walked out the door, needing a break.

Tyler hunkered down against the wind and rain, wrapped his raincoat around him and trudged out to the mailbox. Shoving the mail under his coat, he hurried back to the house and slammed the heavy front door to keep out the elements. Shedding his wet coat, he hung it on a peg near the door. Immediately, a puddle formed below it. Shaking his head, he spread the mail on the kitchen counter. Since few people even knew where he was, the mail consisted of junk and stuff his sisters forwarded from his Seattle water view condo.

Cass's sloppy handwriting was sloshed all over the front of a padded envelope. He ripped it open. He withdrew a small box, already knowing what was inside—her engagement ring. He opened the box and a huge diamond winked at him as if it knew something he didn't.

Tyler turned it over in his hand, examining it from all angles and waited. Waited for the heart-wrenching sorrow, the devastation, the sense of loss. All those painful feelings he'd felt at eighteen when his father died suddenly, the worst loss of his life. Or when Ryan died or Uncle Art. Surely the loss of his fiancée would compare to those losses.

It didn't.

He felt—nothing. Except an odd relief, an ease of pressure, like slowly letting the air out of a balloon. The same feeling he'd felt after winning this last Super Bowl.

Like oil and water, he and Cass had broken up on a weekly basis since they'd met in their freshman year of college. The make-up sex had been worth it, until lately. In fact, Tyler would be the first to admit that he'd proposed to her because he thought it would fix what was wrong between them. Maybe even what was broken inside him. Only Cass hadn't held the key.

There was something final and certain about this time. They were done, and he knew it, as sure as she'd known it when he'd committed to staying on the island.

Marriage had never been in the cards for him. After growing up in a family only seen in 1950s sitcoms, he'd already known he'd never be able to duplicate what his parents had together. So why try?

Nor could he fix a dying teenage boy, a kid who fought for life and didn't deserve to die. Nor could Tyler, who'd once considered himself invincible, give Ryan the one thing he'd wanted most, a future. The fucking unfairness of it all ate him up inside, made all his problems seem petty in comparison. Even anonymously donating one million in cash to cancer research hadn't made Tyler feel worthwhile.

Damn it. Damn it. Damn it. He hated feeling helpless. Regardless, he might be a lot of things, but he wasn't a quitter. Not once he'd made up his mind. He'd see himself through this mess, and he'd do Ryan proud.

Tyler punched buttons on the thermostat, but the old furnace didn't fire up. Damn. It was freezing butt cold in this drafty old dump. He grabbed his cell phone on the off chance he'd miraculously have cell service. No such luck. He'd have to drive into Friday Harbor to call a repairman. While he was at it, he'd call the damn phone company again and the satellite TV service. Not to mention a plumber to look at the leak in the kitchen and a roofer to repair a few damaged spots on the roof.

His foul mood just got fouler. Isolation, boredom, and frustration didn't improve his temper one bit. Hell, he couldn't even surf the Internet or watch a game. Yanking on a sweatshirt, he stalked into the library to build a fire.

"Off the furniture, little shit, or you'll be sleeping on a hay bale in the barn." Hands on hips, legs braced apart, Tyler stared down at the cat. He itched for a good fight. It looked like he'd settle for a cat as his opponent. The cat stared back, blinked his green eyes, and yawned. The little shit stood, annoyed at having his nap interrupted, yawned, stretched, and turned a small circle. Settling into the overstuffed armchair, he kept his back to Tyler.

He'd just been flipped off by an orange fur ball, an uninvited non-guest in his house. "Get off the fucking chair."

No response, not even a twitch of an ear. Bending down, he reached for the interloper. The crazy bastard struck him as fast as a rattler strikes a field mouse. Tyler yelped and jumped back, holding a bloodied hand.

"Damn it! Fucking feline. I knew I hated cats. Worthless little piece of fur-spreading vermin."

The cat stalked off, irritated about God knew what. Grabbing his leather jacket slung over the back of the couch, Tyler dropped the coat over the feline, wrapping it around the little body.

All hell broke loose. The thing fought like a cougar, not an ordinary house cat. Its little legs churned like pistons, claws ripping his coat to shreds. Its body twisted inside the coat, as it yowled.

Ty would've preferred taking his chances in a cage with an ultimate fighting champion. He held on for all he was worth, hurried to the door, opened it far enough to deposit the rabid, coat-wrapped cat on the porch, and slammed it shut. Panting for breath, he leaned against the door.

Sacrificing a designer leather coat was a small price to pay for not being maimed for life.

* * * * *

Lavender stretched in her bed and opened her eyes a crack. Sun poured through the window, a rare sight compared to the rain of the past few weeks.

Cuddling back under the covers for a few more minutes of sleep, her mind drifted to the jock next door. She cringed as she recalled handing him her phone number.

She'd been dropped into a dilemma of her own making—hers and Art's. Damned if she did, and damned if she didn't. She needed Tyler to leave before the ninety days ended, so the Brothers and she could inherit and follow through on Art's dreams. Yet, if he did forfeit, she doubted they could afford to keep the place in its present state, let alone fix it up.

Tyler could afford to do that, but he'd as good as said he wouldn't. Unless she found a way to persuade him. Lavender stopped that thought right there.

She might have a weakness for gorgeous bad boys—and Tyler filled those big shoes easily—but her peace of mind revolved around not indulging her libido. Besides, her various relationships with athletes over the years never led to anything but heartache.

Lavender sighed. Just wait until her grandmother got wind of her new neighbor.

Her grandmother hated jocks so much, she'd go ape-shit when she found out a jock lived next door, and the worst kind of jock, a football player. Not just any football player but one involved in several recent scandals from driving drunk to giving up on the team when they needed him most.

Grandma would probably mount a community protest. At the least, she'd slap a chastity belt on her wild-at-times granddaughter, while her grandfather stood guard with a shotgun. Lavender chuckled at the picture that presented.

Not to worry, Gram. As badly as she wanted to save the mansion, she wouldn't go that far.

Then she heard it.

The cat. Yowling somewhere outside. His bitching came through loud and clear, and he *was* pissed.

All winter the finicky cat next door bitched day and night about the quality of his living arrangements, demanding his house cat status back. In the short time Tyler Harris had lived in the old mansion, he'd ignored the animal, which is why she'd finally intervened on the cat's behalf yesterday.

Harris behaved exactly as she'd expected the arrogant jock to behave. Lucky her, why couldn't he have been a marine biologist or an artist, even a plumber? But a jock? Damn. What a subversive twist of fate. She'd had enough of jocks to last a lifetime, especially one who didn't take his responsibilities seriously. She knew the type.

The jock had been around long enough to shoulder his responsibilities, namely the animal he'd inherited.

Pulling on her clothes, she walked outside. She didn't see the cat anywhere and headed to her neighbors. The gated estate didn't exactly invite strangers, but she ignored the "No Trespassing" sign like always and slid through a gap on their shared fence line. Once on the other side, she traipsed across the scruffy lawn overrun with weeds. The three-story Craftsman mansion dominated its surroundings; even the old Madronas and cedars flanking it seemed small by comparison. Despite needing a good coat of paint, among other repairs, passersby on the nearby country road always slowed to stare at the impressive structure.

Grooming himself on a bench swing under the wraparound porch sat the fat, orange tabby cat. As soon as he saw her, he launched into another litany of complaints. Lavender shook her head and rolled her eyes. The cat had attitude. He was a perfect match for the infamous quarterback living behind these walls.

The feline bitched in earnest, bombarding her with his grievances.

"Damn, you're a drama queen. Well, hang in there, buddy. Lavender's gonna fix everything."

The cat smirked, happy to have his way.

If she expected any peace, she'd need to have another confrontation with Tyler Harris.

Bracing herself, she brought up her hand to rap on the door.

* * * * *

Tyler hesitated and stared at the door. The cat's yowling had stopped, which made him suspicious. Surely, the animal was plotting its next move. He frowned and pressed his ear against the solid wood door and listened. Nothing. Not a sound.

The little shit probably ran over to complain to the neighbor. Next thing he knew, she'd be calling animal control, and it'd be all over the Internet and ESPN. He didn't give a damn what the press said about him in most cases, but he didn't abuse women or animals, nor did he drive drunk or do drugs. *Ever.* End of story.

To keep the gossip mags at bay, Tyler yanked open the door at the exact time purple lady raised her hand to knock. Instead she rapped on his chest. A grin spread across his face as he stared down at her fist frozen in mid-knock on his breastbone. He grabbed her hand in case she decided to punch him in the nuts or something. His eyes locked with her startling brown ones. Unruly red hair framed her pale face with its sprinkling of freckles. His fingers itched to explore the auburn mass of curls.

Tyler gripped her hand tighter. Her palm felt warm against his. His long fingers wrapped around her small hand, engulfing it, making it look fragile. An overwhelming urge to lift her hand to his lips and kiss it like a chivalrous gentleman of old passed through him. As if she read his mind, she wrenched her hand away.

He braced for round two with his diminutive neighbor with the great tits.

"Your cat wants in." Lavender got all huffy and indignant, like she was the cat's protector or something.

"I kicked him out."

"Why? Can't you see how traumatized he is?"

"He's traumatized?" Tyler glanced at the fat tabby grooming himself on the porch swing. He held up his bandaged hand.

She snorted and ignored his injuries. "You need to be a more responsible pet owner."

"Since when are you my conscience?"

"Someone needs to be. Take care of your cat, or I'll be your worst nightmare."

"You already are." He chuckled, goading her for the pure devilment of it.

"Don't you forget it, jock boy. Why don't you go back to the city where you belong?"

"What? And miss the company of a sweet thing such as yourself? Not on your life."

Turning, she stomped off. Tyler stood in the doorway and watched her go. They might not be the best of friends, but damn, she turned him on when she got mad like that.

The cat stalked past him, fucking tail stuck straight up, and interrupted his daydream of Lavender in the buff. The orange shit tossed a screw-you look over one furry orange shoulder and disappeared into the living room. Tyler followed him, knowing exactly what he'd discover.

In front of the massive stone and marble fireplace, the cat stretched out on a mission-style leather couch, one of the mansion's original pieces of furniture. It'd survived over one hundred years.

Tyler hoped like hell it survived an ordinary house cat with the attitude of a cougar.

Chapter 6

Third-Down Conversion

A few weeks later, Tyler stood on the sagging back porch of his piece-of-shit mansion and surveyed his so-not piece-of-shit surroundings. The mansion might need work, but the view sure as hell didn't. Despite his intention to sell the property at the end of his ninety-day exile, a grudging appreciation of the raw beauty wound its way past his defenses.

A pin-prick of guilt regarding the fate of the mansion unearthed his sense of family loyalty. He closed his eyes and waited for a moment of clarity, a sign as to the direction to take, but the answer eluded him.

Taking a gulp of oxygen, he opened his eyes and leaned on the porch railing. Tall cedars crowded the edge of the weed-infested lawn, while Madronas clung to the bank and leaned precariously over the water of Outlaw Bay. On the horizon, clouds gathered and signaled another impending storm. Water lapped at the sand on the small beach and eroded a portion of his restlessness. The old dock creaked as the wake of a powerboat rocked it. In the distance, a small sailboat tacked back and forth taking advantage of the stiff breeze in Hazard Channel, so christened not just for the rocks below the water's surface but for the many smugglers and criminals who plied the waters over the past century. A smile crept across his face as he imagined his ancestors bootlegging whiskey to the mainland. Obviously, he'd inherited their wild streak.

It was hard to believe the Super Bowl had ended only five weeks ago. For a couple agonizing weeks after the game, the sports world buzzed with rumors about Tyler quitting football, his alleged drug and alcohol problems, and his bad attitude. Hiding out on the island might be making him stir-crazy, but it kept him out of the press's sights. The rumors had died down to a whisper here and there, as the fickle press moved onto the next story. He'd become yesterday's news—which for once was fucking fine with him—until the next round of rumors started circulating.

A small smile tickled the corners of his mouth, as an uninvited peace soaked into his bones. He shook it off in an attempt to resist the call of the islands. He wouldn't answer their siren song. He needed stimulation, the constant excitement and activity only a city provided.

Yet he'd been born and raised in the country on a ranch, done some junior rodeo, mucked stalls, bucked way too much hay, and truth be told loved every minute of it. Buried deep a country boy lurked under his city boy exterior, another contradiction in a life of contradictions.

Ryan would have loved it here.

Shaking off that thought, Tyler turned away from the beauty. Walking inside, he ambled down the hallway into the den with its dark wood and massive stone fireplace. A hunk of old-growth cedar served as the mantle. A part of Tyler admired the incredible craftsmanship of the old mansion, how it'd withstood the test of time. Unlike the fickleness of being a football star one day, a goat the next. Another part of him compared the place to prison.

The cat, now christened Cougar in honor of his attitude and Tyler's former college team, sprawled in front of the fireplace and waited for Ty to build a fire. Not that Tyler liked the cat, not at all, but they tolerated each other's presence after the leather coat debacle.

"You're a heat slut, Coug. Know that?"

Cougar blinked at him and stretched his long feline body. Standing, the cat rubbed against Tyler's legs and made a purr-ow sound only cats could make. Tyler bent down and picked up the tabby, cradling him in his arms.

Placing Coug on the couch, he sat down at the antique roll-top desk and checked out the latest issue of a gossip mag he'd picked up at the grocery store. His gaze snapped to a picture of a familiar blonde on the arm of a tall man, both dressed for a Hollywood party. His body tensed. Cass. Once, he'd assumed they'd end up together, like he'd assumed a lot of things.

Such as assuming his invincible father would be around forever. After all, he'd flown rescue helicopters in war zones and survived. And then he'd assumed a miracle would save Ryan, the teenage football player Tyler and his cousin befriended. It hadn't. The brave kid died of cancer a year ago and left a permanent hole in Tyler's heart. Then Art Harris died, the great uncle he'd only gotten to know six short months ago.

Nothing made sense anymore. His brash, self-absorbed costume didn't fit so well. His love of the game dribbled away to be replaced by apathy. Football had been his obsessive focus for so long, quitting didn't seem a viable option. Tyler Harris without football didn't exist. He had no identity unless he held a pigskin in his hands, and right now he didn't even have that.

All this introspection didn't sit well with him.

He needed human company, socialization, maybe a little admiration from the locals, anything to make him feel worthy. He'd hidden out on this estate for almost a month, plenty long enough. An opinionated, demanding cat had been his only company with the exception of a few trips to town for milk, beer, pizza, and cat food, but that was it. Plus, he was damn tired of eating his cooking, which exclusively revolved around an ancient microwave.

A few glimpses of Lavender weren't enough to satisfy his cravings for human interaction. Though those few glimpses kept him going. Like a voyeur, he craned his neck for a glimpse of her curvy body and drool-worthy tits. He even knew her routine. She'd stride out to her makeshift greenhouse every morning and water her plants. One good gust of wind and the shack would be leveled. He snorted. Hell, her dinky little house wasn't much better. It looked like he felt after a weekend drunk.

His sex-deprived brain indulged in various carnal fantasies, each one more deviant than the last, and every one involving the sassy little redhead next door who brought out the worst in him. Tell that to his dick, it didn't care, it just wanted satisfaction.

But a man can't live by fantasies alone. Being as much a social animal as he was an asshole, he sought out attention and conversation. When dusk set in, he headed to Friday Harbor, the largest town in the San Juan Islands, large being a relative term. Time to check out the local women and down a few brews.

Tyler parked his big-assed truck on the main street in Friday Harbor and stepped out. The busy little town of two thousand consisted of a few blocks of shops, stores, and restaurants. He paused, tipped back his black Stetson and did something so rare, it shocked him to his core, yet this was the second time today. He paused to survey the serenity and beauty around him. The storm gave way to an unusually clear night. Stars shone in the sky, more brilliant because of the lack of city lights. Lit up like a cruise ship, a Washington State ferry motored away from the ferry landing bound for the mainland.

Tyler ran a hand over his face and steeled himself against the allure of the island. Turning his back on the view, he walked a half-block and hesitated in front of the veterans club he'd noticed earlier, the same one on the business card Lavender had shoved in his pocket. He thumbed through his wallet for his national membership card, courtesy of his father's service in the military. Finding it, he walked to the door.

He might as well hang with the locals since he was one, at least for now. After all, he'd inherited one of the finest view properties on the island.

Tyler pushed through the door and drew the stares of every bar patron. He signed the guest book and listed his membership number.

Hadn't these people ever seen a tall cowboy before? Casting one last glance around the room, Tyler took a seat at the long bar. He shook his head, wondering what the hell had gotten into him? He'd come to town for company, yet now that he was here, he wanted to be left alone. On any other day in any other place, he'd be sitting at a table surrounded by adoring fans and playing to his audience like the attention slut he was. His gaze swept across the room, past the table of locals speaking in low tones. He caught the words: asshole, selfish, drunk, quitter, and entitled jerk. Shrugging, he turned away. He'd charm their asses off later if the mood struck him. Right now, he didn't want to talk football with anyone.

He did a double-take at the wall of windows looking out over some of the best prime view property in the islands. *Holy shit.* Nestled on a hillside, the bar's expansive view took in the ferry landing and neighboring islands. This place would be worth a fortune even in the current market just for that view.

His sharply honed, womanizing eyes targeted the miniscule woman making a drink behind the counter, her back to him. To call her sexy wouldn't do her justice. Unabashedly, he ogled her backside. Her compact, curvy body differed from the tall, emaciated blondes he normally dated. Her auburn hair fell in a curly mass across her shoulders and down her back. Her tight jeans hugged her round ass, just the right size to fit in his big palms.

Ty grinned. He could use a little island magic.

She barely cast a glance in his direction as she put glasses away. "What can I getcha?"

"How about *you*?"

She turned, and their eyes collided with the impact of a head-on collision. His mouth fell open. The woman rendered him speechless and that didn't happen often.

Shit. It was her, Lavender. Man, she'd cleaned up so well he hadn't recognized her. She looked him up and down. He actually squirmed under her astute gaze. Her brown eyes stripped his defenses bare and found him lacking.

"It's *you*." She beat him to the punch and didn't sound too happy about it either.

"Yeah, babe, it's me. The answer to your prayers. Did you miss me?"

"Members only. You'll have to leave." Her smug smile lasted only a second as he flashed his membership card in front of her face.

"You're not a veteran."

"My father was so I'm a member through him. Aren't you a lucky woman?" He grinned, enjoying matching wits with her.

"You're an ass. Take the hat off."

"Not a problem." He placed his Stetson on the counter. "How about you and me, and you can leave *your* hat on, baby."

Moving closer to him, she crooked a finger. He leaned forward to catch her hushed words, enjoying the husky sensuality of her voice. "Let me fill you in, cowboy. I've heard every line. You're going to have to do better than that."

"Never challenge a competitive man. I don't like to lose."

"Get used to it."

He laughed. She didn't.

The lady was a smart ass. He liked that in a woman. All that attitude made for a fucking good time in bed, pardon the pun.

"What'll you have? I don't have all day." She drummed her fingers on the counter.

"With me it'll take all day, Lavender."

"With you it'll take nothing because it won't happen." Her brown eyes flashed with annoyance. Damn, pissed-off redheads turned him on.

"You're breaking my fucking heart here, darlin'." He held his hands to his chest and cocked his head at her.

"That'll be five bucks in the jar."

"Huh?"

"For swearing. Put a five in the jar." She pointed to a can sitting on the counter, picked it up, and shook it in his face.

"It says a buck on the jar."

"For you, it's five."

Tyler dug in his jeans and pulled out a twenty. Folding it up, he pushed it through the slit in the jar top.

"Do you want change?"

"Nah, consider it an advance payment." With his mouth, he'd need it.

"We don't like your type around here. Why don't you go back to California or wherever you belong?"

"That might be a little difficult, darlin', cuz I ain't from Cali-for-nee-a."

"You sure as heck aren't from Texas. That's the worst drawl I've ever heard."

"Would you believe I'm a rarity around these parts? I'm a native; a true-blue, born-and-bred Washingtonian."

"Dressed like that?"

"Hey, I'm from Eastern Washington. We're all cowboys or farmers over there."

"Like you'd know a horse's ass from its head."

"That'll be a buck for swearing." He smirked at her and tugged on a lock of her fiery red hair. She jerked away from him, and he let the silky strands slip through his calloused fingers.

Pissed, she yanked a bill from her tip jar and stuffed it in the swear jar. He chuckled, having more fun than he'd had in a long time.

"So what'll it be?"

"That's a loaded question." He raised one eyebrow and slid his gaze up and down her body, lingering on those magnificent tits.

"You have five seconds to name a beer, or I'll pick one for you." The lady was definitely not amused.

Lazily, Tyler looked up. He got the point. He *was* picky about his beer. "What's the best dark beer you have on tap?"

"We have a local dark ale, brewed right here in the islands."

"Sounds good." He watched as she poured the beer into a glass and savored the view of her nicely shaped ass. Turning, she scowled when she caught him eyeing her.

"How's the cat?" Lavender slid the beer across the bar to him.

"Why? Has he been bitching to you again?"

"Actually, I haven't seen him at all."

"That's because he's taken my house by siege and relegated me to servant duties."

"You? A servant?" She laughed; a hearty, yet feminine laugh of true amusement. He liked it so much he wanted to make her laugh again.

"Honest. The little shit is more demanding than my agent when he negotiated my last contract." Before she could open her mouth, he dropped a buck in the jar.

"You paid ahead."

"Call it a donation. So what time do you get off tonight?" He reached for her hand and caught it in his much bigger one. She tugged, and he gripped tighter, running his thumb across her palm.

He liked the feel of her soft hand in his. She shuddered and sucked her plump lower lip between her teeth. Their eyes met. For a moment, he lost himself, forgot his problems, and just enjoyed the little jolt he got from being around her.

Lavender yanked her hand away. Her momentary thaw iced over. "You're no better than the rest of them, are you?"

"Actually, I am better. The best, sweetheart. Give me chance." He didn't have a clue who the rest of them were, but decided to let that one go.

"Not unless your IQ is equal to or better than your quarterback rating."

She'd stabbed him below the belt, but he didn't believe in letting anyone see him bleed. "For that to happen I'd need to be above-genius level."

"Too bad, Einstein, the clock ran out, you just turned the ball over on downs." She tossed him a sassy wink and turned away to wait on her other tables.

Tyler stared after her. He made a mental note to toughen up around Purple Lady, while at the same time stepping up his campaign to get her naked.

* * * * *

What a jerk. Lavender wanted to throttle the arrogant jock.

After she'd rejected him, Tyler wandered over to a lone table. He slumped in his chair, propped his long legs on another chair and glowered at the Canucks hockey game on the nearby television. The few people who attempted to approach him immediately backed off when he shot them a fuck-off glare.

Yet, she kept stealing glances at him. He looked like the real deal with his worn cowboy boots, which actually looked like they'd been used in a barn or on a horse. His hat seemed equally broken in. Nothing about him said "money." In fact, his clothes said just the opposite, if she didn't know better. One thing he couldn't hide was his latent sexuality and his drop-a-women-at-forty-paces blue eyes. Of course, there was that professional athlete's body, too. His broad shoulders filled out his flannel shirt quite nicely. His rolled up sleeves revealed muscular forearms sprinkled with dark hair. His big hands were made to grip a football. She wondered what else those hands were made to do.

He was *gorgeous*. While Lavender wasn't adverse to a little recreational sex, she'd made a promise to herself to maintain a jock-free diet. Besides, the cowboy was probably a selfish lover. Unfortunately, the sight of his naked, ripped body might be worth the price of an admission ticket to the rodeo.

Why couldn't she lust after nice guys? Hell, no, she craved bad boys with over-inflated egos and even bigger cocks—Tyler Harris epitomized the bad-boy jock from his strip-her-naked blue eyes to the delectable bulge in his blue jeans. She knew all about his type. As much as she hated professional sports, a girl would have to be a hermit not to know about Tyler Harris. He was a local legend, a Northwest hero, a self-proclaimed asshole and proud of it. Lately, the press had added drunk driver and quitter to his list of attributes. Worst of all, he was her neighbor, the heir to Twin Cedars, the destroyer of dreams and island history, and the current object of her most decadent fantasies.

Unfortunately.

She'd be lucky to make it through the spring with her virtue intact, what was left of it. The bad girl in her desperately lusted after the bad boy in him. They'd be hot in bed, sheet-scorching, bone-melting hot. She'd been celibate since last summer following her aborted relationship with the spoiled son of a wealthy California attorney. Summer ended and so did his interest in her. Another one of her meaningless flings with the wrong type of man. Not that it hurt much because her heart never participated in her sexual relationships. Not anymore. She liked sex, actually she loved sex. Her self-righteous grandmother would drop to her knees and pray for her granddaughter's soul for hours if she knew about the men who'd entertained her granddaughter over the years. Heck, she probably thought Lavender was still a virgin.

The advantage to having a purely sexual tryst with Mr. Touchdown was that she didn't like him, didn't find his particular brand of charm charming, and his residency status on the island was temporary. They'd both be able to get physically involved without any emotional bullshit.

Lavender twisted the bar rag in her hands. *No, no, no.* None of that mattered. She'd promised herself. No jocks, no matter how well she justified it.

Tyler Harris was a football player. A guy didn't get much worse than that. By reputation, he represented the worst football had to offer and that said a lot. Football had wrecked her mother's life for years, and it didn't make hers any easier. Fate played a sick joke on her when the Seattle Lumberjacks bad-boy quarterback inherited the run-down mansion next door.

She wouldn't cut the man any slack, even though he had two redeeming qualities: his body and so far he took good care of the cat.

Despite Tyler's obnoxious personality, conceit, and mastery of the "F" word, her body didn't seem to care. Every time he came near her, said body hummed with pleasure and begged to be set free. Her panties got wet. Her nipples hardened. Her heart sped up. The chemistry between them snapped and popped like a broken power line on a wet pavement.

Heaven help her.

Chapter 7

Autograph Party

Tyler didn't get it.

He drove around the block several times and resigned himself to parking three blocks from the VC. Every closer parking spot was taken.

He walked down the street and rounded the corner. The sight ahead stopped him in his tracks. People crowded in front of the VC's door and formed a jagged line around the block and out of sight. As he got closer, a group of teenagers noticed him and started cheering.

Tyler frowned and slowed down. He glanced over his shoulder but didn't see the object of their attention. *Unless...*

What the fuck? Jim *had* asked to meet with him at noon today at the VC.

His sharp quarterback gaze zeroed in on a hand-printed sign on the side of the building. *Tyler Harris autograph session here today from noon to two. $3 per autograph.*

They were charging for his autograph? Scowling, Tyler pushed past the line at the door and entered the building. He stalked past the meeting room, but not before he noticed a table setup with a stack of photographs just waiting to be signed. *Double Fuck.*

Someone was wading in some deep shit, and he suspected Lavender's boots were sinking deeper. Striding into the bar, he paused inside the doorway to plan his next move. His uncle's attorney, Jim, who'd recently quit smoking, sat in the corner of the bar chewing on gum and shredding a napkin while he stuffed popcorn in his face. The other geriatrics at his table sipped on coffee and watched a basketball game on television. Lavender, his lead suspect, was nowhere to be found.

"What the hell is going on?" Tyler stood in front of Jim wearing his best fuck-with-me-and-you-die expression.

Five pairs of eyes stared at him with mock innocence. Finally Jim spoke, "We're having an autograph party. Didn't I tell you why we invited you here today?"

"Like hell you didn't."

The blind old goat shrugged and added salt to his coffee. "Sorry, I overlooked it."

"You can't charge for my autograph without my consent."

"It's for a good cause." Jim took a sip of his coffee and made a face. He squinted at the salt shaker.

"I don't give a fuck."

Lavender appeared, tip jar in hand. She slammed the jar on the table and faced him with hands on her hips. He stuffed a five in it. As little as she was, she resembled an angry fairy, hardly intimidating. He snorted his disdain.

"It's for the town's senior services fund."

"And that's my problem how?" He didn't like being taken advantage of, he didn't give a damn what the cause was.

Lavender got in his face, or tried to. Instead her nose pretty much hit around chest level even though she stood on tip-toes. Her brown eyes blazed with fury. Tyler glowered down at her, reveling in his height advantage. Nobody manipulated him like this.

"Do you have any idea how the economy has affected the people on these islands? At the same time, the senior service's funding is being cut. We need the funds to provide things like free meals to shut-ins."

"I'm outta here."

Jim stood up and laid the shredded napkin on the table in a pile with the others. His sly smile backed Tyler up a step. "So you're willing to forfeit the mansion?"

Tyler stopped dead in his tracks. "What?"

"Your cooperation is one of the stipulations in your uncle's will."

"Signing autographs? I truly doubt that."

"Yes, the fine print says you're required to participate fully in the island experience as a responsible citizen, activities to be determined at my discretion."

"No. Fucking. Way. I'm calling my sister, the attorney." Turning his back on Jim and Lavender, he dialed his sister, Freddie. The conversation was short and tense. He listened in disbelief as she confirmed the old geezer's claims.

Jabbing the *End* button with his finger, Tyler crammed his phone in his pocket and turned to face Jim and Lavender. "It's against my contract. I can't sell autographs."

"Then you have a problem, don't you?"

"No, you do."

The old goats elbowed each other and chuckled as if this was funny.

"Like hell I do."

"I'm sure your team will understand. Sign or forfeit Twin Cedars."

Tyler waged a silent war with himself. Flipping them off and walking out would give him a moment of satisfaction. On the other hand, he'd be damned if he'd lose the property to these group of idiots.

Turning to Jim, he held out a hand. "Give me a fucking pen."

* * * * *

Lavender wouldn't have believed it if she hadn't seen it with her own eyes. From the second Tyler took his seat and the first nervous fan stepped forward, the surly, pissed off jock morphed into a gracious, attentive celebrity.

Tyler flashed his brilliant smile with those perfect white teeth and won the heart of every female in the room. The teenage girls squealed and jumped up and down like he was a rock star. The middle-aged women didn't show much more restraint. The men engaged him in conversations about next year or any other sports subject they chose. He saved his best for the teenage boys, spending extra time with them, asking about the local football team like he really cared, and posing for pictures.

All in all, he tolerated the inane questions and groping women with ease, obviously basking in the spotlight. The man should run for office, he'd win in a landslide. In the week he'd been coming into the bar, she'd never seen him like this.

Lavender ran interference, keeping the line going and preventing eager fans from monopolizing Tyler's time. The name of this game was quantity. The more people they put through in the next hour, the more money they made. Several fans paid again and rotated back through the line more than once for additional autographs. Tyler mugged for pictures and ignored her attempts to limit the time spent with each fan, almost as if he sought to annoy her. No doubt he did. A little payback for her part in this little surprise.

Meanwhile, Ed and Homer manned the cash boxes, which were brimming with dollar bills and odd change.

The second the door clicked shut on the last fan, Tyler shot to his feet and stalked toward her, an enraged panther stalking a wounded gazelle. Homicide gleamed in his eyes. Lavender fled to the safety of the bar, pretending she didn't see him. He followed her, circling her until he'd cornered her between the icemaker and the beer taps. She backed up a few steps and hit the bar counter, almost knocking over a glass of wine in the process.

"Customers are not allowed behind the bar." She tried for a little steel in her voice, but her words cracked like brittle plastic instead.

"Don't you ever fucking pull that on me again. Understand?" Her body shuddered at the sound of his lethal voice, and her reaction wasn't based solely on fear. Instead, his blazing blue eyes, lowered voice, and tense, threatening stance turned her on. Dang, but she wanted him—every hard, uncompromising, furious inch of him. She wanted him to lift her up on this counter and rip off her clothes then take her hard and rough, demanding all she had to give and leaving it all out on the table—or counter rather.

With a shaking hand, Lavender held out the cuss jar. Tyler batted it away. His fury shifted like a shift in the winds to something more disturbing. His gaze smoldered with a heat not just from anger. She held her breath, even as her fingers itched to bury themselves in his dark hair and yank his mouth down to hers. He leaned closer. His minty breath tickled her nose.

One of the Brothers cleared his throat from several feet away, but none of the cowardly, old men tottered to their feet to rescue her. Not that she wanted to be rescued.

Tyler hemmed her in by putting his big hands on either side of her and resting them on the lip of the counter. His intense blue eyes promised some serious down and dirty fun. His voice dropped a low, sexy octave. "I know exactly what you need."

She bet he did. Her heart seconded it. The rest of her body voted in unanimous agreement. "What I need is for you to leave this island." Boy, did she, before she did something stupid, like give him everything he wanted. And more.

"So not going to happen, sweetheart." He lifted his hand and ran a finger along her jawbone and neck. Her body shook with a mini-earthquake of its own, drawing a self-satisfied smirk from him.

"Why not? Why don't you leave? You don't need the money." Lavender swallowed, hating how her body responded to his. Gathering her courage, she got her head into the game, and smiled sweetly, while reminding herself what an ass he was. Lavender couldn't allow herself to get down and dirty with Tyler Harris, no matter how incredible the packaging happened to be. She'd cure herself of her weakness for gorgeous jocks once and for all. Tyler Harris would be the bar with which she'd measure her success.

"I'm not ready to leave yet. Maybe I'm enjoying it here way too much to leave. Besides, let's be realistic. You and your crew of ancients couldn't even pay one month's taxes on Twin Cedars."

She nodded, knowing he was right. His mouth came within inches from hers. Her body hijacked her brain and wallowed in the jock's bad-boy spell. He smelled so good, so kissable, so male, so very male. His deep blue eyes were the color of a South Pacific lagoon and just as warm. Her heart journeyed down that path into dumb-woman's land while her pulse raced ahead, leading the way. She might as well set the oven to broil and crawl inside to cool off. She was that hot.

He invaded her space. His smug expression turned to awareness of her as a woman, sexual awareness. The man was more than willing to buy if she was selling. She'd be one more notch on his already packed helmet, one more meaningless screw among thousands, one more gullible female. Thoughts raced through Lavender's head of a faceless woman underneath Tyler, her legs wrapped around his waist, as he pounded into her. Once he finished, he'd get dressed and leave, never even knowing the woman's name.

At least he knows my name.

Lavender slapped herself mentally. That wasn't the point. She didn't want to be another easy conquest for a man who'd exceeded his quota several lifetimes over. She'd been too easy in the past, too quick to give her body and then her heart to an entitled jock with an over-exercised cock and an under-exercised brain. Maybe all jocks weren't alike, but the type she fell for certainly were. Tyler Harris made the rest look like rank amateurs.

She wasn't gullible, and she wasn't going to be an easy mark. Not tonight. Not any night. Not anymore. She'd come too far to jump off that wagon. She wouldn't succumb to his charms, even if she did put her toe in the water more than once.

Disgusted with herself, Lavender reeled in her wayward emotions and reminded herself who she was dealing with here. A jock. A jerk. A bad boy. A self-proclaimed asshole who could turn on the charm when the mood struck him, which wasn't often as far as she'd witnessed.

Lavender brought up her knee and gave him a good jab in the groin, not enough to send him rolling on the floor in agony, but enough to back him off. And back off he did with a surprised yelp. A storm raged in those blue eyes. She ducked around the counter and refused to look at him, but she sensed his presence. Busying herself, she cleaned off a few tables. After a long moment, she hazarded a glance at him. He'd retreated to a spot in front of the bar, as he stared at her, slightly bent over at the waist, his face lined with distress and surprise.

Finally, he heaved himself onto a bar stool and snapped his fingers. "Beer."

Slipping behind the bar, she indulged in a brief fantasy regarding where she'd like to shove that beer, but she'd already done enough damage for one night. Instead, she slid a beer across the counter, one of those cheap brands he hated. He grabbed it and drank it down in one long gulp, as if it would ease the pain between his legs.

She slid another cheap beer to him. He frowned at the label and drank it a little slower.

"That was low."

"Sorry, I forgot you liked dark beer." She emptied the tray of dirty glasses into the dishwasher, refusing to make eye contact.

"I meant the hit to my groin." He groaned, as if he'd get any sympathy from her.

"You were in my space. You're lucky your balls aren't hanging in my trophy room."

"You're lucky I'm in a forgiving mood." He shifted his weight, as if having difficulty finding a comfortable position.

"Don't mess with me again. I don't like it."

"Really? Well, I don't like being manipulated."

"Would you have signed autographs if we'd asked outright?"

"Fuck, no." Tyler dropped a buck into the cuss jar. "I don't do this kind of shit. It's bad for my asshole image. People don't want to see me as a good guy, ruins their preconceived notions."

"My point exactly."

Tyler's gaze slid down her body like a bold caress then sauntered back to her face. "I'm falling in dislike with you."

"I'm already there. It's nice to know we're on the same page."

"It's not just a page, it's a whole book."

"Like you would know. Have you ever read an entire book?"

"Sweetheart, I can read your book just fine."

Infuriated, Lavender turned away to tend to her other customers. She didn't know how she'd survive two more months on the same island with this insufferable jerk. Even worse, how she'd keep him out of her bed.

Chapter 8

Goal-Line Stand

Over the next several days, Tyler gained a new understanding of island time. He still didn't have television, phone, or internet service. The roofers he'd hired to repair the leaking roof showed up for work around eleven, took a two-hour lunch, and left about two-thirty. The temperamental furnace worked when it wanted, and the serviceman he'd called seemed in no hurry to take a look at it. Fireplaces didn't come close to keeping this mausoleum heated, even though he kept a fire lit in the den and master bedroom. At least the weather cooperated and hovered in the low fifties and high forties.

Even worse, he'd been reduced to chopping wood every morning to feed the hungry fireplaces. He hadn't chopped wood since he'd been a kid. Funny how things came full circle.

One advantage of being on an island and out of contact with the rest of the world was that his coaches, teammates, agent, and the press couldn't reach him. They'd left tons of messages on his cell, but Tyler ignored every one of them. He didn't want to talk about football or his future. He didn't want to speculate on whether Seattle's finest would press charges. He couldn't answer their questions because he didn't have any answers himself. On the subject of the DUI, they'd believe what they wanted to believe, no matter what he said.

He struggled to come to terms with his future and his past. He needed more time to clear his head and figure things out.

So far, the only thing he'd figured out was that he wanted his sexy, sassy neighbor flat on her back on his mattress, or on her hands and knees, or bent over the back of a chair, or against the shower wall with her legs wrapped around his waist. Pretty much anywhere as long as his cock got satisfaction.

Oh, fuck yeah, he wanted his neighbor. Bad. Really bad.

In his fantasies, he stripped Lavender bare and licked, sucked, nipped, and kissed his way around every curve and valley on her hot little body. He ravaged those full, sexy lips until they were swollen and quivering. Whisker burns reddened her cheeks. Her gorgeous tits begged for his mouth and his hands. Just for fun, he punished her ass with a well-deserved spanking. After which, her shapely legs spread wide for him. His hungry cock slid into her warm folds and found heaven on earth. Oh, yeah, then he fucked her senseless all night long. After which she dropped to her hands and knees and prayed to his dick, pleading for more. He gave it to her. Over and over again.

In his fantasies.

Unfortunately, his fantasies weren't getting any closer to reality. So far, despite a few moments of weakness, she resisted him. Women never resisted him, not for long. How the hell did she fucking do it?

Just thinking about her hardened his cock to the point of physical pain. His dick seemed to be the only part of him still alive and functioning as normal. Cold showers were becoming the norm, and not just because the hot water heater proved to be flakier than the furnace.

Tyler needed a release from sexual deprivation and boredom, or he'd go crazy. Despite his many faults, lazy wasn't one of them. He'd never been one to sit on his ass for long. Looking around at the once grand mansion, he made a decision. If he couldn't rely on the workers, he'd start the renovation process himself. Using the same obsessive zeal he'd once applied to dissecting an opponent's defense, Tyler funneled his pent-up energy toward rectifying the mansion's state of disrepair.

After a trip to town for supplies, he started hand sanding the rail on the oak banister. The chore required infinite patience and days of rubbing, but hell, time happened to be something he possessed in spades for the next couple months.

Cougar sat nearby, a couple steps up, as if Tyler needed supervision. The cat alternated between licking his ass and overseeing Tyler's progress.

A few hours later, Tyler's back hurt like hell, his knees started to give out, and dust filled his nostrils. Tired of crouching on the stairs, he stood and stretched his cramped muscles. His gaze swept around the grand entryway, taking in the one-of-a-kind woodwork and funky interior of the old mansion. Standing back, he admired his work, and it was work, countless hours of painstaking sanding in all the crevices and corners. One of the previous inhabitants of the place, probably Uncle Art, had painted the rooms some bizarre colors, including painting this once-elegant banister lime green.

Thank God, the previous inhabitants' intentions outweighed their ambition. Most of the woodwork hadn't been desecrated. They'd done plenty of other weird stuff, like ripping out all the master bathroom fixtures and never replacing them, enclosing the back porch with plexi-glass by pounding nails into the siding, and ripping up a three-foot square section of teak flooring in the den.

Tyler smiled in satisfaction as he surveyed his handiwork. The majority of his friends and acquaintances considered him as shallow as a piece of paper, a bona-fide asshole. They'd never buy his appreciation for the details which made this old mansion so special or believe he'd enjoy restoring an old place like this. Of course, he'd prove them right and sell it in the end for a handsome profit, placing the almighty dollar higher than any family legacy.

Why was he even bothering with the banister? Too costly to be completely renovated, Twin Cedars would be razed by the next owner and replaced with condos.

A fucking shame, actually. His ancestors probably shook their fists at him from heaven or possibly hell.

Tyler's great-great-great grandfather, Jackson Harris, built Twin Cedars in the early 1900s as a home for his family. A timber magnate, Harris amassed quite a bit of wealth until he retreated to this island to escape the pressures of his Seattle life. Over the years, the estate stayed in the Harris family's possession, even though it'd been leased out for various purposes. It'd operated as an inn with a bar, café, and small marina. It'd also served a stint as a Christian retreat, a hotel, and a home to different branches of the Harris clan, including an eccentric spinster aunt who liked to skinny dip in the bay, beat the local good ol' boys at poker, and scandalize the neighbors. Hell, he'd even heard rumors it'd been a brothel briefly. Maybe that explained the colors.

In the near future, he'd be responsible for erasing a century of family history by reducing this mansion to rubble.

He was no longer sure how he felt about that.

Tyler sank down onto the stairs and rested his hands on his knees. He surveyed the two-story entryway with its huge chandelier. This place had withstood the test of time. Would he? How would he be remembered? What would friends and family say? What would be his legacy? *Great quarterback, but a poor excuse for a human being?*

When did it start to fucking matter?

He knew the answer to that question—Tyler's mind morphed back to the moment a dying Ryan asked him to find his absentee mother:

"I need you to find my mother."

"Your mother?"

"Yeah. Please, Ty. I need to know where she is. I want to see her before—before—well, you know."

"Why didn't you ask Derek?"

"Because I want the truth. Derek's too nice. He'd never tell me the truth if it was bad news."

"And I would?"

"Yeah. You're a tough guy. A badass. You say what you think and to hell with everyone else. I don't want anyone worrying about my feelings. I need to know."

"You think you'll get that from me?"

"Yeah, I will because you won't be concerned about hurting me. You'll just do the job. You take care of yourself; nobody else matters."

Swiping a hand across his face, Tyler rose to his feet. He glanced at his worthless cell sitting on the antique hall tree. By now he most likely had a dozen messages from his agent, but he couldn't access them until he drove to town. The guy must be wetting his boxers in fear his star client might be on the verge of suspension, or even worse—retirement. After all, where does a guy go when he's hit the top of the peak? Twice. Get out while the getting's good, or stay until they kick your ass out cause you're so old no one wants you?

Tyler never wanted to be the object of anyone's pity. Never.

Besides, he didn't know what the hell he was considering. He was still young, only twenty-eight, and healthy, but he'd lost his passion for the game. That fire in his belly. That inexplicable something that drove him to be the best at all costs.

Right now, he felt nothing, not just about football but about his life. Inside, he was one big empty zero. Refinishing this banister or ogling Lavender's ass gave him more satisfaction than his last Super Bowl win.

Picking up the sandpaper, he rubbed harder on the solid oak and used his frustration to fuel his ambition.

* * * * *

Lavender gathered all the glasses onto a tray and wiped the table clean. Behind her Tyler nursed his beer. She felt his eyes on her butt almost like a caress. Holding the tray, she turned back to the bar and filled more drink orders. Hyperaware of Tyler behind her, the counter was the only thing separating their bodies. Distracted, she overfilled a beer glass. Beer ran down the counter onto the floor. Behind her, a soft chuckle raised her hackles.

"What do you find so amusing?" She wrung the towel in her hands and wished it were his neck.

His blue eyes lit up with asshole pleasure. "I make you nervous." His deep voice tugged at something deep inside her.

"Bullshit."

He held out the cuss jar. Lavender dug in her pockets and crammed a buck in the overflowing jar. "That'll be two bucks. One for cussing and one for lying."

"There's no penalty for lying. If there was, you'd be broke."

He rubbed the day's worth of stubble decorating his strong chin. "So you admit to the lying part."

"I admit to nothing, except that you annoy the hell out me." Lavender wiped the beer from the counter and bent down to clean the puddle on the floor. When she straightened, she locked eyes with her insufferable neighbor.

"Nice view. You've got a great ass. I'm a tits man myself, but you could change that. Not that you don't have an incredible rack, because you do. At least what I can see." He sat back on the bar stool, a smug smile spread those sensuous lips apart and revealed perfect white teeth.

"Why can't you just leave me alone?"

"And miss out on all this fun? Not on your life sweetheart." He leaned closer and lowered his voice. Despite her best intentions, she leaned toward him. "I never back down from a challenge, and you're one damn fine challenge."

Grappling with herself, Lavender put her hands on the counter and pushed her body backward a step. "Go away." The tremor in her voice didn't add much bite to her words. He got to her, big-time, and she couldn't seem to do a damn thing about it.

Tyler laughed, the kind of deep belly laugh that sucked others into his web. "Not until you and I have taken care of our unfinished business." He grabbed her hand and rubbed the sensitive spot on the underside of her wrist. She shuddered and yanked her hand away.

"If I believed once would be enough to get you off my back, I'd gladly swallow my scruples for one night."

"One night with me is never enough, darlin'. I'm a greedy man, I have plans for you. Plans that'll fill up the next two months so keep your calendar clear. At least your nights."

"You are the most egotistical, maddening, obnoxious man I've ever met."

"Thank you. I work hard at it. It's nice to see my efforts appreciated." Standing, Tyler guzzled the last of his beer, sketched a salute in her direction, and wandered over to a table. Lavender watched him go, torn between wishing Tyler would hustle his nice ass back to the mainland and wishing he'd stay.

Like iron to a magnet, he pulled her in, teased her with his intense blue eyes, charmed her with his ready smile, came onto her like a master. It was the master part that bothered her. A master at seduction. The more she resisted, the harder he campaigned. The man thrived on competition. She'd unwittingly created a competitive atmosphere for a man who loved the chase as much as the capture.

Tyler signaled to her with a wave of his hand. "I'll take another beer, Vinnie."

She stiffened and studied him for a moment. If she cut him off, maybe he'd go home, and she'd dodge a bullet for one more night. She crossed to the room and sat a glass of water in front of him.

He blinked and looked up in surprise. "What the fuck is this?"

"You've had enough."

"What? I've only had two."

"That's more than enough."

"Why? I'm being a good boy? Wait. That's the problem, isn't it? You like my bad boy side better."

"You only have a bad boy side. And I don't like it. Not one bit."

"There goes that lying thing again."

"You've had enough to drink because I've had enough of you." She wiped the table, snapping his hand with the towel.

He jerked his hand back. "What the fuck was that for?"

She leaned toward him. "I don't like jocks, remember?"

"Awww, darlin', give me a fucking chance."

"In your dreams." She held out the jar. He had three dollars ready for her. "We'll be able to build a new high school with the money you're putting in this jar."

Tyler's gaze slid down her body. "You really do have a great ass."

"You are an ass." She almost smiled. Despite her reservations about him as a person, she enjoyed their verbal sparring as much as he did.

"Thank you. I work fucking hard at it." He dropped another buck in the jar. His eyes danced with pleasure. Instead of getting rid of him, she'd done the opposite. He didn't look like he'd be going anywhere for a while. In fact, he seemed pretty darned complacent.

"You should work on that potty mouth of yours."

"You think I have a potty mouth?"

"Uh, duh. Show a little class."

Tyler frowned, and his brows drew together in a tight line, as if she'd offended him.

"I'll bet you can't go a week without saying the "F" word." She threw out the challenge before she'd given it much thought.

"Really? What's the bet?" He sat up straighter, looking intrigued and wicked.

"A hundred dollars toward the Veteran Hall's improvement fund."

He scratched his chin, drawing her attention to his strong, square jaw line. "That's pretty steep."

"Pocket change to you." She stared at the dark stubble on his face and imagined how it'd feel scraping across her nipples. Lavender fanned herself. One of the brothers must have cranked the heat again.

Tyler's knowing smirk irritated her. He lowered his voice. "What do I win?" The gravel in his voice wet her panties. She tingled in places she didn't know she could tingle.

"You won't win."

"I told you. I'm a competitive man."

"How about a kiss with tongue and all." The words tumbled out of her mouth before her brain engaged.

Tyler looked her up and down, as if considering the challenge she'd laid on the table. His patent slow, sexy grin slid across his face. He dropped his voice to a low rumble and arched one eyebrow. "Just a kiss?"

"That's it. Nothing more." She walked back to the bar and tossed a sassy grin she didn't feel over her shoulder. Inside she cringed at her stupid dare. She couldn't afford to lose for more reasons than money. He followed her, obviously intrigued.

"Trust me. You won't be able to stop with just one. I'm that good."

Only a delusional woman would argue with that statement. "So am I." Her smart mouth needed to go back in a cell where it belonged. She'd just committed herself to a kiss, tongue and all, assuming she lost, then admitted she'd most likely go further.

And damn, she wanted to go further.

"It's a deal then. We start right now." Consulting his watch, Tyler Harris grinned at her, his eyes dark with an animal need, which clenched her insides into a knot and set her libido on fire. Her mind slid into a quick fantasy with his hot, sweat-soaked body sliding across hers while his cock got acquainted with her pussy. She suspected his cock matched his giant ego in size and stamina.

Dang, but she loved sex with a man she hated. No worries about pleasing the other, no concerns over what to do in the morning. Just down-dirty, slam-bam, rough-tumble, get-it-done sex. The best kind in her book.

It'd been ages since she'd let a man get her naked and parallel on a bed. She feared it'd only be a matter of time, and the less she liked him the better the sex.

In that case, sex with the insufferable Tyler Harris would be mind-blowing.

Chapter 9

Standing in the Pocket

A few days later, Tyler wrapped his hands around a beer bottle and watched. Lavender single-handedly managed the bar and juggled orders from the various patrons with her usual sassy efficiency.

He shifted on his bar stool, the same bar stool which should have his name on it. No one else in the small island town dared to sit in his space. If some poor clueless soul parked his ass on Tyler's stool, a regular made sure he vacated it as soon as Ty walked in the door. He liked that about a small town. People got it.

Lavender whooshed by him, balancing a full tray of drinks. He followed her with his eyes, appreciating her many assets. Hell, his fantasies about those particular assets kept him sane. Zipping behind the bar, she whipped up a few martinis with her usual efficiency. Somehow she managed to please all her customers, except him. As long as she wore clothes, he'd be wanting more. A lot more. He licked his lips as her delectable tits bounced with every step she took.

His gaze swept across the room, and zeroed in on a guy watching Lavender as intently as Tyler was. The jerk flirted shamelessly with her, and she flirted right back. A wave of jealousy surged through Tyler, surprising him with its intensity. He tried to shrug it off as a by-product of his alpha-male possessive streak. What's his was his, and no else better forget that.

His? What the fuck. She wasn't his. In fact, they didn't even like each other. Of course, those two little details didn't stop Tyler. He locked eyes with the interloper and pinned him to the wall with a threatening glare. No one lusted after the object of Tyler's current lust. No one. The chickenshit paled and swallowed nervously. Gulping down the last of his beer, the idiot slapped some change on the table, and quickly hustled out the door. Smug with satisfaction, Tyler did another survey of the room. Good, all was as it should be. He settled back and focused his energy on Lavender fantasies.

Tyler's cell vibrated. He frowned, irritated at being interrupted and checked out the caller id, his cousin and best buddy Derek Ramsey. This better be good. He pressed the answer button. "What's up, asshole?"

"I could say the same of you."

"I'm fine. What the fu—fudge are you harassing me for?" Tyler shot a quick glance in Lavender's direction. She stood too far away to catch his almost slip.

Derek cleared his throat, followed by silence on the line. Not a good sign. Tyler's instincts went on red alert. He drummed his fingers on the counter. His cousin remained silent.

Tyler hated waiting. "Aw, shit. Put on your big boy pants and spit it out. Or did Rachel burn them all?"

Derek made an odd noise then finally spoke. "I thought you'd rather hear this from me than from the media."

Tyler sucked in a deep breath and let it out. He shoved his fingers through his unruly hair. He needed to get it cut, but very likely that was the least of his problems. "Oh, crap, what now?"

"There's no easy way to say this, buddy. Brace yourself." He heard Derek inhale then exhale.

Tyler's mind raced through a hundred possibilities. Somehow they did charge him with a DUI. Maybe some woman came forward and insisted he fathered her kid. Or he'd been cut from the team. Or his sisters ran off to South America with what was left of his money. He shouldn't have ignored his agent's many calls. "Dang it. Tell me. What is it?"

"The Jacks signed Zach Murphy to a one-year contract."

Tyler went still inside, rendered completely speechless. He bit the side of his mouth just to make sure he hadn't died from shock. The taste of his blood mingled with disbelief. "Zach Murphy? Are you frigging kidding me?" Across the counter, Lavender raised a brow. He raised a brow right back at her.

"Yeah. I guess Zach took a big pay cut to play for us. He wants to go out with a bang his last year in the league. The poor bastard's played with piece of crap teams his entire pro career. He wants a ring."

Tyler clenched his jaw and ground his teeth together. He wanted to hit something. How could the Lumberjacks do this to him?

He dropped a five in the jar before opening his mouth. He knew this wasn't going to be good. Even if he couldn't use the "F" word, he had others. "Damn it. Everyone knows I can't stand that idiot dickwad, and he feels the same. The asshole is a dirty player. Mother effing dirty. He's tried to take me out more than once."

"Yeah, and he's laid you flat on your back more than any other linebacker in the league. The guy's good." His fuckhead cousin almost sounded amused, which didn't improve Tyler's temper one bit.

"He's old, washed up. There isn't room on the team for both of us."

"Tell that to the Jacks. If you haven't noticed, you didn't get a vote. This is your wakeup call, dumbshit. I'm not the only teammate who noticed your attitude this past season, or should I say lack of?"

Tyler tightened his grip on the cell phone, wanting to crush the life out of this electronic bearer of fucking bad news. He thought he'd been so clever, fooled them all, but his teammates and coaches had seen through his not-so-incredible acting job.

"HughJack loves Murphy's fire. Says the team could use a little of it these days."

"What the hell is that supposed to mean?" Like he didn't know? Maybe they'd disrespected him with this obvious vote of no confidence, but he was also guilty as charged.

"They're doubting your team leadership."

His cousin's words cut right to the heart of the matter.

Tyler jabbed the *End* button on the phone, cutting off his cousin. Without even a backward glance, he stomped out of the bar into the dark, rainy evening, which matched his mood just fucking fine.

* * * * *

Lavender grappled with the large roll of welded wire fencing. It took on a mind of its own and wrestled her to the ground. She was losing the battle when her neighbor decided to be neighborly and lifted the recalcitrant roll off her pinned body as if the heavy wire was a roll of toilet paper. Sometimes brute strength did have its advantages.

She ignored his outstretched hand and struggled to her feet. "Good to see you know how to use those muscles."

"That's how I make my money, babe." A cocky grin spread across his strong, square jaw. His Caribbean blue eyes twinkled with pure devilment, even though she sensed an edge to him.

"Don't call me that."

"Whatever you say, Vinnie." He was deliberately attempting to provoke her.

"Don't call me that either."

"Lilac? Violet?"

She shook her head violently and tried like hell not to laugh, which would only encourage the insufferably obnoxious man. "How about not. Perhaps, I'll come up with something equally annoying to call you."

"Call me anything you want, baby." He reached up and brushed a smear of dirt from her cheek with the pad of his thumb. Her body responded with a revealing shudder. His eyes turned the color of an ocean in a storm, a sexual storm. "Damn, I love it when you get down and dirty."

Lavender sighed and brushed off her clothes, suddenly aware of her innate scruffiness in comparison to his innate gorgeousness. "Did you come over here to exercise your vast wit or do you need something?"

"No, but you do. I couldn't stand watching you fight with the fencing. It was about to deliver the knockout punch." He leaned down, his mouth way too close to her ear. "Besides, if anyone's going to wrestle you to the ground, it'll be me."

"Why don't you exercise your feet and leave?" Before her body exercised its fantasies.

"Seems someone called the phone company and cancelled my request for service. You wouldn't know anything about that, would you?" He propped one foot on the bumper of her pickup truck, more amused than pissed off, which irritated her.

She wiped her face of all emotion, but she was pretty damn sure guilt still came through. "No, not a thing."

"I figured as much. Now I have to wait another few weeks. My ninety days will be up before I get service on this island. Guess what? Maybe I'd just as soon be unreachable."

"Then you don't have a problem. Someone—I'm not saying it's me—did you a favor."

"Perhaps. Being incommunicado does have its merits. But as attractive as it is, I have business to attend to."

"If you leave the island now, you can attend to all the business you want."

He shook his head, not the least bit put off. "Now that's no way to treat a man with a hammer, especially when he knows how to use it." Tyler held up a good-sized hammer for her inspection. For once he smiled a genuine smile, a nice-guy smile oddly out of place on his sinfully bad-boy face.

"Are you offering to help me with my fencing?"

"Yup, just to get a little peace. You're making a fu—, frigging racket." He smirked at his quick catch. The man wanted his kiss. Of course, he'd most likely pegged her right and knew a kiss would only be foreplay to the foreplay.

"Something has me curious." Tyler looked at her so long and hard she started to squirm under his dissecting gaze. "You don't have any animals? What's up with that? Don't you like animals?"

"I love animals." Lavender felt a twinge of jealousy toward her neighbor, not because of his fame or money, but because he was living with the cat, and she had no animals to comfort her or stave off the loneliness. She'd never planned to live in her grandparents' house for this long, but the bad economy and life conspired to keep her under their thumb.

"You could've fooled me."

"My landlady, who happens to be my grandmother, is highly allergic to animal fur. She won't allow any on the property."

"She doesn't live here. You do."

Lavender shrugged. She didn't want to get into details regarding her controlling grandmother and grandfather and all the dysfunctional reasons why she allowed them to run her life.

"So what's the fence for?"

"To keep the deer out of the vegetables."

Tyler gazed pointedly at her woebegone vegetable garden. "I think it's too late."

"So do I, but I promised I'd fence off the garden." Her grandmother expected fresh vegetables, one of the things Lavender of the brown thumb did to earn her keep on this little plot of land.

"Give me the hammer."

"Pound away, jock boy."

Tyler slanted her a sideways look.

"Drag your sorry ass out of the gutter. I meant *with a hammer*." Lavender stood back with anticipation and waited for him to make an ass of himself demonstrating his hammer-pounding talents. Tyler grinned. Perfect white teeth stood out against his dark tan. No one had a tan in the islands this time of year, but Tyler did.

"Go for it. I'd like to see you wield that hammer." Would she ever.

He opened his mouth to speak then seemed to think better of it. He turned to the task at hand and assessed the damage.

Lavender flipped a bucket upside down and took a seat. They were getting along almost too well, so she scrambled to find a subject to ruin his mood. "What's the deal with Zach Murphy?"

Immediately, the shutters slammed shut over his eyes, and he regarded her warily. "You were eavesdropping on my conversation last night."

"I, uh, I just happened to, uh, overhear a bit of it. That's all."

"Then you already know what the deal is."

"Not really, I could only hear one side of it."

"We hate each other's fu—frigging guts. That's the deal."

"So I hear."

"You did? I thought you hated football?"

"Just because I hate football doesn't mean I don't know stuff about it. Why would the Jacks sign someone who has a very public feud with the heart and soul of their team?"

"Maybe they're looking for a new heart and soul." He frowned, as if he hadn't meant to say the words out loud.

"You've done some stupid things lately, like driving drunk."

He glared down at her with a ferocity she'd never witnessed from him. "Have you ever seen me drink too much to drive home?"

Lavender searched her memory. "No, I haven't, but that doesn't mean anything."

"If that's what you think." Rubbing the back of his neck, he looked at an unseen spot in the distance. His expression hardened with determination. "It's my team. He'll learn that soon enough. I can handle the jerk. No big deal."

But it was a big deal, as illustrated by the restlessness she'd sensed in him earlier. It went deeper than the team signing a player Tyler didn't like and rumors of pending DUI charges. Beneath his unease lingered a hint of something, almost like insecurity, or fear, even vulnerability. She shook her head, denying the quarterback possessed a heart with real emotions. The second she acknowledged he might be human would be the beginning of the end of her ability to resist him.

"I'm sure it'll all work out just fine."

"I'm sure it will." He didn't look one damn bit convinced.

Turning his back to her, Tyler picked up a hammer and fence staples. Giving each staple a few solid whacks, he attached one end of the fence to the post. Then he rolled the rest out on the ground.

Lavender stayed out of his way. The man worked like a hummingbird on crack. His hammer strokes were efficient and clean, no wasted movement. He showed her how to stretch the fence tight with a come-along. What would have taken her hours and looked like crap, took him a little over an hour and looked better than most professional fencing jobs she'd seen.

She hated to be impressed, but she was.

* * * * *

Tyler drove in the last fence staple then stood back to admire his handiwork, the most satisfying chore he'd done in the past twenty-four hours. Pushing his baseball cap off his brow, he wiped off the sweat with the bottom of his T-shirt.

He'd walked over here with every intention of starting an argument with her, anything to assuage his bad temper, yet the second he'd seen her down for the count with the fence winning the match, he couldn't suppress his amusement.

"Does that cat always follow you around?" Lavender stood close behind him, too close. Her curvy body enticed his cock. Just the sight of her fueled a lifetime of wet dreams.

"He's not following me." Tyler almost smiled as he caught sight of Cougar sitting on a fence post, casually licking his non-existent balls and faking disinterest in what the humans were doing. Truth be told, the cat followed him everywhere, to the bathroom in the morning, out to the barn, to the garage, anywhere Tyler went the cat showed up. He even followed him to the kitchen every morning and bitched until Tyler put fresh food in his dish. Every time he caught the cat following him, the little orange bastard would sit down and preen as if he wasn't following Tyler at all. Tyler knew better.

"I really do appreciate your help." Her words sounded forced, like thanking him didn't come easily.

"Does this mean you don't hate me anymore?"

"Of course, it doesn't." She lifted her chin, a defiant tilt to her head. One curly strand of red hair fell over her cheek. He wanted to touch it, roll it between his fingers.

"Good, I wouldn't want to end an enjoyable neighborly feud." He moved into her space. His nostrils filled with the scent of lavender and aroused woman.

"Never happen."

"I'm counting on it." He leaned closer and ran the pad of his calloused thumb down her cheek and tucked the rebellious strand behind her ear. "Conflict makes sex even better."

"Too bad you won't find out how good."

"I will, Purple Lady. I promise. One kiss from me, and you'll be putty in my hands."

"You have to win first."

"Honey, I never lose. Winning is encoded into my DNA." He noticed she didn't say she'd stop after one kiss, just that he had to win. He suspected his red-headed tigress would be a wild, untamed animal in bed, the best kind. He was a physical guy with physical needs and a healthy imagination when it came to sex. An imagination he didn't mind indulging. Lavender might not be his usual type, but the chemistry between them snapped and sizzled.

She opened her mouth to respond when an irritated voice from the front of her house interrupted them. Lavender jerked around and tensed immediately.

"Lavender!" A short powerhouse of a woman marched into view from the corner of Lavender's little house, followed by an equally short, fat peacock of a man. She was short, like her granddaughter but had packed on the pounds over the years. Her clothes fit a little too tight, not to be sexy, but like she refused to go up a size or two. Her red hair was a little too red to be natural, and she had this eighties big-hair thing going on.

Panic crossed Lavender's face. She turned to Tyler. "You need to go now."

The ranting woman hadn't noticed them yet. She was too busy bitching to the short guy about the state of the place. Stopping at the side of the house, with her back to them, she inspected the overgrown flowerbeds, never letting up on the steady stream of complaints. Tyler recognized the signs of a nosy, controlling female relative. After all, he'd grown up with more than his share. "Is that your grandmother?"

Lavender nodded and fidgeted with wire cutters. "She owns this place and rents it to me. You really need to go."

"She sounds pissed."

"She's always pissed."

"Oh, shit." Tyler considered his options—stick around and needle Lavender or get the hell out of Dodge. As much fun as it might be to stay, he wasn't interested in getting in the middle of a family altercation, especially when he didn't want to get involved with Lavender on anything but a sexual level.

He grabbed his tools and slipped through the gate in their mutual fence.

Cougar leapt off the fence post and raced ahead, not wanting any part of the crazed woman either. *Smart cat.*

* * * * *

For the next hour, Doris Mead ranted about how her granddaughter wasn't keeping the shack pristine enough. Lavender learned after her rebellious teenage years to nod and say nothing. It made her life much easier. Thank goodness her grandparents lived on the mainland and didn't make the ferry trip to San Juan Island too often.

Doris paused in mid-rant and stared out the back window. "You repaired your fence. It looks good." She motioned to her ever-present husband. "Larry, look at this."

Larry Mead strutted over and peered out the window pane. "That fence looks better than this house."

Lavender held her breath and braced for impact.

"How much did the fence cost?" Her grandmother rounded on her, both barrels blazing. Lavender immediately went on defense, a familiar neighborhood.

"Nothing. I did it myself."

"Don't lie to me." Her grandmother's face looked ten years older when she frowned like that.

"Dishonesty is the work of the devil." Her grandfather, a retired real estate broker and part-time preacher, played the fire-and-brimstone card. Boring but nice, just the type of man her grandmother loved to control. Nothing like her father had been, one more reason why Grandma always disliked Lavender's dad.

"I'm not lying."

"Who built that fence for you?" When her grandmother grabbed hold of something, she hung onto it like a rabid retriever with its favorite ball.

"My neighbor helped me."

"What neighbor? Not the college dropout down the road with the dreadlocks? The one who does drugs."

"Gideon doesn't do drugs. He's just a free-spirit. And, no, he didn't help me."

"Who then?"

She should tell her grandmother to mind her own business, but that rarely worked. She'd come after Lavender like a rat terrier, teeth bared and ready for a fight. "The guy who inherited the mansion."

"Twin Cedars?"

Lavender nodded and busied herself making a fresh pot of coffee. Her grandmother and grandfather walked to the side window and looked out. "The place looks uninhabited."

"He's working on the inside first."

"Who is he?" Doris straightened a picture on the wall and ran her finger across a wood table. She frowned at the dust.

"Just some nice guy." Lavender choked on the word *nice*. If they only knew.

"What's his name?"

"No one you'd know."

"Wait a minute. It's that football player, isn't it? Tyler Harris? I heard about him. He's bad news." Larry dropped the bombshell, and Lavender braced herself for detonation.

Playing dumb seemed the only viable option. "Oh, does he play football? I don't know him well."

Her grandmother's furious expression sent chills down her spine. She was in deep shit. "*Not* a football player. Not Tyler Harris?"

"We're not even friends. We can't stand each other."

"A man you can't stand helped you build a fence? How could you be so stupid as to get involved with a football player? Especially *that* football player. You know how we feel about them. They're—"

Lavender held up a hand. "Gram, he helped me with the fence. I'm not marrying him."

"Good thing. He's in loads of trouble." Larry's helpful addition to the conversation didn't help Lavender one damn bit. "He was driving drunk, ran into a cop car, and resisted arrest. I heard he assaulted a police officer when they tried to cuff him. He's got drug and alcohol problems."

Doris's head almost exploded. "Vinnie, you should have learned from my years of hell to stay away from men like that. Your father—"

"I know all about my father. Let's just drop it. Tyler and I aren't even friends."

"He's no good. I know that without even meeting him. His reputation precedes him. They're all abusive, unfaithful, irresponsible—"

"Gram, I know. I know all about Mom's life with Dad. I do. I'm not interested in the jock. He's just a neighbor."

"Don't call that man '*Dad*.' He doesn't deserve the title. He was the world's worst husband and an even worse father. We've always been there for you."

"It's okay, Doris. I know she appreciates all I've done." Leave it to Larry to lay on the guilt trip.

"I do. Really, I do, but it's my life."

"We hold the mortgage on this house."

"I know, Grandma. I know."

Of course, she knew. They'd never let her forget it.

Chapter 10

Left of Center

Tyler tipped the bottle to his lips. The cold liquid slid down his throat. He savored the rich taste of the local microbrew. Some people, in fact most people, claimed he drank too much and partied too hard. Over the years, he'd built up a pretty good tolerance to alcohol. It took a lot to get him drunk, not that he'd imbibed enough lately to feel more than a decent buzz. Damn, even partying had lost its appeal.

Good thing since the latest sports headlines speculated he was in rehab somewhere.

Still trying to come to terms with the Jacks' latest acquisition and what it meant to his future on the team, Tyler turned off his cell—not that it worked in most places on the island anyway. He didn't want to talk about it, not to his teammates, his agent, his attorney, the front office, or the coaches. They'd sent him a message, and he'd received it. Loud and clear. He might be a two-time championship quarterback, but HughJack didn't tolerate anything less than one-hundred-and-ten-percent dedication. Tyler might fool some people but not his coach. The defense had carried the team this past season, while Tyler stumbled through the motions and rested on his previous laurels.

He'd buried his passion for the game when they buried Ryan.

He'd give anything to resurrect his hunger, his drive. Fu— heck if he knew how. Heck if he could dredge up enough interest to give a damn, which scared the shit out of him. More than anything.

He didn't even give a shit if the police charged him with pissing off an officer, whatever the hell they called it.

So he turned his attention to something he could get excited about.

Tonight was the night. His one-week ban of the F-word was up later in the evening. He could already taste his reward. With his powers of persuasion and his kissing expertise, he'd net more than one kiss. The sexual electricity between Lavender and him could launch the Space Needle into orbit. He'd settle for sending himself and Vinnie into orbit.

Tyler trained one eye on the current karaoke singer and another on his favorite bartender. Lavender bustled around the room, serving drinks, visiting with patrons, handing out encouragement to some and bitching at others. Her luscious mouth kept moving as she worked the crowd, earning her tips. Pretty soon those lips would be making him a happy man. He'd turn on the charm, and his happiness wouldn't stop there. His mouth wouldn't be the only part of his body getting satisfaction tonight. His lips twitched in a half-smile.

"You gonna sing?"

"Me?" Tyler turned his head toward the speaker. Not waiting for an invitation, the Brothers lowered their arthritic bodies into empty chairs around his table. This past week, the old goats haunted him everywhere he went, even showing up at his place at dawn for morning coffee and one afternoon for a poker game. Mostly, he ignored them when he could.

"Yeah, you." With a scrawny hand, Homer scratched out his song pick on a slip of paper. "I'm singing, so you've got nothing to be afraid of. I'm the worst one here."

"Hell, Home Boy, you ever heard Ty sing? He'll shame us all."

Looking at Cliff in his pink striped shirt and orange plaid pants hurt Tyler's eyes. He donned his ever-present sunglasses to neutralize the riot of color. The old guy smirked, apparently considering himself pretty hip with his use of modern lingo.

"Ty-man's got a voice." Jim, obviously craving a cigarette, shredded his napkin in thin strips, adding them to the napkin graveyard on the table.

"I'm not singing, and I didn't invite you to sit at my table either." If they were trying to drive him off the island by annoying the hell out of him, it wouldn't work. Tyler stood and wandered over to the bar with his beer in hand. Sitting his ass on a bar stool, he opened the karaoke book on the counter and thumbed through it. He chewed on his lower lip, wondering if he should sing after all. Maybe try something seductive to reel Lavender in or stick with a more traditional song. Something slow and romantic might melt the pants off her. In a place like this, a guy had to seek his own entertainment, and he'd developed an affinity for purple lately.

Too much of an affinity.

Some guys deluded themselves into thinking that screwing a woman would get her out of their systems. It'd never worked well for him before. Case in point: Cass. Hell, they screwed like rabbits, then broke up just to make up and screw like rabbits again. It'd been this on-again, off-again merry-go-round that kept him interested and coming back for more time after time. In fact, years at a time. Nope, the fuck-her-till-she's-out-of-your-system bullshit didn't work for him, any more than it'd worked for his cousin Derek. Now the dumbshit was tied down to one woman with a wedding ring on his finger.

Not that Tyler had a damn thing against marriage. As long as it was someone else wearing that ball and chain. Sure, he'd been engaged to Cass, even set a date, might have gone through with it.

The long shot odds were against it lasting. He doubted Cass would've been faithful. She didn't have it in her. Tyler would have because of his well-concealed, old-fashioned values that'd been drummed into his head over the years about marriage and faithfulness.

He'd never have a perfect marriage like his parents so he went for the opposite. You couldn't fail if you didn't try in the first place. Safe plan, he figured. Until Cass messed it up by leaving him in the lurch.

A little island affair for the next few months appealed to him.

A soft female voice reached his ears. "You're a sensitive soul confronting demons."

Tyler spun around to locate the owner of the voice. He wasn't sensitive and the only demons he fought were the ones of his own making. A cute, curvy woman of about medium build with streaks of pink in her blonde hair studied him with interest. Tyler resisted the urge to squirm. She saw too much, and he didn't like it. Short curly hair framed her face, making her look like a curvy angel with big boobs. If it wasn't for his current obsession with Lavender, this woman's boobs would've given him enough reason to pursue her. Yet, the thought didn't hold much appeal anymore, regardless of the package.

Tyler's gaze slid across the room and landed on Lavender wearing a tight little sweater and tighter jeans. *Damn.* He shoved his sunglasses on top of his head to get a better look. His cock strained against his zipper to the point where he swore there'd be a permanent zipper imprint on it. He shifted in his seat but couldn't find a comfortable position. Probably because the only position that'd offer relief involved his cock being buried deep inside a certain purple lady. He smiled at the visual of that particular fantasy.

"I'm Xandra with an X." Her voice knocked him back to reality. She held out a hand loaded with rings on every finger.

Tyler ignored her hand, not in the mood to listen to this wacked woman's bullshit. "Wonderful to meet you." Tyler's sarcasm didn't set her back one bit, which irritated him. She'd gotten under his skin with her first sentence. He turned back to his beer, hunched his shoulders, and wrapped his hands around the cold bottle.

"You're very sensitive, in tune to those around you, but you choose to fight it."

"The only thing in tune is my singing voice. I don't give a damn about anyone but myself. Let me guess, you're a psychic?" The damn island was crawling with people like her.

"No, actually, I've retired my psychic abilities, but I can give you something for your skin. You must spend too much time in the sun."

Tyler brought a hand up to his face then quickly snatched it away. "What the fuck is it with you?" He couldn't stop the words as they escaped from his mouth. *Great, just great.* He'd lost the bet, just like that. No kiss, tongue or no tongue.

Xandra held the cuss jar out to him. "That'll be one dollar in the jar."

He fished a dollar out of his jeans pocket and stuffed it in the jar.

"I'll let Lavender know you paid up."

"You do that. Now leave me the fuck alone." He dropped another dollar in the jar. He might as well enjoy his favorite word since he'd screwed up the bet.

Xandra steepled her fingers and studied him. He squirmed as her knowing gaze peeled back layer after protective layer. He jammed the sunglasses back on his face, but they didn't block out her scrutiny. "Stop that."

"You're conflicted."

"Damn right. I'm conflicted about how best to get rid of you without ending up in prison."

"Another dollar."

"I know. I know." He dug in his pocket and stuck a twenty in the jar. "Look, Xtra or whatever you call yourself, I'm an asshole, through and through. I'm a narcissistic bastard. You need to go back to mind-reading school 'cause you have me pegged all wrong."

"I told you. I'm retired, but I'm still perceptive, and I'm not wrong. You, Mr. Harris, are a crappy liar." Her Mona Lisa smile indicated she knew something he didn't, which stretched his tenuous hold on his rising temper.

Now Tyler really took offense. "I'm an excellent liar."

"Afraid not."

Tyler glared at her. She'd gone too far. "I'm an asshole. Ask anyone."

She laughed, enjoying herself way too damn much. "Bullshit. You conceal how much you care because it hurts too much."

With stiff, jerky movements, he gripped the cuss jar so hard it should've shattered and jerked it toward her.

Her brown eyes flashed with irritation. After a dramatic sigh, she emptied out her already empty coin purse and dumped an odd amount of change in the jar. "You consider yourself unworthy. Wonder why good people die instead of someone like you."

He stared straight ahead but couldn't block out the truth of her words.

"You're here because the universe needs you for a greater purpose. Find that purpose. Only then will you have peace and regain what you've lost."

Tyler rolled his eyes and sighed.

"Have you met Jackson yet?" Her change of topic came from his blindside and sacked him for a loss. Tyler glanced around the room, fearing the worst, like maybe this crazy-assed X-girl had an accomplice. "Who the hell is Jackson?"

"The ghost of Jackson Harris. He haunts your mansion."

Tyler rolled his eyes and called a trick play. "Yeah, I had dinner with him last night. Real asshole, obviously it runs in the family. He drinks all my good booze and keeps leaving the toilet seat up." *What the hell was it with these people?* This island obviously attracted a lot of screwballs.

She blinked at him with gray eyes full of mock innocence. "I understand he does that often." How did she keep a straight face and say crap like that?

Tyler glanced around the room for a rescuer. The Brothers were too busy arguing over God knew what. Lavender would be no help. The patrons kept her running like crazy. He searched for her cute ass in the crowd and grinned when he found her listening to one of the Brothers' many stories. Linking his hands in front of him, Tyler leaned against the back of his bar stool and watched Lavender hustle between the tables, hips swaying, her sweater clinging to her full breasts.

"You're destined."

"Huh?" He'd forgotten about X. "Oh, yeah, destined to be in bed together." He'd like nothing more than to strip off Lavender's clothes and take her hard and rough on the pool table across the room.

"It's more than that."

"You've got to be related to Lavender. Your obnoxious personality gives it away."

"Actually, we're cousins." She reached in her huge purse and dug around for a few minutes before handing him a mangled business card. Rolling his eyes, he jammed the card in his pocket.

Waving to the patrons at a nearby table, Xandra glided to the back of the room. Her step was so light and graceful she appeared to be walking on air. She sat down at a table of equally odd people.

Tyler released his death grip on the karaoke book. He'd already crushed a few pages of songs and hadn't even been aware of it. He pulled the card out of his pocket and read it again to make sure he'd seen correctly the first time:

Xandra
Organic Skin Care
Paranormal Investigator

* * * * *

Lavender couldn't suppress a grin as she watched the scowl on Tyler's face deepen with every word Zan said. Her cousin loved to play guys like him. Once Zan sauntered off, Tyler, glutton for punishment, made his way back to the Brothers' table. Sprawling in a chair next to Homer, he glared at the current out-of-tune karaoke singer until he made the guy so nervous, the tone-deaf crooner couldn't even read the words to the song. Tyler propped his legs on an empty chair, crossed them at the ankles, and yawned.

Tonight was the night she should be dreading, but she wasn't—not one bit. All week kissing Tyler haunted her night and daydreams. Just one little kiss to satisfy her curiosity.

As soon as the song ended, DJ Don called Tyler to the mic. Sitting up straight, he glared at the Brothers, who hooted with laughter. Obviously, they'd put in a song for him. With a resigned shrug, Tyler stepped to the mic, attention slut that he was.

Frustrated with how the entire town catered to the conceited ass, Lavender turned away and concentrated on filling drink orders. She grabbed a glass and poured a couple beers from the tap.

A few notes into Tyler's song, she stopped in mid-pour and stared. She couldn't help it.

Tyler held the microphone with the ease and poise of a man accustomed to the limelight. He glanced around the room and his turquoise eyes skipped over hers, teasing but not delivering.

Nothing the man did should surprise her, but his singing did. He sang "The Way You Look Tonight" in a voice that would have made Sinatra proud. The jock had all the moves down, holding the mic close to his sinful mouth and moving his athlete's body to the music. Every woman in the place stopped what they were doing and drooled. Conversations halted. Glasses paused midway to mouths. Men wished they could be him. Women wished they could be naked with him.

Her heart danced to the beat, as his voice weaved a tantalizing web around her. His body swaying in time, foot tapping. Her resolve to keep her distance puddled at his big feet.

Tyler's gaze drew hers and tore the breath from her lungs. One corner of his mouth kicked up into a knowing smile. She dropped a half-full glass, splattering beer all over her sweater but paid it no notice. The man could sing. Really sing. In fact, he sang so well she imagined him crooning a ballad as he slid his cock deep into her or rocked her body hard with a classic rock tune.

"You might want to wipe the drool off your chin."

"What?" Lavender's head jerked around as her hand wiped imaginary drool from her face. Xandra sat on the stool across the counter from her.

"You're mentally ripping off his clothes, girlfriend."

"Zan, in my mind, his clothes are already in shreds at his feet, and he's wearing nothing but an arrogant smile." She'd grown up with Zan, no sense hiding the obvious. They'd had some drunken, wild times together in their younger years. She knew the real Zan behind her mystical smoke screen.

"Your friend has quite the attitude." She indicated Tyler with a nod of her head. "And quite the voice. That gorgeous body should be bronzed and placed in the Smithsonian. Even better, he's hot for you. You should be taking advantage of all he has to offer."

"And here I thought you liked me." Lavender wiped up the beer on the counter, forcing her gaze away from Tyler.

"I do. That's why he's perfect for what you need."

"He's a jock. You know how I feel about jocks. Not to mention, he's a conceited, entitled, obnoxious, womanizing asshole."

"And that's a problem?"

"Maybe not. The real problem is his inheritance."

"You might be able to work out a compromise."

"Fat chance of that happening. He's a selfish, greedy bastard."

"His attitude is all for show. He's nothing like that on the inside, but then I'm not telling you anything you don't already know."

"I know nothing of the sort. He's as shallow as a kid's wading pool and as selfish as his pampered tomcat. What you see is what you get."

"Cuz, you get a lot with him, and there's lot to like."

"Yeah, three things: his body, his body, and his body. But it's look and don't touch." Except for one wagered kiss.

Lavender met Tyler's eyes across the room. A tingle started at her toes and zipped up her body to her lips.

Or maybe it was look and *do* touch.

* * * * *

A few hours later, the Brotherhood headed to their respective homes, DJ Don packed his equipment, and the few remaining stragglers shuffled out the door.

Lavender hadn't seen Tyler leave. In fact, he hadn't paid his tab, which wasn't like him. He might be a jerk, but he wasn't one to sneak out on his bill, and the man tipped well. His coat was still over the back of his chair. Lavender smiled as she fingered the claw marks on the expensive leather. His beer sat on the table he'd shared with the Brothers along with his cell phone.

Lavender walked to the open door leading to the back room, which housed a veterans' museum loaded with memorabilia donated to the club over the years by various members. Tyler stood with his back to her, hands clasped behind him, looking at the exhibits. A picture of a pilot standing near a helicopter had drawn his attention.

"Tyler?"

He tensed but didn't turn around. "Yeah?" His voice sounded strained and tight.

Lavender moved closer, reeled in by the odd tone of his voice. "We're closed now."

He didn't move, just kept staring.

"Are you okay?"

He snorted, as if she'd asked a dumb question. "What do you think?"

"I don't know what to think. Do you know this man?" She pointed at the picture of a pilot standing next to a helicopter.

Tyler sighed and nodded.

"Who is he?"

He was silent so long she wondered if he'd heard her. She moved closer. "Ty?"

"He's a relative." Tyler indicated the small card below the photo. "It would appear Uncle Art donated a lot of stuff to this museum. Hell if I know how he got hold of this picture. My grandfather and he weren't part of my family growing up. I wonder if there's more of this stuff in the attic of the mansion."

"Captain Jason Harris," she read on the card below the picture. "Flew rescue helicopters on Special Ops missions."

Tyler made no comment. He was hiding something, something which troubled him deeply. It'd be to her advantage to keep her distance and maintain indifference.

"If you had no contact with him, why would Art leave Twin Cedars to you?"

Tyler's blue eyes turned cold and distant. A muscle jerked in his jaw. "I met Uncle Artie this past year when he was in the nursing home in Seattle. He contacted me, asked me to visit. I did. We hit it off, and I tried to see him once a week, played cards with the guys. He was ornery, just like me."

She softened a little toward Tyler, despite her best intentions. He'd spent time with his dying uncle when no one else had. *Even her.* "So he left the mansion to you?"

"I guess he figured I could afford to restore the dump when no one else could."

Her momentary good feelings fell away. It didn't take an idiot to figure out he'd sucked up to Artie in order to inherit Twin Cedars. Now it all made more sense. Lavender bristled, feeling protective of the historic old mansion. His irreverent attitude rubbed her the wrong way. "That dump, as you call it, would cost millions to build today, if you could find artisans able to do the work."

His laser blue eyes scrutinized her. He made a derisive sound and uttered something under his breath. "What do you know about craftsmanship?"

"More than you, jock boy."

With a disbelieving snort, he left the museum and strode into the bar. Lavender followed. "I suppose Xtra told you."

"Her name is Xandra. And she told me nothing."

"I lost the bet." He stopped, looking down at his feet, hands in his pockets, resembling a little boy who'd lost his favorite toy.

"You didn't need to tell me that." His honesty impressed her and conflicted with his overall asshole image.

"X would have."

"Actually she wouldn't. She'd make it your decision and leave it up to your spiritual growth."

"To hell with my spiritual growth." His head snapped up, and his hand snaked around her back so fast she didn't have time to draw a breath.

The next thing she knew, he'd bent her over the bar counter and was kissing the hell out of her. She wrapped her arms around his neck, weak-willed woman that she was when it came to a hot man with clever lips. His tongue proved to be as talented as his lips. The man launched an all-out assault that'd put the Marines to shame. He buried his fingers in her hair and pulled her face closer, as if he wasn't already devouring her.

His tongue danced a two-step with her tongue. His thighs pressed against her thighs while his erection rubbed against her stomach, cocked and loaded. *Literally.* Lavender moaned when his mouth slid down her throat, nibbling her sensitive skin and nipping at her collarbone.

Her head swam in deep warm water. The warmth seeped into every cell in her body, drugging her in a haze of sexual need and passion. She wrapped her legs around his back and pulled his upper body against hers. His erection pressed against her crotch. She rubbed against him. A pure moan of male need spiked her own desire. She needed so much more from him. To hell with just one kiss.

She needed a million kisses on every part of her body. Tonight. Definitely tonight. Maybe an encore tomorrow night.

Maybe again the night after that. Oh, hell, how about for the next two months?

She gazed into his eyes. Sure, lust blazed in his depths, but so did something deeper than that. Something which contradicted Tyler's cloak of shallowness.

Lavender slid her hands down his jeans and cupped his butt cheeks. "Did you hear that?" Tyler froze and went on alert. She didn't hear a thing beyond the pounding in her ears.

He straightened and backed up a few steps. His gaze swept the room. He switched to alpha male mode, protecting his territory. Lavender lifted her head, foggy from lust and his drugging kisses. Tyler stood a few feet away from where she lay spread-eagled on the counter. His hands rested on his hips with his legs spread slight apart. His chest heaved as if he'd just run one hundred yards for a touchdown. His blue gaze thundered with the fury of a wild ocean storm.

Lavender sat up, panting and fighting for her bearings and following his gaze. Homer stood nearby, staring at his feet, his face red from embarrassment.

"Sorry, I forgot my wallet."

"Next time fucking knock." Tyler's growled threat sent Homer shuffling to the door as quickly as his old legs allowed. Getting a grip on her sanity, Lavender slipped off the counter and tugged on her shirt to straighten it. She smoothed out her tangled hair with a hand. "You didn't have to be mean to him. He didn't know he'd find us making out on the bar counter."

"I'm an asshole. What do you expect?"

Lavender resisted the urge to touch her lips. "Of course, you are. You're good at playing the asshole." She attempted to resurrect their banter and get her footing back to familiar ground.

"I'm not *playing*. This is who I am."

She looked him up and down. "Have it your way. It's no concern of mine. By the way, I need to close out. Pay your tab, and you'd better leave a good tip."

A predatory grin settled on his lips, and she was the prey. "I'm not done with you yet. You'll get your tip, sweetheart. A big one."

The man wasn't referring to money.

Chapter 11

Holding Penalty

Tyler crossed the room and locked the door. A small detail he should've taken care of before he'd laid Lavender out on the bar, fully intending to fu—screw her brains out. Homer's interruption slapped his horny self out of its lust-ridden stupor.

Earlier in the museum room, Lavender saw his soft underbelly. He couldn't fathom why he'd told her what little he had. The man in the picture was his father, but she'd never know that. Because to know about his family, his perfect family, with their very imperfect son revealed too much of his personal pain. He didn't expose his weaknesses to anyone. Absolutely no one.

She'd caught a glimpse of his vulnerability, and that'd never do. He'd erase that memory from her mind, and Tyler knew just the way to do it. He'd been dying to fuck her smart little mouth and hot little pussy for a couple weeks. Tonight appeared to be the night.

Lavender tossed his bar tab on the counter. Hiding behind his sunglasses, Ty pulled a twenty out of his pocket and gave it to her. She finished her work behind the bar, closed out the till, and walked toward the door.

Tyler followed and blocked the exit with his body. "We have unfinished business. I'll give you a ride."

"I can ride my bike."

"It's midnight." Fine, she wanted to play hard to get. He didn't mind the pursuit; it made the sex that much better.

"This is the San Juans. I'm perfectly safe. I think we've had one murder in thirty years. You're probably the most dangerous thing around here."

A slow smile spread across his face. "I *am* dangerous, but you'll love my brand of danger."

"You take every insult I dish out as a compliment."

"Yeah, so?" He moved into her, put his hands on her shoulders, and slipped his tongue in her ear. He inhaled her scent, that trace of lavender filled his nostrils. She whimpered like a woman about to give in and pulled away from him.

"Fine. Whatever." She flipped the Open sign to Closed then walked across the room to turn off some of the lights. Tyler watched her fine ass in those tight jeans. Damn, he loved those jeans almost as much as he loved her ass. But he was a tits man, and she had that going on, too. She knew how to dress to accentuate her body, a talent he appreciated.

She stopped a few feet from him. "What are you staring at?"

He raised his eyes past her tits with reluctance. "Your tits. Are those things real?"

"What do you think?" Lavender narrowed her gaze, and he braced himself for a butt-chewing. Instead, a calculating gleam lit up her eyes. She propped her hands on her hips and drew her shoulders back in a challenge he dared not misinterpret. If he did, she'd most likely serve his balls on a silver platter as tomorrow's special.

"I don't know. That's why I asked." The rise and fall of her chest mesmerized him. Even in his big hands, she'd be a handful, and he loved big tits, the bigger, the better, as long as they were natural and not silicone, a rarity in his world. Heck, he'd been about to marry a woman with fake ones. While he appreciated their size, he didn't care for how they squished in his hands. There was something to be said about the real deal.

She took a step closer. He held his breath. His groin ached while his twins down south prepared for action. His damn cock hardened as if he'd overdosed on Viagra. Not that he'd ever needed sexual enhancers, he just needed Lavender. Like a rainstorm in the middle of a warm, sunny day, the atmosphere in the room turned hot and sticky. He caught a whiff of female arousal, and his groin muscles constricted.

"Why don't you find out for yourself?" She issued the challenge with a sultry pout of her full lips. He looked up in mid-gawk to catch her expression in case this was her idea of a cruel joke. It wasn't. He knew that look. He'd seen it on several women. He'd never expected to see it on her face.

He watched as the bad girl in her came out to play. Damn, but he loved bad girls. The badder and more adventurous, the better. He'd bet one of his Super Bowl rings his purple lady had both in spades.

"You still hate me, right?" He tested the waters, making sure she didn't have any delusions about an emotional commitment.

"Absolutely. Positively. I can't stand your arrogance, your conceit, your football for a brain. And you're overrated as a kisser."

"What the fuck?" He blinked. Twice. Three times. Women never said that to him. Her insult threw him off-balance, and he didn't like the feeling one bit.

"Yeah, you heard me, jock boy. You're going to have to do better than that." A slight tremor in her voice gave her away. He smiled, knowing he had her back where he wanted her.

"I'll just have to try harder, won't I?"

She glanced down at the large bulge in his jeans and sucked her lower lip into her mouth. "I don't like you. Remember?"

He remembered all right. "All the better. I can't stand you either, but I crave your hot little body. The physical chemistry is hard to resist with no messy emotions involved. Just you, me, and my cock driving into your pussy." His penis hardened to the point of pain. If he didn't give it satisfaction soon, it'd mutiny.

"You are a romantic devil."

"Screw romance. I'm talking sex here. Fucking, hon. Pure, crazy-assed fucking. Any way you want it, baby, as long as it's hot and messy."

"Any way I want it? What if I want to be in charge?" She swayed to the tune of some sultry music playing in her pretty little head, taunting him.

"On occasion, but this is not the occasion."

Lavender walked toward the pool table in the back of the bar, pausing to pull down the shade on the nearest window. "Follow me."

Tyler bolted after her, weaving between the tables. He tangled his legs around a chair and went down on his knees. Lavender laughed at him, but he didn't give a shit. His football-damaged knees protested the abuse. He struggled to his feet, feeling every bit of his twenty-eight years and then some for a brief moment. Then his gaze locked on her body, he became a teenager again.

He caught her around the waist and deposited her butt on the lip of the pool table. She leaned back, supporting her upper body with her hands and looked up at him. He stepped between her spread legs. His erection pressed against her crotch. Undeterred by the two layers of jeans fabric separating them, he ground his cock against her crotch.

She moaned and closed her eyes for a moment. Her little pink tongue darted out of her mouth and moistened her red lips.

"Now, where were we?" Tyler leaned in and licked those lips, tasting her lipstick. She tasted sweet and hot at the same time, like a strawberry margarita with double the tequila. He'd be drunk on her in no time. Her scent soaked into his pores, raced through his bloodstream, and right to his dick.

She buried her fingers in his hair and opened her mouth. Her tongue touched his, flicked against his lips. Lavender circled his mouth with her tongue. He heard a ragged groan and realized a second later it was his. Tyler pulled her mouth closer. His lips rubbed across her lips. He slipped his tongue into her mouth and leisurely explored every sweet recess, holding back with every ounce of control he possessed. His body shuddered in protest, begging for gratification.

Lavender's tongue met his and lit a spark that erupted into a full-blown wildfire. His tenuous control snapped the rubber band of sexual tension between them. Tyler lost it. He couldn't hold back. He attacked her mouth as she attacked his. Kissing her was like kissing a woman raised in the wilds, unfettered by the civilized world. And he loved it.

She locked her legs around his thighs. He marveled at how small and delicate she felt in his arms, compared to his large, hulking body. Panting, he drew back to catch his breath and stared down at her, her mouth slightly open, her lips swollen from his rough kisses, her cheeks abraded by his stubble. Satisfaction surged through him. He loved seeing his mark on her.

Lavender's chest heaved, and his attention snapped to those gorgeous tits. She wrapped her fingers around his wrists and put his hands on her breasts. He didn't resist. After all, he wasn't that stupid.

Filling both hands, he squeezed her through her soft, clingy sweater. *Real.* They were frigging real. One hundred percent female with no silicone. He'd hit the mega-lotto, broke the bank in Vegas, hit for the cycle. He kneaded her soft breasts, savoring the feel of a natural female.

She stopped breathing. A good sign. Lavender wasn't immune to him, any more than he was to her. Tyler fingered her hard nipples and discovered another pleasant surprise. She'd pierced her nipples. Pierced nipples really did it for him. His cock strained against his fly. If he didn't fuck her soon, real soon, he'd cream his jeans. He'd never done that. Never. No woman had ever reduced him to such a state. Not even multiple women catering to him at the same time.

"You like them?"

"Hell, yeah, but I think we need to get to it."

"You wanna do it here or somewhere else?"

Tyler hesitated, wrestled with control of his body, but his cock was winning the battle. His boy didn't like waiting and didn't believe in patience as a virtue. In fact, he didn't believe in virtue at all.

In the next room hung a picture of his father and several other men who'd served their country, including many who'd died doing just that.

Hating himself for caring, for doing the right thing, Tyler straightened and backed up a step. "Yeah, it seems—" He struggled for the words. "—wrong to do it here."

* * * * *

Tyler had just done a noble thing, something Lavender didn't want to acknowledge because it'd lower his asshole status in her eyes. Instead, she followed him to the door. She flipped off the last of the lights and locked the door behind them. The horny jock grabbed her arm and hustled her down the sidewalk. He wrenched open the back door of his big-assed truck and tossed her inside. Zipping around the truck, he crammed both front seats as far forward as they'd go to buy a little space.

Lavender glanced out the windows of the truck, parked in the now-deserted back parking lot. Her wild-girl side trembled with anticipation. She loved sex with an edge, craved doing the forbidden, just to see if she'd get caught.

The chances of anyone being on the streets this time of night were slim to none. Besides, they'd have to walk behind the building and press their faces up against the heavily tinted windows to see inside.

Tyler crawled into the backseat with her. His large body dominated the cramped space.

"Here?" She asked, the thrill of possibly being caught heightened her arousal. She ran her hands down his corded biceps.

"Damn right." He grinned his bad-boy grin, and her body would've followed him anywhere. With the dark stubble and unruly hair, he not only fit that bad-boy mold, but he redefined it.

"In the back of a truck? How high school." She couldn't help getting her digs in. The smart-ass remarks came naturally around him, and they upped the tension. Besides, judging by how his eyes darkened to midnight blue, he relished the conflict.

"I have a cheerleader fantasy." He sat on the edge of the seat and grinned at her. His sexy smile sent little shivers reverberating through her revved-up body. He picked up a lock of her hair and wrapped it around his long index finger.

"Surely you've had plenty of cheerleaders in your day."

"Oh, yeah, starting my freshman year of high school and plenty of them in the backseat, but I've never had a redheaded one."

"Hate to disappoint you, champ, but I was never a cheerleader."

"That doesn't surprise me. I bet you were out smoking behind the bleachers."

Lavender shrugged. "Maybe." So she'd been a bad girl, especially after the divorce when she'd been hurting and wanted to make everyone else around her hurt. This wasn't about the past or the future, but the present and getting satisfaction from a man bent on giving it to her.

"Are you a natural redhead?"

"You'll have to find that out for yourself."

His gaze shifted to her crotch. He lifted his head and a one hundred percent bad-boy smile spread across his face. "My dick can't take much more of this. I want you now, then we'll do it at a more leisurely pace in my bed."

"Oh, jock boy, you have such a wonderful way with words. It titillates me."

"You tit-a-late me."

Lavender rolled her eyes. "Does this?" She grasped the bottom of her T-shirt and pulled it over her head.

"Oh, damn. You are one hot mama." He ran a long finger down her neck, her chest, and into her cleavage. He slid his hands behind her back and unfastened her bra with a practiced flip of his wrist, obviously a man experienced in getting a woman out of her clothes. Grasping the lacy bra, he tossed it into the front seat.

Tyler's quick intake of breath told her more than his words. He studied her breasts with reverence, an art collector appreciating a masterpiece. Lavender preened like a spoiled tabby under his worshipping gaze. She felt desired and desirable, an imperfect fairytale princess with her asshole prince charming, as surreal as any fantasy she'd ever had. And all of it in the back of a big-assed pickup truck in a parking lot in town. To hell with the golden carriage.

"I love pierced nipples. It ups the stakes." Tyler brushed a hand over her nipples, and tremor shook her from her red head to her violet toenails.

"In what way?"

"Gives me more options. Stick around, honey. You'll find out." He fingered the little gold barbells running through each nipple. Lowering his head, he sucked a nipple into his sinful mouth. His tongue played with the little bar piercing her nipple. He tantalized and teased, sucking then licking with light little nips. Holding her creamy skin of her breast between his teeth, he drew it inside and left a small horizontal red mark on the flesh next to one nipple. She moaned and squirmed on the seat as he demonstrated his talents went beyond football. She'd had quite a few lovers, and some were extremely competent. Tyler sucked tit like no man she'd ever been with.

Lavender threw her head back against the headrest and uttered a low groan. She couldn't take much more of this or she blow apart, bones and all, until nothing remained but a quivering mass of lust. She wanted their first orgasm to happen with him inside her, despite the obvious fact he could make her come with just his mouth on her breasts.

"Please. Tyler, I don't want to come like this our first time. I want you inside me when I come. Take me. Hard. The harder the better." She tilted her head downward and rubbed her chin across his short, dark hair. He angled his head to toy with her other nipple. She took advantage and nipped his earlobe.

Tyler growled, a low, guttural cave-man type growl. "The first time? You're admitting there will be more than one time?" He drew back and studied her face. His blue eyes sparkled with lust and pure pleasure.

Oh, crap. She'd blown her cover, but at this point in time, she didn't give a shit. "I bet there'll be more than one time tonight alone."

He nodded, hesitated, and frowned for a moment. "You do hate me, right?"

"I love your body. I just can't stand your mind, what there is of it."

An unmistakable pained expression darkened his features for a moment. It disappeared so fast, she swore she imagined it. Puzzled, she searched his eyes but saw nothing but lust.

"I want to make sure you understand this is about screwing. Nothing else. I don't do relationships."

Ah, that explained it. The jock didn't want her falling for him. "Haven't you been listening? I can't stand you. Even if I liked your mind and stellar personality, I don't do emotional relationships with any man. This is sex, pure, wild, headboard slamming sex. Since neither one of us can stomach the other, it'll be nice, safe sex with no strings."

"Nice? There won't be anything *nice* about it. *Do* you do this often?" He frowned, almost as if he gave a shit about the answer.

"Not as often as you." She slipped her hands under his T-shirt and felt him up, delighting in the rock-hard planes of his muscles and rough texture of his chest hair.

He cocked an eyebrow at her. "Honey, no one does it as often as me."

"I hope you practice safe sex."

He reached in his pocket and whipped out a condom, holding it up for her to see. "Never leave home without them."

"Why doesn't that surprise me?"

"It shouldn't. As you take every opportunity to remind me, I'm a dumb jock, and we walk around with our dicks hanging out all the time in a perpetual state of horniness."

"That about says it." She shook off a twinge of remorse. Something in his tone troubled her, almost as if she'd hurt him with her callous declarations about his kind.

Slipping the condom into the seatback pocket, he unbuttoned the waistband of her jeans and pulled down the zipper. She lifted her hips so he could pull them down her thighs.

"Nice tat." Bending his dark head, he kissed the tattoo of a hummingbird peeking out from under her bikini panties, below her left hip bone. Its little beak pointed toward heaven, and not the one in the sky.

"You like it?"

"Honey, so far I like everything about your body, especially those tits. I'd like to sample a little of your nectar." His large index finger toyed with the elastic on her panties while his mouth went back for seconds on her breasts.

She giggled, sounding way too much like an enamored teenager. In disgust, she turned away from him and composed herself. She'd never fall for a jock. They were entitled, self-serving pigs, just like the one sucking on her tit right now. Not that it mattered. She wasn't in this for love, just lust.

"I like yours, too." Lavender squeezed his shoulder and the Rose Bowl tattoo then kissed the Ryan tattoo on his chest.

A cloud passed over his face but the asshole quickly regained command. "I have one more on my ass."

"On your ass?"

"Yes, ma'am." He grinned and unzipped his jeans. She licked her lips and reached for his waistband, helping him out of his jeans. A couple seconds later, he shucked his underwear and turned his butt toward her, difficult to do in the tight quarters. She stared at the fancy script on his butt spelling out the word *ass*.

"It really does say ass." It just figured the guy would tattoo the word *ass* on his butt.

"You doubted me?" He struggled to untangle his long legs and shift his big body to face hers. "You're still hating me, aren't you?"

"More than ever."

"Good. I'd hate to think you actually liked me."

"Never happen. Quit talking and get to work."

"Yes, ma'am." He grinned his bad-boy grin, which promised all sorts of carnal delights she couldn't wait to sample.

"Good thing you have a big truck with lots of room in the backseat."

"The biggest." His bad-boy grin promised great things.

He turned to fully face her, drawing her gaze to his cock. The man was hung like a draft horse. She'd had some big cocks in her life, but nothing like this guy. He pushed her down on the seat, his hips between her legs, his mouth even with her breasts. His big erection grazed her stomach.

Her pussy wept with desire. Tyler started with her mouth and kissed his way back to her tits. The guy hadn't been kidding when he'd said he was a tit man. His mouth latched onto her other nipple. Little prickles of pleasure shot through her. His teeth abraded the sensitive skin. He flattened the opposite nipple between a thumb and forefinger. He grasped the barbell and rotated his wrist in a slight twisting motion. She yelped in surprise, pinned to the seat by his big body.

Lifting his head, he regarded her with lust-filled eyes. "I'm not much for vanilla sex."

"Neither am I." Lavender gritted her teeth as he grasped her other nipple and twisted.

"Once won't be enough."

"No, it won't."

"But right now, if I don't bury this cock of mine inside that pussy of yours, I may just die."

"I wouldn't want any trouble with the Lumberjacks, so do it, jock boy." Retrieving the condom in the seatback pocket, she tore the wrapper off the package. He reared up, supporting his weight with one strong arm braced on the seat beside her. She slid the condom onto the head of his cock and rolled it down his length. Tyler's eyes rolled back in his head, and he grunted. She slipped her hands under his thighs and cupped his balls.

"Ah, fu—dang. Don't do that. I can't hold out much longer."

Tyler gritted his teeth, the veins stood out in his neck. Lavender placed her hands on his waist and arched her hips, pressing them against him. He positioned his big cock at her dripping entrance. The head stretched her wide open. He paused, even though his clenched jaw looked ready to shatter.

"I really don't want to hurt you." Each strained word sounded as if it was wrenched from his very soul.

"Give it to me."

She flexed her hips and pushed him in a little deeper. It'd be a stretch, a difficult one, but the reward would be worth the pain. She moved her hips in a circular motion, knowing she was teasing him beyond all reason.

"Take me. Hard."

Tyler's control shattered. She saw it on his face. His muscles bunched, gathered, prepared themselves for ramming it home. She wrapped her legs around his waist and urged him on. With one hard, rough, powerful thrust, his huge cock stretched her tight little hole. A sharp pain cascaded through her, but only lasted a brief moment. She cried out, but suspected he wasn't capable of hearing anymore. He filled every part of her not leaving one empty space. She felt him all the way to her womb. Her walls stretched to accommodate him. He stared down at her as he held himself inside her, appearing to savor the moment as much as her.

Sliding out, he slammed into her again and raised her hips off the seat with each successive thrust. Her head tapped against the door as he drove into her body, relentless, demanding, and needy.

She raked his shoulders with her fingernails and dug her heels into the small of his back. The man plunged into her, frenzied and out of control. He rode her hard, taking no prisoners. His mouth came down on hers, growing more crazed with every deep stroke of his cock. Their bodies slapped together. His harsh breathing echoed her own.

The orgasm built inside her, coming on swift and powerful, driving her out of her mind. Judging by his increased rhythm, his was near, too. She screamed her release, shouting his name over and over. Sweat poured off him and mingled with sweat on her body. Veins stood out on his neck. His lips peeled back to reveal bared teeth.

His cock jerked inside her several times. Her pussy tightened around him, as if it could hold him there forever. His hoarse shouts mingled with hers. Her body disintegrated and merged with his, as they shot toward the stars.

Finally, their passions ebbed then floated back to earth.

Tyler wrapped his arms around her and held her tightly in the back seat of his truck on a public street. Lavender closed her eyes and buried her face in his shoulder, allowing herself a few minutes to forget how much she disliked him.

Chapter 12

In the Shotgun

Lavender stirred in Tyler's big bed—the guy didn't do anything small—buried under a mound of blankets. One heck of a storm was blowing in off the ocean. Rain pelted the windows while wind rattled the mansion's old bones. The old lady creaked and groaned but stood her course.

In that place between waking and sleeping, Lavender recalled a night of incredible passion and intensity so strong it would have destroyed a weaker person. Despite being shrouded in mist, the dream seemed too real, right down to the ache between her legs, tenderized nipples, and bones turned to putty.

She lay limp, her limbs too heavy to move, and processed everything in an attempt to separate fantasy from reality. Fantasy came in the form of emotions she didn't want to examine. Reality came in the form of a large hand cupping one breast. A soft snore rumbled in her ear. A hairy chest rubbed against her back. A semi-erect cock pressed against her butt.

Not a dream. She'd done untold things with and to Tyler Harris, and she wanted to do more.

The object of her thoughts stirred but didn't wake. Rolling onto his back, he stretched and smiled a lazy smile in his sleep. She wondered if he was thinking of her or some other woman. After the night they'd just spent together, he'd damn well better be thinking of her.

The man was pure male gorgeousness in the early morning light. As his chest rose and fell in a steady rhythm, she ran an exploring hand over his abs and pecs. She relished the hardness, the sheer maleness of his long, lean body with its well-defined muscles.

His dark lashes were sinfully long, yet didn't look the least bit feminine on him. Nothing on this man was feminine. He exuded one hundred percent testosterone. His chiseled face belonged on the big screen or advertising for the All-American bad boy.

She leaned forward and kissed the cleft in his chin, then brushed a lock of hair from his forehead. His unruly dark hair curled at the ends. She slid a finger across his day's growth of beard. Obviously, shaving wasn't any more of a priority for him than a haircut was. Her breasts tingled as she recalled how his beard scraped across them as he sucked and licked her nipples, the proof of his deeds still visible by the red marks on her breasts.

The two of them connected with combustible chemistry fueled by their differences and their similarities. All purely physical, of course. She didn't like him or the things he stood for.

Lavender rarely lingered in bed with a man after they'd screwed their brains out. One or the other of them left before morning. Hell if she knew why she lingered now. If she had any intelligence, she'd yank on her clothes and head home. That way they could both pretend nothing happened, until the next time. She had little doubt there'd be a next time.

With one last kiss to his cheek, she rolled into a sitting position on the edge of the bed and wondered why she'd felt the urge to kiss him. Kissing on the cheek was a tenderness thing. Tenderness didn't fit her view of recreational sex. She doubted it fit his. Whatever possessed her to give him a chaste kiss couldn't, wouldn't, happen again.

Time to leave.

Oh, crap. Her clothes were in his truck.

A meow sounded behind her head. The orange tabby sat on the nightstand, grooming his pristine white paws.

"How long have you been there?"

The cat smirked, keeping to himself just how long he'd been there. "You watched us?"

Smug and playing it cool, the cat jumped off the nightstand and sauntered from the room.

"You little voyeur."

Next time, she'd insist Tyler shut the bedroom door. She looked back at a peaceful, sleeping Tyler. How he managed to look so angelic and so bad at the same time eluded her.

Lavender loved how her small body fit so well with his big one. Instead of feeling overwhelmed, his sheer size and strength energized her. Despite a level of danger to the man, she trusted him with her body. He'd never harm her physically.

Never.

Emotionally might be a different story.

* * * * *

Tyler yawned and stretched. A satisfied smile lifted the corners of his mouth. The sheets caressed his naked body, while the blankets wrapped him in warmth in the chilly room. He'd rather be wrapped in Lavender's warmth. He reached for her. His hand swiped across cold sheets and found nothing. No warm female body with tits sent from heaven and sinful red hair. And yes, she was a natural redhead.

She must have left sometime in the night. Morning sun shone off the water in the small bay. Rolling to his feet, Tyler walked to the French doors and threw them open, ignoring the frigid air. Unconcerned about his nakedness, he walked out onto the master bedroom balcony.

Tyler breathed deeply, inhaling the fresh salt air and savoring the smells of the island after a good rainfall. Damn, if he didn't watch it, he might actually start liking this place and want to keep the money pit.

Frowning at the thought, he walked back inside and kicked the door shut with his foot. He loved cities, loved the excitement, the parties, the places, the people, the sights, the smells. He wasn't a country guy, never would be and didn't want to be. He'd keep telling himself that, too, until he believed it.

In less than months, he'd be back in Seattle, his life an endless round of parties at night and working out during the day. No more sassy redhead to trade barbs and share his bed. No more Brotherhood with their annoying habits of showing up on his doorstep at all hours to watch his television, play cards, and empty his liquor cabinet. No more finicky orange tabby cat. No more Saturday night karaoke with the gang at the veterans' club.

Life would go back to normal, and so would he.

If he could figure out what normal was.

A cold shower didn't help.

After he toweled off, he wrenched open a stuck drawer on the antique dresser and yanked on clean underwear, a pair of faded jeans, and a sweatshirt. He grabbed a fresh cup of coffee from the kitchen and walked onto the porch. His gaze slid to Lavender's house, but he didn't see any sign of life.

You'd think he'd have had enough last night to last a few days, but his cock didn't agree. It sprang to red alert, ready for action.

Tyler craned his neck for some sign of her piece of shit truck in the driveway. Disappointment flooded through him. She wasn't home, probably volunteering at the senior center or old folks' home.

With a sigh, he walked back to the house. Picking up a sheet of sandpaper, he took his frustrations out on the banister.

* * * * *

Lavender put the dirty glasses in the under-bar dishwasher. Tyler, her only patron, sat at the bar, nursing his first and only beer, one eye on her and one on ESPN. The man wanted some, and he'd probably get it just like he had for the past week. Not that she was complaining. He knew how to find just the right places, places she didn't even know existed.

Tyler stared up at the television, and she followed his gaze. ESPN was interviewing Zach Murphy. The guy, all intense and edgy, discussed his move to a new team and what he wanted out of next season. He fended off the questions about alleged sexual abuse of a former girlfriend, insisting it was bullshit. *Yeah, right.* She snorted out loud, drawing a questioning look from Tyler which she ignored.

"What an entitled ass," she muttered under her breath. The jerk was probably one of those guys who believed women deserved just what they got.

"I heard that. You called the guy an *entitled ass*. I'm wounded." Tyler held his hands over his heart.

Confused, she stared at him. "Why?"

"I thought that endearment was reserved for me." His blue eyes sparkled.

They nearly sucked her in, but she sidestepped their magnetic pull, at least for now. "You're all the same."

"Not at all, honey. I'm unique. Murphy isn't even on the same playing field as me." Tyler leaned forward and wrapped his hands around his beer glass. He studied her, as if waiting for her counter attack. They both relished trading barbs with each other.

What about Tyler Harris? We understand you aren't the best of friends.

At the mention of his name on television, Tyler glanced up and rolled his eyes. "That guy is an idiot."

We aren't the best of anything.

So the rumors about division on the team are true?

Exaggerated. Harris needs to get his head on straight.

Do you believe Harris is in rehab?

Zach snorted. *How would I know? I don't keep tabs on him. As long as Harris leaves it all out on the field and plays with heart, he's none of my concern.*

If he doesn't?

Zach Murphy raised his dark, intense eyes to the camera. *Then we have a problem, don't we?*

Lavender switched the channel to a Mariners baseball game. "We don't need to hear any more of his BS."

"Tell me about it." Tyler rubbed his stubbled chin, watching her way too closely, and looking like a man with something more on his mind than sex or Zach Murphy. "You know, Vinnie, I get hating jocks on principle as overpaid, entitled asses. Your dislike goes beyond the norm. So tell me. Why is it you hate jocks so much? Specifically football players. Is your hatred a matter of principle or based on personal experience?"

Lavender stiffened, and she ground her teeth together in an effort to rein in her smart mouth. He'd hit a nerve, a big one. If he had an ounce of brain matter in his thick head, he'd keep his mouth shut and change the subject. "Do I need to list all the reasons to you? You already know most of them because everything I hate about jocks is reflected in your insufferable personality."

"I'm good in bed." He grinned at her and held out his beer for a refill.

"You *are* good naked, I'll give you that."

"That's all there is, baby, and don't you forget it." Pain flickered in his blue eyes, quickly replaced by his usual arrogant smugness.

Yet, she'd seen it with her own eyes. She'd penetrated his thick skin, which should've made her feel triumphant. A twinge of guilt ruined the usual satisfaction she received by bashing him. "I wouldn't dream of it and ruin our mutual dislike?"

"Never happen." Tyler snaked an arm around her neck and caught her off guard. Pulling her across the counter, he laid a big, sloppy kiss on her. She didn't resist, instead she gave it right back with a vengeance, a grudge kiss, one to prove he didn't serve any purpose beyond a sex partner. They attacked each other like two wild creatures in a mating frenzy of pure animal lust. His mouth bruised hers. Their noses bumped together. His stubble burned her cheeks. His tongue pillaged her tongue. She gave as good as she got by answering his every parry and thrust with a parry and thrust of her own. She'd be naked before she knew it at this rate and going at it on top of the bar. Even more disturbing, she didn't give a shit.

The recently installed bell over the door tinkled, signaling new customers. Lavender retreated to her side of the bar. Homer and Ed shuffled across the room and headed for chairs at their favorite table near the big screen television.

Tyler sketched a salute in their direction. "Hey, Brothers." Both men saluted back.

Lavender had their drinks on the table before they'd managed to lower their creaky, ancient bodies into their seats. "Homer, how's your arthritis treating you?"

"I have good days and bad."

"If you need to go to the VA on the mainland, I'd be glad to take you in my day off." Lavender mother-henned these guys, and they ate it up. "And you, Ed, are you taking your heart medicine?"

"Yes, ma'am." Like he'd dare not take it. The Brothers didn't call her sergeant-major for nothing.

Satisfied they were comfortable, she returned to her spot behind the bar. Tyler studied her so intently, she checked her face in the bar mirror but didn't find anything. He looked too much like a man with something to say, something she might not want to hear. She decided to distract him. "Did you know your cat watches us when we have sex in your room?"

"Cougar?"

"That's what you call him?"

"Yeah."

"He does have the heart of a cougar."

"No shit. Besides, I'm partial to cougars. I played my college ball for the Cougars."

"I know." She busied herself wiping the already clean counter. She knew only too well.

"You do?" He moved in like a cougar himself, circling his wounded prey.

"Everybody knows that." She spat the words at him, as she scrubbed the counter hard enough to rub the finish off the wood top. She was pissed as hell at herself for revealing that fact to him. How stupid could she be? The last thing this man needed to know was her connection to his college football team.

"Not everybody. I thought you hated football."

"Just drop it." Lavender turned her back on him and yanked glasses from the dishwasher. With the same quickness he demonstrated when eluding linebackers, he stepped behind the counter and pinned her in the corner with his big body. His breath tickled her ear. She kept her back to him. Her pulse raced from his nearness not just physically, but emotionally. He'd opened an old wound, one she never wanted to open. Her stomach churned and her head ached.

"Not a chance in hell. Tell me why you hate jocks?" His big hands blocked her in as they rested on the counter on either side of her. Across the room, the brothers turned in their seats to watch. Not one of the cowards came to her rescue. Instead, they whispered among themselves.

"Drop it."

He nuzzled her neck, bringing a low whistle from the Brothers and more whispering.

She tried to escape, but she'd have better luck escaping from a prison cell. "Get away from me."

"Not until I have my answer." Determination reverberated in his voice. His hands encircled her waist. Her body welcomed his touch. Her brain rejected it. She snapped and turned on him so fast, he staggered back a step.

"*Damn you*. Hell yes, I know about football. I know a lot about that so-called game you play. It creates assholes like you, and it tears families apart." Lavender spat out the word 'apart' with vehemence and bitterness she couldn't control. She sidestepped around him, planning her escape, but she was no match for his reflexes. He grabbed her arm and jerked her none too gently against his hard body. She glared up at him, hating him for getting inside, past her defenses, for forcing her to reveal something so personal and painful.

His blue eyes drilled into hers, and she backed away, knowing he'd see the bitter truth lurking there. Tyler lowered his voice. "Spoken like someone who's been there. How? How does it tear families apart?"

Lavender looked him straight in the eye. Her lower lip quivered. She would not cry. Not in front of him or anyone. "My dad is a college football coach."

Tyler released his hold on her as he digested this unexpected information. "Who is he? Would I know him?"

Putting a safe physical distance between them, Lavender wiped all emotion from her face, and met his steady gaze with one of her own. "Oh, yeah, jock boy, you know him. He's the Cougars' head coach."

Lavender ducked behind Tyler and ran for the bathroom, just as the dam broke. She locked the door behind her and leaned up against it. She choked up, her eyes filled with tears, and her gut twisted like a pretzel. Sobs wracked her body.

Oh, God, why was it that after all these years, talk of her father still devastated her? The incredible pain of being abandoned by the man who used to call her *Daddy's princess*, wrenched her in two. Why did he leave her? Never call or write, never acknowledge her birthday? Why? Why? Had she been such a bad daughter that he'd ran like hell and never looked back? Heck, she couldn't blame him for leaving her mother. The woman had been difficult, but what had Lavender done to deserve his rejection?

Losing her mother in a car accident months after the divorce hurt like hell, but there was a finality to it that she'd come to terms with years ago. But losing someone because they chose to forget about you caused a new kind of pain which never totally went away.

In moments of weakness, she missed her dad, missed his wise ways, his gentle yet firm tone. She missed his smile and his teasing. It'd almost be easier if he were dead because there'd be finality to it and an explanation for his absence.

Maybe being abandoned by her father was one of the reasons she'd developed an affinity for old people. Since she'd been in her teens, she volunteered at the nursing home a couple days a week, reading to a group of residents, writing letters for them, or just visiting. Many of them were stuck in these homes and forgotten by their families, just like her father had forgotten her.

And maybe that's why she worked in a veterans' bar. She genuinely enjoyed the old veterans who came into the bar. It did her heart good to brighten their day.

Tyler would never understand the depth of these people's loneliness, and she pitied him for that.

* * * * *

Still reeling from Lavender's admission, he watched her warily when she returned from the bathroom with red-rimmed eyes. He couldn't think of a thing to say. Besides the look on Lavender's face warned him not to go there. He might be a dumb jock, but he preferred life to death.

His college coach was her *father*? But they didn't even share the last name. Her hatred of jocks *was* personal. He'd expected her attitude to have its basis in a jock boyfriend who'd jilted her, not in a coach father. And definitely not his coach. Not in a million years. Fate sacked him for a loss on this one.

He'd admired Coach Gerloch, or Coach as the guys called him. When his father died, Coach took him under his wing, filled the role of a father in Tyler's life, and kept Tyler from diving off the deep end of despair into drugs and alcohol. He'd been there for Tyler, but he hadn't been there for his own daughter? It didn't make sense.

He'd even imagined someday being a coach like Brian Gerloch, one who inspired, taught character while encouraging a competitive spirit. He'd never once heard the coach mention a daughter. A son, yes, but a daughter, never. There'd been no pictures of Lavender in his office alongside the pictures of his current wife and his son. It didn't add up, didn't make sense when compared with the man Tyler knew and admired.

Lavender had just admitted something deeply personal and obviously painful to her. Something emotional, not physical. He'd bet his Super Bowl ring she didn't tell many people what she'd just told him.

Not good.

He couldn't be her confidante. He wouldn't be there for her. It wasn't his style. His style was love 'em and leave 'em wanting more, but never, never get attached. Hell, he hadn't even been that attached to Cass, despite all the stormy years they'd spent together. So why the hell had he even pushed her for an answer to something which was none of his business?

Lavender turned her back on him and busied herself behind the bar. Tyler took advantage of her inattention to escape. He unwrapped his long legs from the bar stool and stood. Grabbing his beer, he sauntered over to the Brothers, sinking into an empty chair at their table. He breathed a sigh of relief. Like a coward, he'd turned and ran when the flames from the emotional heat licked at his ass.

Her pain was personal, and their relationship needed to stay strictly physical. Besides, she didn't want his sympathy or his commiseration, which should let him off the hook. For some reason, it didn't. Empathy was an emotion he rarely allowed himself, and he didn't wear it well. Yet, he was pretty damn sure the nagging ache in his gut didn't come from his crappy dinner.

He avoided her gaze, certain he'd see disappointment in her eyes at his hasty exit to the relative safety of the Brothers. Next to him, Homer and Ed debated the merits of eight-track tapes versus CDs. Hell, Ty wasn't sure he even knew what an eight-track looked like. He feigned interest and steered them toward their predictions for the upcoming NFL draft. Even then, he couldn't immerse himself in the conversation.

He hazarded a glance at Lavender. She swiped at her eyes with a bar towel, kept her head down, and her back turned away from him.

Ah, hell, she was crying. Again. Crying women made him crazy. They used tears as a ploy to get what they wanted since most men caved at the first sign of moisture in a female's eyes. Rarely had he seen genuine tears. Lavender was manipulating him, a typical woman. Yet, even as he tried to convince himself, he didn't believe it. Not really.

She took one more vicious swipe at her tears, squared her shoulders, and headed his way. *Oh, crap.* This wasn't going to be pretty. The Brothers argued on, completely oblivious to the murderous woman advancing on their sacred little oasis. Tyler gripped the edge of the table and forced himself to breathe in rhythmic, deep breaths, and waited.

She stomped over to the table. Hands on hips, she faced him. The Brothers stopped their arguing and stared, dentures clattering and knees knocking together. They knew a dangerous woman when they saw one.

"One last thing, Mr. Harris. Discussions regarding my father are off-limits. You will *never* bring up Brian Gerloch's name in my presence. *Never.* Do I make myself clear?"

The Brothers raised one eyebrow each in tandem, as if they're rehearsed it. They stared at him as if they couldn't believe he'd been so stupid as to piss her off. Ty nodded his head, feeling like the victim in an old episode of *The Twilight Zone*. Not waiting for a reply, Lavender pivoted and stalked back to her safe zone behind the bar.

She meant every word she said, yet at the same time, Tyler knew he couldn't leave it alone. Not until he learned both sides of the story. Not until he understood the situation better.

When the Brothers wobbled to their feet, he escorted them to their cars and got to hell out of Dodge.

He had a lot of thinking to do, and he didn't have a clue where to start.

Chapter 13

Pushed Back

Cussing under her breath, Lavender struggled with the heavy straw bale. After dragging it off the back of her pickup, she tried to push it into the barn. When that didn't work, she attempted to roll it end over end, but it got the best of her and almost delivered a knockout punch. Just as the damn thing was about to crush her, the weight was suddenly lifted from her body.

Hefting the bale as if it weighed ten pounds instead of one hundred and ten, Tyler carried it to the back of her ramshackle barn. Without a word, he returned to the truck and grabbed the next bale. Lavender stood back and watched, not one to bother a man on a mission. Especially when that mission kept her from being a flat spot on the barn floor.

The chickenshit jock had avoided her all week. Even when he came into the VC, he sat with the Brothers and slithered out the door while she still had customers. He hadn't brought up her father, just as she'd asked, yet it hurt her feelings he didn't care enough to push anyway.

Care enough? How stupid of her. He'd done as she asked and not gone there. Still, she wanted him to ask. Unreasonable for her, she knew. She kinda missed the sex, too.

"Thanks for rescuing me from death by straw bales."

Tyler paused from his spot in the bed of her truck, hay hooks grasped in his gloved hands. He looked down at her. "I can't resist a damsel in distress."

"I can't resist a Prince Uncharming."

"Hey, I'm the king of asses." Tyler graced her with his trademark lady-killer grin, as if that'd work on her. Nope. No way. This girl was immune.

Then again—

Her weak-willed body didn't get the message from her brain and melted at his feet. One week was a long time to go without her neighbor's talents. The man played on a mattress as well as he played on a football field.

The muscles in his strong thighs bulged from the weight as Tyler heaved the last bale of straw to the top of the stack as if it weighed no more than a pillow. He flexed his throwing arm then rubbed it, as if he felt a twinge.

"Are you okay?"

He shrugged one shoulder, playing the Mr. Tough Guy. "I'm fine. Just side effects from playing a violent game for a living."

He waited, as if he expected a smart comeback. She didn't have one. Not today. The NFL paid him well for the physical abuse he suffered every Sunday. Those were the trade-offs.

Tyler pulled off his gloves and wiped his hands on his thighs.

"You don't have animals. What's the straw for?"

"For mulch? To lock in the moisture? Heck if I know. Gram insists we have it for the garden."

"I'm all for moisture. Makes things stand up better." His eyes flicked to her drooping garden plants and back. "Moisture looks good on you, too." He traced the sweat trickling down her neck with his calloused finger, not stopping when it disappeared under her T-shirt but following the line down to where her sweaty shirt stuck to her cleavage. Their gazes locked, and she knew they'd be vertical in no time. His blue eyes smoldered, singeing her with the promise reflected in them. Dang, how she'd missed his body. He moved close to her, pinning her against the truck. Grabbing her waist, he hoisted her butt onto the tailgate and pushed her knees apart, stepping between them.

"You've been avoiding me." Lavender ran a hand across his cheek.

His eyes darkened, and he pressed closer. "Yeah, well, my coach being your dad is weird. I'm having a hard time dealing with it."

"I haven't seen him in years. He's a father in name only so don't worry about it."

"Okay." He looked anything but okay.

"Can you deal?" She arched her back and pushed out her breasts, using her body to distract him and get beyond this *too personal* thing growing between them. Lavender had always enjoyed sex, but she'd become a slave to her desires, thanks to this gorgeous, self-proclaimed asshole. She would not let her obsession with getting this man naked temper her emotional dislike of him.

"I'm working on it." Tyler pushed her down on the bed of the truck. His hard cock rubbed against her crotch. He shoved her sweatshirt and her bra up to expose her breasts. She moaned as his warm breath teased one pebbled nipple followed by an even warmer mouth. His tongue drew lazy circles around her nipple as his mouth sucked—now, that took talent. When it came to sexual expertise, the jock stood in a league of his own.

He drew back and admired her generous breasts. "I'm going to buy you some new jewelry for these babies. Something to remind you of me. Maybe some little footballs." She writhed against him, as he toyed with her nipples.

"Anything but footballs. Oh, my. Oh. Ty." Lavender arched her back, loving his touch. He bent down. His mouth covered hers. She threaded her fingers through his thick, dark hair. He tempted her with his lips, tantalized with his tongue, and she yielded to the web he wove. Completely under his spell, Lavender lost herself in the feel of his marauding mouth and did a little marauding of her own.

Cougar leapt onto the truck bed and crawled onto her shoulder. Tyler pulled back when the cat stuck his face between theirs.

"Get lost, Coug." Ty pushed him away. "Get your own pussy."

Coug ignored them and swatted at a lock of Lavender's hair.

She heard the slam of a car door followed by a second slam. *Oh, crap.* Lavender wrenched out of Tyler's grasp, kneeing him in the groin. He yelped and doubled over. Ignoring him, she yanked down her shirt and bra, as she leapt off the tailgate.

"What the fu—fudge?" Tyler ground out through his teeth. Geez, the bet was over, and he was still trying to clean up his mouth. He'd never cared before about his swearing. This wasn't good.

"Grandma and Grandpa just drove up." Lavender smoothed her hair and straightened her clothes. In another few minutes, he'd have been inside her. They would've been humping like rabbits, and her grandparents would've witnessed it all. The grief Doris piled on would've reached epic proportions.

"What? What the hell are you talking about?" Tyler groaned from his bent over position.

"You have to go." She fought to control the panic in her voice, even though embarrassment colored her face a bright red. A grown woman shouldn't allow her family that much control over her life, but most families weren't like her family. Lavender learned to travel the path of least resistance—give her grandmother what she wanted on the surface then fly under the radar and do whatever the hell she pleased.

"Hell, I can't even stand up straight, let alone walk."

"Don't be a wuss. Get out of here."

Tyler looked up, still hunched over. "No." His blue eyes drilled into hers. She cringed at the determination reflected in them.

"Ty, please." She glanced over her shoulder. "They'll be here any second."

"How old *are* you?"

"Twenty-seven." She knew where he was going with this.

"So who cares what your grandmother thinks?"

"You don't get it," she hissed. "You've never cared what anyone thought, even your mother. Never needed to keep the peace."

"You have no effing idea what you're talking about."

"Please, Tyler, out the back door."

"No." Tyler stood up straighter. His face still a little pale from the pain. He put his hands on his hips. His jaw jutted out in a display of cussed stubbornness. She knew enough about him to realize he wasn't budging. "You don't want to be seen with me."

If she didn't know better, she'd suspect she'd hurt his feelings. "Please, she'll be really pissed to see you here."

"So? You're over twenty-one. You're an adult. This is *your* life, she doesn't get a vote."

"You don't understand."

"You're damn right I don't understand. Every time she shows up—and that's a lot—you kick me out or tell me to stay home."

"Tyler, please."

"Nope, I'm staying. Payback's a bitch."

Too late for more pleading, Lavender pasted a fake smile on her face and accepted her fate.

* * * * *

Tyler hadn't a clue why he'd insisted on staying. Maybe just to be contrary. Maybe curiosity about his college coach's ex-wife, or maybe for reasons he damned well shouldn't explore, such as sensing their relationship was about to turn a corner, and he needed to remind Lavender what an ass he could be. Just by the furious expression her face, his message had been received loud and clear. And he wasn't done yet.

Tyler instantly disliked Lavender's grandparents. By the sour looks on their faces, the feeling was mutual. Despite the fourteen-plus inches' difference in height, Doris Mead looked down her nose at him as if he was some kind of vermin infesting her space. Long-festering bitterness added extra lines and years to her scowling face. Maybe she'd been attractive forty-plus years ago before the hatred and anger made her a vindictive old woman.

Larry Mead let his wife do the talking but stood back with a smug, self-righteous smirk on his ruddy face. The guy barely reached Tyler's chin and wore his disdain like a billboard. Obviously, he also ate a little too well, as evidenced by his ample belly. His gray hair was combed back and a little longish behind, like a television evangelist.

"Gram, Grandpa, this is Tyler." When neither of them responded, she turned to Tyler, her expression pleading with him to behave himself. "Ty, this is my grandmother, Doris Mead, and my grandfather, Larry Mead."

Doris sniffed as if she smelled something foul, while fat Larry inspected the stack of straw. If Tyler was lucky, one of the bales would fall and bury the prick. He plastered a fake smile on his face. "Mrs. Mead, it's a pleasure." He nodded to her husband. "Mr. Mead."

"Dr. Mead." Larry rewarded Tyler's rare politeness with a curt nod and continued to poke and prod the stacked hay. Lavender rung her hands together, her eyes full of worry.

"Larry's a psychologist."

Oh, man, her grandfather was a shrink. She'd never mentioned that. He hated being psychoanalyzed because he knew he'd come up lacking.

Catching Tyler's pained expression, Lavender bumbled on. "He's not a practicing one. He's a retired professor from the University of Washington."

Like that made it any better. They were just the type of people who made Tyler feel inferior, and he detested feeling inferior to anyone. He stood up straighter, using his height to intimidate.

"What did you get your degree in?" Larry grinned, as if he already knew the frigging answer.

"I went pro before I got my degree." Hell, with his grades, he'd still be trying to finish his first year if he hadn't joined the NFL.

"You're a football player." Doris Mead spat out the words like some foul-tasting medicine.

"Yes, ma'am." He stifled a grin, enjoying toying with this woman.

Doris rounded on Lavender like a prize fighter going in the for the knock-out blow. "Lavender, haven't you listened to a word I've said? Will you ever learn?"

"Gram, he's just a neighbor. I needed help unloading the straw."

"Larry could have helped you."

Tyler doubted the little prick had the strength to wrestle with a field mouse, let alone those bales. "Mrs. Mead, not to worry. Lavender keeps me around for my brawn."

The woman blanched and turned to her husband. "Larry, perhaps, we should return when Lavender doesn't have a *guest*."

Tyler sprawled in a plastic lawn chair. "Mrs. M, I'm not company. I spend too much time here for that." Tyler grinned with sheer, cussed joy.

Lavender choked and her witch of a grandmother stiffened like she had her broomstick stuck up her ass. "I prefer to be here when you're not."

"Oh, man, I'm sorry. I must stink. Next time you drop in, I'll make sure I shower." Tyler smelled under his arms, and he thought the woman might faint. Damn, needling this hag provided great sport, so why stop now. "You know, it's sure a small world. I had no idea Vinnie's dad was my college football coach until a few days ago."

Lavender's face paled.

Every muscle in Doris's body broadcasted her intent to see him six feet under or sinking into the channel. "We don't refer to that man as *Vinnie's* father. He doesn't deserve the title."

"No, shit? I have the highest respect for your former son-in-law. He was my college coach and a mentor. I would think he'd be an excellent father."

Larry sputtered, while Doris's eyes flashed fire. He might as well have said he idolized a cannibalistic serial killer. He'd made an enemy, or two, but he couldn't stop himself, despite a twinge of guilt over Lavender's obvious alarm.

"You, young man, have absolutely no idea what you're talking about. How dare you defend that man in my presence and my granddaughter's presence." Doris perched her chubby hands on her hips. Larry hurried to her side and stood helpless behind her.

Lavender jumped into the fray. "Please, Tyler. Don't refer to Brian Gerloch as my father. As far as we're concerned he's dead to us. Thanks for the help with the straw." Despite her anger, the pain and betrayal broadcast on her face kicked him in the gut.

Tyler recognized a 'fuck off' when he heard one. His head pounded from all the tension, while Doris's oppressive selfishness smothered him. It was all about her, to hell with her granddaughter and what she wanted. He'd never witnessed such an impressive job of brainwashing, even if his old coach might deserve their ridicule, which he doubted.

Tyler turned to leave when Doris called to him. Turning back, he saw her lip curl into a cruel snarl. "My granddaughter needs a man with integrity, with brains, with a future. She needs a man who has more to show for his life than a Super Bowl ring."

"Two Super Bowl rings." Tyler faked a cocky grin. For a minute, he swore the woman would launch herself at him and start punching.

"Regardless. You are not that man."

With an indifferent shrug, Tyler strolled away, purposely keeping his gait slow and easy, as if these crazy people didn't affect him one bit. What he really wanted to do was beat tracks back to the relative quiet and safety of his mansion. When he passed the gate between the properties, Cougar jumped off the fence post where he'd been waiting and ran ahead to the back door.

Irritation ruffled Tyler's ego, along with a bone-deep fear of his inadequacy. He wasn't good enough for Lavender, wasn't good enough for anyone. He was just a dumb jock. A guy who wouldn't have anything going for him if it wasn't for his arm, his talent for reading defenses, and his ability to make something out of nothing. Not to mention his money.

But money didn't buy respect or piece of mind.

If it wasn't for his athletic ability, he'd be homeless and living under the Alaskan Way viaduct because he'd never have made it out of high school, let alone college. His only marketable skills depended on his muscles and his no-quit attitude.

Except that attitude had deserted him last season, leaving him with a big fat zero in the positive qualities department. Without his killer instincts, his drive, his ambition, he didn't have much else going for him. A blanket of fear smothered Tyler, made it hard to breathe, like he was on the bottom of a dog pile of three-hundred-pound linemen.

He slumped into a chair and stared mindlessly at the flames from the fireplace. Coug perched on the back of the chair. His tail whipped back and forth in annoyance over God knew what. Tyler felt like shit. Not on the outside, but on the inside. He really was a first-class ass, and he didn't deserve all the good things that'd come this way in his life.

Hell, he couldn't even grant a dying kid's last wish. That's how much of a failure he was. And he'd just been a real ass to Lavender and made her life hell when it came to her grandparents for no reason other than to be the asshole everyone expected him to be.

Tyler sighed and wondered if he could sink much lower.

Chapter 14

Broken Tackle

Tyler strode into the VC, pretending he owned the world and everyone in it. His asshole mode served him well, especially when confusion reigned inside his head. At least on the outside, he appeared in control.

He hesitated when he saw Xandra, not Lavender, mixing drinks. He considered leaving, but driven by curiosity, he kept walking across the room. He sat his butt on *his* bar stool. Xandra slid a beer across the counter to him. He stared at the label of his favorite brew and decided not to ask how she'd known what he wanted to drink.

"Where's Vinnie?" He glanced around the bar. The Brothers played cards in the far corner. Except for their table, the place was deserted.

"She's off today. My day to work. She volunteers at the senior center then she makes the Brothers dinner at Homer's house."

"Oh." Tyler had no clue that she cooked for the Brothers or volunteered with seniors. Not knowing this detail of her life rankled him. Not that he cared one darn bit. He smiled to himself, proud that he'd used *darn* not *fuck*, and in his thoughts. Lavender would be impressed, not that it mattered.

"Besides, she's not speaking to you."

Crap. "I figured as much." He scrubbed his face with his hands and took a deep breath, but nothing eased the shame weighing him down.

"Don't you get it?"

"Not really." Which was the crux of the matter. He had questions. Zan, as Lavender's best friend and cousin, should have the answers, at least to the less personal questions—the ones about his coach.

His instincts warned it was best to let sleeping dogs lie and not get any deeper into this. He couldn't. He'd already seen his high school coach accused of points shaving, now his revered college coach appeared to be a deadbeat dad. In the four years he'd been around Brian Gerloch, he'd never mentioned a daughter, just a son who'd played college ball for a few years.

But first he needed to settle a score with Zan. "So what's with this sensitive crap?"

"Being called sensitive disturbs you?" She rubbed a wine glass dry with a towel and gave him one of those all-knowing looks that really got under his skin.

"Hell, yeah. You insulted my manhood."

"Tyler, you are one messed up guy."

He couldn't dispute that fact. His frown tightened the mask of indifference on his face. "I'm not sensitive."

"You are sensitive. It's common for alpha males to hide their sensitivity behind an asshole exterior, but you've honed it to an art form. I've never seen someone so out of touch with their real self."

He decided to ignore her bullshit and cut to the chase. "So you're Lavender's cousin?"

"First cousin." She pressed her lips tight and regarded him with suspicion, reluctant to give too much information. Obviously, she didn't consider him trustworthy.

"Mother's side or father's side?"

"Father's."

Ah, pay dirt. Tyler sized up the defense and did an end run. He wanted more information. "So what's the deal with her dad? What did he do?" Lavender's entire dysfunctional family seemed to thrive on emotional responses, rather than discussing their problems in a forthright, logical manner. Perhaps, he'd find out the truth from her dad's side of the family.

"What didn't he do? We don't like him."

Okaaay. Well. "We?" Puzzled, Tyler tried to make sense of it all.

"My parents, me, the rest of the family."

So much for pay dirt. Hell, even the coach's own family had turned against him.

"Was he abusive?" Tyler braced himself for the truth he may not want to hear. To generate such dislike among people who should love you indicated some form of severe abuse, maybe even sexual abuse. Yet, he had to know what his once-revered coach had done to deserve these people's obsessive hatred.

"Abusive?" She blinked, as if she couldn't comprehend the question.

"Yeah, all of you have such strong feelings about him I figured he'd beaten her or Lavender or both." Tyler held his breath and waited for the answer. He'd take the bastard out himself if Coach had laid a hand on his daughter.

"Oh, no, nothing like that." Xandra studied him like he was fu—flipping crazy.

Relief flooded him even as confusion set in. "Then I don't get it."

"I shouldn't be telling you this. It's really Vinnie's place to tell you what she wants you to know."

"So give me a clue."

She leaned forward and lowered her voice. "He wasn't there."

"He wasn't where?" Tyler didn't have much patience for evasiveness. In his mind, the crime didn't match the punishment. There had to be more.

"You know, he wasn't around. He was never there for Vinnie. He didn't even attend her high school graduation. Never called her on birthdays or Christmas, never even sent a card. He missed every important moment in her life."

"That's it? He wasn't there? I mean it sucks, but it could be worse." He wanted to knock his head against the wall. None of this made sense. The animosity generated by Doris and her followers seemed out of proportion. Not that he could excuse his coach's actions, but damn, he'd heard a hell of a lot worse.

"Isn't that bad enough?"

"The way the family carries on, I figured he was a child molester or a rapist or an abuser."

Xandra sighed, as if he was too dense to get it. "Are your parents divorced, Tyler?"

Tyler snorted at the ludicrous thought, even as he sought to swallow around the lump forming in his throat. "Heck no, not them. My dad died a few years ago when I was in college. Suddenly. Heart attack. He'd been as healthy as a horse." Why he told her this stuff, he'd never know.

"I'm sorry." Her words rang true, not the shallow words most people spoke which meant nothing.

"Up until the day he died, they were as disgustingly in love as they were when they married years ago. High school sweethearts and all that crap. Totally devoted to each other. My mom says she'll never find another man like him, and she's not going to look."

"I think that's incredible. You were very lucky to have a family like that."

Tyler rolled his eyes. "Yeah, right. Try living up to their standards. I don't even attempt it."

Xandra stared at him to the point where he started to squirm. He'd given away too much of what went on inside his head. "You're very proud of them."

Tyler scrambled to steer the conversation away from his personal life. "How long has it been since Coach has seen Lavender?"

"After the divorce about twelve years ago, Uncle Brian took the assistant coach job across state at WSU. A month later Lavender's mom died in a car accident. Uncle Brian left them with the grandparents for the summer. He never came back for them. After that, he made a few feeble attempts to see the kids. Eventually, he never called, never sent them any cards. He just went away. He didn't pay a penny of child support. Poor Doris and Larry struggled to raise two teenagers. Lavender acted out. She was a handful. Her brother, Andy, just retreated into himself. Football became his life."

"Are you sure he never paid child support?" Tyler scratched his head. He didn't know much about child support, but he couldn't believe it was that easy to just walk away and not pay anything, especially when the person earned a state salary.

"Doris told me so. The woman is a good, honest person. Very devout. She'd never lie."

Tyler wasn't so certain about that. The bitch oozed with manipulative dishonesty.

"My Uncle Brian deserted his kids. My mom and dad don't speak to him. No one in the family does, not after what he did to the kids."

"What about the brother? Andy?"

"After he graduated from high school, he went to WSU against his grandmother's wishes, walked on the team and made it. Doris was so furious, she hasn't spoken to him since."

"That's nice of her."

Zan ignored the dig. "She sacrificed everything for her kids. She was always there for them. *Always.* The first chance Andy got, he betrayed her."

"I wouldn't call wanting to have a relationship with your father betrayal exactly." But what the hell did Tyler know? His family came straight out of 1950s sitcom, except his mother actually worked. He'd lived a perfect life growing up, yet he was majorly fucked up. Big time. He had no right to judge anyone else's family dynamics.

"Doris won't compromise when it comes to Uncle Brian. You're either with her or you're not."

"That's too bad." Tyler shut his mouth and dropped the subject. This entire situation didn't add up, and he'd be damned if he'd navigate that emotional powder keg. It was none of his effing business. His relationship with Lavender amounted to sex and nothing else.

Assholes didn't have relationships with meaning. Nor did they get involved in the family affairs of others.

* * * * *

Tyler strode into the bar, and Lavender recognized a man on a mission. By the set of Tyler's jaw, she suspected she wouldn't appreciate this particular mission. She gave him the silent treatment and ignored him as much as possible.

Tyler stayed close all evening, though he made no attempt to carry on a conversation beyond grunting for another beer. Ever since he discovered her father's identity coupled with the debacle with her grandmother, he eyed her with wariness in his blue eyes. Meanwhile, Lavender brimmed with nervous energy during the day and tossed and turned in her bed at night. Ten days of celibacy combined with a hot man next door was a lousy cure for insomnia. Beyond the dark circles under her eyes lurked the fear she just might be missing more than the man's body despite how furious he made her.

Tyler didn't goad her into an argument or make lurid remarks. Nor did he swear up a storm and fill the cuss-jar coffers. Instead, he stayed silent and brooding, not one sign of the asshole persona she'd come to expect and, in a dysfunctional way, appreciate. Except for the day he'd met her grandparents. He'd stepped over the line and sent her grandmother into major control mode.

Tyler emptied his beer, and signaled for another. She poured it and slid it across the counter. His blue eyes drilled into hers, physically stripping away each protective layer. She'd rather he stripped off her clothes than study her as if he knew all her secrets.

This crap needed to stop.

Putting her hands on the counter, Lavender went on offense before his odd behavior put her on defense. "Quit staring at me like that."

"Like what? How am I staring at you?"

"You know."

Tyler rubbed the back of his neck and stretched, as if he hadn't a care in the world. He picked up his beer and took a sip, regarding her over the rim of his glass. "Can't you at least get back to hating me? This silent treatment is making me crazy."

"What makes you think I stopped hating you?"

"You didn't?" He almost smiled for the first time since his close encounter of the controlling kind with her grandmother. He sat back and rested his large hands on his belt buckle, drawing Lavender's gaze downward. She licked her lips as she noticed a tell-tale bulge.

"What do you think? I'm pissed as hell at you for that stunt you pulled with my grandmother."

"But you miss the sex." He tugged on a lock of her hair.

"Now there's the asshole I've grown to know and despise." She ran a finger across his stubbled chin and resisted the strong urge to follow the caress with her tongue.

He worked his jaw, as if considering his next words carefully. "I'm sorry. I was a real ass, even for me."

She shrugged. "Doesn't matter. It's about the sex with us. Just stay out of my family's business from now on."

He looked down, then up again, seeming to weigh his options. "Fine. Just answer one question. What did your dad do that was so bad to make you hate him so much?" Tyler tensed, as if bracing himself for either an ass-chewing or the cold shoulder.

Lavender looked up from the wine bottle she was uncorking. Her face hardened into an emotionless mask which slipped into place every time her father was mentioned. "He was never there."

"You people sure hold a grudge for a long time."

"So you're taking his side." It just figured. Jocks stuck together.

Tyler held up his hand. "Hell, no, just seems weird to me to harbor a grudge for this long. Hell, even I forgive and move on, and I'm an—"

"—Asshole. I know. Listen Harris, my grandfather is the only father I have. He's been there for me, while my real father hasn't. Brian Gerloch is not welcome in my life."

"Is that why you changed your last name?"

"Yes."

Tyler frowned at her. Lavender twisted the ring on her finger. Hard. Any harder and she'd twist her finger off. He watched in fascination as it spun even faster on her hand. He looked up, and she realized she'd been caught. She slipped her hands behind her back and out of his line of sight. A knowing smile crooked the corner of his mouth.

"You do that when you're upset. Really upset. At the risk of getting my head ripped off, tell me why you never call your grandfather 'Dad' if he's the only father you have." He raised one cocky eyebrow in a silent challenge, looking more like his asshole self.

"I—I—just because." Anger rumbled through her like a thunderstorm through a wheat field. "Don't go psycho-analyzing me, Harris."

He snorted and pointed at his chest. "Me? I'm too stupid and shallow for something requiring insight into other people's feelings."

"Yeah, you're just a dumb jock." She volleyed his words back at him.

"It's hard work being bitter." He spiked the ball, almost laying her out on the court.

"What's that supposed to mean?" She came back at him, fearing she'd lost the battle.

"It means you and your grandmother put way too much energy into hating your father. If you really were indifferent, you wouldn't give a shit about him or waste any energy on him."

"You are so wrong." Lavender backed away, needing a moment to regroup. Tyler's words hit home. Hard. Too hard. She skirted around the opposite side of the bar. She didn't like talking about her family. Unfortunately, she couldn't steer clear of the quarterback when she went to pour a beer, since he was sitting right in front of the taps.

"Your grandmother is a control freak." He just couldn't seem to let it drop.

Lavender shrugged one shoulder. "I have no idea what you're talking about."

"For example, you love animals, but you don't have any pets in your house, not a dog, not a cat, not even a fish because of her."

Lavender swallowed but couldn't respond past the lump in her throat. She missed having an animal to keep her company on those endless lonely nights. Animals had always been her family, her comfort, her port in any storm. They loved her without condition and were always there.

"Don't you think that's weird?"

"It's her house. I have to live by her rules if I want to rent it."

"Aw, come on. She could cut you some slack. She's your grandmother."

"Stop it." Lavender's stomach churned. She threw the bar rag on the counter and made her rounds of the tables. Her grandmother might be a little obsessive, but she had a right to be. Maybe others found it odd that she and her grandparents didn't have anything to do with her brother, but he'd betrayed them in the worst possible way.

Nobody understood. If they did, she wouldn't get this kind of feedback from people. She loved her grandmother, and her grandmother loved her. Doris Mead had always been there for her. She couldn't say the same for her father. Even when he'd still been with her mother, football consumed his every waking hour.

She hated all this talk about her father. It put her on the defensive, made her feel guilty for God knows what. She'd done nothing wrong. Brian Gerloch deserted them, left them almost destitute.

Tyler Harris did not fit that mold. Now he was asking too many questions, as if her family mattered to him. They didn't. They couldn't. She knew just the thing to stop this invasion of her personal affairs—another kind of affair. He'd forget his own name when presented with a warm, willing woman ready to engage in a little hard riding.

Casting a sultry look his way, Lavender sashayed closer. Tyler met her halfway, stepping into her space.

"This isn't supposed to get personal, jock boy." She lowered her voice a sexy octave and watched his eyes go from sky blue to midnight blue. Tyler leaned into her and licked his lips. He didn't touch her, allowing her to take the lead.

"Hey, get a room you two," Homer yelled from across the room.

Lavender jumped back. Her pale skin burned as red as a fire engine. Tyler took longer to recover. Finally, he shook his dark head and tipped back on the heels of his well-worn cowboy boots. "Tonight, after everyone's gone, you're at my mercy."

"No, you're at my mercy," she countered, salivating at the thought of being in control of this powerful, muscular hunk of testosterone.

"Is that a promise?" Tyler didn't even blink, instead he looked intrigued.

"For once I'm going to run the show."

"Looking forward to it, sweetheart." He ran a finger over her lips, and she shuddered. With a wink, he sauntered off to join the Brotherhood at a table across the room.

* * * * *

Despite being past their bedtime, the old codgers stuck around long enough to beat Tyler at three hands of pinochle before they finally tottered out the door. Once the door clicked shut behind the final geriatric, Tyler tipped his chair back on two legs, crossed his arms over his chest, and enjoyed the view. Lavender sped around the room, vacuuming, wiping tables, cleaning the counter, essentially putting everything in order for the night. Her ponytail swung as she walked, keeping rhythm with the swaying of her fine ass. Pretty soon Tyler would be grasping two handfuls of that ass as he buried himself deep inside Vinnie's soft heaven. His cock hardened in response. He leaned forward and the chair legs clunked as they hit the floor. He tapped his foot impatiently on the worn hardwood floor.

Lavender finished the last of her closing chores and headed for the door with Tyler on her heels. He held the door open for her but blocked the doorway. She pushed on his chest. He didn't budge.

"It's been too long, purple lady." Tyler leaned in, caught a whiff of lavender, and leaned closer. He slid his hands down her sides and rested them on her hips. Damn, but she felt so fu— flipping good. Everything he'd ever dreamed of wrapped up in one fiery little package. He pulled her against his body, cupping her ass in the palms of his hands. He picked her up, sliding her along his length until her face came level with his. Her red lips parted, revealing a glimpse of white teeth. Her pink tongue flicked out and moistened her lips.

Tyler groaned and bent his head to sample those lips and tongue for himself. He'd always loved kissing as foreplay, but kissing Lavender took the act to an entirely different level. He gave her more than he ever gave with other women, even Cass. At first it might have been the challenge, the mutual dislike, the great chemistry. Maybe it still was all that and more. She drove him wild with an irrational need he couldn't explain, nor did he want to. She made him *feel*. And for a man who'd been buried in smothering apathy this past year, he embraced feelings of any kind, especially those which awakened his passion for life.

Slave to a different type of passion, Tyler backed Lavender against the doorframe. Her mouth opened for his tongue as she sucked on it. He closed his eyes and surrendered to the feelings rampaging through his body, his head, hell, even his big toenail. His brain shut down for the night since he wouldn't be needing it. He had all he needed right here wrapped up in this little red-headed dynamo.

Fingers digging into his scalp, she pulled him closer, held his mouth to hers. Their bruising kisses only sent the flames higher. Tyler resuscitated a miniscule portion of his common sense and dragged his hungry mouth away from his purple lady's equally hungry mouth. Panting and turned on beyond sanity, he slid her body back down his until her feet touched the ground. His cock demanded immediate satisfaction, nothing new there. His boy was legendary for its impatience, but it'd have to hold out a little longer. Wrapping an arm around Lavender's shoulders, Tyler waited while she shakily locked the door. She fumbled with the keys twice. He swallowed a smirk, smugly satisfied with his power to rattle her.

Heady stuff.

"Your place or mine?" He dangled his keys from his index finger.

"Yours, you have a four-poster bed." Her eyes sparkled with little flecks of gold, which he'd only seen when she was aroused.

"Hmmm. So tell me why you need a four-poster bed." The mental images were killing him.

Lavender regarded him for a moment. He stood on the sidewalk, one hand on the side of the brick building as he leaned against it. His casual pose didn't disguise the barely reined-in sexual energy radiating from his every pore.

"You're being punished. I'm in charge, jock boy, just go with the flow."

"Oh, yeah, I will. I definitely will." He pushed off the wall, grabbed her hand, and headed for the truck. His long strides ate up the ground. She ran to keep up. In a few minutes, she'd be calling the shots, and they wouldn't be hurrying anywhere, which was just fine with him.

Chapter 15

Stripped of the Ball

Standing in the doorway to Tyler's bedroom, Lavender scrutinized the gorgeous jock with a practiced eye; at least she hoped it looked that way. Either he forgot who was in charge or he didn't give a shit, he stepped toward her with indecent intentions—the best kind—except tonight was her night. She'd be the one with the indecent intentions.

Lavender held up a hand to back him off. "Not so fast buster, I make the moves. You comply. Got it?"

She held her breath, waiting to see if he'd actually submit. His blue eyes burned into her, sizzling every nerve-ending and rendering her momentarily speechless, which didn't happen often, if at all. His proud stance spoke volumes. The man craved rebellion, walked the unbeaten path, and lived to be his own man and no one else's.

She waited him out, hoping he'd play along.

With a slight nod of his head, Tyler held his hands out, palms up in a surprising gesture of submission. The corners of his mouth slowly turned up until they formed a full-blown grin. Surrendering control to her didn't seem to set him back in the least or compromise his manhood. She smiled back. Something to be said about a sexually adventurous man. In fact, a lot to be said.

"Strip and get on the bed." She faked her best dominatrix voice, not that she knew what a dominatrix sounded like, but Tyler stayed on task and didn't challenge her authenticity.

"Yes, ma'am." His clothes went flying until he bared his body in all its hard muscled nakedness. He might be playing along, but she got the distinct feeling that ultimately she wasn't the one in control.

Her gaze dropped to his body. Long, lean muscles bulged in his calves and thighs. Slender hips, a tight butt, and a flat stomach came next. Not to mention that cock. She hesitated and licked her lips then forced her gaze higher, following the trail of chest hair past his six-pack abs to his sculpted chest and widening to broad shoulders. A strong neck led to a hell of a chiseled face framed with thick, unruly dark hair. Nature didn't make men better than this. Not a pretty boy, but a man's man, ruggedly handsome and sexually charged. And all hers, at least for the night.

Lavender cleared her throat and rubbed her sweaty hands on her jeans. Her labored breathing stuck in her throat.

"You're supposed to be a little nervous. A little afraid. Get it?" Her voice cracked and betrayed who was actually nervous. She slapped her hand against her thigh for effect. His mouth quivered, as if he was suppressing a grin.

"Yes, mistress, your wish is my wet dream." Those rebellious blue eyes followed her every movement and contradicted his compliant stance.

Lavender sighed. The man was so not playing his part. "Puhlease. A little uncertainty, insecurity." She snapped her fingers. His eyes sparkled with devilment.

"I don't do insecurity or uncertainty." He blew her a kiss.

"You must place your body in my hands."

His grin grew wider. "Absolutely, Mistress L." He hopped on the bed and lay on his back, spread-eagled. His cock stood up ramrod straight and hard, ready to be called into action. "Take me. I'm ready to be abused."

Lavender rolled her eyes, but her heart rate broke the sound barrier. "Do you have any equipment here?"

He pointed at his cock. "Honey, I have all the equipment you'll ever need right here."

She heaved an exaggerated sigh and shook a finger at him. "You know what I mean, you're being insolent."

"Bottom drawer on the bureau." The man didn't bother to ask what type of equipment.

Why was she not surprised? Lavender pulled open the drawer and stared. "You have to be kidding? You brought all this stuff from the mainland?"

"It's my seduction kit. Never leave home without it." He shifted his hips on the bed and put his hands behind his head.

"Seduction kit? Seriously? Where did this come from?"

"I ordered it a day after I met you."

"Presumptuous of you." This man needed to be taught a lesson, and she was just the woman to do it, assuming he let her.

"I prefer to call it industrious and efficient. Oh, and also confident."

"I'd call you obsessed, opportunistic, and cocky."

He shrugged. "There's an outfit in there for you, assuming you want to immerse yourself in your role."

"Immerse, huh?" Most likely she'd be the one drowning, not him.

"Yeah, I've been reading the dictionary in my spare time."

"You can read?"

"Naw, someone reads it to me." A gray cloud dimmed Tyler's sparkling eyes, but it passed as quickly as it came. The man didn't like references to his dumb jock status one bit, even though he perpetuated the myth.

"Good. I wouldn't want to ruin my image of you."

"Never happen. I'm simple. It's all about sex with me." Again, that flicker of something. Lavender looked away, refusing to give credence to her suspicions.

She held up a small leather outfit, complete with boots. "You are prepared. I'm impressed."

"Not as impressed as you'll be by the time the night ends."

A rogue wave of excitement rippled through her body. Exiting to the bathroom, Lavender pulled off her clothes and stepped into the little number. Leave it to Tyler. The thing was barely there, emphasis on barely. A pair of thin leather suspenders covered her hardened nipples and not much else. The suspenders wrapped around her neck then came together below her belly button. A small strip passed between her legs and between both ass cheeks. A band around her waist held up the back. Oh, yeah, it was sexy and a size too small, an oversight she'd bet her booty was intentional.

The feel of the leather rubbing against her crotch caused her pussy to weep with anticipation. She pulled on the high-heeled leather boots, examined herself in the mirror, then sashayed into the bedroom.

"Holy crap!" Tyler shot up in bed, forgetting his subservient status.

"Don't move." She pointed at him. "Or you'll be punished."

"What if I want to be punished?" His pupils dilated, and his nostrils flared. His cock waved in the breeze, not that there was a breeze.

"Just play along." He was so not getting this.

"Okay, fine. Please, please, don't punish me." He spoke with absolute insincerity and laughed out loud.

"Don't give up your football career to be an actor."

He said nothing, just perused her body like the connoisseur he was.

Lavender returned to the bureau and pulled out a flogger. "You use this?"

"Honey, I'm pretty much game for anything. I told you that. I don't have many scruples when it comes to sex."

"None?"

"Well, very few. Have it your way." He spread his arms wide. "Make me hurt so good."

Digging through the drawer, she removed four sets of pink-fur-lined handcuffs, still in the packaging. She ripped them open, littering the hardwood floor with the cardboard. Leaning over the bed, she clicked the first cuff in place over Tyler's big wrist—it barely fit—then fastened it to the four-poster bed. Tyler didn't seem to mind the pink, not one bit. She fastened the other wrist and both legs to the bed, spread-eagled, and rendering him helpless. Well, helpless as long as he played along. She'd no doubt he could break the handcuffs if he wanted with one flick of his wrist. This game wasn't about physical control but mental control.

Crawling onto the bed, the mattress sagged a little under her weight. Tyler glanced down at the flogger and back at her face. They locked gazes momentarily. She dragged the flogger over his body. He shivered and closed his eyes, as if at her mercy, but she knew better. Tyler Harris would never be at anyone's mercy. His entire body tensed, but he held stock still, as if he feared any movement would make her stop. Lavender rolled the flogger around in her hands. She'd never really used anything like this, but her naughty girl took over.

Lavender slid the leather lashes of the whip over his cock, and it jerked in response. Moving it back and forth, she caressed his erection and balls with the leather strands. He groaned and tossed his head back and forth on the mattress. She brought the whip up and lightly slapped his flat stomach in the vicinity of his navel. He squeezed his eyes shut.

"Aww, damn, that feels good." Tyler flexed his hips and thrashed on the bed.

Gathering her courage, she adjusted her stance and slapped the strands across his upper thighs and over his cock. Lightly, but it had to sting, at least a little.

"Harder." He spoke through gritted teeth, but she doubted it was because of the minor pain she'd inflicted. Closing her eyes— she'd never make a good dominatrix—she struck him again, but it was a pansy-assed strike at that. He gasped and growled like a wolf challenging his mate. How she loved a feral man.

"Harder." Tyler ground out the words with a mixture of anticipation and dread. Beads of sweat stood out on his body. His chest rose and fell as he writhed on the bed. He tugged on his restraints. His eyes rolled back in his head. His cock grew bigger, more rigid, if that was even possible. Tyler fisted his hands and braced himself.

Lavender considered her options. So far she'd played right into his plans, given him what he'd asked for. Sitting back on her haunches, she perused his body with the expertise of a dedicated window shopper. "No."

He snapped his head up and stared at her incredulously. "Why not?"

"Because you want me to." Lavender brushed him with the flogger, refusing to strike him, and turned him into a writhing, groaning mass of lust and muscle. She feared he would come right then and there. She watched him fight to control his body's reaction, feeling a bit evil and a lot naughty.

"Aww, man, you are tough."

"Don't you dare come until you're buried inside me." Lavender closed her eyes for a moment, fantasizing about the very moment he'd fill every empty corner of her body and soul.

"I'm trying not to. You're good. You ever done this before?" His voice was thick with passion and tight from the strain of holding back. The veins stood out on his neck, while his cock twitched as if demanding some satisfaction.

"Nope. I'm winging it." Lavender grinned and traced the flogger across his balls and up his cock to the tip. She drew circles on the bulbous head until a few drops of pre-cum appeared.

"Damn. You're a natural, Vin."

"Thanks, I think." She bent down. Tyler held his breath, still as a bronzed statue of a Greek god. Her red hair grazed his stomach, his abs, his pecs. She tasted his body from his neck to his belly button. The man exerted incredible self-control as she did her best to bring him to the brink then yank him back from the edge. His magnificent body was strung tight, rock hard and trembling.

She swirled her tongue in his belly button. He groaned and arched his back, biting down on his lower lip. When her mouth touched the velvety tip of his cock, he arched his hips and dug his heels into the mattress. After sucking off the bead of precum, she licked the soft flesh, tenderized by the flogger torture/pleasure.

He thrashed his head on the pillow and uttered a series of unintelligible grunts and groans. His body broadcast that his ability to control his desire was razor thin, and she did *so* want to feel his big cock inside her swollen pussy.

"Come here." He beckoned her, his deep voice like a male siren song, reeling her in, pulling her toward her fate.

"You're in no position to give orders."

His blue gaze drilled into hers. "I could be in the right position in a second." He tugged on the restraint on his left hand a few times to prove his point. The flimsy pink cuffs wouldn't withstand his strength if he chose to end the game. Despite the illusion of her being in charge, he'd never relinquished control. She craved to hang onto that illusion a few more minutes. Evidenced by the fact that he didn't break his bonds, he chose to let her. Her heart warmed at his selfless act, the type of gift she'd never have expected from a strong-willed, very male Tyler Harris.

"But you won't." Lavender pointed out that obvious fact since he hadn't broken free. She'd give him a little taste of being the submissive partner, her own unorthodox gift.

Leaning across him, she opened the nightstand drawer and pulled out a condom packet. She tore open the package.

Tyler watched her, eyes shining with a raw hunger and something deeper than that. Her gaze lingered for a moment on his handsome face. So rarely did he allow anyone to see beyond his mask of bravado, yet he'd lowered it for the moment, let her see the man beneath, just a glimpse, a hint of who he really was. A soft smile spread across his face. She smiled back.

"Fuck me." He whispered. His low, sexy voice weaved the spell of intimacy tighter, pushed the intensity higher. Lavender leaned down and sheathed his cock in a condom. Straddling his hips, she held the base of his cock with one hand and rested her other hand on his chest to balance herself. She lowered her body until the head of his cock brushed her pussy lips. Rubbing her pussy across the tip, she got as much enjoyment out of it as he did. He shifted beneath her, alternating between cussing and groaning. Tyler lifted his hips in an effort to push his cock deeper. Lavender raised up, avoiding penetration.

"Fuck me. Dammit," he ordered, and the man was not in a position to order anything. He jerked on his bonds, ready to break them.

Lavender leaned down over him. Her large breasts close to his mouth. He tried to catch a nipple with his lips, but she eluded him. Straightening slightly, she held his cock upright and slid down about one inch. Tyler fought harder against the handcuffs. Much to her surprise they held. He flexed his hips and raised his ass off the bed. She let him take her another inch deeper. Inch-by-painful inch she lowered herself down, taking her time, enjoying his total dependence on her. Knowing he hated and loved it at the same time.

But she had her own needs. When he was halfway buried inside her, she surprised him by slamming her body downward the rest of the way. He uttered a guttural growl of pleasure. She leaned back, letting his big cock fill the places only he could fill, not just physically but in ways which scared the living daylights out of her.

Lifting herself up halfway, Lavender dropped down on him again. He jerked his hips upward to press their bodies tighter together. She established their rhythm, pumping up and down on him until the twitching of his cock inside her warned of its impending release. His eyes squeezed shut and his jaw tightened.

"Ah, woman, just give it to me. Now. Harder. Harder. Harder." His begging eroded her sanity.

With each stroke she slammed down harder on him, while he met her halfway. She felt his release inside her body and somewhere even deeper in her mind.

Her own release overwhelmed her like an undertow pulling her out to sea. Waves of pleasure swept them into the ocean in a warm rush. Lavender collapsed on top of his sweaty body and rested her head against the crook in his neck.

A second later, his deep breathing indicated he'd fallen asleep. *Typical man.*

* * * * *

Tyler didn't want to wake up. Every time he had sex with his purple lady, he swore it couldn't get better than that, and then the next time it did.

Tonight she'd taken charge and screwed his brains out. Damn, but he did love a woman in control. At least for a while. He'd never concede total control to any woman, but once in a while the novelty proved worth it. Lavender sent him beyond "worth it" into the "incredible" zone. He wanted more, greedy bastard that he was. Good ol' Uncle Artie must have known what he was doing when he'd willed this place to his horny nephew. Tyler would bet his Super Bowl bonus the old guy knew his brother's grandson would get off on the hot chick next door. And not just once, but multiple times. Get off and be gotten off on.

Tyler sank into the mattress. He let his body melt into a state of ultimate relaxation, a place he never went without Lavender's assistance. He planned on taking that vacation several more times before his island exile ended.

He pulled the layers of blankets up to their necks to ward off the chill in the room. Funny, he'd never noticed how cold it was earlier. He blew out a breath, expecting to see puffs of air crystallizing to ice. The damn furnace must have quit again. Tyler glanced at the empty fireplace across the room, wishing he'd built a fire earlier, but he'd freeze off his cock if he got out of bed to build one now. He had better uses for said cock than to turn it into a Popsicle.

He pulled purple lady's body closer to his. The heat generated by Vinnie's body should put his temperamental furnace to shame. Of course, the piece of crap had no shame.

Damn, but she felt so good, all soft and silky and pliable in his hands. Hell, despite his fourteen-inch height advantage, she fit him well. He'd always avoided short women, now he wondered why he'd been so shallow as to have height as one of his dating requirements. But then he'd been shallow about a lot of things.

"Ty?" Lavender rolled over and lay across his chest. Damn, her body warmed him like an electric blanket turned on high. Maybe working furnaces were overrated. He grinned in the darkness.

"Tyler." She jabbed him in the ribs to get his attention.

"Hmmm?" He frowned. Not liking the tone of her voice.

"What are you thinking?"

He mulled the answer over for a minute. "Actually, I'm thinking about all the Harrises who lay in this room and stared at this very ceiling. I wonder what they thought about? This house could tell some good stories."

"If your ancestors were anything like you, I'm guessing it could." Her small hands curled in his chest hair. "Twin Cedars is your family's legacy. What are you going to do with this place?"

Ty stiffened. "I might hang onto it until things turn around, but I am selling it eventually."

"If a developer sank his claws into this property, the first thing he'd do is raze this mansion. Could you live with that?"

The idea of the Harris mansion being reduced to a pile of rubble disturbed him. He'd grown a little fond of the proud old lady, which is how he came to think of the mansion. Yet, he wouldn't get sentimental when it came to his bank account. "Do you have any effing idea how much this place will be worth once the economy recovers? I'll make a shitload of money."

"Is that why Artie left this place to you? So you could make money off it?" Lavender raised up. Even in the darkness, he felt her accusing gaze on him. Tyler knew what Twin Cedars meant to his father and grandfather. To his family. Yet, Uncle Artie had left it to him with no stipulations on what he could do with it, other than his ninety-day banishment from civilization. Obviously, the old coot trusted his judgment, though Tyler couldn't fathom Artie's rationale when it came to requiring Tyler live here.

"It's all about the money with you, isn't it?" Lavender's disapproving voice bothered him more than he cared to admit.

"Damn right. You can't be surprised." *If she only knew.*

"I'm not, but I am disappointed. Your uncle must be tossing in his grave." She plucked at his chest hairs until he captured her small hands in one big hand and held them away from his body.

"He's not in a grave. He's in Hazard Channel."

"Smart ass." Annoyed, she slapped at his chest. He tucked her hands against his warm body. She was trying to have a serious discussion, and assumed he just wanted to screw. Let her think that. He wore his asshole costume well, no reason to take it off now.

"Me? I'm just a dumb, over-sexed jock. I haven't a clue what you mean."

Lavender sighed. "Artie used to talk about giving something back. He wanted to make an affordable retreat here on the island for veterans, soldiers, and their families."

"Why the fu—fudge would he want to do something like that?"

"Because most veterans and soldiers can't afford a vacation in the San Juans. He wanted them to feel the peace he felt here. To heal a little."

"Whatever." Tyler mumbled. "And you mean to tell me the Brotherhood could afford to fix this place up and rent out rooms for less than they were worth to needy veterans?"

"No, they can't."

"If this veterans' home was so important to Uncle Art, why'd he will the place to me? He knew me. I'm a selfish, greedy bastard."

Lavender rose up to look him in the eyes. Her brown eyes challenged him—to what he didn't have a clue. "Maybe he does know you. Maybe that was the point. Maybe you don't know yourself."

Tyler groaned and rolled his eyes. He shifted his body underneath her. "Oh, crap, I know where this is headed."

"Do you? Where is it headed?"

"You want me to hand this place over to you and a bunch of goofballs. No way in hell. I'm not giving up millions of dollars."

"Is that all this place means to you? Just dollars? What about the heritage, the history behind it? You don't even know a thing about the people who built this place, even though they're your damn ancestors."

"You're starting to piss me off. If we're going to get personal and discuss long-lost relatives, why don't we discuss your dad?" He braced himself for the explosion.

Lavender shot to her feet and evaded the arm that snaked out to grab her. "So you can dish it out but you can't take it, can you? If Twin Cedars means nothing to you, why are you restoring the banister?" His look of surprise seemed to give her confidence. "You care, Tyler. About a lot of things. The question is why do you spend so much time pretending you don't?"

Before he had a chance to mount a counter-attack, she grabbed her clothes and ran for the door, slamming it behind her. A rush of cold air swirled around him, like a cold hand on his shoulder. He shivered and sat up in bed, rubbing his eyes.

Being a jerk had never affected him before.

But now it did.

Lavender saw through him. Just like Ryan had. Tyler swallowed the lump in this throat as he pictured Ryan looking like a skeleton in that hospital bed. He'd hugged the kid's fragile body one last time. As he turned to leave the last words Ryan ever said to him were: *Ty, I was wrong. You do care. About people.*

Those words ripped his gut apart. He'd cared, alright, cared that for all his blustery confidence, he hadn't been able to do a damn thing about the cancer destroying Ryan's body or convince Ryan's mother to leave her stripper job in Vegas for one last goodbye to her son. As dysfunctional as families were, they were still family, no matter what. If only Lavender got the importance of mending those fences. Any moment might be the last moment she'd ever have.

After that, there'd be nothing but a lifetime of regrets.

Chapter 16

Picked Off

The pounding on the door roused Tyler from his stupor. He bolted upright in his chair, sending Coug flying off his lap. Coug stood, shook himself off, and shot the offender an indignant look. The tabby marched over to the fireplace hearth and proceeded to groom himself—his third favorite thing to do next to eating and sleeping.

Ever since Lavender ran out at sunrise, Tyler worked on the woodwork in the grand entryway, but the painstaking physical labor did nothing to alleviate his bad mood.

Taking a lunch break, he'd sat down in his favorite chair and drifted off, something he rarely, if ever, did. Yet given his lack of sleep in the past twenty-four hours, not a surprise. The more he screwed Lavender the more he wanted, and not just her body. This thing was getting out of control. At first, he'd wanted nothing but sex. Yet he kept pushing the limits of their relationship beyond the physical and so did she by meddling in his personal life. Her interference pissed him off. What he did with Twin Cedars was none of her business, any more than her relationship with her father was his. So why did he keeping pushing her? What did it matter to him if she ever reconciled with her father?

Tyler didn't relinquish control to anyone, but he had to her—physically and emotionally—and enjoyed every effing minute of it. *Literally.* Despite claiming indifference toward her on an emotional level, he kept sliding into his personal no-man's land by caring about her as a person, granted an annoying, irritating person. Stepping over that line had to stop. Their relationship was about their bodies, nothing else.

The pounding started again and snapped him back to the present. Irritated, he glanced at his watch. Late afternoon. He wasn't expecting anyone except for his truant carpenters, and they'd never show up for work this late in the day.

Walking into the two-story foyer, Tyler peeked out the side window and frowned. *Well, crap.* Three vehicles littered his driveway. He recognized at least one of them and seriously considered a lights-out, no-one's-home strategy, but only a coward retreated. Besides with limited hiding spots on the island, the assholes would hunt him down.

More pounding. The big double doors rattled in their frame.

Heaving a sigh of resignation, Tyler yanked on one side of the solid oak front door. The damn thing stuck as usual. Grabbing the antique door handle with both hands, he wrenched on it. On shrieking hinges, the door gave way and slammed against the opposite wall. In the process, the force catapulted him across the room on his ass.

Shit. Damn. Fuck.

His unwanted guests' hearty laughter bounced off the walls of the entry. Cussing a blue streak, Tyler shot to his feet with his ego bruised and his butt stinging. *Sacked by a door.* How fu—frigging embarrassing.

A half dozen members of the Seattle Lumberjacks loitered on his front porch.

"Well, are you gonna let us in or roll around on the floor all afternoon? Not much fun I might add unless you've got a woman with you." Derek Ramsey, his best buddy, cousin, and the Jacks' all-pro wide receiver didn't wait for an invitation. Instead, he pushed past Tyler.

"Who the hell invited you dickheads?" Rubbing his ass, Tyler stood back to allow them in, as if he could stop a couple tons of muscle.

Derek smacked him on the back. "Don't need an invitation. You missed the Super Bowl parties so we thought we'd bring the party to you."

"About two months too late." Tyler pointed out the obvious, but none of his teammates seemed to give a shit. "You're really here to mooch off me and get a free vacation on the island."

"Fuck, yeah." Bruiser Mackay, the team's starting running back and a bigger party boy than Tyler, followed Derek through the door.

"Hey, we should sign that door to a contract. It laid Harris out flat." Hoss Price, Tyler's Center and a smartass, grinned with unrestrained amusement. Three more guys pushed through the door, rookie defensive end LaDaniel Crates, tight end Spin Statler, and cornerback Bryson Lewis. Tyler started to shut the door but someone else prevented its closing.

"Not hard to do, considering it's Harris." Zach Murphy shoved the door open and strutted past Tyler. The man wore a cloak of attitude that even did Tyler proud, except the jerk was his nemesis.

"What the fuck are you doing here?" Tyler swung around and blocked the linebacker's path. Murphy looked him up and down as if to say *you and what army?* Tyler stood his ground. He couldn't let a dick like Murphy get even the slightest inkling he might have the upper hand. Sure, he outweighed Tyler by thirty pounds, bench-pressed elephants for fun, and ate rookies for lunch. That didn't impress Tyler. The Jacks were his team, not this interloper's.

"Fostering a little team camaraderie." Murphy dropped his duffle bag near the rookie's feet and leaned against the banister. He studied Tyler like a poker player sizing up his opponent.

"Foster it by getting the hell out of my house." Tyler ignored his teammates gathered round, as they waited for bloodshed.

"Is that any way to welcome your new teammate?" Murphy stepped forward, invading Tyler's personal space until they stood toe-to-toe. No one got in his space. Especially not a washed-up tool like this guy.

"Hey, guys, let's play nice." Derek pushed between them, the whimpy-ass assuming the role of peacemaker, as usual.

"How about I spare his life if he gets the fuck out of here in the next five seconds." So much for curing his potty mouth.

Zach held his hands over his chest. "I'm so fucking scared, I'm shaking."

The guys snickered, especially the defensive players, who no doubt idolized the asshole. The offensive players traded nervous glances, even as they bit back amused smiles.

Assholes, all of them.

Tyler flexed his fingers, itching to plant a fist in the smug bastard's face. How the hell could the Lumberjacks sign this guy considering the public knowledge of how much the two hated each other?

Murphy found this way too amusing. "The boys invited me to hang with them for the weekend." With a smooth, quick move that left Tyler standing flat-footed, the all-pro slipped around him and joined his teammates in the entry. Tyler growled his disgust.

Murphy jumped on it, making Tyler look like an idiot. "Losing your step there, Harris. Along with your killer instinct."

Derek turned a complete circle in the two-story entryway. "Damn, this is some place."

Murphy grunted and faked a yawn. Tyler snarled. The rest of the team played dumb and nodded or murmured agreement with Derek.

"Yeah, the advantage to being on an island is it deters unwanted guests." Ty leaned against the banister, crossed his arms over his chest, and ignored Murphy, pissed he'd let the guy get under his skin and in front of *his* team.

"Where the hell have you been?" LaDaniel, the stupid rookie, couldn't keep his trap shut.

"The rumor going around the league is that you're in rehab." Bruiser ran a hand over the sanded banister. "We had to see for ourselves."

"I might be a lot of things, but I don't do drugs."

"I knew better, unless there's an ego rehab." His chickenshit cousin stepped between Tyler and Murphy, keeping a wary eye on both of them.

"That's not what's been stuck up his ass all season. It's worse. The word on the street is you've lost *it*." Murphy's dark brown eyes glittered with undisguised animosity. Tyler damn well knew what defined *it:* a guy's indescribable love of the game, his hunger for the next win, his obsession with all things related to the pigskin. Doubly worse, Tyler was guilty as charged, and Murphy had seen right through his posturing.

"The only thing I've lost is my patience—with you. Get the fuck out of my sight, asshole." Tyler took a step toward Murphy, but Derek put a restraining hand on his arm. Two defensive guys did the same to Murphy. Then there it was, plain as day, the division. The defensive players stood next to Murphy, while the offense gathered around Tyler. Their personal feud had already divided the team, and they were months away from playing their first down.

"You two pussies need to get over it. We're all on the same team." Exasperated, Derek squeezed Tyler's arm so hard he should have left fingerprints.

"Just remember, dick, how many Super Bowl rings I have." Tyler flipped him off with both hands. "And you have? What is it? Zero?"

"I'm going to have one by the end of next season, or I'll hold you personally responsible." Zach looked him up and down, a sneer on his ugly mug. "You're right about one thing. I don't have a ring. This is probably my last year. Twelve years in the NFL and not one ring. I took fifty percent of what I could get anywhere else to win that ring. There's no way in hell an asshole like you is going to ruin it for me."

"It'll be tough to win three in a row." Bryson the wiry little cornerback stared at Murphy like he was the second coming.

"Depends on Harris. A QB without a killer instinct might was well take up knitting and leave the game to us real men." Murphy turned back to Tyler, straining against his teammates' hands on his arms. "I'm going to make your life a living hell."

"Yeah, bring it on, asshole. That just scares me shitless." Tyler leaned into Murphy, ready to smash in the jerk's face, but Bruiser and Derek held him back.

Murphy hesitated then flipped Tyler off and strutted from the room like a frigging turkey the day after Thanksgiving, having survived another year.

It was going to be a damn long football season.

Breathing hard more from anger than exertion, Tyler glared in the direction Murphy had gone. The rest of his team vacated the area, following Murphy down the hall. Tyler heard the sound of a hockey game going in the den. Obviously, Murphy had found the remote and made himself at home with Tyler's newly installed satellite service.

Tyler spun around and launched an attack on his idiot cousin. "Why the fuck did you bring that fuckhead here?"

"Because he'll be our defensive team leader next year. You need to settle your differences if we're going to do a three-peat. Hell, he's warming up to you already."

"I could tell, like a hound dog warms up to fox."

His cousin glanced over his shoulder, as if eavesdropping could be added to Murphy's long list of offenses. "He's a tough nut to crack. Kinda like you."

"Two assholes on the team is one too many. By the way, where's your ball and chain?" Ty didn't see his cousin's wife anywhere. Hell, and here he'd thought they'd joined at the hip when they'd said 'I do.' Rachel sure as hell castrated the poor bastard. She'd pussy-whipped Derek to the point where he actually believed he enjoyed being married.

"Helping HughJack evaluate talent for the upcoming draft. We're losing a lot of veterans to free agency this year."

HughJack was the Seattle Lumberjacks fiery young coach, who'd led the team to two Super Bowls in two years. He'd lead them to a few more, if Tyler could get his game back. At least, Murphy pissed him off, which beat not giving a shit about football.

Tyler made a point of glancing at his watch. "You have plenty of time to make the next ferry."

"This is a guy weekend. We're not going anywhere."

"Fucking fantastic." Tyler muttered and headed toward the den. He needed a drink, make it a double. His pansy-assed cousin dogged his heels.

"Ah, come on, you love hanging out with the guys, downing some beers, losing your ass at poker."

Tyler didn't need the team to do that. The Brothers kicked his ass almost every week. He grabbed a couple beers from the den refrigerator and popped the tops.

Derek snagged the beer offered to him. Murphy stole the other without even a grunt of thanks. The rest of the guys jostled for the remaining beers in the fridge or dug into his hard liquor in the bar cabinet. Bruiser, who ate like he had a hollow leg, opened a couple bags of chips. Seconds later, the entire group of uninvited guests sprawled all over his couch and chairs, eating his food and drinking his booze. Each one talked louder to be heard over the din of the conversations.

Obviously annoyed by the noise, Murphy cranked up the sound on the hockey game. His brother played on that particular hockey team.

Pure chaos reigned. Usually Tyler instigated any bedlam related to his team. Today he stood off to one side, an observer instead of a participant, and way too reminiscent of how he felt after winning this last Super Bowl.

These guys weren't leaving anytime soon. With a long-suffering sigh, Tyler took a thirsty gulp and hitched a hip on the corner of the antique bar stool. His cousin studied him, most likely reading his expression pretty damn accurately.

"You missed all the Super Bowl parties." Derek pulled out the other bar stool and plopped his ass on it. He took a pull on his beer, and Tyler braced himself for whatever the hell came next.

"Been there, done that. Besides, my car shoved its nose up a cop car's butt. I had a little explaining to do."

"Yeah, you sure have a nose for trouble."

"You let the team down again by driving drunk so you're hiding out here." Murphy inserted himself into Tyler's private conversation. How he'd managed to hear over the din, Tyler couldn't fathom. He shot the jerk a glare. Murphy just raised one eyebrow and saluted Tyler with his beer can.

"Seriously, why *are* you here? A little scandal's never driven you out of town before." Derek turned his back on the rest of the team, blocking Tyler's view of Murphy. An intentional move, no doubt.

"Some obscure great uncle left me this run-down piece of crap, but I have to live here in hell for ninety days before I take ownership." Even Derek didn't know about his friendship this past year with Uncle Art.

"It's rustic but not really a piece of crap, just needs some cosmetic work."

"I'm working on restoring it." Tyler appraised the den, imagining it from his cousin's neutral position. Faded wood paneling, he wasn't even sure what kind of wood, but definitely exotic and expensive and most likely irreplaceable, covered the walls, along with an impressive array of scarred wood trim, hardwood floors in need of buffing, and worn area rugs. Arranged around the massive fireplace, pieces of antique furniture were scattered, and not dainty shit either, but furniture made for men to use. Good thing, considering the size of the men currently sprawled on his furniture.

"You're doing the work yourself?" The asshole Murphy frowned at the television then jabbed at the remote. The picture on the television showed nothing but squares of color, a digital snowstorm.

"Some of it." Tyler hated admitting to manual labor, not good for his image.

"What the hell's wrong with this damn TV?" Murphy shook the innocent remote, obviously wishing it were Tyler's neck instead. *Well, back at you, dickwad.*

Tyler fought back a grin. "Give it up. My TV service goes in and out. It's all part of living on the island. Welcome to my life without working electronics."

Murphy picked up his phone.

Tyler chuckled, loving Murphy's initiation into island life. "No cell service either."

"How the hell do you stand it?" Murphy paced the floor a few times then grabbed another beer. Grumbling, he slumped in the armchair by the window, shoved on his earphones, and ignored them all. Coug helped himself to Murphy's lap, his paws kneading on the linebacker's leg. Murphy yelped when the cat's claws dug too deeply.

"You can leave anytime. Let me show you the door."

"And miss out on all the fun. Not on your life." Murphy leaned forward and snapped his fingers at Bryson who'd found a deck of cards. "Deal me in, Bry." Bryson scrambled to do so. Tyler rolled his eyes at the pathetic way the defense catered to Murphy.

"So how's it going? Really." Derek lowered his voice and leaned closer. Tyler could have sworn Murphy's ears pricked up, even though the guy faked disinterest.

"Just counting down the days until freedom."

Derek shrewdly assessed his cousin. "You don't seem to mind it here that much."

"I hate it. I'm just being a good sport."

"You *are* never a good sport." Derek knew him too well. He didn't buy Tyler's bullshit. "Hiding out isn't going to give your attitude a kick in the ass. Plus as soon as you come out of hiding, the press will be all over you."

Tyler sucked on his beer and didn't answer. Tolerating a weekend with these assholes required a lot of beer. He'd send the rookie to the store for several more cases.

Derek changed tactics. "What's with the cat? You hate cats." Coug, the traitor lap slut, luxuriated on Murphy's lap. The man petted the cat absently as he stared at his poker hand.

"I was taken hostage and turned into slave labor."

Derek's grin turned ruthless, the rat bastard. "Ah, I get it. You've met a woman, and she's into cats." It wasn't a question, but a statement of fact which hit too close to home.

Ty shrugged, not about to give away anything.

"You have. You're an animal lover, but not cats. Never cats. They're not manly. It'd ruin your bad boy image. So who is she?"

"No one you know. Have you seen Cass?" He patted himself on the back for his deft sidestep.

"Nope, she left town right after the Super Bowl and never looked back."

"Oh, well." He meant it. He didn't really care, sad but true. He'd spent years with the woman, and she'd barely caused a blip on his emotional radar. He'd bet the feeling was mutual.

"She was all wrong for you, Ty. You were toxic for each other."

"Yeah, no shit." Tyler put the empty bottle in the bar sink. He popped the top off a cheap beer and handed it to Derek then opened a microbrew for himself.

"I liked her, but not for you." Derek stared at the beer and frowned before taking a sip and making a face.

"Weird thing is I don't miss her."

"Not even the makeup sex?"

Tyler shrugged and his cousin studied him with shrewd appraisal. Even Murphy turned his head to hear the answer.

"Ah, ha. I knew it. There's someone else."

"I've found a hot body to warm my bed."

"Just a hot body? That's all?" Derek's skeptical expression said it all. He considered Tyler full of shit. "By the way, Steve wants to know what the hell is up with you?"

Tyler sighed. His cousin was an annoying bastard and his agent, Steve, even worse. "Look around you. I'm stuck in nowhere hell."

"That doesn't stop you from returning your calls."

"It does when I have to travel five miles just to get cell service."

"What's stuck up your ass, anyway? Don't think I didn't notice your attitude during our last playoff run and the Super Bowl."

"I always have attitude. I'm the king of attitude."

"No, actually, it was the lack of attitude which worried me and everyone who knows you. You were on auto pilot, and you were just good enough to pull it off."

"No one really knows me."

"I do." His cousin stared him straight in the eye, his gaze unwavering. Ty knew he'd been outed.

Derek did know him better than anyone, yet even his best buddy didn't know what lurked in Tyler's murky depths. Most times, Tyler didn't know himself.

"Ty, you won the Super Bowl on pure technical ability. You weren't bringing it on the field. Our defense won the game for us, and you know it."

Ty looked away, unable to answer his cousin's question because he didn't know the answer himself.

"What's wrong, Ty? Hey, man, if you're not leaving your heart out on the field every game, you need to hang up the cleats."

The room had gone unusually quiet. Murphy grunted his agreement, but for once, kept his mouth shut. The rest of his teammates studied their cards and pretended they didn't hear a thing.

"Nothing's up with me. Nothing." And that was the problem. He felt like a big fat nothing. The only time he felt alive was with Lavender, but that was a spring fling. As soon as his ninety days were up, he'd haul ass to the first ferry out of here, sell the place, and never look back.

Never.

* * * * *

Lavender snuck through the gate between her property and Tyler's, more than a little peeved at him for bringing up her father once again. For a man who insisted on keeping their relationship purely physical, he sure got himself involved in her family dynamics. She didn't know what to make of the mixed messages he kept sending.

Several vehicles were parked in the circular driveway. Each one bigger and more expensive than the one before it. Tyler had company, a team full of company, and curiosity drove her to check them out, while admittedly, check out whether or not a house full of gorgeous women came with his hunky guests. Hey, she was sleeping with the guy, and he'd damn well better not be messing with other women while he was sleeping with her. It was one of her unwritten rules. Regardless of how *casual* their relationship might be.

One of the guys who'd hauled a duffle bag up Tyler's steps earlier looked so much like Tyler she knew it had to be his cousin, Derek Ramsey, consummate good guy and Tyler's exact opposite. The straggler of the group wore his bad attitude for all to see, just like Tyler. Every one of them was big and built. Judging by the pushing and shoving as they jostled onto the front porch, they'd come ready to party.

Since Tyler wouldn't come to the team, the team came to Tyler.

Lavender paused in mid-knock and listened. The noise inside the large mansion reverberated against the thick walls and shook the window panes. They'd never hear her. She turned the door handle of the unlocked door and let herself inside.

Following the racket to the den, Lavender hesitated in the open doorway. Several guys had draped their big bodies in Tyler's overstuffed antique furniture. Many held cards in their hands, others played pool, a few more watched a hockey game. Well, attempted to watch since Tyler's television reception went in and out. All of them drank. Tyler and his cousin sat on a couple bar stools and attempted a conversation over the racket.

The big guy with the attitude lounged on the leather couch. He looked up and caught her eye. A slow smile crossed his ruggedly handsome face. His brown eyes lit up as he did a slow perusal of her body. Remote in one hand and cards in another, he muted the television and stood. An inch or two shorter than Tyler, he moved his husky body with incredible ease and grace for one so large. Despite her declarations against any football knowledge, the coach's daughter in her recognized the infamous Zach Murphy, the best linebacker in the league, perhaps ever. The man's handsome face was plastered all over the gossip mags and the web due to his notorious reputation and racy underwear ads.

"Well, pretty lady. Come on in." Zach held out his hand to lead her into the room. The jock's compliment dripped with country boy charm.

She'd picked her clothes carefully before coming over and knew she looked pretty darn good in her form-hugging green sweater and best blue jeans. She'd tied her unruly hair back in a ponytail and put on a little makeup, anything to give her the edge in a house full of randy jocks.

Upon hearing Zach's words, Tyler jerked around and almost fell off his bar stool. Something akin to jealousy and possession shone in that blue gaze. He literally vaulted across the floor in a few long strides, reaching her before his teammate even knew what hit him.

With a possessive gleam in his eyes, Tyler pulled her to his side and held her there. Zach stopped a few feet away and regarded them with undisguised amusement. Tyler glowered back, gripping her so hard she fought for her breath. She'd walked into a powder keg fueled by male testosterone and professional dislike.

Refusing to be the pawn in anyone's game of revenge, Lavender stomped on Tyler's toes and elbowed him in the ribs. He yelped and loosened his hold just enough for her to escape. She walked forward and accepted Zach's outstretched hand. "I'm Lavender, and you must be the nefarious Zack Murphy."

Zach held her hand in his big paw and stared into her eyes. "Nefarious. I like that. And I like you, you just might be my favorite color."

Lavender laughed and yanked her hand from his. Her back bumped into Tyler's unyielding chest in the process. Tyler's hot breath tickled the back of her neck. His body shook with barely controlled fury. She could feel the heat of his anger radiating from him to her shoulders, down her spine, even her butt. His big hands locked onto her shoulders. He'd claimed possession, which was nine-tenths of the law.

Regardless of what he might need to prove to his teammate, no man treated Lavender like his personal piece of property, especially one who continually made it clear their relationship was physical.

Tyler Harris did *not* own her.

While she harbored no interest in Zack Murphy or any of Tyler's other teammates who gathered round and introduced themselves, Tyler didn't need to know. The obnoxious jock deserved a little discomfort in his privileged life.

"So, boys, are you going to invite me in for a drink?" The guys fell all over themselves as they moved aside and offered her their recently vacated seats. She sat down on the couch. Zach immediately claimed the spot next to her. Tyler rousted the rookie from the other spot and sat down on the opposite side. His arm on the back of his couch, he tucked her close to his side.

Derek grinned and winked at her. Tyler's cousin enjoyed this as much as she did.

Turning to Zach, Lavender blessed him with her best smile. "Deal me in."

Zach wagged his eyebrows. "How about a little game of strip poker, honey."

"No fucking way in hell." Tyler's warning didn't deter Zach one tiny bit. In fact, it egged him on. A few of the other guys cringed, while others just chuckled.

This might be the best fun she'd had in a long while. Tyler Harris was certainly off his game tonight, and Lavender had the better game plan.

Chapter 17

Fumbled Return

After a few rounds of poker, in which Lavender lost her shirt, figuratively speaking only, she left the boisterous, drunken group of jocks and escaped to the privacy of her little home. Tyler walked her to the door, still pissy and behaving like a cave man, and incredibly sober. He'd had the gall to demand she leave her door unlocked. She'd half a mind to latch every deadbolt in the place, but in the end lust won out. Sex with a hot and angry Tyler appealed to her way more than it should. He'd become her chocolate-dipped-strawberry craving, her weakness, her secret yearning.

After unlocking the back door, she sat down on her bed in her lonely little room. At first the silence had welcomed her, now minutes later it smothered. She missed the rowdy noise of Tyler's team.

Tyler. What the heck was she going to do about Tyler?

Tyler, the self-proclaimed asshole who wore his bad attitude like a merit badge. For almost two months she'd fooled herself into believing she was a much better person than the arrogant, entitled jock could ever dream of being. Yet, Coug attached himself to Tyler as if it was his cat-given right. The Brothers embraced him as one of their own, whether he liked it or not. Tyler's teammates cared enough to travel to the island to spend some time with him. Tyler might pretend they were pains in his ass, but she knew better. He liked having them there. Well, except for Zach. He hated Zach, but that was another story.

She'd crashed his jock party tonight to pay him back for bringing up her father yet again. Unfortunately, her strategy turned inside out. Sure, she'd ruffled Tyler's feathers by flirting with Zach.

Unfortunately, all those jocks sitting around reminded her of her younger years. In her father's high school coaching days, his team filled their house. Guys came and went at all times, day and night. Her father's door had always been open. As a result, he'd given so much to the team, he'd left very little for his family.

Even so, Lavender had been daddy's little girl, a star female athlete sure to get scholarships for softball or volleyball. Brian Gerloch had doted on his princess until the day he packed his suitcase and walked out of her life forever when she was fifteen. She locked herself in her bedroom all weekend and cried, completely inconsolable. At first she blamed her mother for nagging so much she drove him away. After Mom died, she saw the light and put the blame on her father. She never picked up another ball and never went to college on a scholarship or otherwise. In fact, for the remainder of high school, she drowned her disappointment in alcohol and partying. Her grades sucked. She struggled for a year at community college and dropped out.

Always drawn to senior citizens because of a wonderful set of now-deceased grandparents, she worked in various nursing homes and swore she'd find a way to better their lives. Now that dream was swept out with the tide, thanks to Artie's one-eighty in his will, and Tyler's selfish intentions. Despite all those disappointments, ultimately she could only point a finger at herself. She'd believed the promises of the people in her life, instead of creating her own good fortune.

No more. Especially when it came to Tyler Harris and her father.

Viciously, Lavender swiped a hand across her cheek to remove the one lone tear. Why thoughts of her dad still brought tears after all these years, she didn't know. He'd been a no-show in her life for twelve years. She'd buried her pain so deep, not even her controlling, over-protective grandmother suspected how much Brian Gerloch's absence shaped the woman Lavender had become.

If her own father didn't love her enough to stick around, why would anyone else? Maybe she'd driven her dad away, caused all of this somehow. Or maybe her father, a jock himself, made typical jock choices and never once regretted his decision to walk out on his son, daughter, and wife without so much as a look back. Obviously, they didn't fit into his new life as a Division 1 football coach.

Well, guess what, Brian Gerloch, you don't fit in mine.

Tyler didn't fit in her life either, despite her screwed up fascination with him. Sexual attraction she could handle easily, but she'd be kidding herself if she believed that's all there was. Not that she'd fallen in love, she still didn't *like* him. The jock did have a few minor redeeming characteristics, if a girl looked hard enough. Like those hard, lean muscles, the way his hair stood up on end after a wild night in bed, or how his blue eyes sparkled when he was giving her shit. Or his soft spot for animals. And maybe he wasn't as dumb as she'd first thought. In fact, his sharp mind impressed her. None of it mattered because, she'd never attach herself to a man with a sports career. Athletes were married to the game and the game only. Everything else fell by the wayside in the endless pursuit of the next championship.

That empty hole expanded in her chest, a hole she'd never be able to fill because she gave her heart to men who didn't deserve it, not that she'd given Tyler her heart. Tyler would never know she'd softened a little toward him, nor would her father realize how much she missed him. She didn't do vulnerable—not anymore.

Sliding under the covers, she pulled the blankets up to her chin and closed her eyes. The tick-tick of the clock echoed in the empty room. Lavender tossed and turned for several hours, unable to shut off her brain in order to sleep. She finally heard the click of the door as it opened and shut. Her heart thudded in her chest, tapping out a welcome beat.

"Hey."

"Hey." She spoke into the darkness of the room as Tyler's tall body loomed in the doorframe.

"You're awake." He sounded haggard. Tired. She'd never heard such defeat in his voice.

"Yeah." She sat up and squinted into the darkness, as he crossed the room in a few heavy-laden strides.

"You'd better be naked."

"More naked than you." Being a smartass kept her tender emotions at bay.

She heard the sound of a zipper and the rustling of clothes, the crackle of a condom wrapper, the snap of the rubber as it stretched to fit over his erection. A second later a warm, naked body slid under the covers next to her. Tyler reached for her with a desperation so strong it crackled in the air like a live wire on a power line. Every muscle in his body tensed, as if strung too tight and on the verge of breaking.

"You didn't have to flirt with him." His muffled words, laced with hurt, reverberated against her shoulder. His warm mouth pressed against her collarbone.

"I wasn't flirting with him. He was flirting with me."

"Well, you didn't have to like it."

"Who says I did." She closed her eyes and bit back a moan as he bit at her shoulder, most likely in retribution for her sins.

"I was there. Remember? I saw you." He moved lower, leaving a trail of rough kisses that inflamed her body.

"You couldn't see anything beyond your dislike of Zach, who I'd like to remind you is now your teammate."

He raised his head, staring at her in the darkness. "I wish you wouldn't remind me."

She couldn't make out his expression. Lowering his head, he ran his tongue over her hard nipple, teased the nipple jewelry into his mouth. When she gasped, he closed his mouth over her nipple and sucked. Hard. She rocked her body underneath him. His stubble abraded her skin like sandpaper. Her head swirled from the sensations slamming into her. His tight body told the story. He might be mad at her. He might punish her for playing him, but she'd enjoy the hell out of any penalty he extracted. He pinched her other nipple. Then he twisted it just short of real pain, and a shot of pleasure catapulted through her. Removing his mouth from the other nipple, he grasped it, too, and gave it a sharp twist. The air rushed from Lavender's lungs.

"Oh, damn. Tyler."

"Are you attracted to Murphy?" He spat out the linebacker's name in disgust. His sinful mouth moved within inches of her face. He kissed her chin, her neck. He applied pressure to her nipples with his fingers.

"No. I just wanted to pay you back for toying with my grandmother and siccing her on me." She cried out when he grabbed a bit of skin on her neck and bit down, surely leaving a mark. His mark. An alpha male marking his mate. Except she wasn't his mate. She was only his island screw for a month more.

"Stay away from him." Tyler spoke with absolute authority, as if he expected obedience, so not Lavender's thing.

"You don't get a vote when it comes to what I do." With his mouth on hers and his fingers milking her breasts, she wanted to promise him anything.

"You sure?" The rawness in his voice undid her. He pushed her thighs apart with his leg and positioned himself between them. Her pussy wept with joy. His greedy mouth came down on hers, harsh and demanding. His tongue and lips invaded and conquered. She surrendered completely, lost in the heat.

Lavender wrapped her arms around his neck and her legs around his waist as he covered her with his big body. "Positive."

"I don't feel like taking it easy tonight."

"Then don't." She pressed closer to him, wishing she could absorb him, all of him, and keep him like this forever.

"I don't want to hurt you." Yet his expression indicated he might be beyond the turning point. Sweat dripped off his face, and his arms shook.

"You won't. I'm stronger than I look." She didn't care if he hurt her, emotionally or physically. She just wanted him inside her.

"I know that."

"Then fuck me." She writhed under him and grasped his ass in her hands, squeezing hard.

"Watch that mouth, darlin." Tyler grabbed her thighs with his big hands and raised her legs over her head. Spread wide, he held them there. "Good thing you're flexible." He actually chuckled, which warmed her heart.

"I can still do the splits."

"I'll hold you to that before the night is over." His ever-ready cock pushed at her opening. "You're wet."

"I've been wet for hours, but I was beginning to think you weren't coming."

"Oh, I'm coming honey. I'm coming. So will you." He slid in a little further and held himself over her. The muscles in his arms bunched from the strain of holding his position.

"I'm sure you won't—uh—disappoint."

"Never." His blue eyes glittered like stars in the night sky. This indefinable chemistry between them arched, snapped and sizzled like an electrical current gone rogue. She witnessed the exact moment his control surrendered to his animal instincts. With a powerful thrust, he reached pay dirt and began his enthusiastic assault. Taking no prisoners and making no apologies, he drove deep and high, retreated, and plunged homeward again, each lunge harder and faster than the last. Digging her fingernails into his back, Lavender urged him on, swept along in his frenzy and building a frenzy of her own. She arched her back, reveled in how deep he reached with each stroke.

He grunted, his hot breath burning her neck, igniting her fire. His mouth sought hers, lips bruising while his tongue plundered. She gave back everything he threw at her.

Harsh, labored breaths signaled his orgasm. He wouldn't fly solo. She'd be right there with him. Shuddering from the power of their emotions, his cock spasmed inside her. Her walls tightened around him. Her juices flowed. His eyes never left hers.

For one magical moment, Lavender wriggled past his tight defenses, slipped into the depths of his most secret places. With him buried inside her, the world stood still for them. As if they were poised on an edge, about to bungee jump off a bridge, fall to their fate, only to be saved at the last minute by the bungee cord, their only thin link to sanity. Lavender didn't want sanity. She wanted Tyler stripped raw and bare, ready to reveal his body and soul to her, but an instant later the door slammed shut. Lust trampled the moment, sweeping her away in a stampede of the physical.

Tyler didn't give her a moment to recover. His control blew up in a frenzy of wild animal hunger. Lavender closed her eyes and sank into oblivion with him.

What a way to go.

* * * * *

Tyler's eyes snapped open. He stared at the ceiling, suddenly wide awake. If he didn't get out of Lavender's bed and sneak back into the mansion before sunrise, he'd get no end of shit from the guys, especially from Murphy. He shouldn't give a shit, never would've before, but he wasn't sure he'd be able to tolerate the hassle in his current state of mind.

Lavender stirred beside him. She didn't awaken but snuggled closer. She buried one small hand in his chest hair. The other gripped his bicep. He almost smiled, almost forgot his worries, she looked so damn cute and sexy. Especially sexy. Dang, his cock hardened in response. He'd have thought his dick wouldn't have anything left after last night's marathon. Obviously, his little head possessed more try than his big head did anymore.

He sighed and closed his eyes. The last twenty-four hours rolled through his mind in a blur of impressions and reactions, covering a gamut of emotions. But, hell, at least he'd gone beyond numbness to feeling something, even if so far it was limited to anger and lust.

Tyler dreaded more time with his teammates, fearing they'd see what he already knew, along with his cousin and that asshole Murphy. He'd misplaced his indomitable will to win, and he doubted he'd be able to pull off another season of faking it. Already he caught the guys staring at him, wondering if he'd quit on them in the middle of an important game.

Murphy's smirk said it all. He'd be more than happy to take Tyler down if his teammate didn't leave his heart and soul out on the field. Tyler wasn't sure he had a heart or soul left to leave.

Lavender rose up and regarded him with sleepy eyes. He tucked a lock of hair behind her ear and gazed at her for a moment. A fleeting instant of contentment crept past his defenses.

Glancing up, he caught his expression in the mirror on the dresser near the foot of the bed and did a double take.

Tenderness? What the fu—heck? Tenderness? He forced his face into his standard arrogant mask.

"Had you ever been to Twin Cedars before Artie died?" Her question from out of the blue caught him off guard and unbalanced.

Tyler battened down the hatches, not willing to give away anything. A muscle ticked in his jaw. His voice sounded tight to his own ears. "My dad spent his summers here for years growing up. After my grandfather and my dad had their final falling out, Dad quit visiting the place. Then Grandpa died and Uncle Artie inherited."

"Did you ever visit the islands as a kid?" Annoyingly, she pried, obviously in an attempt to get beneath his surface armor. *But why?*

"Plenty. But never here. Never. All this happened long before I was born." He thawed slightly. "And you? How did you end up here?"

"I grew up on the mainland not far from the ferry landing. My dad—Brian—coached high school football in Mt. Vernon. This property was in his family for a couple generations, but Mom got it in the divorce."

Tyler rubbed his fingers across his rough stubble. "I went to WSU because your dad was there. My dad used to hang out with him when he came to visit the islands as a kid. They were college roommates. I bet you never knew that."

"I didn't."

"Small world, huh?"

She nodded and visibly swallowed.

Tyler rolled over onto his side and propped his head up with his hand. He studied her in the rare morning sunlight peeking through the curtains. "You know, Vinnie, my dad never reconciled with his father. I guess he thought his dad would always be there, and he'd get to it someday. After Grandpa died, he said not seeing him one last time was the biggest regret of his life. I know I'd give anything for the chance to see my dad again, to have him in my life."

She tensed in his arms, but he plowed onward. "Vinnie, you have a dad who's still alive. You're throwing away the chance to have a future with him in it."

"He threw away that chance, not me. He abandoned me."

"What if he didn't? At least not to the extent you've been told. What if you've just been made to believe he did?"

Her eyes narrowed, she slammed the shades shut and boarded up the door and windows in an attempt to keep out the truth—a truth she most likely didn't want to face regarding her grandmother's role in all this. "We've been down this road. I told you. Brian Gerloch is off-limits." She grabbed the blanket and swung her legs off the bed, sitting on the edge of the mattress with her back to him.

"You might try to see both sides." He stroked her spine with gentle, sure strokes. He'd shoved his problems to the back burner and focused on her pain.

"I've seen both sides. My father is wrong." She hugged herself, tightly, rocking back and forth, and softening his heart.

"Nothing is that black and white."

"This is." Huddling forward, she gripped the blanket tighter around her, as if it would insulate her from a lifetime of pain.

"Why do you let your grandmother run your life?"

She couldn't voice the answer, but Tyler knew the answer already. Her grandmother's love was conditional, like Ryan's mother's love had been, always conditions, do this and I'll love you, do that and I won't. If she didn't cave to her grandmother,

Doris Mead might go away like her father, mother, and brother had. At least that's how he saw it.

When she didn't answer, he spoke again. "You're a stubborn brat."

"You're an obnoxious asshole."

His big hand snaked around her waist and pulled her back down onto the bed. "I resemble that remark."

"You sure do." She wriggled around until she faced him, her body draped across his chest.

"So that's it. You won't even reconsider?"

"That's it. Done. Finished."

"It works both ways. You don't try to psychoanalyze me, and I won't you." He smiled; triumphant he'd proven his point.

"Deal. All we have together is sex. We need to keep it that way."

"Does this mean you like me?" He teased her, hoping like hell she'd maintain her distance as he attempted to do.

"Not at all. I still can't stand you. You're an arrogant, self-serving jock."

"You forgot entitled. That's my favorite insult. I like being entitled." He buried his face in her hair. She smelled so damn good.

"Sorry. My Bad. Entitled. Absolutely. I can't stand entitled jocks."

"Good. Dislike makes the sex hotter. If we got along, it'd be boring as hell."

"No chance of that."

Yet there was a chance, a chance this thing between them might be slipping out of his control. He took her mouth in his, slipped his tongue inside when she parted her lips. Tyler lost himself in her soft naked body rubbing against his harder, rougher one, hard being the operative word. His cock stood poised at the starting gate, raring to go. Rolling onto his back, he dragged her with him, still kissing her. Hey, it was a talent.

"Ride me, baby."

Lavender pulled away and sat up, straddling his torso. She rewarded him with a sexy, sultry smile. She grabbed a condom packet from the nightstand and unrolled it on him in record time. Raising her hips, she lowered herself onto his waiting cock.

"Oh, fu—fudge. Heaven. Frigging heaven." He groaned and bit down on his lower lip. Her wet pussy sheathed his cock inch by incredible inch. Her muscles clenched around his dick. Waves of pleasure circuited from his body through his malfunctioning brain and back to his erection. Nothing about his cock was malfunctioning, which was a damn good thing. She lifted her hips until only the head of his cock rested inside her moist entrance. His balls tightened almost painfully. She held herself above him, teasing the tip of his cock with her hot pussy.

Enough of this shit.

Tyler grasped her waist and slammed her hips downward, shoving his dick deep inside her.

She screamed out and arched her back, pressing her hips into his. "Tyler. Ty, oh, yeah, that feels so incredible."

"Then ride me, baby, like you're riding for your life, and the devil is on your heels." He loosened his grip on her hips, allowing her to control the pace.

"The devil isn't on my heels. He's underneath me." Her mass of red curls tickled his chest as she leaned down and claimed his mouth. Damn, but he loved an aggressive woman.

"You got that right, honey."

She lifted up her ass and slammed back down, upping the pace with each rise and fall of her hips. The air whooshed out his lungs and stole his breath, rendering him incapable of speech. The smell of sweat, sex, and Lavender filled his nostrils. They kissed like two uncivilized creatures, mindful only of the moment, and driven by the most basic of desires. Their bodies slapped together in rhythm, followed by a sucking sound on the upstroke as her pussy gripped his. Faster and faster. Harder and harder. Deeper and deeper.

Tyler opened his eyes and met her gaze. Usually he didn't meet a woman's eyes during sex. He avoided the intimacy. With Lavender, he couldn't look away, couldn't save himself from falling until they melded into one being with one purpose: to experience ultimate pleasure.

And their screwing did just that. His control shattered. He came, shouting her name to the treetops. A split second later, he heard his own name over and over.

They collapsed in a pile of spent arms and legs, not moving for several minutes.

Shaking off the after-sex high, Tyler stood and started pulling on his clothes. "I need to get back before I'm missed."

"Yeah, we don't want anyone to think we have something between us." Her attempted smile didn't reach her eyes. Guilt stabbed at him, putting a dent in his sexual satisfaction.

"Oh, honey, we do have something between us, namely my cock and your pussy." His attempt to keep it light faded when she stared back at him, her eyes devoid of the warmth he'd witnessed a few minutes ago. Tyler's grin faded. He averted his eyes for a moment and gnawed on his lower lip. His fingers hesitated on his zipper. He wanted to say more, put the smile back on her face. "Vinnie, I—"

"What?" Her hollow voice stabbed at his heart, made him feel like a true asshole.

He shook his head, changing his mind. Nothing he could say would ease his guilt, a guilt he didn't understand. Tyler hesitated in the doorway. A slit of sun peeked through the curtains and shed light on one side of her face and left the other side in total darkness. Somehow that seemed appropriate because part of her was completely concealed to him. She only let him see what she wanted him to see. Just like he did with her.

They were one hell of a pair.

Chapter 18

Naked Screen

Tyler grimaced and suppressed his inclination to barf.

The Brotherhood and several other bar patrons surrounded Tyler's cousin as if he was the second coming. It was disgusting. Derek, who normally didn't like being in the limelight, basked in their attention like Cougar lying in the one spot of sun streaming in the living room window. Sure, Derek oozed kindness and concern in nauseatingly high doses. Even worse, his sincerity attracted people in droves. He loved everybody, and everybody loved him. If his cousin had an enemy, Tyler hadn't met him yet. He suspected Dare hadn't either.

Even worse, his butthead cousin was telling stories about Tyler's past escapades, stories which painted Tyler in a way-too flattering light and endangered his asshole reputation.

Insulated by the other defensive players, Murphy slouched in his chair and watched the entire scene with an eagle eye. No doubt the butthead filed every detail away for future ammunition to nail Tyler's ass. Derek told him to cut Murphy some slack. The guy just wanted a Super Bowl ring before he retired.

Whatever.

Tyler frowned and flipped his chair around to concentrate on something more intriguing than his cousin's bullshit, his teammates' amusement, and the local residents' hero worship of Dickwad Ramsey.

Propping his long legs on the chair next to him, Tyler watched Lavender's fine ass while she bussed a couple tables. Damn, he loved that ass of hers, loved the feel of it as he held onto her while banging her brains out. His mind drifted to even better visions.

"So Harris, you ever play any sports other than football?"

Tyler's feet landed on the floor with a bang. He snapped his head in Murphy's direction, pissed the has-been linebacker interrupted his fantasy concerning Lavender, purple silk sheets, several plump strawberries, and a large can of whipped cream. "Huh?"

"He sure did, All-State in three sports. Coulda played in the majors if he'd wanted." Derek inserted cheerfully.

"Why didn't you?" Murphy probed, obviously looking for signs of weakness.

Tyler curled his lip into his baddest sneer. Murphy didn't even lift one eyebrow. "Football *was* my passion."

"*Was* being the operative word." The bastard sneered right back.

Tyler cringed. He'd effed up. "I meant *is* my passion."

"Too late now, fuckhead. Every one of us heard you with our own ears. Didn't we, guys?"

The defensive players nodded, diving right into Murphy's web of dissension. The offensive side looked everywhere but at Tyler. He'd dropped a notch in their eyes, thanks to their newest teammate.

Derek separated himself from the Brothers. With a heavy sigh, he interceded. "Gentlemen. Nothing good is going to come from picking sides. We're all in this together."

"Some of us are." Murphy snorted, and Tyler itched to wipe that smug smile off his ugly mug.

Tyler rose to his full height. Planting his hands on the table, he leaned down and got in Murphy's face. "Why don't you fucking go to hell? This team did fine without you. We don't need an asshole like you parading like he's the fucking team savior. You wanna talk about *try*, fuckhead, we'll talk about try. Tell me—just how many playoff games have you won in your way too long career? How many MVP awards? Why don't you hang it up, and admit defeat, Murphy? Rather than ripping *my* team in half with your bullshit." Tyler took a moment to glare at the defensive players, driving home the point that they were part of *his* team, not Murphy's. The cowards looked everywhere but at Tyler.

For emphasis Tyler slammed his fist into the table, causing the Brothers to jump. Spinning around, he crossed the room before he turned the arrogant asshole into whale bait and threw his mutilated body in the Straits of Juan De Fuca. Some unfortunate sucker with crappy timing sat on Tyler's favorite bar stool. One murderous glance sent the jerk diving for cover. Tyler swung a leg over the seat and stared at nothing.

"You could be nicer to him, you know. He's just trying to figure out where he fits in with the team." Lavender stood near his bar stool, an empty tray in one hand and a pitcher of beer in the other.

Tyler rubbed his sore knuckles and glowered at her. "I don't do nice when it comes to assholes." A predatory smile lit up his face. "But I could be convinced to be nice to you for a price."

"Sorry, jock boy, I wouldn't be interested if you were free."

"You didn't say that last night or this morning." He inhaled a whiff of her perfume. His brain fell into a fog. Some of his anger fell away. "I was really nice to you."

"We don't even like each other. Remember?" The gleam in her brown eyes promised untold pleasures. She ran a finger across his lips. He cleared his suddenly parched throat.

Oh yeah, he remembered. In fact, last night had been filled with tons of dislike. "How about we practice being enemies some more tonight?"

"Sorry. Not unless you agree to be nicer to him."

Damn, she was a frigging tough negotiator. "What do I get out of it?"

"Besides team unity?"

He rolled his eyes. "Fat chance that'll happen as long as both of us are breathing."

"What do you want?" Lavender put a finger under his chin and pulled his face close, real close. He could smell mint gum on her breath.

"I'm a greedy bastard. I want a lot." He did want a lot. He wanted something unexplainable, something unfathomable to his asshole self-programming. Yet, he wanted it. He didn't know what the hell *it* was, but he'd know it when he got there. He also knew Lavender might be his best ticket to that destination.

The truth slammed him to the ground harder than a tackle by a three hundred pound lineman.

She could help him find the missing piece of his empty life. Somehow she'd been dropped on him when he needed what she had to give. He hated to go all Zen on himself, but he believed in intuition and instincts. They'd served him well over his football career. Without them, he'd be just another quarterback instead of a future Hall-of-Famer with two Super Bowl rings and a few more left in him. At least he hoped there was gas left in that tank.

He met her brown eyes and recognized a kindred spirit, someone who hid pain behind a brash exterior, just like he did. He looked away, uncomfortable with what he was feeling.

Last night she'd seen him at his most vulnerable. She'd sidestepped past his asshole front and right into his soul. That didn't set well with him.

Sex. This thing between them had to remain about sex and only sex. He craved her body. Her sassy attitude challenged him. Her imaginative approach to sex made him harder than a bronzed penis. But it stopped there.

It had to stop there.

* * * * *

Lavender watched Tyler as he bent over his iPhone and texted some anonymous person. Anonymous to her, obviously not to him. A smidgen of jealousy settled in her stomach.

Tyler looked up and caught her staring. She flinched, fearing he'd read her face. Try as she might, she couldn't save herself and look away. Only when he held his phone up for her to see the screen did she avert her gaze to the phone. He'd been texting his mom.

He knew. He knew she'd been jealous. Just like he'd been yesterday almost to the point of losing control. In order to be jealous a person needed to care at least a little.

She glanced back at him. He locked gazes with her. His blue eyes burned so intense and powerful, she fell back a step. Something between them shifted and leaned off kilter, teetering and unbalanced. They crossed an invisible emotional boundary, stuck a toe in water beyond their comfort zones.

Lavender shook off her crazy thoughts. She shoved them out of her mind and away from the temptation to want something more out of this relationship, the temptation to consider there'd ever be something more.

She didn't believe in love. She'd seen its effects as it turned her mother into a bitter woman and removed her once-beloved father from her life. She'd suffered its effects each time she'd allowed herself to fall for the wrong guy. *No thank you.* She didn't need that shit. Leave love to the dreamers and fools. She was no fool.

Tyler was a jock. While she'd admit not all jocks were bad, Tyler *was* one of the bad ones. He wore his cockiness and attitude for all to see. Besides, Tyler shared some of the same traits as her father, good and bad. They loved sports, were married to the game, and any woman in their lives would always take a backseat to their sport of choice, be it basketball, football, or baseball, or even ping pong. A jock lived for the game. Even after he quit playing, he coached or announced. Whatever he chose to do, the sport dragged him away from home, leaving behind the ones he professed to love—not the way to a successful marriage and certainly not a great way to raise kids with an absentee father.

She knew. She'd lived that story. She'd never willingly live it again. She wouldn't wait at home for her husband to return from practice and a night of analyzing game film, just to see him for a few minutes each day. Then he'd be up at 6 a.m. and back to the practice facility to start the process all over again.

Sex she needed, and sex Tyler Harris provided. The man redefined insatiable. She didn't need to love anything else about him. Keep it simple and physical, that was the plan. She'd deviated from that path lately, time to walk the straight and narrow, no detours, and not cross any emotional borders.

Lavender headed behind the bar, Tyler hot on her heels. He backed her up against the counter. His hips pressed against hers.

"You're making me crazy. I can't get enough of you. All day long, I think about having sex with you. I wake in the middle of the night and think about it some more."

"You've been getting your fill." Lavender slid out from the counter and grabbed a bar rag to wipe the tables.

"I can never get my fill." His blue eyes turned midnight black. A lock of dark hair fell over one side of his forehead. She wanted to touch it, brush it back. He shoved his fingers through his hair, pushing it off his face. He cornered her again, cutting off her escape route.

"Your team's watching."

"Yeah, so? I'll get rid of them." Ty strode across the room, tossed the house keys at his cousin. They exchanged a few words. A few seconds later, the guys filed out the door, but not before Derek winked at her over his shoulder.

Zach hesitated, as if ready to go another round with Tyler. Instead, he turned his attention on her. He tossed a broad grin in her direction. "Hey, Lav, honey, when you get tired of this pussy and want a real man, give me a call."

Tyler growled, but Lavender stepped between them and smiled sweetly at the man. "I'll be sure to do that, Zach."

Zach kissed her cheek, lingering a little longer than necessary. Then he, too, followed the rest of his teammates on the door.

Tyler stood near the doorway, hands fisted, legs spread apart, as if debating whether or not to go after Zach.

"Drop it, Ty. He's trying to get to you, and you let him."

Frowning, Tyler turned back to her. "Yeah, I know, but you won't be calling him."

She considered taking exception to his order but decided to drop it. "So, you've chased them all out, now what did you have in mind?"

"I have a lot in mind. Dare told me to go to your house, said he doesn't want to be kept awake all night."

"You told him we'd make noise?"

"I didn't need to. He knows me. Let's get out of here. Your bed's waiting."

"My bed? I had something more daring in mind."

Tyler grinned, always game for sex in unusual places. "Tell me."

"It's your turn. Come up with something."

He ran his thumb across his lips. "Yeah. I have just the place." He nodded and starting putting glasses in the dishwasher. The sooner they cleaned up, the sooner they could get naked.

"For wild, monkey sex?"

"Oh yeah. I love how your mind works."

Lavender leaned forward and milked his erection through his jeans. "I bet it's not my mind you love."

"Oh, baby, you have that right. Minds are overrated. Give me an X-rated body any day or night."

A second later, Tyler hopped behind the wheel of her car. They sped down the road to an unknown destination.

* * * * *

Tyler drove easily, maintaining an aura of nonchalance. To be honest, he didn't know where the hell he was going. He figured he'd drive until he got there. Sex in an elevator was out. He didn't think there were any on the entire island. A back alley didn't do it for him because of the dumpster smell. Plus, it seemed pretty damn tacky. He craved something more. He struggled for the right word, but the only word that came to mind was *romantic*. Being romantic was so not him. Yet, he kept coming back to the word, a foreign—yet intriguing—concept.

A full moon shone in the clear night sky. He pictured Lavender's naked skin illuminated by the soft light of the moon. Unseasonably warm weather and windless conditions resulted in temps in the balmy low sixties. Sex outside would be in the realm of comfortable possibilities. Not that he and Lavender couldn't generate enough heat to be comfortable in below-freezing temperatures.

Purple Lady didn't make it easy on him or his rough-and-ready cock. She stroked him through his jeans, making it damn hard for him to concentrate on his driving. He skidded around one corner a little too fast. His distracted driving didn't deter her. She unbuttoned the top button on his jeans and slid down the zipper.

He raised his hips to give her easier access, even as he bared his teeth and bit back a primal groan.

Her hand slid inside his jeans. She cupped his balls, squeezing lightly.

"Oh, yeah, baby, keep that up, and we'll screw right here on the double-white line."

Her soft laughter touched his heart. Damn, he loved the sound of her voice whether it was soft, sexy, sassy, or demanding.

Rounding a corner on the two-lane road, Tyler spotted a sign indicating the entrance to a county park. He grinned and slowed down the car. Rescued at last.

"Here?" Lavender's fingers froze between his legs. She stared into the dark woods at the side of the road.

"Why not, Vinnie?" Hell, any place was a good place for sex, especially with Lavender.

"The park is closed for the night." His bold little vixen turned into a shy, proper lady. He knew better. She was anything but proper. With a slight tremble, she pushed her red hair off her face and stared out the window.

A little thing like a locked gate never stopped Tyler. He pulled off the side of the road and parked the car. "You got a blanket in this thing?"

"In the backseat."

"Grab it and let's go." He didn't want to keep his boy waiting. It'd been patient for way too long. He unfolded his long legs from the driver's seat and hopped out, checking his wallet for a condom and found three. He couldn't stop the grin from spreading across his face. His dick twitched, reminding him to get back to the matter at hand.

Lavender hung back. "Tyler. Are you sure? What if someone comes along?"

"Then we'll give them a show, won't we?"

"This is so not a good idea."

"This is an excellent idea. Since when are you a coward?"

She glanced nervously at the gate and twisted that damn ring. "I'm not. It's just—"

"Get the blanket."

He expected her to balk at the authoritarian tone of his voice. She didn't. Good thing. She'd had her turn being the boss. Lavender grabbed the blanket from the backseat and followed Tyler. He stood near the gate and waited for her. He hooked his arm over her shoulders and guided her down the dark path.

Lavender stumbled, but he caught her, hugging her to his side. "Do you have any clue where you're going?"

"Nope. I'm not one to hang out in parks."

"This is such a bad idea."

"I like this idea. Great outdoors. Communing with nature. All that crap."

"You can't be that horny. Let's go home, or at least to the car."

"I'm in a perpetual state of horniness." He might be horny, but he loved the anticipation, the craving, the torture of wanting something, and yet controlling his lust until it finally exploded like the grand finale in a fireworks display.

She sighed as if he'd asked her to work a double-shift or something. Little faker, she wanted this as bad as he did.

"Watch your step, baby." Tyler stepped over a log, and she clung to him. He liked that. A lot. Rarely did Lavender depend on anyone, so even a small gesture like this one made him feel needed. He liked the feeling.

The path opened up into a clearing. He stopped at the edge of a patch of grass near a picnic table. Beyond the grass, a steep, rocky bank dropped down to the waters of the Straits of Juan De

Fuca. Yeah, this was the place. Taking the blanket from Lavender, he spread it out on the tabletop.

"A picnic table?" She stepped back as if ready to flee. Not a chance in hell would he let her disappear on him.

"What's wrong with a picnic table?"

"Nothing."

"You're worried about doing it here? Hell, we've done it in my truck."

"I know, but there were windows to steam up and protect us from others watching us."

"Vinnie, no one is around. The park is closed. We have it all to ourselves." He lowered his voice a notch, cajoling her. "Don't you crave the forbidden, the possibility we could get caught. Doesn't that turn you on?"

She lifted her face to his and dug those sexy red fingernails into his arm. "Yes. A little."

He rubbed his cheek against hers, tugged on her earlobe with his teeth, finding that spot which drove her beyond sanity. She gripped his arm harder and turned her head to seek out his lips. He covered her mouth with his, sucked on her tongue, applied perfect pressure calculated to drive a female crazy. Oddly, the only female he cared about driving crazy happened to be his purple lady.

Panting, she drew back and looked up at him. Way up. She was such a petite little thing. The determination in her chocolate eyes weakened his football-damaged knees, while his dick jerked inside his unzipped jeans. "Just screw me. Anywhere. I don't care. Just bury your big guy inside me and drive down the field."

"Impatient, aren't we?" With a grin, he put his hands on her waist and lifted her up so she stood on the bench, which put them eye-to-eye. "If it makes you feel any better, waiting hurts me as much as it hurts you."

"I doubt that. You're the epitome of calm." She rested her hands on his shoulders and gazed into his eyes. He gazed back, liking what he saw.

"It's my game face. Trust me. Inside I'm a raging ball of lust."

She raked her gaze down his body and back up again. "I want you."

Oh, damn. If she looked at him one more time like that, it'd be all over. "You'll get me, but tonight I'm in charge."

Tyler unzipped her hoodie and pushed it off her shoulders. "Let's get you a little more comfortable." He unbuttoned her blouse, and it, too, followed the sweatshirt to the grass. Lavender leaned toward him in an attempt to press her body against his. "Don't move or you'll face the consequences."

"Don't tempt me."

"Oh, honey, just play along. It'll all be worth it in the end."

She nodded and stood straighter, hands clasped behind her back.

"Good. Keep your hands there."

With an exaggerated sigh, she thrust out her breasts and stood still before him. The breast thing tantalized him and tugged at his control.

Getting back to the job at hand, he unzipped her jeans and slid them down her legs, taking his time despite the need throbbing through his groin area. She stepped out of them without him asking. Standing back, he surveyed her almost naked body. A hot pink lace bra barely confined her big tits. Her nipples stood out under the lace. He couldn't discern their outline in the moonlight, but his imagination filled in the blanks. His gaze dropped lower to her curvy hips and pink panties. They didn't cover much more than a G-string. Pretty soon those panties wouldn't cover anything.

Tyler leaned his head close to her until their breath mingled. Holding her face in his hands, he traced her lush lips with his tongue. She moaned in response. Her hips rubbed against his. He found himself smiling, loving the power he had over her, even as he acknowledged she possessed a similar power over him. His cock strained against the fly of his jeans, demanding attention. He forced it to wait because tonight was about Lavender, not him.

The realization gave him pause. With Cass and other women, he'd made it about him. Sure, he met their needs at the same time. He was just that good, but he'd never focused solely on a woman's pleasure and forced his desires to take a back seat.

Her mouth opened to his tongue. He closed his eyes and let his talented tongue work its magic. Their mouths mated, starting slow and working to a fever pitch, a fever he'd better rein in if he planned on taking this slow.

Pulling away despite her protests, he worked his way down her body. Lingering at those mouth-watering nipples, he scraped his tongue across them through the thin lace barrier of her bra. She wiggled and pressed herself against him. He took one in his mouth, sucking on it, wetting the lace, sucking harder. He switched to the other, gave it the same treatment.

Holding her waist to keep her from moving, he knelt down and kissed a path to her belly button then lower. Until he found the treasure trove between her legs. He slid the panties down her legs and ran his hands up the inside of her thighs. She trembled, wavered a little, as if her knees wouldn't hold her up. He parted the folds of her pussy and buried his head between her legs, seeking out the moist heaven concealed there. He used his tongue to toy with her clit. She couldn't keep her hands behind her back and dug her fingers in his hair. He took her clit in his mouth and sucked. Her body shook with a spasm. He sucked harder. Her hips pumped, grinding her cunt into his face. She came with a rush. Her sweet juices coated his face. She cried out into the still night and sank downward.

Tyler caught her before she fell off the bench and laid her on the blanket.

His turn.

She lay still, limp and spent. Her legs splayed out to the side, opened wide for his pleasure. Her wet pussy glistened in the moonlight. Tyler rubbed his shirt sleeve across his wet face. His cock demanded some action. A tremor shot through his body in warning. His fine thread of control was in danger of snapping.

He closed his eyes for a moment and breathed deeply. *In. Out. In. Out.* Oh, man, that made it worse. All he wanted to do was plunge his cock in her tight wet pussy and forget the rest of the world existed. When he was with her, nothing else *did* exist.

She blinked and raised her head slightly to look at him. "Screw me."

He nodded. His head hurt from the strain of holding back. It was time to give his cock some relief. He unzipped his jeans and dropped them to the ground. Moving close, he guided his cock into her entrance.

"Give it to me. Hard. Don't hold back."

Ah, hell. How could any sane man resist that invitation? He let loose with the fury of a man who'd waited too long. Slamming into her, he took up a rhythm and went with it. Hard, fast, and deep. All control gone. She writhed under him, crying out words of encouragement pushing him into sweet insanity until the world exploded and took them with it.

Chapter 19

Kicking it Away

Tyler stared out the window at Lavender's house. Usually she was home by mid afternoon. She cooked an early Sunday dinner for the Brothers at Homer's house. Those old goats couldn't stay up much past 7:30.

Behind him, Derek read a sports magazine on his tablet. Murphy ignored them both and stared mindlessly at the television as some reality show droned on and on, while he stroked Coug. Not only was the asshole alienating his team, but he'd sucked the cat into his web. Tyler should've stuck with dogs. Dogs were loyal. Cats were too much like women.

The rest of the guys had gone whale watching and would meet Murphy at the ferry landing. Tyler couldn't wait to get rid of the jerk. How they'd managed to avoid beating the shit out of each other, only the football gods knew.

Derek put down the iPad and stood next to him. After a long silence his rat bastard cousin got to the point. "I've never seen you like this before. You need to get over it, Ty."

"Get over what?" Tyler stared straight ahead and ground his teeth to the roots.

"Ryan."

The word hung between them, binding them together in mutual pain, yet driving them apart. Tyler said nothing. He glanced at Murphy, but the guy had the television cranked so loud no way could he hear them.

Derek sighed and leaned his forehead against the window pane. Finally he straightened and faced Tyler. "Hey, his death ripped my heart out, too, but it's time to let go and move on. Ryan wouldn't want you like this."

"I should've dragged his mother back. I should've offered her so much money she couldn't refuse. I didn't because I wanted her to do it for Ryan, not the money." He met Derek's kind eyes. "You know what? Ryan saw through me. No one sees through me. He did. When he was laying there in that hospital bed, he told me he loved me. I remember every word of what he said next: *I was wrong. You do care. About people.*" Tyler's strangled voice sounded like someone else's. "Oh, God. I don't deserve all the good that's come my way. What the hell have I done with it? Any of it? I've squandered it away. Wasted it on my own selfish pursuits. Good people like Ryan make a difference in people's lives. I don't. I use people and throw them away."

"You're finally growing up. That party boy/asshole role isn't so easy to hide behind, is it?"

Tyler didn't even bother arguing or playing the tough guy. His cousin stared out the window at the bay, having said his piece. Tyler's entire body ached as if he'd played a brutal double-overtime game—only the game was life, and he didn't have a clue how it would end.

"Lavender is good for you." Derek words came out of left field. He studied his cousin over the rim of his beer glass. "I like her."

Tyler snapped his head around so fast a sharp pain shot up his neck. He reached up to rub the affected area. "So what? You like everyone."

"I like her, too." Murphy walked up beside them. "But I don't understand what she sees in a fuckhead like you."

"Guess what, assholes. I don't give a shit about your opinions or anyone else's for that matter."

"Bullshit and you know it. It's all an act, Ty. This is your cousin you're talking to, your life-long best friend. I know what's under the hood of that hard skull of yours. Why don't you date her? Take her out? Treat her like a real girlfriend?"

"Yeah, she deserves to be more than your fuck buddy." Murphy added his unwelcome two cents.

"She's not my girlfriend. I don't even like her outside of the bedroom."

Derek threw back his head and laughed. "Coulda fooled me. You love how she calls bullshit on you, argues, pushes your patience to the limits."

"Why would I love that?"

"There's no figuring how your messed-up mind works. I can only guess because she's a challenge, keeps you guessing, while Cass only challenged you in bed and spent your money."

Derek hit too close to a truth Tyler hadn't yet admitted to himself. He didn't like to be the last person clued in on something, especially when it pertained to him. "Are you two packed? The next ferry leaves at 5:30 p.m."

"Trying to get rid of us?"

"Damn right. Especially him." Tyler pointed at Murphy, who'd already gotten bored with the conversation and returned his attention to flipping channels on the television.

Derek just grinned, way too immune to Tyler. "Not a problem. We're tired of your company anyway. You're just jealous because the Brothers like me better than you."

"Take them with you, too, would you?"

"What and deprive you of their company? I don't think so."

"Damn, I need to get off this fucking island." Tyler ran his hand through his hair, considering his options. He didn't like any of them.

"You're not a prisoner here. Just pack up and go." Murphy grabbed another one of Tyler's good beers and leaned against the bar.

"And let Vinnie and the dufus brothers get this place. No effing way."

Derek watched him like a man who knew him too well. "Make them a deal. Sell it and split the profits. Homer knows a good realtor."

"Homer is a realtor."

"Let him sell it. Then everyone's happy. They have money, and you never have to come back here again."

Tyler didn't answer. He clamped his jaw shut, not certain if Derek truly believed he should sell the place or if he was needling him.

His cousin took a step closer and stared at him. Really stared. "I know that look."

"What look?"

"You don't want to sell this place. It means something to you."

"Like hell. I'm not a sentimental fool like you. Unfortunately, the economy's too bad to get a decent price for it right now."

"Yeah, sure." Derek wasn't fooled. "You're a sentimental fool, Tyler Jackson Harris."

Tyler refused to meet his gaze. A month ago, he'd have sold his family's legacy in a heartbeat.

Now? Well, yeah, he still would, given the right offer, just like he'd sold his soul one too many times.

* * * * *

Lavender stared at Tyler standing in her doorway. His big body filled up the entire door frame. The rain dripped off the rim of his Stetson, puddling on her miniscule, saggy front porch. He wore a dark blue sweater which matched his eyes, butt-hugging jeans, and his cowboy boots. Damn, but the boy did look hot. Sexy hot. Scalding sexy hot.

"So cowboy, looking for a rodeo?" She cast her come hither look his way.

His eyes darkened as a slow, sexy smile changed the harsh landscape of his handsome face. "I hear you're a champion bull rider, darlin'."

"You heard right. And I hear you're a champion bull."

"Comparisons between the size of my boys and a bull's privates have been made on occasion." He pushed past her into the small living room and tossed his hat on a chair. Turning, he stepped into her, filling up every square inch of the room with his presence.

"Show me." She stood on tiptoes and scraped her teeth across his jaw.

"Keep that up, honey, and we won't even make it out the chute." With a heavy sigh, he put his hands on her shoulders and held her away from him. "I'll take a rain check. First, I'm taking you out to a nice dinner."

"You're taking me out?" In the two months he'd been on the island, he'd never asked her out for a measly cup of coffee, let alone dinner. Of course, she didn't care because she didn't like him.

"Yeah, I'm taking you out." His crooked smile melted her heart. She spread her palm over his chest. He covered her hand with his then wrapped his fingers around hers and lifted her hand to his mouth. He kissed it, palm up, gentle and careful. His sweet reaction turned her on more than any of the raunchy, headboard-banging sex they'd had to date, and that was saying a lot. A damn lot.

"Why?"

"I'm hungry and I don't like to eat alone."

"I have to think about this. Where?"

"The Partridge Inn." Those dark blue eyes pinned her down and rendered her breathless.

She swallowed and struggled for her voice. "Are you serious? That place is so expensive they don't have prices on the menu."

"Don't worry. I think I can afford it this once."

Lavender studied his face. He looked away, shuffled his feet, seemed almost embarrassed. His behavior was completely out of character. "I still don't get it. Why?"

"Because—Because I don't want you to think that you're just a good lay to me. You're a damn fine lay. Besides, a good argument always whets my appetite." He still wouldn't look at her.

"Fine. I'm all for a free gourmet meal."

"I hope you're hungry."

"Hungry? I'm starving. I haven't eaten all day. I've been weeding that damn vegetable garden. Give me a few minutes to take a shower and clean up."

"Sure." He sank onto her couch and started flipping through the channels.

Not caring how anxious she appeared, Lavender vaulted over a pile of clothes on the floor and dove into the bathroom. Clothes flying, she turned on the water and stepped into the combination tub/shower. She couldn't believe one little date with a man she'd been sleeping with for a month could affect her this much, but it did. Not only that, but it made her day.

The hot water ran down her face, sluiced across her naked body. She closed her eyes and let it flow. Tyler asked *her* out. Sure, she'd be stupid to think this date meant anything beyond this island, but she didn't care. She'd live for the moment and deal with the painful aftermath down the road.

Lavender picked up the bar of lavender-scented soap—was there any other kind—and started to soap her body until it was stolen from her hand. She groaned as Tyler pulled her against his hard male body.

"I guess dinner can wait." Her mumbled response faded into the mist of the shower.

Tyler lathered up her stomach, upward to her breasts, and across her shoulders, taking his damn sweet time. She leaned back against him and closed her eyes. The heat of the water combined with the heat of his body until she didn't know where one started and the other ended.

He ran his hands back down her body. Pushing her gently against the wall, he soaped up her back and ass, sliding his hands between her legs and rubbing her thighs. Lavender flattened her hands against the wall and slid her feet back a few steps. She spread her legs and bent down. Water streamed down her back and funneled off her erect nipples.

"Someone wants some cock." Tyler slid those masterful fingers up the insides of her thighs.

"Duh." She sputtered on a mouthful of water.

"How bad do you want it?" His hips pressed close behind hers. His dick tickled her crotch. He reached around her body and caught her tight nipples in his fingers, teasing her, driving her out of her mind. Capturing each taunt nipple between his thumb and forefinger, he squeezed, hard, until she whimpered for him to stop or go or, hell, what the heck did she know? She just wanted more.

"Bad. Really bad. I want you."

"Yeah? Show me." One big hand slid between her legs. She shuddered. His index finger slid with ease into her wet pussy. He pumped his finger in and out as she pressed her pussy against his hand, angling for him to hit her sweet spot. He pushed another long finger inside her and took her fast and furious with his fingers. She shattered like a china cup on a slate floor. Just like that. No prelude. Just a weak-willed body, weaker knees, and a quivering pussy.

A few seconds later, his big cock powered into her in one swift, hard stroke, no time for recovery. He filled her completely. Thoroughly. Incredibly.

Hands gripping her hips, Tyler held himself there, as the water ran down both their naked bodies. Lavender fought to regain control of her spiraling emotions. No such luck. She'd lost her sanity the second he'd set foot in the shower.

He pushed high and hard into her. Touching her in those places only he could touch her, which she'd begun to realize had nothing to do with the size of his cock or how full she felt with him buried inside her.

Hell, no, it went deeper than that. Deeper than anyone had ever touched her, physically and emotionally.

Tyler Harris had her number. If only she had his.

He started moving in and out of her. His motions were controlled and constricted, as if he knew he'd snap at a moment's provocation. Her fuzzy brain whispered something about a condom, but she'd gone past caring minutes ago. Then he held her from behind when he let himself go. His cock jerked inside her. He withdrew and rammed back into her. Hands pinching her nipples, he rode her hard and rough, until his body spasmed, and his release came.

Together, they leaned against the wet shower walls, chests heaving, sanity slowly returning, bodies weak but satisfied.

"I didn't wear a rubber." He panted.

"It's okay, I'm on the pill." She squinted at the wet wall but couldn't see straight.

"Why the hell didn't you ever mention that before?" He relaxed against her.

"I don't know." She did know. Doing it without a condom seemed more intimate. She felt his seed inside her, felt it dripping from her wet slit, knew he'd left a part of him with her.

She'd never had sex without a condom before. Never in her life. But then, she'd experienced a lot of firsts with her arrogant jock.

Straightening, he smacked her ass, and she yelped. "Get ready for dinner."

On that note, he exited the shower and left her alone to get ready. Lavender slid down the wall and buried her face in her hands. She'd given him something tonight, and he hadn't a clue regarding the significance of her actions, the kind of trust it invoked.

But Lavender knew.

Chapter 20

Turned over on Downs

Tyler glared at Jim, but the old man didn't blink through his coke-bottle glasses. Obviously, he needed new spectacles because Tyler had used his best you're-in-deep-shit-glare. Jim sipped his drink and studied the cards in his hand, as if he could see them. The rest of the Brothers ignored him. Nothing interrupted their poker games, not even a two-time Super Bowl quarterback.

"You fucking—" Five pairs of eyes looked up at him. "—frigging can't force me to miss mini-camp. The rumor sluts everywhere will be certain I'm in rehab or about to be traded or just don't give a shit."

Jim raised one bushy eyebrow. "No one's stopping you from going."

"Yeah, and you and your buddies will be taking over my mansion—as if you haven't already." Tyler couldn't help notice Jim held a full-house in his hand.

"Nah. It's not worth much beyond bull-dozing. No one has the money to restore that place." Homer muttered. "If you'd just let me sell it for you. I have several—"

"—potential buyers lined up. I know. I know." Tyler bristled and rose to their unintentional challenge. Maybe he'd restore the damn dump to its former splendor if it took every penny he had just to spite them all. With a few more prime endorsements, he'd garner a chunk of change and just might earmark the cash for mansion rehab. He snorted to himself. Easier said than done. To keep those endorsements coming in, he'd need to win.

"It's not just mini-camp; the awards ceremony for the Pacific Northwest Athletic Association is that evening." Missing mini-camp and the awards would send the national media into a feeding frenzy, especially since he'd most likely get Northwest Athlete of the Year for the second straight year.

"Go for it. The last ferry back to the Island sails at eleven p.m., you'll need to be on it each night. No overnighters on the mainland."

"How will you know if I come back or not?"

The Brothers looked at him as a unit and glanced at Lavender hustling between the tables.

"Fine. I'll charter a seaplane." Tyler downed the last of his beer and snapped his fingers at Lavender for another. She rewarded him with an eff-you scowl. He grinned, pleased that he'd managed to get under her skin with his little display of chauvinism. Hopefully, his surliness wouldn't backfire, or he'd end up wearing the beer instead of drinking it.

"Fine, as long as your feet are on the island by midnight." Jim held the cards six inches from his nose. The man really was blind.

"Midnight? Are you fucking kidding me? What's up with that? Will I turn into a damn pumpkin?" Tyler's sarcastic tone didn't faze the guys either. Lavender appeared by his side, the tip jar in one hand and his beer in another. He dug in his pocket and stuck a twenty in the jar. He grabbed the beer and chugged it. The stuff tasted like crap, absolute crap, He choked on it and turned his irritation on purple lady. "What the fuck is this garbage?"

"Light beer. You're getting a little pudgy."

"I am not." Tyler frowned and looked down at his waist. Lavender laughed at his reaction. Her sassy humor turned him on even when he happened to be the brunt of it. Maybe he could goad her into a good argument later. Fighting made him hornier than hell for make-up sex.

"Clean up your potty mouth. I bet your mamma didn't raise you to talk like that."

Tyler didn't have a comeback for that. His mother sure as hell didn't allow cussing in her presence. "Hey, I've been working on it. I'm wounded that you haven't noticed."

"Work harder. When you get pissed, your swearing comes back with a vengeance. It's as much a part of you as your throwing arm and insufferable personality."

Stupidly, he took the bait. "I went cold turkey for a week. Remember?"

"One whole week. Impressive. You use the 'F' word so much it's lost its effect."

"Whatever."

"You can't stop, can he, guys?" The old geezers nodded, not about to cross the Sergeant-Major.

"You want me to quit. No problem." Tyler regretted rising to her challenge. "We're just talking the 'F' word, right? No other swear word?"

Lavender nodded, looking awful damn cute thinking she'd gotten the best of him. "We'll take it one step at a time."

"Fine. I'll stop. No big deal, but what do I get out of it?

"The satisfaction of a job well done."

"That's it?" Annoyed, Tyler turned back to Jim. "I can't even spend one night off this fu—fricking island?"

Unconcerned, Jim continued to stare at him. "Those are the terms of the will. You're allowed off-island excursions, but you must be on the island by midnight the same day. Oh, and you'll need to take a chaperone appointed by me."

"A chaperone? What the fu—fudge do I need a chaperone for?" Tyler's temper flared, but he reined it in. He gripped the back of a nearby chair, seriously wanting to throw the damn thing across the room. This senior citizen attorney tested his severely strained patience.

"To keep you in compliance. Lavender will go."

"What?" Lavender sputtered and shook her head. "I'm not going to Seattle with him. We don't like each other."

"Except for the sex part, honey. We like that just fine." Tyler grinned when she smacked his arm.

"Shut up." Lavender's glare didn't faze him. He'd be wearing the next beer, of that he was certain. The old men hooted and slapped their hands on the table. Lavender turned her homicidal glare on them, and they hushed immediately. She faced Tyler. "I'll miss a few days of work. This'll cost you."

He pulled out his wallet and waved a credit card in her face. "Does this help?"

She snatched it from his hand and shoved it in her pocket. "You'll be sorry."

"I doubt that." His dirty mind worked overtime. Flying back and forth to the mainland had its advantages, especially at night. He'd initiate Lavender into the mile-high club—not that they'd be flying quite that high—but it was the spirit of the gesture that mattered the most.

"I'll see to it."

Damn, but he loved it when she threatened him like that. Her sexy butt swayed with each step and mesmerized him until one of the brothers cleared his ancient throat.

"It's settled then." Jim turned back to his poker game. "I fold, guys." He tossed his full house on the table.

Tyler shook his head at Jim and walked away with a definite lift to his step. He wandered into the back room where the military museum was housed, avoiding the picture of his father. Instead, he painstakingly looked at each picture and exhibit item, reading each description before moving to the next. His dad's picture kept calling to him. He felt its invisible pull. No matter where he stood in the room, he was acutely aware of the eight by ten of Jason Harris.

The picture sucked him in until he stood staring down at it. His father stared back. The empty hole inside him grew bigger. Like a physical thing, it hurt like hell. It hurt to breathe, like the time Murphy had sacked him so hard he hadn't been sure he'd ever get back up.

Damn, he missed his father, missed his sensible guidance, and missed shooting the shit with him. They'd sit up for hours after a game and analyze the hell out of it, giving both wins and losses equal attention. If only his dad had lived to see him play college ball, win the Rose Bowl, and two Super Bowls. If only—

Tyler heard purple lady laugh in the next room, acutely aware of her. His father would've enjoyed Lavender, especially her irreverence toward his son's jock status. His sisters and mother, heaven forbid, would enjoy combining wits with her on how best to take Tyler down a peg. He'd be in deep shit if that ever happened. Of course, it wouldn't. He kept his fu—sex buddies and his family separated.

His rarely-used conscience smacked him up the side of the head, claiming foul. Tyler disregarded that nagging voice demanding to be heard. If he listened, he might be forced to admit Lavender meant more to him than a willing body. Even worse, he might be forced to examine what he really wanted out of life and why none of his accomplishments to date amounted to more than a pile of crap.

He looked into his father's blue eyes, so much like his own. Even after all these years, a lump of grief settled in his stomach. "Do you think I'm a failure, or are you proud of me, Dad?" He croaked in a hoarse voice.

The man in the photograph didn't answer.

"Tyler, who were you talking to?" Lavender stood in the doorway, keeping her distance, emotionally and physically. If she didn't tread carefully, she'd do something stupid like fall for the obnoxious jock. How she'd survive a couple days flying back and forth crammed into a float plane with him, she couldn't imagine. The credit card did soften the blow, though.

Tyler stiffened and kept his back to her, a very fine, broad back with incredibly wide shoulders and one fine, fine ass. For a moment, she closed her eyes and time-travelled to last night, and their first "unprotected" sex.

Sure, she was on the pill so in a way she was protected. Regardless, she'd trusted him in ways she'd never trusted a man, jock or not, to be clean. Feeling his penis inside her, skin unguarded by a condom and then his seed filling her boiled her blood, pushed all her hot buttons, and worse of all, labeled her as a sappy fool. She'd gotten in over her head with this boy, and no lifeguard on earth could rescue her.

"Ty?" She touched his shoulder, and he flinched. "Ty, are you okay?"

"Yeah." He didn't sound okay. In fact, he sounded like a man who'd lost his best friend. Her gaze followed his. He stared at the same picture of the helicopter pilot he'd been fixated on a few weeks ago.

"Who is this man?" She scrutinized the photo. The same intense, deep blue eyes as Tyler's looked back at her. The chiseled good looks, strong jaw, proud mouth, and dark hair were all mirrored in Tyler's face. *A relative. A very close relative.* She wrapped her fingers around his bicep. "He means something to you."

"My father." His feeble attempt to keep his voice flat and emotionless didn't succeed in masking the pain.

"Your father?"

"Yeah, I miss him." His troubled gaze met hers. Pain written clearly on his face. She didn't see an over-confident jock. She saw a confused, vulnerable little boy. Someone battling his demons and trying hard to make sense of life, just like her.

In that one moment, Tyler wound his way around her heart so completely she'd never be the same. "You look a lot like him." She slid her arm around his waist and held him close to her. He laid his cheek on top of her head.

"Thank you, but that's where the resemblance ends. I'm no hero, but he was."

"Your father was a hero. That's a fact. But in your own way, you're a hero, too." She couldn't believe her own words, yet she meant them.

He pulled away and shook his head. "What have I ever done? I'm just a dumb jock, a football player." His upper lip turned up in a sneer of self-loathing.

Lavender reached up and wrapped her arms around his neck. He stared straight ahead. "Ty, you're not just a dumb, jock football player. First of all, you're not dumb. Second, you bring a lot of joy to people following the team. You've given us regional pride, brought the area together. Perfect strangers stand in line at a grocery store and talk about the Lumberjacks. Third, you do a lot of good for the community."

Tyler snapped his head downward to glare at her. "Who told you that?"

"Your cousin."

"He's full of shit. I'm no hero. To anyone. I'm just a guy gifted with athletic talent. I get paid well to do what I do. Now my dad, he was a hero. He got shot down and managed to stay one step ahead of the enemy and get to safety. He carried his injured buddy on his back and saved his life. That's a hero. Then Ryan, the kid was dying of cancer, but he was stronger than any of us right to the end. Upbeat, positive, a true fighter."

"There are different kinds of heroes, Ty." The revelation dawned on her like the fog lifting on Rosario Straits. "That's what this is all about, isn't it? You thought a second Super Bowl win would prove your worth to yourself, but it didn't change things in your mind, did it?"

"You have no idea how much I hate all the attention showered on me. I don't deserve it." He pulled away from her and stared out a window, his face carved in stone.

Lavender absorbed his words and realized how little she really knew Tyler Harris. In fact, how little anyone knew him. "You? You're an attention slut."

He looked at her sadly, as if he expected her, of all people, to see the truth. "Not really. It's all a front. I don't deserve any of this. The money. The fame. None of it. I'm a fake. A failure."

Cocky Tyler Harris—a failure? How could he possibly think such a thing? "You're not a failure. You're a good guy just doing the best you can." Her heart fell at his feet over the admission. He'd opened up, let her in, something she suspected didn't come easily, if ever to him, which moved their relationship beyond casual sex and scared the crap out of her.

"I'm an ass, remember?" He looked at her then. One corner of his mouth twitched in a sad smile.

Encouraged by his attempt at humor, she dared to say more. "You pretend to be an ass so you never have to measure up or be held to the high standards you've set for yourself."

"Is that what you really think, Doctor Vinnie?" He straightened the crease on an American flag folded into a triangle on the table.

"That's really why you're here, isn't it? You're hiding because you've somehow minimized all your successes and feel unworthy. You don't know where to go from the top."

"You know what they say. Once you're on top, the only way to go is down."

"Tyler, how many men in this entire world get to be Super Bowl winning quarterbacks?"

"Uh, twenty-nine or so."

"You've managed to do something very few men have ever done, and you did it twice. You did it because you don't give up. You believed in yourself and your team. That first year, you carried them on your back, made them play beyond their ability. *You* did it. Your leadership qualities and your strength of will did it."

"And you know this how?" His blue eyes searched hers, stripping away layer after layer.

Lavender squirmed a little. "I'm a closet Jacks fan. But let's not go there now." She didn't want this to be about her. It needed to be about Tyler. "I'm proud of what you've accomplished, and I'm sure your father is too. And so is Ryan. Whether you led your troops on the battlefield or the football field, you have a chance to do some real good in this world. You have the power to make a difference, to influence others. Use it wisely then you can be proud of yourself."

"You think it's that easy?"

She nodded. "I think it could be. You need to be the real you, instead of this asshole image you've adopted because it's not working so well for you anymore." He smiled and put his arm around her, hugging her close. "My dad and Ryan would've loved you. You ground me."

"Thank you."

Lavender looked away so he didn't see the tears in her eyes.

Chapter 21

Third-Down Conversion

Tyler stood on the practice field waiting for the no-pads scrimmage to start. He should be listening to the offensive coordinator's instructions. Instead, he stood off to one side. He stifled a yawn and tried to look engaged. Behind him, Lavender sat in the small set of bleachers. Thanks to his big-mouthed cousin, the guys knew about his chaperone and gave him no ends of grief in the locker room. Assholes all of them.

Even worse, her presence distracted him from his job, one more piece of evidence pointing toward his waning interest in the game. In the not-too-distant past, a woman would've never registered on his radar when he had football on his mind. Unfortunately, football wasn't on his mind. Lavender was, along with tonight's airplane ride. He shifted his stance as his cock rose to the task. *Down boy. Not yet.*

A small group from the local press core crowded nearby. They'd jostled for his attention all morning. He'd been a no-show at every press conference since the Super Bowl, and they wanted answers he wasn't willing to give. Earlier he'd snarled at them, and they'd backed off somewhat. He doubted for long.

Damn, but he was in a crappy mood. Murphy made it all the crappier. The defense gathered around the jerk like he was the fucking god of football. Especially the young guys, they ate up his every word. Their hero worship of the interloper didn't sit well with Tyler. As long as Zach Murphy wore a Jacks' jersey, team unity was shot to shit. Somehow he'd find a way to get the guy traded or cut before the first regular season game. He'd show the front office Murphy didn't have it anymore. The guy's ancient joints couldn't withstand the rigors of another season. You can't win on heart alone. Tyler frowned, uncomfortable with his own thoughts. Obviously, you could win without heart, as evidenced by his own uninspired play last season, but he doubted there'd be a repeat if he didn't get his game back.

"Harris! Get your head out of your ass." The offensive coordinator slapped his clipboard against his thigh. "Are you ready?"

With a sheepish shrug of one shoulder, Tyler swallowed and faced his pissed-off coach. "Uh, could you run through that one more time?"

"For the love of—What the hell is it with you?" Exasperated and obviously nearing the end of his patience, Coach Carter slammed his clipboard to the ground, a trait he'd picked up from the head coach over the years.

Tyler clamped his jaw and kept his mouth shut. No excuses, he was guilty as charged for letting his attention wander. His offensive line grumbled comments questioning whether certain parts of his anatomy were male or female. His receivers stood to one side, arms crossed over their chests, disgusted they'd have to suffer through a lecture by the coaching staff courtesy of their quarterback. Several feet away, Murphy watched the exchange with more than a casual interest. His defense gathered around him, glaring at Tyler with defiance, something they never had the guts to do pre-Murphy.

Hubert Jackson, the Jacks' fiery, young head couch stalked over to add his two cents. *Wonderful. Just wonderful.* Tyler braced himself for an old-fashioned ass-chewing, one of HughJack's signature traits, along with clipboard throwing. His coach wasted no time stepping into Tyler's personal space, not intimidated by the quarterback's height advantage.

"What the fuck is up with you, Harris? Get your head in the game. I know it's just a scrimmage, and maybe you think you're too fucking good to be bothered. Maybe you'd rather get your nails painted or get your hair highlighted or some other pansy-assed thing. We're here to play football. The only person impressed with your past accomplishments is you. I'm about today and tomorrow. We compete every day, every hour, every minute. Either you're with us one hundred percent or get your sorry ass off this field."

The old Tyler would've lit into his coach and gave it right back to him. This Tyler took it and said nothing. HughJack stared him down. Tyler stared back, willing the smallest emotion from showing in his face. The accusing eyes of several dozen teammates burned into his back. Tyler looked away first. He shoved his helmet on his head and turned toward the field. *Wrong move.* HughJack snatched his facemask and wrenched Tyler's head around. He swore he heard something snap, most likely a vertebrae.

His coach lowered his voice so only Tyler and Coach Carter could hear. "I'm watching you, Harris. I don't give a fuck if you're the best quarterback in this league, if you don't leave it all out on the field, I don't want you. I let it go last season, figured you'd work it out on your own, while the rest of the team picked up the slack. Not this year." HughJack pointed toward Murphy. "We signed Zach to give this team some dedicated leadership, the type we used to get from you." HughJack jerked on Tyler's facemask a final time for good measure then stomped off.

Anger flowed through Tyler's bloodstream, but anger at himself. He turned on his teammates. "What the fuck are you guys staring at? Get to work." He bellowed, giving them a glimpse of the old Tyler. The guys shuffled their feet and kept their distance, their expressions ranging from sympathy to annoyance. Turning his back on them, Tyler bent his head over the offensive coordinator's clipboard and studied the plays.

A few minutes later, he stood behind center. The offense avoided his gaze, while the defense's contempt shone in their eyes. Murphy's blatant disrespect and the coach's dressing down undermined the team's confidence in their quarterback, not to mention the rampant speculation by the sports media as to his mental state. His leadership role was in serious jeopardy. When it came down to it, he'd no one to blame but himself.

Determined to prove them wrong, Tyler took the snap and stepped back into the pocket. He ran through his options but didn't see one open man. The next second, he was slammed to the ground with the wind knocked out of him. As soon as he filled his lungs with oxygen, Tyler shot to his feet.

Murphy grinned at him. "Sorry, man, I couldn't stop fast enough."

"You fucking asshole. You did that on purpose." Tyler stood toe-to-toe with the jerk. The chuckles of his teammates infuriated Tyler all the more.

Murphy shrugged one shoulder. He knew as well as anyone this was a no-tackle scrimmage. "Just like old times, huh? Aren't you glad I'm on your team now? I won't be knocking you on your sorry ass during real games."

"I don't want you on my team, asshole. You're washed up."

"What does that say about you, since I knocked your ass clear to I-5, and I'm not done yet." After delivering his final words like a slap in the face, Murphy laughed and strutted back to his tight group of defensive players.

Teeth clenched, Tyler called the next play. He took a quick step back. Derek sprinted across the middle heading for exactly the right spot, an easy first down. Tyler hesitated a split second too long. Realizing his mistake, he hurled the ball at his cousin. Too high and way off to the left, Derek dove for the ball at the same time as Murphy. Their helmets slammed into each other. Both men were slow getting up.

Derek rolled his head around then rubbed the back of his neck. Breathing hard, he stalked back to the huddle and turned on his cousin in a rare moment of temper. "You fucking idiot. That's the kind of throw you complete in your sleep."

Wide-eyed, the rest of the offense stared at the best friends. Tyler flicked his gaze to HughJack, who hadn't missed a thing. His coach balled his fists and glared at him. It was going to be a damn long practice.

Murphy laid him out on the ground two more times during the scrimmage. He fumbled once, and Murphy recovered. HughJack and his coaching staff never said a word to Murphy about his over-zealous sacking of their quarterback.

Meanwhile, Tyler did nothing to prove Murphy was too old to play. His passes fell to the ground, overthrown and underthrown with an inaccuracy uncharacteristic of him. When he finally managed to throw a few on target, his receivers dropped every one of them. To add insult to injury, Murphy intercepted the last pass of the day and ran it back for a touchdown. The guy zipped all over the field like a one-man wrecking crew. HughJack paced the sidelines and barked orders, slamming his clipboard to the ground several times. Not a good sign.

The torture finally ended. Head down, Tyler pushed past the rabid media and into the locker room. His teammates stayed clear, even his cousin. Murphy gloated from his corner, enjoying every minute, as he recounted the day's events loud enough for everyone to hear.

After his shower, Tyler sat on the bench in front of his locker and laced his shoes. When the usual locker room ribbing and jaw-jacking faded to silence, he glanced up.

HughJack strode across the room, heading straight for him. With a sigh, Tyler waited for his next ass-chewing.

His coach looked him up and down, as if he'd never seen him before. "You were forcing it out there, not making wise decisions, and you let Murphy get to you. Pollard takes the snaps tomorrow in scrimmage. Maybe he can make something happen." HughJack spoke with a quiet intensity, which scared the crap out of Tyler more than the man's trademark temper tantrums.

* * * * *

Lavender followed Tyler to the back of the floatplane. He squeezed into the back window seat. She took the one next to him, the sole passengers on the eleven p.m. flight to the San Juan Islands. The pilot settled into the cockpit separated from them by a door-less bulkhead and a few rows of empty passenger seats.

The pilot donned a pair of earphones and set about his job. A few seconds later, they taxied across the water on Lake Union then built up speed for a takeoff. In no time, the plane was airborne. Below them, the lights of Seattle illuminated the night sky through the haze of rain.

Shoulders slumped, Tyler stared outside. He'd wallowed in self-pity all evening. They'd eaten a tense dinner at a seafood restaurant on the water. Tyler spoke little and ate even less. Lavender attempted conversation a few times, but the man only grunted in response. Eventually she lapsed into silence and let him brood.

But now she'd endured enough of his silent treatment. Smacking sense into him didn't seem the right thing to do. Seeing his cocky façade ripped away to expose vulnerability brought out an inexplicable tenderness in her.

"Tyler, please don't take your day out on me." She reached for his hand and held it. He wrapped his fingers tightly around hers in response, almost as if she were his lifeline.

A muscle worked in his jaw. "I'm sorry. It was one shitty practice."

"I know. I was there." She lowered her voice and stroked his palm with her thumb.

"HughJack and Murphy made me look like a rookie. I played like crap."

"Then find a way make it better. You're not a quitter." He wouldn't get sympathy from her. That wasn't what he needed.

He turned toward her, confusion rather than anger in his troubled blue eyes. "I never was before. Now it's all on me. I'm losing the team, and Murphy is leading the mutiny, but I gave him the ammunition."

Lavender held his face in her hands, searching his eyes for some sign of the man she knew he was. "Get them back. Be the guy you know you can be. Be a fighter."

"I'm trying. The harder I try, the worse it gets, the further I get from where I used to be." He broke his gaze away from her and stared back out the window. His jaw tensed, his body tightened into an unyielding knot of despair.

"You're trying too hard. You need to relax, let it flow, rediscover the joy you once had for the game." She ran a hand down his arm. The muscles bunched, hard as concrete. "Take a deep breath. Find your zone."

"If only it was that fucking easy. It's the zone that eludes me." He rested his head on her shoulder, seemingly oblivious to his use of the forbidden word. "I'm tense and tight. I'm forcing throws, not seeing open receivers, not using my instincts. I made it through last season on technical skills alone."

"Your technical skills are the best in the league."

"Technique won't be enough. Not this season." Frustration forced his voice into a tight rumble in his chest.

"What am I going to do with you?" Lavender nuzzled his neck. The man needed to relax before he shattered into pieces. Tyler sucked in a breath and rested a hand on her thigh. His fingers tightened around her leg. He lifted his gaze and met hers again. She touched his model-worthy face, ran a finger along his strong jaw line, uncompromising lips, and over the cords in his neck. Reaching up, she slipped her fingers through the silky strands of his shaggy dark hair.

"When I'm with you, I forget all this shit." His blue eyes sliced through her. "Help me work on that relaxing thing." His voice sounded hopeful, somewhat out of breath.

"How do you propose we do that?" She swallowed as her body tingled in anticipation, suspecting and dreading the implication.

Tyler pulled her onto his lap. The vulnerable guy of a few moments ago replaced by the in-charge, take-no-prisoners asshole. "Perhaps a little sexual therapy in the sky would help."

Her eyes popped open wide as she guessed the direction his mind was taking. "Tyler. What are you doing? The pilot—" She cast a nervous glance in the direction of the cockpit. The pilot paid them no mind, as he worked the controls and talked on the headset to an unseen person.

"You started it."

Tyler had a point. She did start it but merely to comfort and not to have sex on an airplane. Well, maybe she did consider such a thing, but just a little. "Really, let's wait until we land."

"He won't notice." Tyler ran a finger across her lips and parted them with the tip of his index finger.

"Won't notice? I'm noisy, remember? And so are you. He'd have to be deaf not to notice." Despite her feeble protests, she parted her lips and sucked his finger into her mouth.

Tyler groaned and closed his eyes for a moment. "Now do that to my cock, darlin', and you'll make me one happy man."

She grasped his wrist and removed the finger from her mouth. "Tyler. We can't."

"Sure we can. Our best sex happens when you're pissed at me, or we're pushing the limits. You don't hold back, and I fucking love it. If you prefer, I could do something to piss you off. I excel at that." He grinned, his wicked, to-hell-with-everyone-else grin and slid his hands up her sweater. "How's this?"

The jock knew her hot buttons, and he pushed more than a few as his fingers did a little tango along her rib cage. Her eyes rolled back in her head, and she rewarded his "unwanted" attention with a sultry groan.

"Am I pissing you off yet?"

"Very much so." She did nothing to stop him, couldn't if she wanted. Lavender gripped the waistband of his jeans, pulling him closer, rather than pushing him away. She pressed her shoulders against the back of the seat in front of her and gasped as he pushed her bra and sweater up to her neck. The cool air pebbled her nipples into hard nubs.

"Are you furious yet?" He grinned at her, looking every bit like the obnoxious Tyler she'd grown to appreciate.

"Absolutely. I've never disliked you as much as I do now."

"Good, I'm doing my job then." His husky voice exposed the ragged control he had over his emotions.

"Oh, yeah." She'd become putty in his big hands. If he asked, she'd strip naked and do him in the center of Pike's Place Market.

Yeah, that's how much she disliked him and his ripped athlete's body.

"Honey, I can make you really mad at me. We're going to fu—uh, screw while we fly thousands of feet in the air. It's our destiny."

"That'll do it. I'll heap tons of passionate fury on you." She rolled her head back and allowed his mouth easier access to her neck. He jumped on the opportunity, mauling her with a combination of lips and teeth. Most certainly, he left his mark more than once.

"I like the passionate part. Yeah. Really like it."

Bending his head, Tyler covered his bases. He sucked on one nipple, squeezed the other with the fingers of one hand, while his other hand slipped between her legs. He unzipped her jeans, banging his elbow on the armrest. He cursed a blue streak, grabbed her around the waist and raised her off his lap into a standing position. Yanking her jeans down to her ankles, he pushed the soaked crotch of her panties aside.

"Honey, thinking of me and not Murphy better be the reason you're so fu—effing wet."

"What do you think, buster? I like Murphy, which makes him boring. I don't like you."

His warm chuckle gave her heart a boost. "Keep it that way. I'll make you forget the man's name."

"Whose name?"

He threw back his head and laughed. She loved his hearty baritone. Nothing like the promise of sex on a plane to bring a man out of his funk and send a woman flying without needing wings.

"Get these damn things off."

She didn't wait for a second invitation. She kicked off her shoes. The jeans and panties followed. Pressed against the cramped quarters of the space between the two seats, he'd effectively fenced her in. She couldn't move.

Her bones melted under his touch. Her open thighs welcomed him, inviting him to do as he wished. She suspected he wished to do a lot. Parting the folds of skin, he slid his index finger inside her soaked pussy. The droning of the engine and whirring of the propellers drowned out most of Lavender's whimpers and cries. Tyler expertly worked her pussy with his fingers until she almost came, then he withdrew. She protested, pissed as hell that he'd stopped. He had a habit of doing that just to torture her. Panting, she leaned back against the seat and wiped the sweat from her brow.

"Ride me." He ordered, holding his breath, most likely in hope she wouldn't balk at his alpha-male posturing.

Hesitating, she glanced over her shoulder. Tyler did, too. The pilot seemed oblivious, which amazed her. The sexual sparks arcing about the plane should've lit up the cockpit's dashboard. Maybe he'd seen it all.

With shaking hands, Lavender unzipped Tyler's jeans. "Condom?"

"Pocket."

She slid her fingers into his pocket and pulled out the square packet. Tearing it open, she rolled it down the length of his hard erection.

"Aw, honey, I love it when you do that. Now make me a happy man."

After one last uncertain glance, she straddled Tyler's thighs, facing him. Legs spread wide, she lowered herself down. He guided his hard cock into her soft pussy. Once the head penetrated her opening, her common sense and remaining modesty flew out the window and drowned in the Straits of Juan De Fuca below.

Tyler grasped her butt cheeks and pulled her down on top of him until she was fully impaled. His pubic hair abraded her smoothly shaved pussy. He shoved his hips upward and held her down at the same time, driving deeper. His blue eyes shone with passion and unrestrained lust. They shone with something else, too. Something in opposition to their claims of mutual dislike. Something she didn't want to acknowledge.

Damn, she loved the feeling of fullness, being stretched to her body's limits by his impressive cock. Every time her body managed to accommodate him.

They moved together, settling into their now-familiar rhythm, bodies slapping together. Tyler grunted with each thrust, while Lavender bit down on her lip to keep from crying out. The emotions built inside her, like a flash flood sweeping her away down the mountain. The pressure built inside her.

Lavender plummeted head first into the spell woven by the joining of their two bodies, by the depths of heat in Tyler's blue eyes, and by the inexplicable connection between them.

Denial wasn't working anymore.

It wasn't just about the sex.

* * * * *

Tyler couldn't remember ever being so turned on, and that was saying a lot considering this past month he'd spent fucking—okay screwing—Lavender in every possible location and position. He stared at her, locking his gaze with her own, as he grasped her hips and pressed her down onto his cock.

"Tyler. Ty. I need you to make my day." Her throaty whisper did more for him than any screams of passion. Damn, but he craved sex with this woman, any time, any place; he'd be there, locked and loaded like a good little soldier. All she had to do was call out his name just like she was doing right now.

Never one to disappoint a woman, Tyler held her waist in a vise-like grip. He banged her up and down on his cock in rapid succession.

He nipped at her shoulder, and she cried out, obviously beyond caring about the pilot. He pumped harder, faster, driving deep and hard with each hungry stroke. Their bodies collided in an unrestrained frenzy of slapping and thrusting. Positioning Lavender's legs over his shoulders, he drove in deeper and harder. She begged for more. Oh, yeah, his lady liked it rough at times. This happened to be one of those times. Ignoring his aching muscles and protesting cock, he rammed into her over and over. She slammed her incredible pussy down onto his dick until it ached in the most freaking incredible way.

His balls tightened, his dick jerked. Leveraging her upward, he slammed her down and ground his cock deep and high inside her. She shuddered and leaned back, pressing him even deeper. Her legs wrapped around his waist with surprising strength for one so small.

Her pussy tightened around him as he came in a fevered eruption of passion. Emptying all that he was or would be inside her, he left it all out on the field with a fervor which eluded him when it came to other aspects of his life. She shuddered on top of him and came, the incredible high written all over her face. Obviously, it was as good for her as it was for him.

He slipped into a temporary lust-induced coma. Holding her close, he whispered nonsense in her ear, terms of endearment, sweet promises of devotion, crap he never said to any woman.

He bit back the most terrifying phrase of all: *I love you.* Even as it sat on the tip of his tongue.

Buried in the haze of incredible sex, his brain played tricks on him. It had to be.

He looked up to meet the pilot's eyes. The man winked at him and went back to his business.

Chapter 22

Blown Coverage

Lavender sipped wine and swapped stories with Derek's wife, Rachel. They'd become fast friends after meeting in the bleachers earlier in the day. Nearby Tyler and Derek stood together, drinking beer and making small talk with the athletes and media gathered in the reception room following the Seattle area sports awards. For the second straight year in a row, Tyler won Athlete of the Year. He mustered up his expected panache and gave a rousing speech thanking his teammates, namely his offensive line and his receivers. Then he accepted the award on behalf of his defense, christening them as the real heroes of the season.

Lavender swelled with pride for him. It'd been a tough weekend, but he'd survived. Zach Murphy might be a thorn in his side, but the guy would goad Tyler out of his self-induced indifference or die trying. She couldn't hate the man for wanting the old Tyler back on the field even if she didn't agree with his in-your-face methods.

Between the awards and last night's plane ride, the weekend wasn't a total loss. Sex at a few thousand feet about sea level exceeded even the high expectations she'd set when it came to sex with Tyler Harris. Her man delivered once again.

Lavender froze. *Her man?* When had she started considering him her man? They weren't a couple. They couldn't be. They had too many strikes against them. They'd never be the type of couple that friends and family mentioned in the same breath as if they were one unit.

Just to torture herself, she tried linking them together in her mind.

Lavender and Tyler. What a mouthful. Vinnie and Ty. Much better.

Yeah, she liked the sounds of that. Too much. Their situation blurred her firmly held line between sex with a jock and a relationship with one. She'd be a fool to blur it even further in her mind.

Tyler interrupted her introspection by moving to her side and claiming her hand. He seemed relaxed and content for once. Rachel slid next to Derek, who hooked an arm over her shoulder and pulled her close. An unexpected twinge of jealousy shot through Lavender. She wanted what they had with a powerful surge of longing that set her back on her heels. Heaven help her if she fooled herself into thinking she'd have an emotional connection with Tyler.

"Having fun?" Tyler grinned down at her. He wrapped a lock of her hair around his big finger.

"I would be if the man of the hour asked me to dance." She gazed up at him, and her insides turned weird, all soft and sticky, like a great caramel chocolate bar left too long in the sun.

"It'd be my pleasure." He offered her his tuxedo-clad arm, and the man did look fine in his form-fitting tuxedo that emphasized his broad shoulders and hugged his fine ass.

Derek elbowed Tyler and caught his attention. "Hey, don't look now, but Coach Gerloch is headed our way."

The smile dropped off her lips. Cold fear sliced through Lavender. She snapped her head around in the direction Derek was looking.

Her father.

Tyler had promised her he wouldn't be in attendance. "Did you plan this?" So much for the chocolate bar. She glared at him, reeling from the hurt and betrayal.

"No, I promise. I didn't think he would be here." His apology was cut short as his college coach's long strides ate up the distance between them. Her father's unfathomable eyes never left her face. Tyler stepped in front of her in an instinctual protective gesture.

Oblivious, Derek's face broke into a grin at the sight of their old college coach. The two shook hands vigorously then Derek introduced him to Rachel. Expectantly, they turned to Tyler and Lavender.

Coach nodded at Ty and stuck his hand out. Tyler snubbed him, refusing to shake it. He stood taller, chin jutted out in stubborn defiance. Lavender stepped to his side, not allowing him to fight her battles. She'd handle her father.

"Good to see you, Ty." Gerloch's brow furrowed as he regarded Tyler with wary watchfulness. He turned to Lavender, the moment of truth. She'd give anything for a glass of water as her mouth dried up like a pond in a drought. She twisted her ring, the one he'd given her for her sixteenth birthday, and the only item from her father she'd kept. His quick glance downward indicated he noticed.

Brian Gerloch clutched a wine glass in his hand and swallowed. The pulse in the side of his neck throbbed. He'd gotten older since she'd last seen him. The lines on his face and gray in his hair didn't diminish his good looks. Her convictions caved slightly at the sadness in his eyes, but she shored them up and braced herself.

"Vinnie, honey, how are you?" He made a move to hug her, but Tyler pulled her against his body, coming to the rescue.

As much as she wanted to call him Brian, she couldn't bring herself to do it. "I'm fine, Dad, but you wouldn't know that, would you?" All of the hurt and anger she'd kept bottled up for years bubbled to the surface. Like a volcano building to the big eruption, the emotions had festered inside her. Derek and Rachel swapped shocked glances.

"Honey, I'm sorry. I'd like to talk to you." He slumped slightly and seemed so lost, so vulnerable, his expression so at odds with the strong, fearless man she'd known.

Emotions clogged her throat and threatened to reduce her to blubbering mass of sobbing, weak female. Exactly what she didn't want to do. Instead, she'd get the hell out of there before she embarrassed herself and gave her father a clue as to how much he'd hurt her.

"I have nothing to say to you." She turned on her spiked heel and ran from the room before she did something stupid, like forgive him.

Not waiting for the elevator, she ran down the stairwell, out the door of the hotel to the sidewalk. The rain pelted her body, drenched her evening dress, and wilted her carefully styled hair. She hailed a cab and was opening the door by the time Tyler caught her. He pulled her into his arms.

"Vinnie, where are you going?" His blue eyes brimmed with concern as he gazed down at her.

Dumb question, Harris. "Back to the island."

"I'm coming with you." The determination in his eyes didn't allow argument.

She argued anyway. "Please, Ty, I need to be alone. Let me go. I'll see you tomorrow." Her voice cracked. He raised a hand and wiped her face with his finger, even though it was damn difficult to know where the tears ended and the raindrops started.

"Are you sure?" He didn't look convinced in the least. "I can't leave you alone."

"Please. If you care even a little bit for me, give me space. Besides, if you leave in the middle of the party, that'll start more rumors."

"I'll deal with it."

"Ty, please. Stay for me. Okay? I'll be all right. I've been through this before. I appreciate your concern, but take care of yourself."

"I can't—" He clamped his hands on her shoulders.

"You can. I'll see you tomorrow. I want to go home to the island and get away from this city. You need to stay here and show the world Tyler Harris is still a force in Seattle sports."

Tyler's mouth covered hers. For a moment, she forgot what she was running from. Lavender wrenched away from him and slipped into the back seat. He let her go. "See you soon."

Tyler bent down and handed the taxi driver some cash then gazed back at her. "Do you need airfare?"

She shook her head and forced a grin. "I still have your credit card." On that note, she signaled to the taxi driver to take off. Lavender looked over her shoulder. Tyler stood in his tux on the sidewalk, rain pouring down around him. He stayed there as the Taxi drove out of sight.

Chapter 23

Block in the Back

Tyler stood in the pouring rain, not moving until Lavender's taxi turned the corner and disappeared. Riddled with guilt for not going with her when she needed him most, he walked back into the hotel lobby and shook the rain off his tux.

He'd rather follow Lavender, maybe cajole her into another round of in-flight sex, which would make both of them forget their problems, at least temporarily.

Maybe he'd leave as soon as he went back inside to grab his trophy. The press would crucify him if he left it on the table. They use it as one more piece of evidence regarding his lack of dedication, or they'd claim he drank too much to remember he'd gotten an award. Lavender was right about him staying. They'd be all over his ass for skipping out early.

At least camp was over, for now. He could crawl back to the relative obscurity of the islands and lick his wounds. It'd been another shitty day at mini-camp. He'd paced the sidelines and watched as his backup, Sam Pollard, took all the reps. The fact that he felt inclined to pace was somewhat encouraging. At least, he cared enough to be frustrated, definitely a step in the right direction.

Murphy did everything except stand on his head to make sure Pollard looked good. Under Murphy's influence, the defense missed easy tackles and let receivers beat them. Judging by the quizzical look on HughJack's face, he'd noticed their lack of effort, too. Instead of ranting on the sidelines, he observed it all, as if biding his time. Hell if Tyler knew for what, but HughJack did everything for a reason.

Tyler's uncharacteristic ineptitude and lack of desire for the game troubled Tyler more than being benched. Two plus months on the island hadn't glued those broken pieces back together. Somehow, he'd hoped mile-high sex with Lavender might help cure his woes, even perform a miracle. Instead, once the incredible high wore off, he found himself mired in doubt as the situation between them grew more complicated.

Lavender added one more complex piece to his confusing life.

Oddly enough, Tyler didn't enjoy his return to the city as much as expected. Several times during the evening, he'd checked his watch, doing a mental countdown until the limo picked them up to take them to the floatplane. He'd spent the first half of the evening, imagining getting Lavender out of her little black dress, pushing down those the thin shoulder straps and lifting up that tight little skirt to nothing underneath. Maybe a repeat of the night before. His greedy cock had signaled its approval of that plan. Then Brian Gerloch's appearance ruined what should've been a perfect night for them. The hypocrisy of the man cut deep, as Tyler witnessed firsthand the damage her father's indifference did to Vinnie.

A feeling of protectiveness overwhelmed Tyler. He wanted to do battle for Lavender and make this man pay for the emotional wounds he'd inflicted on her because of his own selfishness.

Hell, he didn't blame the guy for avoiding that controlling bitch Doris, but he did blame him for deserting his daughter. She deserved better of her father. Coach preached family and commitment, but he sure as hell didn't live it. That didn't work for Tyler.

Brian Gerloch wasn't the man Tyler thought he was. Did anyone in this world measure up with the exception of his father?

Tyler frowned. His dad was unapproachable when it came to hero material and much more deserving than a man like Gerloch. Fuck, Coach was even less of a hero than Tyler was.

Except Lavender considers me a hero. The thought warmed his heart and gave him hope.

Slipping back into the ballroom, he made a beeline for the bar and ordered a double whiskey.

A few seconds later, Derek grabbed his arm and whipped him around. "What the hell was that all about? Coach Gerloch has a daughter? He's Lavender's father?"

Rachel flanked Derek, her hand on her husband's arm and her green eyes filled with concern.

"I guess you could call him that. He donated the sperm, but not much else." Tyler threw back his drink and grabbed another off a waiter's tray. He scanned the crowd, ready to pull a disappearing act if Gerloch headed his way. He hated hiding, but it beat planting a fist in the man's face and ending up on the evening news.

Derek shook his head, in denial like Tyler had been earlier. "No fucking way."

"Oh, yeah. Big fu—flipping way. She hates him and so does her family. He abandoned her and right after her mother died. Really messed her up." Of course, Doris contributed big-time to the overall picture, but right now he could only deal with one of Lavender's dysfunctional family members at a time.

"Wow, I never pegged him as the kind to shirk his responsibilities."

"He didn't just shirk them; he acted as if they never existed."

"Well, brace yourself. He's coming our way again, and he looks none too happy."

His escape cut off, Tyler leaned nonchalantly against a wall and pretended he hadn't a care in the world. His chickenshit cousin and his wife slipped away, leaving the two men to settle their own differences.

"Who shoved a football up your ass?" Coach kept his voice low, not wanting to be heard in the crowded room. He sipped a glass of wine; his other hand shoved in his pocket. By all outside appearances, their conversation was nothing out of the ordinary. Yet, tension crackled between the two of them like two Pro-Bowl linemen facing off on fourth and inches.

"It appears you did." Tyler fisted his hands and crammed them against his sides in an attempt to keep from beating the shit out of a man he once respected. He squared up to his coach, legs slightly apart, body tense with anger. He fought the urge to wipe the arrogant expression from the asshole's face. "I've got better things to do than waste time with you."

"Harris. If you're one thing, you're straightforward. Quit beating around the proverbial bush and say what you fucking want to say. You've never been one to hold back."

"I inherited Twin Cedars. You familiar with it?"

Momentary surprise flickered in eyes. He hadn't known. "Of course, I am. I wondered what happened to that place. I guess it stayed in your family."

"Sure as hell did. Your daughter is my neighbor. I've heard all about you—the side you keep hidden."

The man's face fell, a look of profound grief sunk his features into his face. Tyler almost felt sorry for him. "I'm betting you've met my ex-wife's mother, too." Coach's shoulders slumped. In less than two seconds he became a shell of the man he once was.

"I've had the *pleasure*."

Coach rubbed the back of his neck and stared out the window at the Seattle nightscape. A muscle twitched in his jaw. "Fuck. Is nothing sacred? She destroyed my relationship with my family, my closest friends, pretty much everyone but my son. Even he was under her spell for a while. Now she's trapping my former players in her web."

"You deserted your daughter when she needed you most." Tyler refused to be swayed. The man was full of bullshit.

"I did, but not because I didn't care. By the tone of your voice, we have nothing further to talk about, you've convicted me without hearing both sides."

"What the fuck am I supposed to do?" Tyler's head pounded as his confusion battled with self-righteous anger.

"Form your own opinions once you have all the facts."

"You were my mentor, the guy I wanted to be someday. You held me up when my dad died unexpectedly. You filled in for him, kept me sane." Tyler's voice cracked. He backed up a step, no longer feeling combative, just betrayed and puzzled.

"Ty, I can't begin to explain all this. You'd never believe me if I did."

"I don't know who to believe."

"It's not a matter of believing, it's a matter of judgment. You need to weigh your experiences with me against what you've been told. You need to decide based on what you know about me as a person." Coach raised his eyes to meet Tyler's. "Listen, let's talk somewhere alone. Meet me in the bar in ten minutes?"

Tyler hesitated then nodded. He had to hear the story from his coach.

A few minutes later, Tyler hunched over his beer and waited for Coach to join him. The hotel bar was dark and private. Only a few people sat at tables scattered around the room. No one paid him any attention. That should have bothered him. It would have a few months ago, but Tyler found the privacy oddly comforting.

He didn't wait long. He'd only taken a few swigs of beer when Coach slid into the seat across from his.

"I heard about your Uncle Artie. I'm sorry. He was a great guy and a big supporter of the athletic program at WSU. So Twin Cedars is yours now? It's a beautiful place."

His coach's knowledge of Twin Cedars threw Tyler off his game. He couldn't come up with a response.

"So tell me how well you know my girl. You're not dating her, are you?" Coach raised one eyebrow and leaned forward, staring Tyler down, as if the man had a right to ask about his daughter.

"Worried?" Tyler shot back, knowing his reputation made him any father's worst nightmare.

"Wouldn't you be if you were a father?"

"Damn, I'd never let my daughter near anyone like me." Tyler chuckled and the ice between them cracked a little.

"Yeah. Are you going to be charged with a DUI?"

"Hell no. I wasn't drunk, and before you ask, no, I wasn't fu— frigging in rehab either. Drugs and alcohol are not on my extensive list of vices."

"Good to hear." Gerloch sighed, as he folded and unfolded the bar napkin. "I hoped—prayed, actually—if I ever ran into Vinnie she'd hear me out. Maybe agree to give me a second chance." His expression softened, grew tender. "She looks good. She's happy with you."

Tyler said nothing, but guilt gnawed at his gut. What made him any better than her dad? He'd desert her, too, once he returned to his life on the mainland. He wasn't any good at real relationships because the last true fairy tale couple died with his father.

"I'm betting you've gotten an earful about me from Vinnie and her grandmother, too."

"Good guess."

"Not a guess. The woman hates the air I breathe."

"That's an accurate statement."

"She never liked me when I was married to her daughter, made my life hell with all her interfering. She despised me once I got a divorce. So you've heard her stories, which explains it all."

"Don't you want to defend yourself?" Tyler popped a pretzel in his mouth and chewed. Despite it being stale and tasting like crap, he stuffed his mouth full of a few more.

"I gave up on that long ago. The woman is a master manipulator. Doesn't matter what I say, people believe her. She even turned my own family against me. I've heard all sorts of crap she's spread about me, and there's plenty I'm guessing I haven't heard."

"Then hit me with your side of the story." Tyler slouched in his seat and propped his feet on a nearby chair.

"Do you think it's a coincidence my daughter just happens to live next door to your family legacy?" Coach fidgeted with his coaster. Tyler couldn't recall ever seeing Coach fidgeting. Pacing the sidelines with pent-up energy, yeah, but fidgeting? Never.

"More like family albatross. But yeah, it did occur to me how strange fate is."

"Not fate exactly unless fate's name is Art." Coach tore a piece of the corner of the cardboard coaster then ripped it into even smaller pieces. Fidgeting, again.

Tyler sat up, dropped his feet to the floor. He signaled for another beer and leaned his elbows on the table. "You knew Uncle Art?"

"I was born and raised on that island on the very property next door to Twin Cedars. I graduated from high school on the island. My family's old homestead burnt down years ago though. I was a high school football standout, your grandfather and uncle helped me get a scholarship. When my pro career didn't pan out, I coached a high school on the mainland. By then your grandfather had died."

"I never knew my grandfather. He was at odds with my dad so we never met." Regret seeped into Tyler's voice, and he fought to keep his tone neutral. This was not about him.

"I know. That's tragic." Coach now bent and re-bent what was left of the coaster.

Tyler pushed his own coaster across the table to Gerloch. "This from a man who abandoned his daughter?"

"That's tragic, too." Coach rubbed his face with his hands and sighed. "Artie played a large role in my career. He and your grandfather were big Cougar fans and convinced the current coach at WSU to give me a chance. I took the assistant coaching job a few years before you went there. I worked my way up to head coach by the time you attended." Now all four corners of the coaster were torn. A little pile of coaster guts littered the table. Coach reached for Tyler's coaster.

"I didn't know about that connection."

"Artie didn't want you to know. He never missed one of your home games. Flew over those mountains from the San Juans for every game."

"Why didn't he contact me? My dad died before my freshman year. I was pretty messed up. I could've used someone." Tyler tried to make sense of his family dynamics and come to terms with the situation. Maybe his family did have a chink in their perfect armor.

"I tried to convince him, but he was funny like that. He pushed me to recruit you. Not that I wouldn't have anyway. Every college coach in the nation was salivating at the chance to sign you." Coach attacked the second coaster, murdering it with his bare hands.

"When you recruited me, you played on my family loyalty, how a long line of Harris's had been Cougars."

"Sure I did. Art gave me the information I needed to have one up on the other schools. Of course, it helped that your dad was an alumni there, too."

"Yeah, Dad really pushed me to attended Wazzu." All the locals called Washington State University by the nickname of Wazzu. At one time the new president of the university attempted to ban the usage of the nickname because it wasn't complementary. After a backlash, he conceded and gave it his blessing.

"I'm sorry your dad and grandfather didn't get to see you play. They'd have loved that." Coach looked up and caught Tyler staring at the pile of coaster pieces on the table. He shoved them out of the way. But his fidgeting didn't stop, pretty soon he swirled the beer in his glass around and around.

Time to steer this conversation away from Tyler's family and back to Gerloch's family. "How did your ex's mother end up with your family's homestead?"

"She didn't." Coach seemed confused. He tipped the beer up to his lips and took a good swig.

"What do you mean she didn't?"

"Not for lack of trying. Lavender's mom knew how much I loved that place, which is exactly why she went after it in the divorce." At the mention of his ex, Coach's face turned hard, like it did when his team couldn't score in the red zone.

"But it's Doris's."

"If it was hers, it would've been sold by now. She knows that I pay all the bills. She doesn't pay a damn thing."

"But Lavender pays her rent."

Gerloch shook his head and scrubbed his hands over his face. "Damn. That bitch never ceases to amaze me. She has no right to collect rent on that property. It's mine, not hers. When we divorced, I put it in trust for the kids."

Tyler didn't know whom to believe, but he knew how to find out. Once he got back to the island, he'd research Coach's claims. "Go ahead, tell me your side of the story. I've heard the ex's."

Coach stared over Tyler's head, silent for a long moment. Finally, he drew in a breath and blew it out. He picked up a wine list and bent the corners. "What's to tell? It's an old story. I'm the bastard according to Doris, never paid child support—which is bullshit—never contacted the kids—bullshit again—had a problem with alcoholism and drugs, which is why her daughter divorced me—more bullshit. We divorced because she refused to move across the state. Not to mention we fought like cats and dogs and could hardly stand each other. I tried to stay in touch with the kids. After their mom died, they begged to stay with their grandparents for the summer. Then Doris and Larry filed court papers for full custody. Our battle over the kids was destroying them. She made their lives miserable whenever I tried to see them. Tore them in two, claimed they were disloyal. No matter how I looked at it, it was a lose–lose for them and me."

Tyler signaled the waitress for a drink. "I wouldn't have let that woman win. I'd have fought her with every penny I had."

"Easy for you to say. As long as I was in the picture, Doris put the kids through hell. They were already reeling from their mother's death. I didn't want to pull them out of school and away from all their friends to move them across the state. I always sent birthday and Christmas cards and presents, called several times, but Doris claimed the kids didn't want to talk to me. Several years ago, I received a letter from Lavender telling me to go to hell, essentially."

Tyler absorbed his coach's story, feeling more confused than ever. He wanted one person to blame for this mess, but right now, he faulted all three of them.

"I respected Lavender's wishes even though it broke my heart. I haven't talked to her for years until tonight. My son—her brother—Andy, called me a few years ago, and we met. We talked. He went away for a while. Then he came back. He'd done the research and confronted his grandmother on her lies. When he chose to reconcile with me, Doris wrote him off and convinced Vinnie to do the same. Andy misses his sister and grandmother, but I can't talk sense into Doris. Her love is conditional. You're either with her or you're not. A relationship with me, the enemy, means betrayal and exile."

Closing his eyes for a moment, Coach leaned his head against the wall of the booth. Finally, he opened them and continued. "Then there's my daughter. Do you have any clue how it feels to be excluded from every facet of your child's life? I was specifically told not to attend her high school graduation. That's a memory I'll never get back. My own sister took sides and has nothing to do with Andy or me."

"That's crazy. What grandparent wouldn't want a child to have contact with a parent?"

"My new wife, Sarah, and I have asked ourselves that a hundred times. We're attending counseling as a family with Andy. There's no cure for what's wrong with Doris. It even has a label, actually several, and it's affected children of divorce for decades. But in the end the results are the same, the child is alienated from one parent, usually the non-custodial parent, and made to feel guilty and disloyal if they want a relationship with that parent. It's really a form of brainwashing. It can even go so far as to alter the child's memories of that parent."

"Are you serious?" Tyler couldn't imagine such a thing.

"Yeah, unfortunately, I'm very serious. It's way too common with children of divorce. The person doing the alienating honestly believes they're in the right. They're on a mission to do what they believe is best for the child, which makes it even more difficult to treat."

"Damn." Tyler's head spun with conflicting reactions. He needed time to weigh what his coach was telling him. He didn't have any experience with divorce in his perfect family, but he sure as hell knew how much it hurt to lose a parent.

"Look, I gave up a long time ago trying to convince anyone that this black and white situation is really gray. It's not to say I wasn't faultless in this screwed-up mess. I let my ex mother-in-law get to me. I gave up. I went away. I'd like to say I did it for the kids, but I did it for my own sanity, too. I didn't fight for them like I could have, maybe should have. I don't know if it would've changed anything or made their lives more unbearable. I suspect things would've ended up the same. I'd have still gone away so they could have some sense of peace in their lives."

Tyler scratched his pounding head, tried to fit all the pieces together to get to the real truth. "Vinnie misses you. I know she does."

"Tyler, be careful. Don't get in the middle of this. You won't win with Doris. Her hold is too strong. Let it be." Now the menu was missing corners.

"I can't." Tyler stared into his coach's stricken eyes. He saw how difficult this had been for him. "I still don't completely understand why you gave up and went away. Why you didn't fight."

"Because it hurt too much to try. Doris didn't make it easy for me, but I chose to walk away. That's on me."

"Her grandmother is so convincing."

"Andy filled me in on some of her stories. Judging by how he continues to keep me somewhat at arm's length, I'd say he's still uncertain who's telling the truth."

"Damn."

"Tyler, form your own opinions. All of this state's court records are online. Check it out for yourself. Run a background check on me. A bad ass like me should have domestic violence charges and DUIs, not to mention some kind of criminal record."

"I'll do that." Tyler shook his head as he stared at the now shredded menu.

"Will you do one last thing for me?" Coach squirmed a bit in his chair, so unlike the confident man Tyler knew and once idolized.

"I might." No way in hell would he commit to anything yet.

"Tell my daughter I love her."

Picking up the tab, Coach walked out, leaving Tyler to sort out fact from fiction.

* * * * *

Tyler's floatplane touched down at 11:58. He half expected the Brothers to be standing on the runway with watches, hoping he'd screw up. They weren't.

Pausing on the large front porch of Twin Cedars, Tyler craned his neck to see Lavender's house through the trees. The lights were out. He missed her. Too much. And they'd only been apart for a few hours. He fought the urge to go to her.

Not tonight, because for once it wasn't about him. He'd give her the space she'd requested. Besides, he had work to do.

He walked in the door of his chilly mansion. Coug sat on the arm of his leather chair and bitched his head off. After he took care of the opinionated cat, Tyler called his mother and got her out of bed. Groggy as she was, she listened to the entire sordid story about Lavender's family dysfunction. Her advice was simple. *Follow your heart. Do what you think is right but be prepared to live with the consequences.*

Tyler conference-called his sisters next. He wasn't surprised to find out they were still up at this ungodly hour. He explained the situation to them, minus the part about Coach's daughter being not just his neighbor but his lover.

Unearthing dirt and getting to the truth happened to be a hobby of theirs. Being two of the nosiest women he'd ever known with type triple-A personalities, they were on it like an all-pro defensive end on a rookie quarterback.

Instead of going to bed, Tyler did his own research. He found the county website for property information and typed in his coach's name in the search field. Brian Gerloch owned 142 Twin Cedar Lane. Not Vinnie's grandmother. Not her grandfather. But her *father*. He'd caught Doris Mead in an out-and-out lie. He suspected one of many.

Tyler rubbed his eyes and glanced at the clock. Four a.m. Shit. Yet he couldn't stop, not now.

Searching online he uncovered summaries of court records, no details. He ran a few background checks on Gerloch and came up with nothing. No protection orders, no records of domestic violence, no DUI's, no drug charges, nothing that substantiated Doris's claims. If she lied about legal issues easily proven false, what else would she lie about?

His sisters with their connections would get to the bottom of it. His job would be to figure out what to do with the information once he received it. Any way he looked at it, it wouldn't be pretty.

A sick feeling took root and grew in the pit of his stomach. This may not end well for Lavender or him.

Several hours and no sleep later, he had lots of questions and no answers.

Chapter 24

Protecting the Blind Side

When it came to Tyler Harris, Lavender embraced dishonesty—with herself.

For example, she didn't perk up when she heard his deep, teasing voice. And certainly, she would never crane her neck to get a glimpse of his to-die-for body. Nor, did she live for matching wits with him. Last of all, she'd never lay awake at night wondering where he was. Yup, definitely a first-class liar and a lousy one.

That very morning her grandmother invaded her privacy and spent the better part of the next few hours raging at her about jocks, how foolish Lavender was to fall for one—which Lavender denied—and hadn't she learned any lessons from her mother. Then Doris delivered the ultimatum: *Dump the football player or find another place to live. I'm doing this for your own good because I love you and don't want to see you hurt. I know you'll do the right thing.* The implication hung heavy between grandmother and granddaughter. I'll disown you if you don't do as I say—just like she had Andy.

Lavender didn't want to do the *right* thing, not yet. Nor did she want to lose her grandmother. After all, Doris and Larry were the only family she had left. Once Tyler headed back to the mainland, the problem would solve itself. Until then she'd keep her gram in the dark.

Lavender glanced up when the bar door opened. She'd been doing a lot of that all afternoon and evening. Tyler walked through the door, looking as male and gorgeous as ever in his usual faded jeans, scuffed cowboy boots, and well-worn, long-sleeved T-shirt. Her heart caught in her throat and took up residence. She breathed a sigh of relief. He'd been MIA since last night's disaster at the awards banquet.

Last night when Lavender had caught a seat on a floatplane just as it was about to leave Lake Union, she recognized the pilot as the same one from the night before. He recognized her. His knowing smiling indicated he'd seen more of her than she'd hoped, which only added to her misery, as fate plotted against her. The older lady sitting next to her chattered non-stop about knitting and cooking all the way back. Lavender smiled and nodded through her pain, not hearing a word the woman said.

All she'd wanted to do was curl in a little ball and cry herself sick until she'd run dry of tears and fallen asleep. A few hours later, she did just that, except for the sleep part. Then her grandmother disrupted her pity party. She cringed to think how crazed Doris would have been if she'd know about Lavender's brief encounter with Brian Gerloch.

By the time Tyler parked his fine ass on his favorite bar stool, Lavender was dragging. She poured a beer and slid it across to him. He thanked her. His steady gaze held hers as he worked his jaw, a sure sign something was on his mind.

Finally he spoke. "I'm sorry about last night. Coach wasn't supposed to be there." He leaned across the counter and took her small hand in his large calloused one. "I'd never put you through that on purpose. I hope you know that." A flicker of regret substantiated the sincerity of his apology.

Lavender looked away, choking up again. She cleared her throat but still couldn't find her voice.

A sad smile floated across his lips. "Vinnie, I'm sorry. I really am."

She nodded, pulled her hand free, and turned away, wiping at her face with a napkin. The weekend had shaken up her house of cards, and she doubted it would survive.

"You know, Vinnie, you should give him a second chance."

She turned around and faced him. "I can't. You don't have a clue."

He looked at his beer as if it held life's answers, then raised his gaze back to hers. Dark circles ringed his eyes and weariness shone there. Stress creased his handsome face. "I do have a clue. More than you can imagine."

"You talked to him after I left, didn't you?" Betrayal stabbed deep. Leave it to jocks. They always stuck together, just like her grandmother warned. Tyler didn't understand. No one understood except for her gram—according to her gram. A sliver of doubt crept past her well-shored defenses and settled deep in her gut.

Warily like a man walking through a den of snakes, Tyler spoke with quiet determination. "Yeah. There are things you should know."

"The only thing I need to know is that I love my gram, she's always been there for me, and he wasn't." Grabbing a bar rag, Lavender walked around the counter.

"Vinnie, I—" He stood and held his hands out in a gesture of surrender, looking so lost she almost caved and ran into his arms.

"Drop it." She snapped the bar rag and hit him on his thigh, dangerously close to his prized possessions. He jumped back, obviously fearing for his boys' well-being. He tried one more time by taking a half-step forward. She snapped the bar rag again. He yelped as it narrowly missed his crotch.

"What the fu—hell is wrong with you? You're nuts. Just like your effing grandmother."

Oh, low blow. By the look on his face, he regretted the words as soon as he said them.

"Get. Out." She twisted the towel in her hands.

Keeping his eyes on her, Tyler backed to the door with Lavender dogging his every step towel at the ready. He lunged out the door and slammed it so hard the windows shook.

How dare he compare her to her grandmother? She'd never be that bitter and vindictive and unforgiving.

Never.

No, not her.

Oh, crap.

The cold hand of truth wrapped its fingers around her neck, choking her. Out of site of the patrons, Lavender sank to her knees behind the bar and gripped the counter.

That's exactly what she was—just like her grandmother.

* * * * *

Tyler stood on the back porch on a rare sunny day and sipped his cup of coffee. Lavender drove out her driveway and never looked his way.

He sighed. He'd screwed up again and been an insensitive ass as usual. For two days, he'd stayed away, let her cool down.

But damn, he missed her.

He'd never worn regret well, but regret his actions he did. A lot. In fact, so much he felt like crap inside. Dredging up this stuff about her father hurt her deeply and uprooted her life. Damned if he knew whether it'd be worth it in the end for all of them.

A smart man would butt out, just as Coach warned him, but Tyler's pigheadedness outweighed his intelligence. Always had.

Tyler's father died without reconciling with his own father. Ryan died unable to say goodbye to his mother. If he'd learned anything, he'd learned life was too short for such bullshit. Too short for regrets. Better to try and fail than to regret not trying.

Maybe he should follow his own frigging advice. Live so you won't have regrets on judgment day.

And what would he regret when his ninety days on the island were up?

Tyler leaned on the railing and stared out at the peaceful bay. Sun shone on the water, and the old dock creaked from the wake of a passing motorboat. A seagull dropped an oyster on the dock to break it then dove down to collect his reward. A smile twitched at the corners of Tyler's mouth.

Smart bird.

It was a beautiful spring day, warmer than usual, and Tyler decided to take a walk around the estate and make a list of outside projects.

He liked it here. This place gave him peace. It felt like home more than his ritzy Seattle condo ever had. For two more weeks, it *was* home.

Gravel crunched in Lavender's driveway, and his heart sped up a beat. Expectantly, he swung his gaze back to her little house. Her grandmother's car turned into the driveway, as disappointment flooded through him.

While Larry sat in the car reading a newspaper, Doris walked up the front steps and tried the door. The door opened, and she disappeared into her granddaughter's house. Larry continued to read the paper, as if he expected to be there a while.

Tyler waited, expecting Doris to exit in a minute or two. She didn't. His eyes narrowed. The woman had to be up to no good. The minutes ticked by. He checked his watch. Twenty minutes passed.

Unable to stand it any longer, Tyler slipped over to Lavender's and opened the unlocked door.

With her back to him, Doris Mead rummaged through the contents of a file cabinet. Silently, Tyler watched as she picked up a folder of pictures and sorted through them. She wadded one up into a ball and tossed it in the nearby garbage can.

What the hell?

"What are you doing here?"

Doris spun around at the sound of his voice, hackles up and ready for a confrontation. "I could ask you the same thing." Her gaze drilled into his, as if a mere dumb jock could never intimidate her.

"The door was unlocked. I knew Lavender wasn't home. I'm a good neighbor and thought I'd check it out." His gaze never wavered but neither did Doris's. Like two prize fighters, they sized up each other.

"Well, you've done your good deed for today now get out." The woman pointed at the door and stepped in front of the desk in an attempt to block his view. He'd already seen what he needed to see.

"Does Lavender know you're going through her stuff?" Tyler pointed at the open file folders on the desk. "Just because you took care of her doesn't give you the right to invade her privacy any time you please."

"It's my house." Doris snarled at him like an enraged lioness.

Tyler almost grinned. Armed with his newly-discovered information, he relished having it out with this bitch. "You're not the only one who's nosy. This isn't your house. It's her house. It *was* her grandparents' house, *paternal* grandparents." He bent down, retrieved a wad of paper from the nearby wastebasket and uncrumpled it. Doris stiffened and looked ready to kick the crap out of him. He bit the inside of his cheek to stop the laughter. He had her where he wanted her.

"I wonder how this ended up in the garbage." Tyler waved a picture of Lavender and her father in front of Doris's face. It was like waving a red flag in front of an enraged bull.

"She must have thrown it away." Doris fixated on the picture in his hand. "Lavender makes bad decisions. I have to watch out for her best interests." Doris charged, lunging for the photo, but Tyler held it out of her reach, not hard to do since he towered over her by several inches.

"You mean you have to control her."

"I care about her."

Tyler shrugged, which infuriated her further. "She'll never learn to stand on her own two feet, if you keep propping her up, but then you don't want that. You want her dependent on you. You need absolute control."

"I don't have to explain my actions to you. I'm a protective, loving grandmother."

Doris's contemptuous glare didn't faze him. In fact, he kinda liked getting under her skin. "You're a selfish, narcissistic bitch."

"How dare you." She raised her hand, and Tyler braced himself for a slap across his face. Strained silence stretched between them. Tension clawed the air. The sharp sting never came. Doris lowered her hand and walked behind the table.

"Yeah, whatever. You're a piece of work, lady. You should butt out of your granddaughter's life. You're the one with issues. Lavender's relationship with her father is private between the two of them, and none of your business."

She whipped back around to face him. If she'd had a knife, she would have gutted him from neck to bowels. "Lavender doesn't need a relationship with her father, and she never will as long as I have anything to do with it. I'm only looking out for her best interests."

"You need counseling." Tyler advanced on Doris like Coug stalking a mouse. He gave her credit for not flinching. Instead, she stood up straighter and stared him down—or up actually, considering the height difference. *Crazy-assed woman.* The table separated them, which suited Tyler just fine. He preferred to keep his balls intact.

"Get out." Doris pointed toward the door. Her pudgy fingers shook with anger.

"Don't tell me to get out. You get out. Neither one of us has a right to be here without Lavender's permission."

"I have every right. She owes me rent."

"You lying bi—you should be in jail for collecting rent on a place you don't own. I know for a fact this property is owned by Brian Gerloch and put in trust for his kids."

"How dare you accuse me of dishonesty." Doris's face turned crazy-assed ugly. She clutched a vase as if preparing to throw it at him.

"I'm not accusing you at all. It's a fact."

"I'll have you out of Lavender's life."

"Just like you did her dad? I'm shocked you didn't put out a hit on him. You're that wacko."

"The man is an alcoholic. He's emotionally abusive. He's toxic to the kids. Unfortunately, Andy fell under his spell."

The door slammed open, hitting the wall with a bang. Tyler spun around as Lavender burst in the door. Chickenshit Larry slinked in behind her and stood in a dark corner of the room, out of the line of fire, and wisely keeping his mouth shut.

"What's going on here?" Lavender looked from Tyler to her grandmother. "What are you doing in my house? Both of you?"

Doris lost it. Like a hyena on crack, she bared her teeth and threw a glass vase at Tyler. Athletic as he was, he dodged it. It slammed against the wall behind him and shattered. "Get out! Get out now! You're causing problems. Brian Gerloch needs to be out of our lives for good. I hate him."

"Maybe your grandkids don't." Tyler yelled right back in his loudest quarterback voice in an attempt to be heard over Doris's high-pitched screech.

"He stole my grandson. Abandoned my granddaughter. He wasn't good enough for my daughter."

"Yeah, but really, it's all about you, isn't it?" Tyler shouted so loudly his temples throbbed.

Doris's face turned so red Tyler expected to see the top of her head blow off. "You're as toxic as he was. You drink too much. Chase women. You're no good. Just like him."

"You don't know a thing about me." Tyler's loud and booming baritone clashed with Doris's high-pitched screech, like a discordant grade school band.

Lavender jumped on a chair and screamed to get their attention. "Stop it. What's going on here?" They both started to talk at once. "One at a time. You first." She pointed at Tyler.

Smugly, Tyler winked at Doris. She clenched her fists and most likely fantasized about planting her knuckles in his mouth. Larry stepped up beside her and tried to put a restraining hand on her shoulder. She slapped his hand, and the wimp flinched.

"I saw your grandmother over here, and knew you weren't home. I found her going through your file cabinet." He pointed at the open drawer on the file cabinet and waited expectantly for Lavender's reaction, her anger at being violated by someone she trusted.

Lavender looked at her grandmother and sighed, as if this had happened before. "Gram, you know I hate that."

Open-mouthed Tyler gaped at his purple lady. "Don't you care that she's invading your privacy?"

Doris sputtered, still recovering from her fit. "And it's a good thing I did. Someone needs to watch out for you, honey. You're too susceptible to men like your father and *him*." She snatched the folder from the desk and waved it in Lavender's face. "What are *these?*"

With a dramatic flair, the crazy woman threw the folder in the air. As it fell to the ground, pictures of Lavender's father fluttered to the floor. Hands over her mouth, Lavender watched in horror, like a little girl being caught snitching candy from a candy store.

"Gram, I forgot all about those." Her apologetic tone knocked Tyler on his ass. She shot Tyler one of those *keep your mouth shut* glares.

Doris switched from crazy woman to concerned grandmother in a manner of seconds. "We've worked so hard to heal after all that man has done to tear our family apart. How could you keep such personally painful memories of him? This isn't good. I'm just concerned about you, honey, and it appears I have every right to be."

"I'm sorry, Gram." Lavender hung her head, like she'd been in the wrong. *What the fuck?*

Tyler stared in amazement at Doris. She'd somehow turned this into being about Lavender and not about her control issues.

He knew better than to involve himself in a family dispute, but he did it anyway. "There's nothing wrong with wanting to have some pictures with you and your dad." Tyler had spent several hours with his sisters yesterday going over copies of paperwork they'd dredged up, proving Doris a liar on several fronts, such as child support, ownership of this very property, and court papers filed on more than one occasion by Brian alleging that Doris interfered with visitation, countered by her claims of emotional abuse and neglect.

"Tyler, stay out of this. Please." Lavender's eyes pleaded with him to understand, to drop it. He did understand. She wanted to keep peace with her grandmother but at what cost?

Doris stepped forward, patting Lavender's hand and sucking her back in her web. "Honey, we're just concerned about you. A relationship with your father would be damaging to you. You know the man is harmful. Why would you want to see him?"

"Listen to your grandmother, Lavender. She knows what's best for you. Don't disrespect her by going against her wishes." Larry blurted out the words. He glanced at Tyler, cringed like a frightened pansy, and retreated to the safety of his corner.

Tyler shook his head in an attempt to clear it, totally baffled. Doris and Larry worked their own kind of black magic on Lavender. He'd never seen anything like it. He clamped down on his lower lip and savored the taste of blood, wishing it were theirs. He couldn't fight this battle for her. She needed to stand up to them, but she wasn't.

"Vinnie, hon, I know this is tough for you. A child naturally wants to have a relationship with her parents, but the man who donated his sperm to your existence gave up his parental rights after your mom divorced him. He never paid a penny of child support. Larry and I gave you all our love. After all we've done for you, how could you be so disloyal? We've always been here for you." Doris clenched Lavender's hand.

The stench of her flowery perfume wafted around the room, like being buried in dead flowers. Tyler hated the smell. He'd never date a woman who wore that scent. *Ever.*

He ground his teeth together until his jaw hurt. He wanted to yell, to scream, to throw things at the injustice of it all.

A knot of anger gripped his stomach in a vise. Oh, yeah, at first the manipulative witch had sucked him right into her web of hatred. He'd believed every word Doris uttered until his sisters had uncovered a shitload of information on his old coach and his ex-wife's parents. Facts don't lie. Maybe he should've minded his own business, but it'd gone way beyond that. Lavender deserved the truth, despite the possible repercussions. While his coach wasn't entirely blameless, the guy was also the victim of a vicious, vindictive grandmother obsessed with her hatred.

Turning on him like a wounded animal, Lavender pointed toward the open front door. "Go home, please. We'll discuss this later."

Tyler hesitated. The lead weight in his stomach warned he might have stepped out of bounds on the last play of the game. His arguments would make matters worse right now. Lavender needed to come to her own conclusions in her own time.

He flashed back to the last few months and how far they'd both come, how much he looked forward to being around her, how she made him see things about himself no one else ever did. She'd turned his image of himself upside down and inside out.

Lavender thought he was worthy, thought he made a difference. She didn't see him as a failure. Just by her kind words, he'd gained back a piece of his self-worth, started to see his life for what it was and how he could make it better. She'd given him hope. Even more, she'd given him something so fragile and precious, he refused to put a name to it for fear it would slip away. When she was around, he felt alive, content, passionate yet comfortable. Things seemed so right, like they'd known each other for a lifetime, not a few months. She'd taught him so much about himself without even trying. When she wasn't around, her absence left an empty hole only she could fill.

Now her expression told him to go away, and her rejection hurt like hell.

Frustrated and powerless, Tyler shot one last menacing glare at Larry and Doris. They might have sacked him for a loss on fourth down, but he'd be damned if they'd win the game.

* * * * *

Lavender sported the Super Bowl of all headaches. Her grandmother ranted for what seemed like hours, forcing Lavender to cancel her shift at the VC. Finally, Larry managed to coax Doris into leaving so they could catch the next ferry. Lavender almost felt sorry for him as he trudged out the door behind her grandmother, who still hadn't stopped screeching.

Angry, frustrated, and looking for someone to blame, she sprinted across the field to Tyler's house. She'd set him straight on getting involved in this mess between her grandmother and father. She'd managed to keep peace with Doris—no easy feat—until Tyler came into their lives. Now he'd sliced open those old wounds, and there'd be hell to pay for months to come.

Not bothering to knock or ring the doorbell, Lavender wrenched Tyler's front door open. She stalked down the hallway into the den. He sat in his chair, drinking a beer, and watching a basketball game, as if he hadn't a care in the world. Cougar was draped across his chest.

Tyler glanced up at her, his expression closed and unreadable. "Hey."

"You shouldn't have interfered."

"What? And let her dig through your stuff? What right does she have?" Tyler sat up, and Coug slid off his lap. Irritated, the cat shot a glare at Lavender like it was her fault.

"She owns the place, and I'm two months behind on my rent. That gives her the right." She hated making excuses for her grandmother's behavior, but criticism of her gram always made her defensive. *Maybe because the truth hurt?*

"Well, guess what, honey? She doesn't own the place. Your father does. It's in trust for you and your brother. She has no right to charge you anything."

"You're lying." Lavender couldn't believe his words. Gram wouldn't deceive her that badly. Would she go that far? Lavender stomach churned and her throat went dry as a cornfield in a drought. Buying time to think, she crossed to his bar and poured a glass of water.

Tyler stood up. Instead of approaching her, he parked his fine body in front of the window. "Why would I lie? What would be in it for me?"

"You don't like my grandmother, and you've taken my father's side. Jocks stick together."

"Yeah, you're right, we do. And we're all assholes." His blue eyes froze to ice, even as he blasted her with his angry words.

"All you want is sex." She pushed him, halfway hoping he'd deny her accusations. "My grandmother knows all about guys like you. I should've listened to her."

"Your grandmother doesn't know shit, unless you're referring to pure, hateful vindictiveness. She wrote the book on that." The muscles in his arms bulged, probably from the stress of holding his body under control, but he didn't dispute the all-you-want-is-sex part. She died a little inside.

"Don't badmouth my grandmother. My father's filled you full of shit." Intense pain clawed at her gut, making her a little nauseous. Her head ached from confusion and fear—fear she might be wrong.

Tyler lowered his voice. "Maybe she's the one who's full of shit. I talked to your father after the awards banquet. I got a totally different story from him—one that checks out." A hint of regret mixed with sadness burrowed into the grim lines around his mouth.

Lavender fought the urge to throw herself in the comfort of his strong arms and let him make the pain go away. Instead, she rose again to her grandmother's defense, even as doubts clogged her thought processes. She'd been defending her grandmother for so long it came as second nature. "He doesn't give a damn about me. He hates my grandmother. What better way to hurt her than to take me away from her. My grandmother is a saint. I love her, even with all her faults."

Tyler softened his tone, tempering it with sympathy, which pulled the plug on her temper. "I'm not questioning your love for your grandmother. I know you love her. I'm not trying to drive a wedge between the two of you. I would never do that. It's not healthy anymore than it's healthy for you to be forced to pick between your father and grandparents."

Pretty insightful words from a guy who claimed to be selfish and uninvolved.

"My dad was never home. It was always football, football, football." Lavender paused, wiped at her eyes and blundered forward. Despite the strength of her words, her resolve stumbled like a blind man in an unfamiliar place.

Tyler cocked his head as if listening intently. He caught her hand and squeezed it, his touch gentle and almost caring. He nodded for her to continue. Lavender gripped his hand, and stared at the glass in her other hand.

"Here's something you don't know about me. I played sports." She lifted her gaze, wanting to gauge his reaction.

He opened his mouth like a fish, but no words came out.

"Don't look so shocked. I was a female jock, assured of getting a softball scholarship to a D-1 school. When my dad got the big job, he left us in Mt. Vernon and never looked back. Then Mom died. Dad promised he'd come get us, but he never did. He stayed in touch for a while then the calls became non-existent." Her voice wavered then cracked. She paused, took a sip of water, and drew strength from his fingers wrapped around her hand.

"He didn't exercise his visitation, too much bother I guess. I went into a downward spiral, partying, drugs, drinking. I quit softball, never played another game. I lost all chance of a scholarship. My grades tanked. I went from a top student to barely graduating from high school. Through it all, Gram was there. When I hit rock-bottom, they picked me up and got me straightened out. I owe her my loyalty, and I owe Grandpa. They sacrificed their sanity for me." There she'd said it, gotten it all out. A couple tears slipped down her cheeks. She ignored them.

"You don't have to defend your grandmother to me. I'm not on your dad's side or your grandmother's side. I'm on your side, and your side of the story tells me that you miss your dad. It's time to forgive both of them." Tyler wiped away her tears with the pad of his thumb. She leaned into him without thinking.

"My grandmother doesn't need my forgiveness."

"She should." Tyler shook his head, weariness etched lines into his face she'd never noticed before.

"What's that supposed to mean?"

"It means this black and white situation is neither. The villain in this scene is much more complicated, and you deserve to know the truth. Your grandmother made it so difficult for your dad; he went away rather than put you and your brother in the middle of a contentious situation. I'm not excusing his part in this, but she played a part, too."

"I don't want to hear this. My grandmother has always had my best interests at heart." Despite her words, the cold hand of truth clutched her throat, almost strangling her. Yanking free of Tyler's grasp, she covered her face with her hands.

"Are you certain of that? I think you're afraid she'll cut you out of her life just like your brother. Her love is conditional—*Do this for me, and I'll love you. Don't do this, and I won't.* That's bullshit. Pure and simple. Healthy parents or grandparents encourage their children to have a relationship with the other parent. They don't do their best to poison it."

"You don't know anything." Lavender hugged herself, praying she didn't throw up.

"You're an animal lover with no animals. I know you walk on eggshells around her. You pretend to be a rebel on the surface but it's all show. Underneath, you conform to everything she asks you."

"You're so wrong." Her stomach churned and bile rose in her throat, as the obvious truth blindsided her.

Tyler crossed to the antique roll-top desk in the corner of the large room. He opened it and removed a large manila envelope.

"Take a look at this stuff. My sisters did some research for me. It's all here. The records for child support your grandmother claimed your father didn't pay, the deed on the property, all of it." Tyler shoved the envelope into her hands.

Lavender stared at the bulging envelope. Her hands shook. If she looked inside, life as she'd come to know it might change forever. Truths she took as the gospel might be shaken to their very foundations.

She couldn't look, couldn't take that step.

She stalked to the fire, and tossed the alleged damning evidence into the flames. Whirling around, she rubbed her hands together, squared her shoulders, and spoke clearly. "That's the last I want to hear of this subject. Please drop it. It's too painful for me right now. I'm not ready."

His face changed. The hard rigid lines gave way to affectionate concern. He managed a sad smile, but his brow furrowed with worry. "I'm sorry." He moved close to her.

Those two little words came across as so heartfelt, so genuine, Lavender's heart wrenched and tears flowed down her cheeks. Obviously assuming she was crying because of her family drama, Tyler wrapped her in his strong arms. She tried to push him away, but he didn't budge. He rubbed her back with gentle hands and murmured words of comfort in her ear. His husky voice tickled her insides and uninvited tenderness seeped to the surface. Caving, she buried her head in his chest and sobbed for all she'd lost and was about to lose in her life, most of all for this man.

Sure, she'd been pissed as hell at him for interfering, for shaking things up, for dredging up painful memories, but he'd done it with the best of intentions. A woman couldn't hate a man for caring.

Caring?

He cared? Well, of course, he cared. At least a little because as much as she tried to convince herself otherwise, Tyler Harris was a good guy. Sure, he had his asshole moments like when he baited her grandmother. Despite his best or worst intentions, the nice guy shone through. She almost laughed as she clung to him. He'd be appalled at how well she saw through him, so she'd keep it her little secret.

Lavender breathed in the alluring scent of soap and man. She could get used to not being so strong all the time and letting him carry the load for a little while.

Yet, precious times like these were fleeting and temporary. The man caused as much mayhem in her life as he did joy. She didn't need the brand of rollercoaster romance that happened to be Tyler's signature.

Still, for tonight and the next few days, she'd throw her hands in the air and scream for the thrill of it as that rollercoaster careened around the corners on the wildest ride of her lifetime. And she needed that wild ride right now so she could forget the pain.

"Just make me feel better. Please."

For a second, Tyler almost looked like he would turn her down, but his little head must have won the battle. Instead, he grabbed her and threw her over his shoulder as if her weight was insignificant. From her position, she zeroed in on his fine ass and took advantage of the situation. Raising her hand, she smacked one firm butt cheek with the palm of her hand. His fingers tightened around her thighs in response.

"You're going to regret that." He put his growled threat into action and smacked her butt. She yelped and tried to wiggle out of his grasp. Impossible. The man's muscles held like a steel trap. He smacked her again.

"You know I like that."

"I'm always one to give a lady what she likes."

"Is that a promise?"

"You bet your sweet ass it is."

And just like that the queen of denial mounted her throne and did what she did best—avoided the real problems in her life and substituted sex as a short-term solution.

A long-term resolution would have to wait for another day.

Chapter 25

The End Run

Tyler stared beyond the protected Outlaw Bay to the waters of Hazard Channel as he had countless times before.

His eyes didn't register the beauty as his thoughts focused inward.

He wanted to rip his hair out by the roots in frustration. He couldn't recall dealing with a weirder situation, and he'd had some doozies over the years. He didn't know how to get through to Lavender. Her grandmother was hopeless, but the Lavender he'd come to know and lo—

Love?

Tyler slammed the brakes on that thought.

Cass had been a fixture in his life for years, yet he'd never called what they had together love. In fact, he'd never told Cass he'd loved her, not even when he sort of proposed. Could he have fallen in love with Lavender, an obnoxious, pixy-sized woman with a passionate temper and fire red hair? Hell, if he stuck around her much longer, he'd have major back problems from bending down all the time. Her head barely came to his midsection. A wicked grin slid across his face. Of course, her height did have its advantages.

Oh, yeah, they enjoyed each other's company in and out of bed. The bantering between them made life exciting and unpredictable. She kept Tyler on his toes. They had a lot in common. Animals took up a soft spot in both their hearts. Come to find out, Lavender was actually a sports fan, too, and quite knowledgeable, even though she denied her interest in sports, especially football, every step of the way.

Last night had thrown him off his game completely. He'd bargained for some down-and-dirty sex and had not been disappointed. Yet, somewhere in all the grunting, sweating, thrusting, and sliding, a seed of compassion took root. He didn't quite know what they'd planted, only that even as they screwed each other's brains out, this thing sprouted and grew, leaving him wrapped in a blanket of warm contentment for hours afterward.

When he finally came down out of the stratosphere and regained his senses, he attempted to convince his brain—both of them—the entire thing had to be a fluke, a bi-product of mind-blowing sex and nothing of substance, not like the utter devotion he'd witnessed over the years between his parents.

Still, he conceded Lavender had given him something special. He was bound and determined to give as good as he got.

In a few days he could leave the island for good, head back to the city with all its excitement and bustle, so many things to do and places to go.

His gaze settled on the bay and the channel beyond it, the same bay his great-great grandparents sailed into so many years ago and decided to stay. They'd raised their children here. They'd laughed, loved, and cried here. Hell, they'd even bootlegged whiskey here back in the prohibition days. And they'd buried their dead. Oh, yeah, he'd found the headstones of the small overgrown family cemetery a week or so ago. He wondered about the people buried there. What would they think of his plans to destroy his legacy? Their love of this place was coded in his DNA.

His decision to sell seemed so simple almost three months ago. He swallowed past the lump in his throat. Once he returned to Seattle and his old life, he'd gain some needed perspective.

But for now, he wasn't in any hurry to move back to the mainland. Lavender's birthday was coming up, the same day his ninety-day exile ended, a weird coincidence not wasted on him. He wanted it to be special, one last hurrah before they parted ways, and they had to part ways. Tyler hated long-distance romances. He needed his woman available when the urge struck and not on some island in the middle of fu—effing nowhere.

Still...

Crap. Was this how love felt? This inexplicable need for another person, to be so close that even when physically separated she was still there. In his heart.

Tyler pressed his forehead against the cool window, striving to clear his head of all these contradictory thoughts. As a man schooled in snap decisions, he'd never been so conflicted. He'd figure out his future when the moment presented itself, and trust his instincts. They'd served him well in the past. But for now, he had some planning to do for a birthday she'd never forget.

He knew exactly the perfect present. She may not appreciate it at first. But if he knew his Lavender, she'd thank him later, once the smoke cleared. Her initial reaction wouldn't be pretty, but he was a big guy, and he'd handle it, even if he couldn't handle five geriatric men with no manners and an orange tabby cat.

Speaking of the devils themselves.

Tyler sighed, as Homer and Jim sauntered into his den. "Don't you two know how to knock?"

"Why should we knock?" Jim squinted at him and mistook the cat for a pillow. Yowling in protest, Cougar slid out from under Jim, shook himself off, and glared at the old man over his shoulder.

"So for what reason did you break into my house this time?" Tyler adopted a long-suffering expression normally reserved when addressing his sisters.

The two men looked at each other, as if they'd forgotten why they were harassing him. Tyler waited them out as they consulted with each other in whispers.

Finally Jim turned back to him. "We want you to keep this place."

"Really?" Tyler suppressed the urge to laugh and had no clue what he found so funny.

Homer ran a hand over the now-finished banister, gleaming with a fresh coat of varnish. "I can offer my services to oversee the renovations."

"Okay, but why?"

Again that quick look between the two men. "We like you. This island needs some young blood and so does Twin Cedars. The Harrises have long been a fixture around here. It's time for the next generation to pick up the torch."

"You make it sound like an Olympic event."

"Restoring this place might as well be."

They'd get no argument from Tyler on that point.

"Artie had a method to his madness when he left the place to you. He knew if he forced you to stay here, you'd fall in love with it like he had, like your grandfather and your father had. And like all your ancestors before them." Jim bent down to study the banister more closely. "Wasn't this orange?"

"Lime green." Tyler corrected him.

"If he'd left it to us, we would have sold it or lost it. It would've been bulldozed. Artie didn't want that, but he couldn't afford to restore it either. You can."

Could he afford it? Yeah, probably if he handled his money better, played five more years, quit wasting his life on parties, women, and material stuff that didn't make him feel any better.

Tyler didn't react on the outside, but on the inside, he staggered backward as if punched in the gut.

He couldn't sell Twin Cedars.

It needed to stay in his family and generations of Harrises to come. His sly old uncle had known exactly what he was doing when he'd written the ninety-day requirement into the will. Uncle Art knew him better than he'd known himself.

"So you guys want to help me out with renovations?"

"Well, when we have time. The Widow Chandler's been giving me the eye. At my age a guy goes for the bird in the hand." Homer winked at him and slicked back his hair, preening like a peacock in the antique mirror hanging on the wall.

"She's not giving you the eye; she's giving me the eye." Jim pushed him out of the way to squint at the mirror, even though Tyler doubted he could actually see his reflection.

"It's me she's sweet on. What would she want with an old coot like you?" Homer pushed back and postured in front of the mirror, flexing non-existent muscles in his skinny arms.

"You're both old coots." Tyler settled the argument, or so he thought. No such luck.

Both men ignored Tyler and continued their arguing over who would win the favors of some blue-haired old lady. Tyler cranked the sound on the television and settled into his chair, listening to the sounds of home.

Tyler grinned, finally grasping the true value of the important things in his life. Things he'd denied himself in the past as being unworthy. Things money couldn't buy. Putting his heart on the line scared the crap out of him, but he'd handle the fear and be a better man for it.

Ryan would approve, and so would Tyler's dad.

* * * * *

Bundled in a heavy sweatshirt, Lavender leaned her head on Tyler's broad shoulder. The dock rocked gently underneath them as the current from the incoming tide pushed against the floats. A thick quilt protected them from splinters and offered some cushion from the wood planks. Stars twinkled in the night sky and frogs croaked cheerfully in a nearby pond.

A crisp breeze scented the spring air with a combination of fir trees and salt water. A bottle of wine sat between them, along with two wine glasses. Tyler draped his arm across Lavender's shoulders, the gesture seemed casual, yet a niggling feeling warned Lavender it was more than that.

She saw herself sitting here with this man on this dock through all the seasons until their hair turned gray and their wrinkled faces attested to the happy life they'd led together.

In her wildest dreams.

She recognized an illusion when it bit her in the butt. Her recent battles with Tyler regarding her family opened a void between them and rammed home the impossibility of anything lasting. Despite the inevitable hanging over them, she embraced the moment as if it might be their last, because some intuitive part of her understood it was.

Even though she'd fallen in love with the loveable asshole.

In a few days, he'd leave her and her shattered heart for the mainland and his old life. She'd stay here and dream of things that could've been and never would be. And she'd do so without regrets because a life without risks wasn't much of a life at all. She'd cherish every moment they had together. Tonight the beauty of the islands weaved its magic around her heart. The moon's soft glow bathed them in a golden light. Breathing life into their doomed relationship, she'd cherish this fleeting moment in her life forever. Tyler sipped his wine, seemingly content to just be and not ruin the spell with shallow words and unrealistic promises. His body warmth flowed through him into her, keeping her cozy on this cool spring night.

"Are you going back to football?"

"I don't know what else to do." He stared out at the water, but a muscle jerked in his jaw, betraying how conflicted he still was on that subject.

"Tyler, do what you love for the right reason, or you'll no longer love it." She touched his strong jaw with a finger and let it bump along his ever-present stubble. "What's the reason you play football, Ty? Is it the money, the fame, or something else?"

He mulled her question over for a minute, as if trying to figure out the answer. "I've never wanted to do anything else. It's always been football as long as I can remember. When I was a toddler I slept with a football. When I was in junior high school, I watched every game I could on TV. My dad and I would analyze every play, every move made by a quarterback. In high school, I knew I wasn't just good; I was one of the best. Call me arrogant, but a top-level athlete better be arrogant on the field because once you get to the pros, everyone's operating with essentially the same skill set and athletic ability. So the other ninety percent is mental."

"And that's been your problem. The mental."

"Yeah, lately. Since Ryan." His voice sounded choked, as if a vise squeezed his heart.

"Tell me about Ryan." She entwined her fingers with his.

Tyler tensed and stared out at the water. He blew out a long breath, seemed to consider his options, then answered. "I never let myself get involved, especially with kids. I get tons of requests to see kids, especially sick kids. I usually find time but keep it on a superficial level. Ryan wasn't superficial, and his death made me question everything I'd ever believed about myself. When my life is over, can I honestly say I've done my very best and used the tools and talents at my disposal to make other people's lives richer? Would this world be improved because I'd been in it for a short time? But I'm off subject. You asked about Ryan."

Lavender nodded. He gripped her shoulder tighter.

"Ryan was a high school quarterback and a good one. Derek got to know him through Mitch."

"Mitch?"

"Rachel's brother. Mitch coached the kid in high school, an up and coming star. Several months before his senior year, Ryan was diagnosed with cancer and given six months to live. When he was pretty much wheelchair bound, his mother, a local barfly and worse, skipped out on him. None of us knew he was living alone until Ryan fell out of his wheelchair and couldn't get back up. He called Derek to rescue him. After that, Mitch took Ryan in. The team adopted him. The players' wives took turns keeping an eye on him during the day and the players hung out with him in the evening. He became everyone's little brother, especially for Derek and me."

"I didn't know. I mean I'd heard about Ryan, but I didn't know how involved the team was with him."

"He was the little brother I never had and always wanted. I got pretty attached to the kid. He asked me to find his mother so he could say goodbye to her. I found her stripping in Vegas. She refused to come back." Tyler's voice cracked. He rubbed his hands over his face. "The team was just walking off the flight after winning the division title, next stop the Super Bowl when we got the call. Ryan was in the hospital for one last time. He wouldn't make it out. Derek and I raced there as did the rest of the team. The kid died a few minutes later. I got to say good bye to him. He told me he loved me and that he saw through me, that I did care about people. I didn't know how to take that. I felt like a fake. I died that day, too, but I pushed through the next two weeks in a haze, a man on a mission. I swore we'd win the Super Bowl for Ryan or die trying. I've never wanted anything so badly in all my life."

Tyler looked at her, his eyes misty with unshed tears. He shook his head, as if still in denial Ryan had died. "I think I used all my try in that game because after it was over every ounce of emotion drained out of me and left this big, empty hole nothing could fill. Not football. Not friends. Not women. Nothing."

She opened her mouth to talk but he held up a hand to silence her. Tyler faced her, taking both her hands in his. He stared at her as if he'd never really seen her before. Tenderness shone in his eyes and left her lightheaded. "Until I met you."

Lavender choked with sadness and pride for this stubborn, wonderful man. "Tyler, I—"

"No, listen. At first, you flat-out pissed me off, but at least it was something. Then there was the lust. Now that was really something." He almost smiled. "But somewhere along the line it became so much more than that. More than I bargained for. You gave me back a piece of what was missing. You made me see that even though I don't put my life on the line, I can still make a difference. I can influence so many people. I can be the man my father always wanted me to be. You did that for me. You gave me purpose."

"I'm happy for you, but I didn't do it. You did that for yourself."

"No, you showed the way, like a beacon in the night. You're good for me. I like having you around."

"This ends when you leave the island." Lavender held her breath, prayed for an argument from him, a declaration of how much she meant. He wanted her in his bed and to be his companion, but love didn't enter into it. She couldn't be with him on a long-term basis if he didn't love her. She needed so much more from him than he was willing to give because somewhere in the past few months she'd fallen in love with him despite her best intentions and denial no longer made the feelings go away.

It was what it was.

"We don't have to end it." His hopeful expression almost changed her mind, but she stuck to her guns.

"No, you were right the first time. We've been down this road before. It won't work for so many reasons. Let's start with location and end with family—as in mine can't stand you." Even as she outlined all the reasons it wouldn't work, she hoped he'd convince her it would, but he didn't.

Tyler focused his gaze back on the water. The moonlight reflected off his handsome face, which seemed to have turned to granite once more.

Lavender buried her face in his tense shoulder and wished life could be different, that somehow a little island magic could survive and show them the way.

She didn't know how that could be possible.

* * * * *

Tyler sighed and tucked Lavender against his side. He closed his eyes and let his intuition make the decision. The answer came through loud and clear. He wanted to keep Lavender in his life. For how long, he didn't know.

He thought he loved her but couldn't say the words. Not yet. Not until he was sure.

Sure, he'd resisted and been the one to insist their relationship had to end, but this wouldn't be the first time he changed his game plan when the pending outcome didn't work for him. He didn't want to let her go. He'd been stubborn and stupid. For once, he'd take the emotional risk and lay it on the line tomorrow night on Lavender's birthday.

Fate dealt him an odd hand. What better way to celebrate the end of his exile and the beginning or something new than to give Lavender the best gift he could think of and one money couldn't buy? He couldn't wait to see the look on her face. She'd steered him back onto the right path, he'd give her the one thing she wanted most.

Tonight was theirs. Tomorrow night belonged to their future. A smile tugged at the corners of his mouth. Oh, she'd be pissed, but she'd get over it. It'd all work out because he'd make it work out, just like he'd made the team win games by carrying them on his back. He was a strong guy. He could handle it.

Since nothing he said seemed to come out right, tonight he'd show her how much she meant to him in the only way he knew how.

Lifting her chin with a finger, he stared down at her. The sadness in her eyes struck him like a blow to his heart. She'd accepted their fate, he hadn't and wouldn't. Not without a fight.

He brought his mouth down to hers. Soft and gentle, he moved his lips across hers. With feather light kisses he tasted her, breathed in the lavender scent surrounding her as it mingled with the fresh scent of the islands. Scents he'd never forget. They whirled around him like a magical spell, absorbing his cynicism and creating a soft layer of comfort and belonging. He hadn't belonged anywhere in a long time, but he did here.

Water lapped against the pilings of the dock and rocked them gently. She opened her mouth, and he accepted the invitation. When she tried to ratchet up the desire, he held back. Tonight wasn't about animal lust; it was about tender, sweet emotions. Holding her face between his two hands, he took his time tasting her lips, exploring her mouth, teasing her tongue. She pressed against him, wanting more just like he wanted more. Just not the kind of "more" she assumed he wanted.

He'd lower his defenses, show her how much she meant to him because the words wouldn't do his feelings justice.

Tyler lay her down on the blanket, pushed up her sweater, unhooked her bra. Freeing her nipples, he bent to the task. She moaned underneath him as he slowly kissed his way from her neck to her nipples, like a connoisseur of fine wine, he took his time. Her soft skin felt like satin against his tongue. Her sweet scent filled his nostrils and gave him a heady thrill. Closing her eyes, Lavender wriggled and threaded her fingers through his hair. She tried to push him into something harder and faster, but not tonight. Nope, tonight was all about slow and easy.

Tonight was about them.

Tyler sought her mouth, his kisses gentle, yet powerful. She held him close. Her legs wrapped around his waist. Her heels dug into his butt. He floated on a cloud somewhere, as the dock swayed. He slipped his tongue in her mouth and explored the moist recesses.

Sliding his hands down her sides, he fumbled for the button on her jeans, unfastened it, and pulled down her zipper. She helped him out by lifting her ass off the blanket and pulling her jeans down those shapely legs of hers. He slid her underwear off and sat back on his heels. Damn, but she was a fine sight in the light of the moon.

She gazed up at him. Her eyes sparkled with a sheer joy of living. His lips kicked up into an answering smile.

"You next, jock boy."

Tyler nodded and shucked his own jeans and underwear in a single move. He slipped the condom out of his pocket and slid it onto his rock-hard cock. He lowered his body over hers and slid his cock into her with excruciating slowness. He set a leisurely pace, determined to keep it gentle and show her what tender really felt like. He controlled his breathing at the same pace as his measured thrusts. Her walls hugged his erection, milked it, coaxed him to go faster. Tyler resisted. He stayed with the pace he'd set.

Almost completely out then slide back in with deliberate, unhurried strokes. Then he'd hold himself deep inside for a beat. Or two. Or three. And start the process all over again.

He strummed her body with sensuous music like a well-played violin. He stroked her in places he'd never tried before. Her body told him all he needed to know. A thin, silken thread joined them, united them. One mind. One body. One mind-blowing natural high.

Oh, man, he'd never felt such a connection to another living being. Not like this. Her breathing became his breathing. Her needs were his wants. Her body mirrored his body. Their blood mingled and flowed in each other's veins.

They clung to each other, heading to the stars and beyond. As he thrust a final time, and his released followed, he took her with him. They floated away, wrapped in bliss and contentment.

This was it, that thing his parents had together for so many years, that piece of life he'd assumed would always elude him. Yet, here it was.

With Lavender.

Chapter 26

Clashing Helmets

The next night Lavender opened the door to her little house. Tyler dwarfed her entryway with his size and presence. Outside, rain battered the single-paned windows, while wind rattled the walls. Water dripped down Tyler's face and matted his hair to his head.

She couldn't stop the huge smile on her face. She'd never been one to take sex slow and gentle, but after last night, hard and raunchy might be vastly overrated. He'd shown her a place she'd never imagined existed, swept her into an ecstasy so sensual she felt as if they'd left their bodies and the earth behind. For a moment that lasted forever, yet didn't last long enough, she bonded with Tyler, soul to soul. She saw his hopes, his fears, his dreams, and she knew him like she'd never known anyone.

Then it was over.

And she wished that it could work, wished they could find a way to make it work. A girl shouldn't give up on chemistry like this. And now it was her birthday and his ninetieth day, both causes for celebration and mourning. He'd be free to leave now.

Lavender threw her arms around the waist of the gorgeous man gracing her doorway. "Hi, baby, I missed you."

He grinned, as he literally bounced on the balls of his feet. "It's only been what a few hours or so."

"Too long." She sounded like a sappy teenager in the first throes of puppy love, but she didn't give a shit.

"Happy birthday, Lavender. I have a surprise for you."

She caught a flicker of uncertainty in his eyes. Holding her breath, she almost expected him to drop to one knee and profess his undying love like any good prince charming. Only Tyler didn't drop to one knee, didn't turn into a fairy tale prince. Instead, he moved to one side.

And her prince became the worst kind of frog.

Lavender looked beyond Tyler to the man who stood behind him on her front porch. Her stomach lurched. Her knees wobbled. He heart stopped beating. She grabbed the back of the chair and froze, unable to move, to talk, to think. Still grinning and oblivious, Tyler motioned to the hesitant man at his side. The two men entered her house, uninvited. Her legs refused to function. Her voice deserted her.

The door clicked shut, sealing her inside with the man she never wanted to see again in her life, or so she told herself.

Her father.

With the exception of those few fleeting seconds at the awards banquet, she hadn't seen him in years, except on a television screen during a football game. He looked older, more tired, sadder. A million images flashed through her brain: his laughing eyes as he told his infamously corny jokes, sitting in his lap as he read her a bedtime story, watching him roam the sidelines coaching his team, and shouting encouragement to her from the stands as she stepped up to bat.

She shut out the pleasant memories and focused on the pain of a father who'd missed her graduation, ignored her calls, disappeared from her life when she needed him most, and turned her brother against her and her grandparents.

Her next coherent thought involved murder. Tyler Harris was her intended victim.

"Happy birthday, Lavender," Tyler announced in his big, booming voice. His grin collapsed into a confused grimace as he took note of her scowl.

"Vinnie. Happy birthday." Brian Gerloch stepped forward, rubbing his hands on his jeans then holding his arms out to her. His fingers shook slightly. "Andy says hi. He'd like to see you."

Lavender backed away from his outstretched arms. "What are you doing here?"

He dropped his arms. "Tyler invited me." He continued to smile, but it stopped south of his eyes.

She whipped around, finding it easier to take her wrath out on Tyler. "How dare you butt into my business. *Again.*"

"Don't blame him. It was my idea." Her father started to step forward but the look on her face appeared to stop him.

She truly doubted Brian Gerloch concocted this asinine plan, especially considering the guilt etched across Tyler's face. "You're not welcome here. Ever."

"I just want a few moments to talk. To explain myself." Her father stood his ground, which angered her all the more.

"No, it's too late for that, *Brian.*"

He cringed at the way she said his name with such venom. Her hard heart cracked a bit. Her father looked so pathetic, so lost, so not in control. She'd never seen him like this. Fighting her reaction to this man she'd once called "Daddy," she shored up her defenses.

Lavender shot a murderous glance at Tyler who shifted his weight from one foot to the other, his eyes hooded and his mouth pressed in a tight, firm line.

"Please, honey, just hear me out. Can you find some room for a little forgiveness?" Brian laid his pride at her feet like a sacrificial lamb.

"Not now. Not yet. I'm not ready." She resisted, even as she longed to hear his story.

"Lavender, just listen to what he has to say." Tyler, the traitorous bastard, reached out to her.

"Butt out. You've interfered enough." She turned on Tyler then back to her father. "You gave up the right for forgiveness years ago."

The man sighed and ran his fingers through his damp hair. "You're too much like your grandmother."

"I am not." She shuddered inside, fearing he might be right.

Brian slumped slightly and backed up a few steps. "This was a mistake."

"You're damn right it was a mistake." Lavender twisted her ring until her finger ached. How could Tyler do this to her?

"Look, honey, I know I wasn't there. I admit I gave up to easily. I didn't fight for you like I should have. I just don't know if it would've turned out any differently if I had. I didn't want to put you and your brother in the middle of a contentious situation. It would've torn you in two. So I backed off. I honestly don't think it would've worked out any better if I'd fought. I think either way you'd end up hating me. I hoped someday you'd come around, ask to hear my side. Your brother did." Her father stared down at his feet, but not before she caught the stark and vivid pain in his eyes.

"Yeah, look where it got him. He's lost his grandparents and a sister." She lashed out like a wounded animal, hating herself for being vindictive like her grandmother, yet enjoying her power in a perverse way.

"Andy shouldn't have to lose anyone. Neither should you. There's room for both of us in your lives. No parent should make a child feel like they have to choose."

"My grandmother did the best she could. You deserted us."

His face fell. He gnawed on his lower lip and closed his eyes for a moment. "I didn't. Believe me, I didn't." He held a large envelope out to her. She ignored it. "If you'd only take the time to look at the items in here."

"I'm not interested." She crossed her arms over her chest and hugged herself tight, but nothing eased the ache of her broken heart.

Brian laid the envelope on the table. Lavender ignored it.

The door crashed open, and Doris Mead threw herself into the room and at Brian like a crazed she-wolf. Larry was on her heels and grabbed her before she made contact. Lavender backed up a step, while Tyler watched Doris with wary concern.

"How dare you show up here and try to lure my granddaughter away with your lies. You're no-good, a dead-beat dad. Get out of here. Now!" She flailed her arms and struggled to get free of Larry's hold. No way was her grandfather letting go of his wife.

"You're kicking me out of my own house?" Brian stood his ground, facing his ex mother-in-law.

What? His house? Could it be true?

"It's not your house. My daughter got it in the divorce." Doris visibly controlled herself and elbowed Larry. He released her but kept one hand on her arm. She stood up straight and took a few steps until she was only a foot or two from Brian. She glared up at him.

"That's a lie, and you know it, Doris. It's in trust for the kids." Brian held his voice steady. Lavender grudgingly admired his remarkable restraint.

Larry swallowed and tightened his fingers into a death grip on Doris's arm. Lavender stared at her grandmother's face, twisted and ugly with hatred. In her rage, she looked inhuman, like a wild animal. Lavender never wanted to look like that.

She needed to diffuse the situation and fast before it escalated into something even uglier, if that were possible. She turned to her father. "Please, you need to go." Lavender couldn't take the conflict. She never could. Her grandmother's relentless harping usually wore her down until she did as the woman wanted just to buy a little peace in her life. This time would be no different.

"I'll leave, but honey, I love you. I've always loved you. I'm not giving up on you again, I'll be waiting when you're ready."

Lavender jabbed a finger toward the open door. The wind blew rain inside, but she didn't care. "Please. Just leave." A sob welled up in her throat. Unshed tears blurred everything, except she still saw sorrow in Brian's eyes. It almost undid her.

His body caved as if it'd been deflated, his expression that of a broken man. He shuffled to the door, and she almost went after him, almost threw herself in his arms. One glance at her grandmother stopped her.

Doris kicked the door shut behind him. "This is your fault." Her grandmother unleashed her fury on Tyler.

Tyler's blue eyes blazed with anger. He clenched his fists, widened his stance, and scowled at Doris, his expression so fierce, Doris retreated a few steps, while Larry hid behind her.

Doris turned her attention on the person she'd have better luck controlling. "We'll come back once you get rid of him. Make it permanent. Look at the grief he's caused our family, and do the right thing."

Tyler stood up straighter. "No, I'll go. I need to pack anyway. I'm leaving in the morning."

He stopped in front of Lavender and looked down at her, his expression unreadable. "If you want me to stay, I will."

For tonight? Or forever? She longed to know the answer.

For a moment, gazes meshed and held. She saw things she'd never thought she'd see in his eyes, crazy things like love. In the next moment, she convinced herself she'd only seen what she wanted to see, nothing real.

A million things ran through Lavender's mind, their fights, their bickering, Tyler's control issues, his vulnerabilities, his gentle loving, his enthusiasm, his wicked sense of humor. His mastery of the F-word and attempt to break his bad habit. All of it. She glanced at her grandmother and saw the ultimatum in her eyes.

"Tyler, please go." Tears blinded her and she rubbed her eyes. Her heart broke open and the contents shattered at her feet like broken glass on concrete.

"Are you sure? I won't be back."

"I'm sure." She choked on the words, a sob strangled her.

Without another word, Tyler left. The door clicked shut behind him. Lavender sank onto the worn couch and buried her face in her hands, as the floor fell out beneath her.

* * * * *

Lavender watched from her window as Tyler locked the front door of the mansion. For a moment, he stood on the veranda and gazed around him. Then he walked down the front steps to his truck. Unable to stop herself, she trotted across the muddy field and slipped through the gate between the two properties.

Tyler saw her coming and paused, his expression guarded, his eyes hooded.

She met his gaze and held her chin high. "I'm furious at you for what you did last night, but I still can't let you go without saying goodbye."

"You're furious because I tried to fix what's broken. I get that. It was a stupid move on my part." His hard blue eyes never wavered from hers, and his asshole mask was held firmly in place.

"You can't force everything to be the way you want it to be."

"Why not? It's worked for me in the past." He skirted around her and threw his duffle bag in the passenger seat.

"There are some things you can't control." She stood behind him. When he turned around, she effectively blocked him in.

"Tell that one to your grandmother, though she sure as hell does a good job controlling you. You fell right into her web."

"My grandmother is not a spider. And she's not evil."

"I don't think she's evil either. Not anymore. I'll admit I did at first. She needs help, Vinnie. She's convinced herself she's doing what's best for you. She doesn't understand how much she's hurting you and your brother. Don't you see how abnormal her behavior is?"

Lavender heard the truth in his words, but her mind wasn't ready to accept them. She'd championed her grandmother for so long, defended her, put her on a pedestal, she couldn't change her behavior overnight—even if she wanted. Tyler tried to force Lavender to see her grandmother as human with flaws. She couldn't do that, not yet.

"I think it's time you left." She stepped away, but he stepped forward into the space she'd just vacated.

"I'm going, but I'll be back. I'm keeping this place, Lavender. You can't run from me and your life forever." Tyler leaned forward, filling her nostrils with his clean, woodsy scent. Her entire body angled toward him, even as she kept her head thrown back.

"I'm not running. I'm walking away."

Determination glinted in his eyes, the same determination she'd seen in television interviews just before his first Super Bowl. "When you decide to live your life, not your grandmother's plan for your life, you know where to find me."

"Goodbye. You won't know where to find me. I'm moving."

"But that's your place. You know that now. Not your grandmother's."

"It's also my brother's and my father's place. I can't stay here."

"You won't leave the islands." He spoke with such conviction, it irritated her. He knew her too well.

She'd given up too much to stay here and take care of her senior citizens, including an education and a more lucrative career. But it was home, and she loved it as much as she loved her old people. "There's more than one island in the San Juans. We'll be separated by a body of water, and it might as well be another country."

His mouth settled into a thin line.

"Tyler, do one thing for me."

He stared down at her a long, long time. Regret, need, and sorrow showed on his face and he made no attempt to conceal his emotions.

"Find your passion. If it's not football, retire, and don't give up until you find out what it is."

"I *have* to go back to football."

"You don't have to do anything. You could retire if your heart's not in it."

"I don't want to retire." He spoke softly, almost reverently, almost as if he'd just discovered the truth for himself.

"Then go back to your team and show them you're in this one hundred percent."

"I could stay a while longer, if you'd only make this between you and me and not your grandmother."

She bristled at his mention of her grandmother, feeling protective and defensive. "It is about us, and it'll never work. You need to go back. There's nothing holding you here."

"You are." He touched her face. The look of tenderness in his warm blue eyes sucker punched her.

She shook her head, fighting back tears and feeling torn between the jock she swore she'd never fall for and a grandmother whose love came with tough conditions.

"We don't start training camp for a few more months."

"Is Zach at the practice facility working out right now with the young guys?"

"Yeah, every day, so I hear." He regarded her warily, as if he knew what was coming.

"Go back. Go to team headquarters, start working out, throw yourself into it with all you've got. Show the doubters it's still your team, and you aren't giving it up without a fight."

Hands on her shoulders, he studied her for a long time. He made no attempt to hide his feelings from her. He'd definitely come a long ways. Had she?

"You're pretty special, Tyler Harris. Let the rest of the world see what you let me see. Be the person you can be, and you'll find your passion again."

His deep blue eyes searched hers, peeling away her defenses layer by layer. His gaze trapped her, chipped at her armor, made her believe in miracles. "I think I love you, Rebecca Gerloch."

"Don't say things you don't mean." Lavender shuddered at his use of her given name even as her heart danced at the words until she wrapped her brain around his actual words. He *thought* he loved her. But that wasn't enough. He needed to *know* he loved her.

"You love me, too." With a confident nod, Tyler stepped back and released her, as if he knew something she didn't.

No sense denying the truth. "Love isn't enough. We have too many strikes against us. Football is a greedy mistress. You and I will never work out." Eventually he'd leave her just like her father had, and she'd be left without a family and without him. She'd be all alone. She didn't think her heart could survive, so it was better to get it over with now.

"You're right about one thing, the two us will never work out—as long as your grandmother controls your life. You have to learn to follow some of your own advice. Be your own person. Stand up for yourself." With a sigh, he planted a chaste kiss on the tip of her nose, and turned back to his truck.

"Tyler."

He hesitated, hand on the door handle. "Yeah?"

"I'll miss you. Make your dad and Ryan proud."

He nodded and swallowed. "I have, and I will." On that note, he got into his truck and shut the door. Cougar stared at her through the window from his place on the back of the seat. The cat's accusing gaze said it all.

You're a coward.

That she was.

With one last sad smile, Tyler pulled down the driveway. She watched until his truck rounded a corner and disappeared out of sight. A lump sat in her throat almost choking her. She was a coward of the worst kind. She refused to see the truth because hiding behind lies and assumptions made her life easier in the short run, even as it ate her up inside a little bit more every day.

She trudged down to Twin Cedars' dock. A storm moved in. Dark clouds brewed angrily in the distance. Waves crashed against the rickety dock and rocked it. She braced her legs apart to keep from falling into the swirling waters. The wind whipped at her hair. Rain peppered her face, but she didn't feel any of it.

Instead she recalled a night of passion on this very dock on a calm, starlit night and a man who made love to her with such profound tenderness, it rocked her to her very soul.

The ever-changing waters rolled onto the beach then receded, only to return again. Like life, the waves altered the landscape by pushing driftwood up the beach, cutting away at the rocky bank, carving a new shape to the islands, adding some here, taking away there. A constant evolution, ever adjusting to nature's demands.

Wiping a tear from her face, Lavender splashed through the mud puddles back to the house, ignoring the rain, which found ways past the protective shell of her raincoat. A blast of heat welcomed her as she opened the door. She removed her coat and shook it out on the vinyl flooring of the entryway. After hanging it on a peg near the front door, she wandered into the small living room. Slicking back her wet hair, she pulled a bulging envelope from its hiding place under the couch.

She stared at it for a moment then stashed it back under the couch. She wasn't ready yet. For a lot of things. She wondered if she'd ever be ready for the truth.

* * * * *

Tyler ground his teeth so hard his head throbbed. A vein pulsed in his neck from the tension. He pulled his truck onto the ferry. Shutting off the engine, he leaned his head against the headrest and closed his eyes. Coug climbed over his shoulder and purred in his ear. He rubbed his face against Tyler's five-o'clock shadow, as if loving the scratchy feel of Tyler's chin.

Tyler's laugh rang hollow to his own ears, as he spit out a mouthful of cat hair. He pulled Coug onto his lap.

"Damn cat." He stroked the animal's soft fur, while the ferry engines thrummed as the boat pulled away from the dock.

"We're going home, buddy. You'll like the place." The cat stared at him. "Okay, maybe you won't. No mice, and you can't go outside in the city. You'll get used to it."

Yeah, but would he?

Dang, he'd told Lavender he *thought* he loved her. Maybe not the best choice of words. They'd just bubbled from his lips. As soon as he'd uttered the three scariest words known to man, he knew he'd meant them. He didn't just *think*, he knew. She hadn't even batted an eye, but swatted him down like a pesky fly. Even worse, she'd chosen her psycho grandmother over him. He gritted his teeth harder, which didn't help the pounding in his head. Nor could he drown out that cracking sound, which surely signaled the splintering of his once-hard heart.

Damn, he fu—effing hated this. He never let down his guard. He never let a woman inside his most secret places. Never. But he'd let Lavender in, and she'd messed with him. Okay, so maybe shoving her dad down her throat as a birthday present might qualify as a stupid-assed idea.

Still, she'd thrown his words back in his face, as if she didn't believe him. That hurt worse than anything else because for once he'd been honest about what was in his heart.

He guessed honesty didn't count.

Chapter 27

Red Zone

Tyler put his hand over his mouth to stifle a yawn. The dim-witted, gorgeous blonde model glued to his side posed for a photographer and stood on tiptoes to kiss his cheek. All the while, she kept her face turned toward the camera. Once the photographer moved away to other celebrities, the brilliant smile plastered on her face turned upside down into an ugly scowl.

Tyler raised an eyebrow at her. She pouted and tapped one toe on the marble floor of whatever Hollywood mansion they happened to be partying in that night. He was way too sober to deal with this brainless twit. He regretted agreeing to escort the silicone babe, but his agent pushed until he'd conceded.

"I'm bored. Let's move on." She stuck out her lower lip, which had so much botox pumped into it that it looked like a landing pad.

"Be my guest." Tyler couldn't wait to ditch her, the sooner the better.

"Be your guest?"

"Yeah, I've had enough. I'm flying home. Tonight." He added for emphasis. He shook her off his arm and strode toward the door. She ran after him and yanked him around.

"You can't walk out on me like this. I'm somebody, and I need an escort for the evening even if you are a dumb jock."

"Well, this dumb jock doesn't give a shit if you're the fu— effing Princess of Wales."

"You're an ass."

"Thank you. I'm glad you noticed." He tipped an invisible hat. Tyler headed toward the door only to stop dead at the sound of a familiar voice.

"Ty. How are you?"

Tyler turned around slowly. "I'm good, Cass. And you?" He waited for the old feelings of desire and raw hunger to come flooding back to him. And waited. And waited. Nothing happened.

"I've never been happier. This is my husband, Sam."

The two men shook hands. Tyler felt not even a twinge of jealousy.

"Congratulations, I'm truly glad for you." He meant every word. He smiled at Cass, a genuine smile. She looked good, actually happy, as she clutched her husband's arm. The man gazed down at her like a man in love. Cass returned her husband's look, devotion shone in her eyes. She'd never looked at Tyler like that. They'd either been fighting or making up, but never anything in between.

Stepping forward, Cass hugged Tyler, and he hugged her back. Her familiar scent tugged at his heartstrings, but more melancholy than regret.

"Well, I just wanted to say hi when I saw you across the room. Take care." An awkward silence set in, and Tyler took the hint.

"Good to see you, Cass." He escaped out the door and signaled for his ride. He settled into the limo and stared out the window, digesting it all.

When he saw Cass and her husband together the only thing he felt was envy. Not envy because he wanted Cass, but envy because he wanted Lavender to look at him like Cass looked at her husband. He wanted Vinnie on his arm as they walked through a black-tie affair, making it clear to everyone they were a couple. He wanted it all, but she obviously didn't feel the same, at least not enough to take a chance on a reformed asshole or sacrifice her relationship with her grandmother.

For the last two months, Tyler had dived into football, the first one at the practice facility in the morning and the last one to leave at night. The tension with Murphy didn't subside; if anything it worsened, dividing the team even further.

He didn't have his game back, couldn't get in the zone but he improved a little bit every day. That's all a guy could expect. Tyler wasn't giving up. It'd take some work to win back his old confidence and the team's respect and trust.

In his spare time, he volunteered with a couple of veterans' organizations, visiting VA hospitals and nursing homes, not to mention working with young cancer patients. He played cards with a group of veterans once a week, and they loved to raz him about anything and everything. The kids at the children's hospital lit up when he walked in the room, reading to them or just hanging out playing video games. He felt good about himself for the first time in a long time.

He rarely had more than one drink a night, left the parties early and alone. They weren't part of his life anymore. He didn't get any satisfaction from superficial crap. He'd cut way back on his spending, invested his Super Bowl bonus instead of blowing it, and sold a couple vacation houses to help fund the mansion rehab. All in all, his bank account started its slow recovery from anemic to financially secure.

Tonight he'd fly back to Seattle and his fu—frigging cat. Hell, he'd even managed to confine his use of the F-word to special occasions.

Either time would heal his wounds—and so far that wasn't working for him—or make Lavender's heart grow fonder, fond enough she'd hunt him down.

And if she didn't hunt him down, he'd know the truth behind her feelings. Proud men didn't beg. If he had one thing left, it happened to be his pride.

* * * * *

For two months, Lavender denied everything. She denied missing Tyler. She denied her grandmother may not have been straight with her about her father. And she denied that she wanted to know the truth.

She immersed herself in her work with her seniors and enrolled in a correspondence course in the gerontology field. Eventually she'd get a degree.

A summer storm hit her little house forcing her inside. Across the pasture, the workmen hurried in and out of the old mansion, carrying tools and supplies. She'd love to see the inside, but she kept her distance.

The envelope she'd stashed under the couch two months ago beckoned to her, Lavender hesitated. In this case, ignorance might be bliss—or not.

Setting her jaw, she got down on her knees and rummaged under the couch. She pulled out the over-stuffed envelope and shook the dust bunnies off it. Housekeeping had never been her strong suit. Ripping open the envelope, Lavender poured the contents onto the coffee table and began to rifle through them.

Unopened letters and cards addressed to Lavender from her father were scattered across the old coffee table's marred surface. *Return to sender* was scrawled across each one in her grandmother's handwriting. A decade of birthday and Christmas cards Lavender had never received. The cold blade of betrayal sliced through her. She felt physically ill, like she'd come down with the flu or some kind of bug. Yeah, the betrayal bug. Clutching her stomach, she stumbled to a chair and sat down with a thud.

Her grandmother led her to believe her father didn't care, that he'd abandoned her, in order to keep her granddaughter under control and her father out of her life. The selfishness of it overwhelmed her.

Her hands shook as she picked up another piece of paper, an accounting of the child support her father paid over the years. Another of her grandmother's lies shattered by cold, hard proof.

The deed on the property came next. Another lie unveiled.

An opened envelope addressed to her father in her grandmother's handwriting caught her attention. The postmark indicated a date just before her high school graduation. She pulled out the one-page letter and read it.

Lavender asked me to write to you. Please do not contact her. She wishes no further contact with you in any way, shape, or form. She does not consider you her father. Please do not cause our family any further pain with your selfish actions. Leave us alone. Doris.

Icy cold ran through her. A tear slipped down her cheek and onto the letter, blurring a few words. Lavender crumpled the letter in her fist. It slid from her fingers to the floor. She hugged herself and rocked back and forth.

She'd sat on that stage at graduation and watched for her father, growing more and more depressed as each moment passed.

Selfish? Her grandmother called her father selfish for attempting to contact her? She'd swallowed her grandmother's lies. All these years, she'd been denied a relationship with her father and brother because her grandmother couldn't let go of her obsessive hatred of her former son-in-law. Lavender had gone along, because she'd feared Doris would disown her, like she'd done Andy.

Doris had lied about everything.

Lavender stared at the proof littering the top of the table. She'd patterned her life according to her grandmother's wishes. Her grandmother forbade her to have animals in the house so she'd lived a lonely life in this house. She'd kept the peace by not asking questions, by going with the flow, by letting her grandmother have her way, by losing a part of herself. She'd even let her grandmother dictate whom she should love.

Now it was time to live her life, not her grandmother's version of it, and damn the consequences.

* * * * *

Lavender paced the floor and fretted, twisting her ring harder than ever. One thing at a time. First her grandmother. Then her father. Then Tyler?

Tyler had been right; she needed to get her personal life in order before she'd be able to have a successful relationship with him.

Doris swept into the room, barking orders at Lavender. Larry slinked along behind her. "The garden is full of weeds. The lawn needs mowing. This house is a mess."

Tight lipped, Lavender stood as tall as a short person could and approached her grandmother, the crumpled letter in one hand. Without a word, she gave it to Doris. Doris glanced at it. Her face turned white as she recognized the contents.

"Lavender, I can explain. I did this for your own good." Doris reached out for her granddaughter, but Lavender backed away. She saw her grandmother's actions as they really were, just another way to manipulate her.

"No, Gram. You did it for you. Not me." She twisted her ring harder, ignoring the ache in her finger and her heart.

"Honey, everything I do has been for you. I've sacrificed everything for you." Doris's words rang false, draining her grandmother's power to control.

"Does that include hiding this stuff from me and collecting rent on a property you don't own?" Lavender pointed at the various cards and letters littering the table.

Doris blanched and went on the defensive. "You've been talking to your father."

"No, I haven't, but I'm going to." She stared her grandmother in the eyes. She'd taken control of her life and was standing up to her grandmother. As hard as it was, she felt empowered.

"You wouldn't betray me like that. I've always been there for you." Doris's cold voice contained a warning, but Lavender had prepared for the worst.

"It's not a matter of betrayal, Gram. If you won't support me, at least tolerate my desire to have a relationship with my father. Be happy for me. Don't make me choose. I want you both in my life. I wish you'd see it that way." Lavender's voice broke, but she held to her convictions.

"I don't see it that way. Not at all. You've disappointed me and broken my heart." Turning on her heel, Doris grabbed Larry's arm. "We're through with that ungrateful brat."

Casting an apologetic glance over his shoulder, Larry followed Doris out the door. Her grandmother made her choice and Lavender would make hers. She didn't cry. She didn't break down. She found an inner strength she didn't know she had and made a phone call. One she should've made years ago.

Chapter 28

Final Seconds

Tyler stood next to his locker. He listened to the sounds of men getting ready for the third pre-season game. The veterans razzed the rookies. Cleats clattered on the floor. Familiar smells filled his nostrils, and a little tendril of excitement ignited his soul.

He couldn't kid himself. So far training camp was tough. The first two pre-season games even tougher. For a few weeks, the press dogged his every step, resurrecting the rumors of a fictional DUI and his time in rehab. No charges were filed for the lip he'd given the officer after ramming his car. His attorney insisted he was off the hook. The rehab rumors might be tougher to overcome, but he'd cleaned up his act, and his improved attitude spoke volumes.

Tyler didn't miraculously get his game back overnight, but he was on the right path. Maybe HughJack couldn't see it. Maybe Murphy still questioned his dedication and his fire. Maybe the team still treated him with guarded respect.

Tyler would battle his way back and push aside the doubts. He'd learn to relax, let things happen, not force them. He'd find the zone again, that space where the best athletes went in their heads, time slowed down, and every move became crystal clear.

Tyler strapped on his pads and stared at two small photos taped to his locker: his father in his pilot's uniform stood next to his helicopter and Ryan, in healthier days, holding a football.

At that moment *he knew*.

You are proud of me, aren't you, Dad? Ry?

Yeah, they were and so were Uncle Art and all the other Harrises whose blood ran through his veins and all the Harrises yet to come. Yeah, they'd grow up loving Twin Cedars and preserving it for the next generation and so would he.

Tyler had refocused on the game, at peace with himself and his direction. Training camp didn't tell him much. Some of his passes reflected the quarterback he once was, others not so much. Regardless, he'd resurrect his old killer instincts and relentless drive to succeed or die trying. He'd had some great practices, taken no prisoners, and forced the Jacks' defense to do their job, especially Murphy. The old guy huffed like a rusty industrial fan as he chased Tyler around the practice field trying for a sack.

Speaking of the devil...

Murphy walked up to him and blocked access to Tyler's locker. They glared at each other, eye to eye, man to man. "I don't like you very much, and I sure as hell don't respect you."

"I don't fucking like you either." Hey, the conversation merited use of the F-word. Tyler sneered at the ass. He did respect Murphy. The guy was everything Tyler used to be. Murphy left it all out on the field.

"I'll be watching you, fuckhead. Let's see if you can play like the champion you're supposed to be."

Tyler rolled his eyes. "Whatever." He pushed Murphy aside to get his cleats from his locker. Murphy stepped back, not causing a scene in front of the team. Both men were fully aware that several sets of eyes absorbed their every move.

"I want that ring. I want it so bad I can taste it like the metallic taste of blood in my mouth. I want it so bad I'd give my left nut for it. Hell, I'd give both nuts. I want a ring. If you fuck this up for me, I'll destroy you. I promise."

"Damn, I'm scared." Tyler held his hand over his mouth in a yawn. "Can't help it that you've been a loser all your life. Don't hold me responsible."

"You and I need to spend some time in the ring."

"It'd be my pleasure. I'd love to whip your ass once the season ends."

Murphy nodded. His face set in stone. The linebacker turned back to his locker and his posse of young players.

Tyler snorted with disgust. He reined in his emotions, forced his mind back on the game, nothing but the game. Murphy didn't deserve to be a blip on his internal radar. Tyler sat on the bench, head down, and closed his eyes. He practiced every technique he knew to get in the right state of mind.

The guys left him alone, knowing he needed time to focus and visualize the game. Instead, he kept visualizing purple.

Damn.

He missed Lavender like he'd miss his throwing arm. When he'd first come back from the islands, he'd expected her to call, been certain she'd call. Instead, nothing. Silence. Nada. As the days turned to weeks and months, he'd become less certain. Yet, something told him they weren't finished. Not yet. If he knew his purple lady, and he believed he did, she missed him as much as he missed her.

They had unfinished business. She'd left an empty hole in his heart, even as she'd helped him fill the emptiness since Ryan's death and even his father's death years ago. Football had filled that void once. And once again, it was all he had.

After the season ended, he was going after her.

"Hey, Ty, it's time." Derek slapped him on the shoulder pads.

"Yeah, right." Tyler stood and jogged after his teammates down the tunnel leading to a packed stadium of rabid Jacks fans. The team surged around him, running onto the field. He paused at the tunnel opening. His fingers flexed on the helmet in his hand. The stadium roared. Blue and gold towels waved in the crazed crowd. The green turf spread out before him. Eagerness thrummed through him. Anticipation churned in his gut.

This was his stage. His. He owned it. He'd owned it since the day he'd first picked up a football and toddled toward his father with it clutched in his tiny hands. He'd own it this year.

Several plays later, Tyler stood on the sidelines and watched the defense crush the Saints, pinning them back to their own 15. Grudgingly, he admitted Murphy was brilliant. The guy was everywhere, barking orders to the defense, sacking the quarterback, stuffing their opponents running game up their ass. Murphy played like a man with something to prove, and he played like a guy in his twenties. No way in hell would Tyler give anything less on the field than the Jacks' pain-in-his-ass defensive captain.

The Saints punted. Special teams downed the ball on the Jacks 45. Tyler strapped on his helmet and sprinted onto the field. Derek flanked him. Bruiser Mackay, his running back, dogged his heels, constantly yammering to carry the ball. Tyler called the plays, his confident tone and aggressive stance demanded respect. He got it. At least to a point. The guys watched him warily. He'd disappointed them before. Now he'd work twice as hard to gain back their trust.

Things were as they should be.

Maybe.

He waited for the rush of adrenaline and wasn't disappointed. It coursed through his veins, stampeded over his earlier doubts. He could do this. He wanted to do this.

His teammates stared at him from around the huddle and waited for the play. The stadium crackled with electricity.

Tyler Harris took his position behind center. He didn't like what he saw and audibled a different play. He barked the signals, set the team in motion. Pads smacked against pads. Linemen grunted as they protected the pocket. Receivers ran their routes. Tyler scanned the field, spotted his open man and snapped the ball into the air. The tight end hauled it in for a first down and then some. Tyler marched his team down the field until a quick toss to Derek in the end zone netted their first score of the game.

The crowd erupted with their approval. A slow smile crossed Tyler's face. Satisfaction warmed his insides. Determination flowed through his veins. His body thrummed with pure joy.

He loved this game.

He was back.

* * * * *

Lavender sat in the stands between her brother, Andy, and her father. Andy taught high school on the Eastside and following the family tradition, coached football and baseball. Lavender had made several of his high school games, even though the ferry ride to the mainland every weekend proved to be time-consuming.

So much had changed over the past few months. She'd called her father and arranged a meeting with him and her brother. They talked it out, had a good cry and agreed to forgive and move on. Her grandmother found out and threw one of her maniacal fits, but Lavender didn't cave this time. She held her ground.

Together with her brother, she met with Doris and Larry a few weeks ago. They told Doris they'd like to have a relationship with her, but regardless they'd be having a relationship with their father also. Doris would hear nothing of it. Larry, on the other hand, surprised them. After Doris stormed out of the room, he promised them he'd get her into counseling. He'd keep the lines of communication open with them.

The old mansion was a flurry of pounding and sawing as carpenters and craftsmen worked to restore it to its former splendor. Homer supervised the remodeling when Tyler's sisters weren't in residence. The two women sent the workmen cowering for cover.

Lavender accepted her father's invitation to attend a Jacks game for a couple of reasons. One, to be with her father and brother. Two, to see Tyler. She missed him. He'd been right about a lot of things, and she owed him an apology.

Hopeful that she could have it all, Lavender watched the last piece of her life's puzzle on the field below. Tyler Harris commanded his team, the picture of absolute confidence. When the defense went in, Tyler didn't sit on the bench. He roamed the sidelines and shouted encouragement to the defense when needed and chewed ass when deserved.

She stole her brother's binoculars, ignoring his annoyance. Tyler looked good. Really, really good. She'd stalked the Internet for the past months and found little gossip about him. He'd been laying low, working out, studying the game. She'd expected nothing less. One small article she read made her proud. Tyler had become a regular at several veterans' facilities in Seattle over the past few months, along with the cancer ward at the children's hospital. She gave herself a little credit for pointing out to him the good he could do as a local celebrity. He'd obviously taken her advice to heart.

He'd either be happy to see her or snub her. She didn't know what his reaction would be; she only knew that if she didn't try, she'd wonder for the rest of her life what could have been.

One step at a time. First, she'd confronted her grandmother with the truth. Then she'd reconciled with her dad. Now she'd figure out where she stood with the Jacks' sexy quarterback.

Selecting Tyler's cell number, she texted a picture of Tyler on the field and a picture of her in the stands, hoping he hadn't changed his number in the past few months. As soon as he checked messages in the locker room after the game, he'd know she was there.

She'd tell him she loved him. Then the ball would be in his hands, literally.

* * * * *

Reveling in their victory, Tyler wasn't in a big hurry to leave after the game. He stood in the locker room and savored the moment. The place buzzed with excitement and the promise of a new season and a new beginning. Hell, yeah, it'd be an uphill battle to win a third championship. The entire league gunned for them, but Tyler believed in his guys. He hoped they believed in him.

As the locker room started to clear out, he made his way over to Murphy's locker. The guy shoved his wallet in his pants then met Tyler's direct gaze.

Tyler held out his hand in a peace offering. "Good game."

"Don't expect me to say the same of you." Murphy snubbed him, ignoring his outstretched hand and concentrating on the contents of his locker. "Your receivers caught some uncatchable passes."

So that's how it'd be played out with Murphy. "You're an asshole." Tyler growled at the jerk. Hey, he'd offered a truce. The guy threw it in his face. "Your attitude, not mine, is going to damage this team. If we lose the championship, it'll be on you." He moved closer, getting into Murphy's space. "You know what? I think you're disappointed I had a good game."

Murphy studied him long and hard. "For the average pro quarterback that performance would've been good. For you, it was mediocre."

Tyler's eyes widened in false shock. "Murphy, you're getting soft, man. That sounded suspiciously like a compliment."

Murphy narrowed his gaze, irritated most likely with himself. "You're a prick." He grabbed his jacket and stalked out the door.

Shaking his head and chuckling, Tyler yanked on his navy Jacks sweatshirt and grabbed his car keys. He paused to look around the empty locker room. This season would be his biggest challenge, but he felt up to it. Rejuvenated. Ready to face the world. Either Murphy would come around, or he wouldn't. People used to say Tyler had a chip on his shoulder. Murphy sported a boulder. Tyler didn't give a shit. They'd win with the jerk or without him.

He was getting his game back. Today he'd bask in the win, enjoy the journey, just like Lavender suggested. At the thought of her, the now-familiar ache built in the pit of his stomach and radiated outward. He'd started to dial her number so many times in the past month and chickened out. He sighed and pressed his forehead against the wall for a moment.

His cell phone chirped, indicating a text message. Tyler pulled it out of his sweatshirt pocket and tapped the screen. His blood stopped circulating, his lungs quit pumping air, his finger froze as he saw Lavender's name on the message. He tapped the picture and opened it. A picture of him on the field. He tapped the next picture. Lavender in the stadium.

She's here. In Seattle.

His soul sang for joy, and his body hummed in response. Licking his dry lips, he tapped the screen to dial her number. And waited. It seemed like a lifetime, but the phone only rang a few times with an eternity in between each ring.

Her soft voice, sounding a little uncertain, a little apologetic, answered. "Tyler?"

"Uh, yeah." His glib tongue deserted him and tied itself in knots.

"Where the hell are you? I've been waiting for over an hour."

A slow smile spread across his face. "Where the fu—fudge are you?" *Please God don't let her be heading for the ferry.*

"At the ale house across from the stadium."

"On my way."

Tyler sprinted out of the locker room, out of the stadium, and across the street. He shoved open the door and paused to let his eyes adjust to the dim lighting in the room. The door slammed against the wall. People glanced up, realized who he was and cheered. He sketched a salute, as he skimmed the room for a diminutive redhead.

He spotted her at a corner booth. Weaving through the rowdy after-game crowd, he high-fived guys on the way to her table.

"Hey." He slid into the seat across from her. She looked great in a Jacks jersey, his number he noted, and her red hair in a sassy ponytail. Her face was flushed, and her eyes danced. She was happy to see him. His heart raced with joy. His head tamped it down, warned him not to get too excited.

"Hey to you, too." She offered him a tentative smile. "Great game. You looked better than ever out there."

"I wouldn't go that far, but I felt good. You came to my game." He rubbed his sweaty palms on his pants.

"With my brother and my father."

"No shit?"

"No shit." He heard the smile in her voice, as well as saw it on her face.

"How did that happen?" He glanced around the room. "Where're your dad and brother?"

"I sent them back to the hotel. Said I had some important business to take care of." She started twisting her ring.

Some things never changed. "Lavender, I—" He stopped when she held up a hand.

"Just hear me out. You were right, you know."

He shot her his trademark cocky grin. "I'm always right."

She rolled her eyes at his regression into his asshole role. "About my grandmother. I read the paperwork Dad left me. I see things more clearly now. I always thought it was one hundred percent my father's fault, now I see it's more fifty–fifty. My grandmother made it really hard for him. She told a lot of lies. I've talked to Grandpa. He's attempting to get help for her. Right now she's not speaking to me."

"I'm sorry, Vinnie. She'll come around. Despite her faults, her grandkids mean a lot to her. I don't believe she'll chance losing both of you."

"It'll take time. Right now she accuses me of betraying her."

Tyler took her hand and squeezed it, stopping her ring twisting. Her hand felt so small and delicate. "And your dad and brother? How's that going?"

"It's going well so far."

Swallowing around the lump of emotion in his throat, he looked up and took the plunge. "And me. Where do I fit in?"

"Where do you want to fit in?" She met his gaze, her eyes full of hope and more.

He held her hand to his heart. "Right here." His voice gave out making him sound like a croaking frog.

She choked back a sob of joy, lifted her gaze to his, tears streaking down her face.

"I miss you." He grabbed her other hand and squeezed. She squeezed back.

"I miss you, too, you lovable asshole."

"Reformed asshole."

Lavender laughed and leaned forward, and Tyler met her halfway across the table. His mouth captured hers, and he lost himself in one hell of a reunion kiss until someone shouted "Get a room."

Tyler pulled back a few inches. "So—you think you could grow to love an asshole like me?"

"No, I don't think I could."

His heart cracked, his brash armor crumbled. He stood to go, his pride not allowing him to stay. Leaping to her feet, she grabbed his arm, surprising him by her strength and pulled him to her.

"You didn't let me finish. I can't grow to love you because I already do—love you." Lavender wrapped her arms around his waist.

"Are you sure?" His breath stalled in his throat.

"Yes, I'm absolutely sure. I'm stuck with you, and you're stuck with me." Love lit up her eyes.

"What about the islands? You don't like cities."

"I'm not leaving the islands, but I'll live here during the season until you retire. After that, we're going to be permanent residents at Twin Cedars."

"My dad and Uncle Artie would like that."

"Yes, they would."

"I'm making part of the mansion into a B&B for veterans and kids with terminal illnesses. Did you know that?"

"No, but I'm not surprised. I knew I could count on you to do the right thing."

Tyler pulled her against him and hugged her tight. The crowd in the pub hooted and clapped. Lavender wrapped her arms around his neck and kissed him soundly.

When she drew back, he grinned like a damn fool. A happy, contented damn fool who'd finally found his missing pieces, along with the love of his life.

And don't miss Zach's story, coming soon!

After twelve years in the league, all Zach Murphy wants is a Super Bowl ring. He's been about hard hits not smooth manners, about breaking quarterbacks not making small talk at cocktail parties. But now he's shattered something else. After dumping a tray of drinks on the team owner's snooty daughter and accidentally feeling up the Governor's wife, his tenure with his team looks perilously short. And things are getting worse.

Life is looking up for Kelsie Carrington-Richmond. A onetime beauty pageant star and mean girl, she only recently stopped living out of her car. But both those times have passed. Her Finishing School for Real Men has a real shot, and the Seattle Lumberjacks have hired her to polish up their roughest player. Except...it's Zach. Long ago she broke his heart. He's just the beast she remembers—gruff, protective—but she's nothing like the beauty from his past. Yet, getting knocked down happens, and getting back up makes a contender. And they both have the hearts of champions.

DOWN BY CONTACT
Jami Davenport

Early 2013

AUTHOR'S NOTE

I often get plot ideas from a news story that intrigues me. Such is the case with Lavender's plot line in *Forward Passes*.

A few years ago a story made national news that caught my attention. A woman returned to South America taking her young son with her. A short while later she died. Her father (the child's grandfather) refused to return the child to his American father. A legal battle ensued for several months ending in the child eventually being returned to his father, even as he claimed he'd rather stay with his grandfather. As I recall, the grandfather, a psychologist, stated he could turn any child against his/her parents using the principles of parental alienation. I never heard how that story ended up, but I never forgot it.

I'm always looking for a good subplot for my next book and decided to research the concept of parental alienation. I met several people in the process who had varying degrees of horror stories, the worst extreme involved the mother killing the father in order to keep him away from his children. I learned that parental alienation is more common than I'd ever imagined, often brought about by loving parents or grandparents in the heat of a divorce or the aftermath. Some parents, grandparents, and children get over it and move on, others never do. The different behaviors exhibited by Lavender's grandmother are based on a list of the common things an alienator does to alienate his/her children from the other parent or grandparent.

ABOUT THE AUTHOR

An advocate of happy endings, Jami Davenport writes sexy romantic comedies, sports hero romances, and equestrian fiction. Jami lives on a small farm near Puget Sound with her Green Beret-turned-plumber husband, a Newfoundland cross with a tennis ball fetish, a prince disguised as an orange tabby cat, and an opinionated Hanoverian mare.

Jami works in information technology for her day job and is a former high school business teacher and dressage rider. In her spare time, she maintains her small farm and socializes whenever the opportunity presents itself. An avid boater, Jami has spent countless hours in the San Juan Islands, a common setting in her books. In her opinion, it is the most beautiful place on earth.

FORWARD PASSES

With two championships in as many years, superstar Tyler Harris is the best quarterback in the league. Gorgeous and rich, he's at the top of his game. But everyone's looking to take him down. There's a building media frenzy around an unfortunate accident, and the only safe place seems a rundown mansion deep in the San Juans and owned by his late great uncle. There, Tyler gets sacked by the sassy redhead next door. It's more alive than he's felt in years.

Lavender Mead has a good reason to dislike jocks, namely an absentee father who deserted the family to coach college football. Maybe that explains her penchant for bad boys who play ball for a living and break hearts for a hobby. Her new neighbor seems just the type. Yet, something is different about Tyler, and sometimes love requires a Hail Mary. You draw back your arm, pray…and give it all up to fate. And sometimes you win your ring.

 **Boroughs**
Publishing Group

Did you enjoy this book? Drop us a line and say so! We love to hear from readers, and so do our authors. To connect, visit www.boroughspublishinggroup.com online, send comments directly to info@boroughspublishinggroup.com, or friend us on Facebook and Twitter. And be sure to check back regularly for contests and new releases in your favorite subgenres of romance!

Are you an aspiring writer? Check out www.boroughspublishinggroup.com/submit and see if we can help you make your dreams come true.

www.ingramcontent.com/pod-product-compliance
Lightning Source LLC
Chambersburg PA
CBHW062026170626
46813CB00001B/307